THE BEQUEST

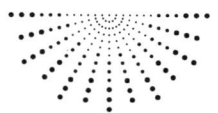

HOPE ANIKA

Copyright © 2002, 2015 Hope McKenzie

All rights reserved.

No part of this book may be reproduced in any form or by any electronic or mechanical means, including information storage and retrieval systems, without written permission from the author, except for the use of brief quotations in a book review.

Other books by Hope Anika:

The Getaway
Aequitas
In Plain Sight
Evolution: Awakening

To Dan
For Believing

PROLOGUE

When he dreams, it's always of the desert.
Of the sun, baking him slowly and turning his skin into blistered rawhide. Of the wind, scouring his flesh as effectively as steel wool. Of the sand, encrusting his skin so deeply he knows it is possible to drown in a pool of miniscule golden grains.

Dusk descends, and the sky is breathtaking in its intensity: gold and pink, orange so deep it could be pure flame. A disorienting paradox; hell should be ugly and bleak and without hue. That such brilliance washes the horizon infuriates him, an empty promise no one will keep. The mockery of night is no better: stars glitter like a sea of diamonds, and the thick, glittering twist of the Milky Way pulses as if sentient. It tempts him to believe.

In something. *Anything.*

With every return to this patch of earth, he notices details he missed. Little things: the faint vibration beneath his feet as the helicopter approaches, the small hole on the bottom of his left boot, the Boston Red Sox bandana Hogan is wearing. Nothing of significance. Nothing important.

Nothing that will stop what is to come.

"Fucking wind, fucking sand, fucking shit hole!" someone snarls.

Kent, maybe. Or Hogan. He doesn't know. The wail of wind that surrounds them like a keening child is almost deafening, the sand a maelstrom that swallows them whole. His eardrums throb to the beat of the rotors of the incoming Apache helicopter.

"Life with Alpha Team 6 sucks ass today," another adds.

No one disagrees. They are exhausted. Homesick; heartsick. Tired of the sun, the sand, the blood. The rhetorical struggle in which they find themselves engaged: one god pitted against another, a fruitless argument over existence where death is the only victor.

"They're early," Hogan mutters. His hands are chapped and blistered as he straps the wooden crates tightly together. The lettering painted across the top of the warped wood is oddly beautiful; a biting irony. "Command confirmed 2100."

Hogan's unease trips his own, a switch that immediately puts him on full alert, but they can see nothing beyond the whirl of sand and darkness. The sky is hazy, an endless black blur broken only by the infrared lights mounted on the copter's steel frame as it grows near. Next to them, Kent and Rye are carefully stacking the last of the crates, their faces stark with tension behind the bandanas they wear in effort to hold the sand at bay. Pale with dehydration, skin reddened and chapped, limbs fatigued from swimming through sand.

These are *his* men. His brothers; his family. They have followed him relentlessly, with such unwavering belief it astounds—and sometimes shames—him. Into every nook and cranny of this godforsaken country, down every IED and mortar strewn road. Without question or protest. They are good men. Men he would die for.

He claps Hogan on the shoulder, but when he speaks, his reassurance is harsh, crushed glass in his throat. "Could be the storm."

Hogan shakes his head once, a decisive rejection. "Feels wrong, boss."

He knows he should turn away and conduct another security sweep, but the power of Hogan's rebuff uncoils and stabs deep, rooting him to the hard desert ground he occupies. They remain alive in this land of sand and death only because they do not discount their gut; instinct is a far more useful tool than any weapon they've been given. And he trusts Hogan's gut.

He squints at the incoming copter, seeking reassurance through the surge of sand and grit, but his heart pounds with breathtaking force. The winds grow stronger, a wild, feral howling that feeds his growing disquiet. Foreboding whispers down his spine as he glances at the crates—simple wooden boxes that house death. Coveted and hunted by every faction under the sun, from pole to pole.

The Apache is upon them now; he can feel the steady *whoosh whoosh whoosh* of the rotors pulse inside his skull. His gut is thick with acid. Deep inside, where his soul clings to tenuous life, a cry of panic wells.

"Fall back." He gives the order abruptly, instinct pushing through protocol. "Get to the fucking ridgeline. *Now.*"

The stark wall of sandstone is steep, but riddled by narrow canyons and deep crevasses in which to hide. They know these hollows intimately, as familiar with them as with the underbelly of their armored Humvee or the firing mechanisms of their weapons. They are the only haven to be had in this hellish land.

"Boss?" Rye questions.

"To the ridgeline," he repeats and steps next to the crates.

Inside his skin, dread swells like a corpse bloated by death. "Go."

His rank overrides the argument he can see in their gazes, pitting their need to stand with him against the indoctrination of their training. That disapproval is the very thing that leads him to protect. He goes *first*. Always.

His men fall back as the Apache lands. The sandstorm is intensified by the circling blades, and he is swallowed by a suffocating golden cloud. Grit fills his throat as he lifts his night vision goggles and straps them into place. Blood roars in his head, a dizzying rush as the sand pummels him.

The copter bobs as it hits the desert floor and creates fresh chaos. A brutal storm of sand and rock and desert scrub pelts him, tearing unprotected flesh. Poppy petals whirl into flight like confetti. Behind the thick lenses of his night goggles, he tries to make sense of the figures who are jumping from the copter.

He can hear nothing but the rotors—*whoosh, whoosh, whoosh*, the jackhammer of his pulse, the sickening rush of his blood. As he watches the figures grow closer, Hogan's words are a drumbeat in his skull.

Wrong. Wrong. Wrong.

Two things happen in that moment. First, he realizes the Apache is not powering down; the rotors circle ceaselessly, their speed unabated. Second: the men who have disembarked the copter are not wearing fatigues. Or SEAL gear. Or any military issued wear.

He turns; his gaze clashes with Hogan's as the first the bullet tears through his flap jacket, burrowing into his back to pierce his left lung. A cry of warning lodges in his throat, coated by blood and fury.

Go.

But it does not escape.

The second bullet plows into his right hip and drops him where he stands, next to the crates. Fire bursts to life in his lungs. His breath whistles through his lips, and he can feel blood, warm and wet, streaming down his back, his thigh, filling his lung. He rolls over, and his hip threatens to separate from its socket. He flirts with oblivion, but in his brain the knowledge that if he sleeps, he dies hammers at him. So he grits his teeth and blinks it away, blood spewing from his mouth to sprinkle the sand like flower pollen. And he focuses.

His weapon is heavy, but he clasps it tight, squeezing so hard the steel cuts into the flesh of his palm. It steadies him. Behind him, Hogan is screaming—*fury given sound* —and regret threatens to undo him. He forces himself to his knees, but his hip gives and he wobbles like the Yoda bobble head Rye once glued to the dash of their Humvee. He wrestles for breath, struggling to suck in enough oxygen to stay conscious. Blood pools next to him, black and oily in the night.

He lifts the SSAR-15 and fires, but his aim is wild, an unsteady arc that sends his shots sharply to the right; he kills nothing but a stray Creosote bush. He grasps futilely at the sand in effort to find purchase, but the grains collapse beneath him. He pulls the trigger again and knows a fleeting, intense moment of satisfaction as three of the bodies heading toward him fall. But when he moves to fire again, buoyed by his small success, a third bullet shatters his right forearm and a broken, enraged sound tears from his throat, expelling the last of his remaining air. His hip gives, and he falls back, his body convulsing beneath the onslaught of blood loss, oxygen deprivation and massive trauma. His weapon disappears into the sand.

Darkness beckons, but he clings to the only lifeline left: consciousness. His goggles are askew, but he can see the booted feet of the men who have come for the crates, who will take them.

Steal them. Sell them. Use them.

They speak in low, guttural tones of Arabic, but he doesn't recognize the dialect, can't make sense of their words, and as they step over his body, one of them kicks his wounded hip hard enough to shatter what little is left holding him together. It is everything he can do not to react. To stare sightlessly into the storm, unblinking, blood seeping from his mouth to drool down his jaw. To deny himself breath.

Because he will live; *there will be vengeance.* Violent, malicious, soulless retribution.

A laugh echoes around him. Husky, low. And there is something in that sound that marks him, a wound deeper than any other, a memento more effective than any of the scars that will mar him.

I will know you. And death will follow.

The crates are gone, leaving nothing but perfect squares stamped into the sand. The Apache lifts, abandoning the bodies of the fallen to the harsh desert landscape, where they will be perfectly preserved in their murderous glory by the dry air. A licentious act—symbolic of identity—and he tells himself to *remember.* As the Apache fades from sight, a plume of glittering gold sand drifts down over him like a silent eulogy.

Hogan is sprawled on the sand only a handful of feet away; he is missing most of his skull. Just beyond him, Rye lies in a pool of blood so profuse it seems impossible that it was ever contained in only one body. Kent and Axel have fallen to his left, their heat signatures fading into muted splotches of pale pink, weapons still clutched in hand.

Dead.

War has taught him that life is altered in an instant, a span of time so quick it cannot be comprehended, but still, he is stunned they have disappeared so quickly, so thoroughly, from existence. Erased. And the rage that has kept him awake and alive steeps into every breath, every cell, until his pores bleed black with hate. Purpose is born; a need for vengeance so deep there is no consideration of failure.

Live. Live to kill.

Around him, the night is as black and still as the death that has come for them. There is no sound beyond his own rasping battle for air—no moans or groans or twitching limbs. No hope.

Dead.

All but him.

The temptation to follow beckons sweetly, but he does not deserve to live a life none of them will have. He is their leader; none should have gone before him.

Not one.

And for a moment he can only think it is better to let his blood stain the hard desert ground here, now, than to exist in the shadow of their obliteration. Better to give up than to go on.

But the purpose born within him will not allow such an easy end.

Get the fuck up and live. You have people to kill.

Retribution must be his lifeline. That his vision swims with inky streams, and his thoughts break apart, shattering as quickly as his bones have beneath the onslaught of bullets, makes no difference. He will push himself to his feet. He will make it to the village beyond the ridge.

Because he is the only one left. No matter his pain, his rage, the grief that chokes him like a murderous hand. He is all there is: the only one who can sound the alarm that the crates have been taken. The only one for whom blood will be the sole recompense.

As he reaches out and pulls himself across the barren land—like fucking nails, shredding his flesh—his eviscerated soul is rewoven, dark and feral and starved for vengeance. *Justice.*

Life for life.

Someone he trusted has betrayed him. Someone he will find. Someone he will kill.

CHAPTER ONE

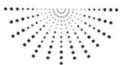

"Dead?"
"Dead."
"As in...kicked the bucket? Bought the farm? Sleeping with the fishies?"
"Er...yes."
"Huh," Cheyenne Elias said. "Well. Better late than never."
The punctuated silence on the other end of her cell phone spoke for itself—silencing people was something at which Cheyenne was proficient. The sad fact of it was, shutting people up was ludicrously easy, because they were usually so full of foolish expectation.

Death brought the expectation of grief. But grief was a product of loss. And this was…

Plus column all the way, baby.

"I contacted you because you are named in Ms. Humboldt's will," the voice on the other end continued, rather doggedly. "To inform you that you have been designated as guardian to her minor son."

Shock jolted through Cheyenne.

Shoe meet other foot.

"Huh," she said again. Which was better than *Have you lost your goddamn mind?* Or *Ha ha ha! Suck it.*

Grossly inappropriate, even for her.

"I quote: 'In the event that my son, Rafferty Humboldt, is a minor at the time of my death, I hereby appoint Cheyenne Elias to be the Guardian of his person. My Guardian shall be held solely to the standard of good faith in the performance of her duties, and shall exercise her authority without the necessity of obtaining the consent of any court.'"

Cheyenne filed through the words and tried to think of something to say. A toxic, jumbled mix filled her throat, unfit to speak. Her cell crackled, static filling the silence she couldn't.

Georgia Humboldt, dead. Six feet under and pushing up daisies...

Try hemlock.

"I realize this is probably a shock. I'm sorry. I urged Miss Humboldt to contact you, to send you a copy of these documents, but she was insistent that you not be notified unless she..."

Died. Unless she died.

"...well, only if it became necessary. I'm afraid her reluctance has left her son a temporary ward of the State of Wisconsin, and if you decline to act as his guardian, he will remain so until his eighteenth birthday."

Too bad, so sad.

"Balls," Cheyenne said. Because she wasn't really that callous. She *wasn't*. No matter how easy it would be.

"You can decline, of course. But Miss Humboldt had been confident you would take the boy in."

Had she now? Well, wasn't that special?

"Hardy-har-har," Cheyenne said.

"I'm sorry?"

Talking to herself—while simultaneously talking to

someone else—was one of her worst tendencies. An old, bad habit of simply thinking out loud, born when there was no one listening. But sometimes people thought she was nuts, and according to Phil—her anger management counselor—that was the idea.

You deliberately put people off, Cheyenne. Why do you think you do that?

Because people are assholes, Phil.

"Georgia's idea of a joke," she clarified. "*Hysterical.*"

The voice (whose name she couldn't remember—Smith? Jones?—attorney at *law)* replied, but it was inaudible, courtesy of the fact that she was halfway up Sleeping Indian mountain, and backcountry trails were generally not good cell receptors. She smacked her phone once, twice, knowing it wouldn't help, but it felt good. Then a handful of words materialized. "..afraid...don't follow...meaning?"

"You wouldn't be the first," she said and sighed.

Chuck, her three-legged blue heeler, stood a few feet ahead at the crest of the trailhead. He cocked his head at her as she muttered to herself, painfully aware that her peaceful existence had just been blown to smithereens. *Again.*

"Shouldn't have answered the damn phone," she told him.

What had possessed her? Answering an unknown number was a no-no—and something she *never* did. Because she hated dealing with people. Any kind of people, but especially strangers. *You have the social skills of a leper,* her publicist, Whitney, had once observed. *It's like you were raised by hyenas.*

Not exactly. But close.

"Look," Cheyenne said, trying her best to sound reasonable. *Human.* "Georgia and I—we weren't...anything. You need to call someone else."

"There isn't anyone else," came the reply, oddly clear. "You are the sole guardian she named. If you won't take the boy, he will go to the State."

"Not my problem," Cheyenne retorted bluntly. But she felt something—a ping? a pang?—that might have—*maybe*—been shame. Dismissing Georgia was nothing, like throwing out holey underwear. But the kid... The Kid. She'd been The Kid, once.

"You won't reconsider?"

"Ha," she said, but then—*ping*! Damn it. "Where's his father?"

"I don't know. Miss Humboldt didn't see fit to share his identity with me." The voice was faintly disapproving and touched by a Midwestern accent Cheyenne knew intimately: the diction of a Cheesehead. One too many lagers, and she'd sound just like him. "Miss Elias, you are this child's only hope."

Well, that was just profoundly stupid. Who would make *her* anyone's only hope?

Ah, Georgia. The hate that had once lived in Cheyenne's heart had long since faded to indolence—or perhaps apathy, because really, why expend the energy?—but this...*this* was almost funny. Almost. Except for the whole kid thing. And the whole "ward of the State" thing. And the whole "you are this child's only hope" thing.

Fuck a duck.

"Son of a nutcracker," she said.

"I take it you and Miss Humboldt were no longer...close?"

Cheyenne could only laugh, a harsh, bitter bark that hurt her throat. She had no words. What she'd once been—what *they'd* once been—bore no relation to what they'd become.

"No," she said, so cold an unknown part of her shivered. Chuck growled softly in response. And then—*ping.*

"I'm afraid I don't know what to say," said Smith/Jones.

Which made two of them.

Georgia had given birth?

Cheyenne could not even begin to comprehend it.

"To what?" she wondered. "Rosemary's Baby?"

"I'm sorry?"

"Nothing," she said.

"I am sorry to be the bearer of such unexpected news, Miss Elias. I was under the impression that you and Ms. Humboldt were...friends."

"Not in this universe." Then, in spite of herself, "Where's the kid now?"

"At the DHS temporary placement center, Haven House."

Bile surged with sudden, violent force. The response was wholly visceral; she stumbled back a step, lost her footing, and fell ass-deep into the sagebrush, her heart thumping wildly in her chest. Chuck wandered over to sit beside her, his body warm against her thigh. In the distance, the Grand Teton Mountain Range rose from the valley floor like a row of stalwart, granite infantry lined up for battle, and high above them, the sky was pure, azure blue.

She saw none of it.

Haven House.

The crumbling red brick building bled into her brain in rivulets, streams that ebbed and flowed until the image coalesced into the hellish homestead of her childhood, shockingly familiar in all of its dilapidated glory.

White walls and scarred wooden floors and windows barred by steel. Sirens and screams and cold, angry hands. Blurred faces, hollow words, pain, pain, pain—

Cheyenne shook herself. Struggled to breath. Put her hand over her heart in futile effort to ease its breakneck pace. Chuck put his paw in her lap.

"Fuck me," she said.

"Miss Elias?"

Another bark broke from her.

A kid and a mental breakdown. The gift that keeps on giving.

"Cheyenne?"

"Haven House," she croaked. The scent of urine and Lysol spray flooded her nostrils; mildew tickled the back of her throat. Her stomach clenched in rebellion. "Shit-boy-howdy."

"Er...do you know it?"

Like the back of her scarred hand. *Tied to a truck and dragged down memory lane.* What had she done to deserve this?

Try being born.

"Not funny," she whispered, her knuckles aching where she gripped the phone.

That it had such power—that all she'd become could dissolve so quickly into what she'd once been...she never would have guessed. Everything she'd considered conquered merely lay dormant, existing in stasis, mute until its reawakening.

Like the plague.

"I am sorry, Miss Elias. Clearly this is an unwelcome surprise."

Unwelcome. What a pale, weak word for Georgia's last hurrah. So mild and understated, the antithesis of who she'd been. Like declaring the sun lukewarm. Or the ocean a bit briny.

"Perhaps you should take some time and think it over?"

"Negative." *Over and out.* But—"How old is he?"

Stupid, Cheyenne thought. She didn't want to know. She didn't care. The entire conversation was like rolling naked in poison oak. But her mind's eye—insolent and defiant and gleefully giving her the finger—drew him in startling, painful clarity: *thin, like Georgia had been; all angles and sharp edges. Narrow and slight in his mother's shadow, a whisper to her scream. Hushed and anxious in a prison of rusting iron bars and inhuman chill.*

Yeah, sure, why not?

"Just make it up as you go," she told herself.

"I'm sorry?"

"Nothing."

Smith/Jones sighed. "Rafferty is currently ten years old."

"Ten," Cheyenne echoed tonelessly. At ten, she'd been shooting craps and sneaking into R rated movies. Vandalizing freeway underpasses and drinking stolen beer—with this kid's mother.

Goddamn irony. Someday she would figure that shite out. But not today.

"Miss Elias, even with the best of foster families Rafferty's existence will be…difficult. Children are all too often lost within the system and left to fend for themselves. I would urge you to take some time and consider this. A decision need not be made immediately."

You must learn to control your impulses, Cheyenne. They do you more harm than good.

Bite me, Phil.

"I don't want him." The words were harsh, stark, unflinching. *Truth.* Next to her, Chuck whined softly. "Not today or tomorrow."

"I see." Smith/Jones went cold. "Well, I apologize for bothering you. I will let family services know you have no wish to serve as Rafferty's guardian, and they will act accordingly. Good day, Miss Elias."

And then he was gone.

Cheyenne stared down at her phone. Then she turned and threw it into the sagebrush.

"The Kid is *not* my problem," Cheyenne told Chuck an hour later.

They sat at the summit of Sheep's Mountain, also known as Sleeping Indian, in the exact spot where the Indian's arms crossed his chest. Below them, the Jackson Hole valley spread like a picturesque landscape painting, spires of pale gray granite interspersed by waves of brilliant, aspen green and swells of dark pine that hugged the low alpine like an artfully draped scarf. The Snake River wound sinuously along the base of the Teton Range, a glittering ribbon of sun-flecked gold.

"It's a play," she continued. "Georgia was a textbook sociopath. Games defined her, and if she could destroy someone's life, she did. Just for kicks."

Chuck grunted, content atop the small boulder they occupied, his gaze sharp on the hills of sage below them, ever vigilant for the possible chisler sighting.

"I don't care *why* she did it. Doesn't matter. I know what she's doing—but I let that go a long time ago." Which might not have been—strictly speaking—entirely true, because really, how did one let the complete and utter annihilation of everything they ever were—*the stripping of their bones to their fucking soul*—go? "I refuse to rise to the bait, Chuck. Because that's what he is—bait. And I'm not biting."

There was no doubt in Cheyenne. Not about this. Georgia had been many things: selfish, greedy, vain. Frighteningly intelligent. A woman who was wholly incapable of empathy, sympathy, or compassion.

What appeared to *be* was only illusion. Manufactured deception was a skill at which Georgia had excelled. Even at sixteen—the last time Cheyenne had seen her—she'd been capable of building a house of lies so vast, so intricate, that determining her end game was nearly impossible. But there was always an end game.

One where everyone but Georgia lost.

That realization had come late to Cheyenne. In spite of

every malevolent act she'd witnessed in their decade of friendship, every machination Georgia had played out around her. Every lie told. None of the pain had mattered, so long as it wasn't hers. And then, it was.

Sirens screaming and blood spilling down—

"The Queen of Fuckery, smiting her subjects." A hand down Chuck's silky, brindled coat, a deliberate release of the tension. She had to tread carefully—the memories of blood and death and terror slept fitfully within her and were easily woken.

As proven by The Incident, which had led to The Counselor, followed by The Interrogation and—inevitably—The Diagnosis.

You have serious anger management issues, Cheyenne.

And you, Phil, have serious halitosis.

No, the memories were not something she could afford to let control her. All the more reason she should get up, haul her ass off this mountain, and forget. Problem was, The Kid was real. And *she* had done that, had colored in the lines and made him whole. She had allowed it.

Why? Why had she done that?

She didn't want to know him. Nothing said he wasn't as damaged as his mother had been, just as capable of evil. No one could claim he'd been born uncontaminated by her malice, her cruelty. There were no guarantees he wouldn't mistake a scream for a symphony.

Besides, she was hardly fit to be a parental figure. Cheyenne knew herself well. She was short-tempered, impatient, intolerant of stupidity, and wholly antisocial. That she had been cursed with a soft heart was just another mystery of life—like the Bermuda Triangle or Bigfoot. But there was a difference between adopting a three-legged cow dog—or a one-eyed cat, or a goat with a bad attitude—and taking responsibility for a child.

Especially the child of a woman she'd once fantasized about clubbing to death with a tire iron.

"That's just not healthy," she said. Chuck sighed and rolled over to offer his white belly, his gaze glinting like polished amber as he watched her.

"Don't," she told him. "We can't. She did this for a reason —some fucked up, crazy-ass reason—and I won't go there. Not again. *She almost killed me.*"

Anger vibrated, deep, steady, eternal. Another thing to add to the unfit list: incessantly pissed off. And while Phil considered that *"problematical,"* Cheyenne saw no problem with it at all. Except when it slipped its leash. When it became rage. When she *acted.*

No kid deserved that. And she would know.

"I came from crazy," she said and gave in, rubbing Chuck's belly. "I have no business even contemplating this."

But she was. Jesus, she *was.*

Not for the reason Georgia assumed she would. And not because revenge was best served to a ten year old. No, her consideration was born solely of one unarguable truth: *because it was the right thing to do.*

Doing the right thing hadn't mattered in the first half of her life; surviving had superseded any morality that might have shaped her. But she no longer had that excuse. Her life had been changed by one man's act, and the sole price for receiving that boon was to one day pay it forward. It was the only thing he'd asked of her, and she could no more refuse than fly to the moon. That the opportunity had arisen here and now—when she'd begun to think it never would— attached to the one person whose memory still had the ability to infuriate her really shouldn't have been a surprise. *Goddamn irony.*

But while Cheyenne knew it was the right thing, that didn't make it the smart thing. Because she *was* damaged. Her mother had been certifiable, her father a complete unknown. She was scarred—inside and out—and what she felt toward Georgia was...toxic. *Dangerous.* And she wasn't at all certain she was any better than those who'd produced her. Perhaps that was just fantasy born of her own need to believe. Was she capable of punishing a child for his mother's crimes? Would the anger that had become so deeply engrained within her use him as its outlet?

All pertinent, important questions—none of which she could answer. Not unless she acted. Not unless she leapt.

....even with the best of foster families Rafferty's existence will be...difficult. Children are all too often lost within the system and left to fend for themselves...

As she had done. First with the rusty edge of a serrated blade and later with her rage. The only difference between her and Georgia—as she'd reluctantly come to realize in the years that followed—had been the simple fact that Cheyenne *felt.* All of it. And her reactions had been the result of emotion, not the cold, inhuman premeditation with which Georgia had calculated the world.

Sometimes, Cheyenne wasn't sure which was worse.

So she knew what The Kid faced. And part of her thought, *Hell, I survived it. So will he.* Which was probably true. But another part, the one coerced into life by a man who'd demanded only her best, that part understood that who she'd finally become owed itself entirely to that patient nurturing, to that unbendable belief in *her,* to the utter refusal to allow her to be anything less. And everyone deserved that. Everyone.

Even The Kid.

Now, there was a chance—similar to that whole pigs flying thing—that some exemplary foster family would come along and provide that cultivation. It *could* happen. Allegedly. And who said she wouldn't be destroying that opportunity?

Who said her need to pay it forward wasn't simply egotism in the guise of charity?

"The odds are screwed," she said to Chuck. "Damned if I do, damned if I don't."

Which left only…instinct. And since she *was* thinking pretty seriously about getting on a flying boat and embracing legal responsibility for the child of her nemesis, well, instinct had spoken. Loud and clear.

Anger was her one consistent, her companion; her fellow man-at-arms. Fear was not something she'd experienced since she'd awoken in a cold, hard hospital bed at fifteen, her body reshaped, her soul rewoven in hate, but she felt it now.

For The Kid, because she had no idea if she had the ability to give back what she'd received. For herself, because to fail in this would not only mark her, it just might erase what she'd fought so hard become. But most of all, she feared the motives behind this sequence of events, the manipulative, malicious hand which took such pleasure in arranging the pieces and watching them fall.

"All bets are off," she muttered. Chuck thumped his tail, his gaze conveying all of the unknown secrets of the universe, his delight in her unhidden.

Stupid dog.

Cheyenne pulled her phone from her pocket, checked the signal and dialed.

CHAPTER TWO

*B*lood coats his teeth.
 His lung gurgles and threatens to send the acid in his belly surging up his throat, onto the hard ground around him. The air is frigid, turning his exposed skin to ice, stiffening his limbs. He is dying as he drags himself across the merciless scrub and sand and broken rock. One dark, pulsing thought drives him forward, and he clings relentlessly to the life that drains from him with every shallow, bloody breath—

William Blackheart woke with a violent start, a howl of pain and fury and grief wedged in his chest. Cold air sliced through his lungs, piercing them as effectively as the bullets he dreamt of. Sweat matted his hair and trickled down spine; his hip ached as though he'd caught the business end of an angry mule. The throb of his arm echoed the hammer in his skull, and he could still feel the cold weight of his weapon cutting into his palm as he dragged it through the desert sand.

Next to him, the clock's obnoxious green display read 4:35.

He pushed from the bed, ignored his pain, and lit a cigarette. His heart beat like a heavy, angry drum, driving the furious rush of his blood. Adrenaline pumped through him like the slide of the finest whiskey.

Fifteen weeks, six days, and seven hours had passed and still, the sand continued to cling. The air—like raw earth—remained in his nostrils. The shriek of the wind—lunacy given sound—was a song that haunted him.

The pain was ripe, fresh and new; this, he accepted. *Enjoyed.* Because it meant he yet lived, that the promise of retribution had not been stolen. But the sand, the air, that wail of madness...those were not things he'd expected to live on, to trail behind him like a deep, dark wake. To hunt him.

Mock him.

Fury was a raw, living thing within him, and their echo only fanned the fire, like careless children teasing an animal kept chained. The wrath swelled against his flesh, and his skin ached at the effort of keeping it contained. The darkness born within him wanted to unleash the fury and revel in the destruction. The darkness wanted screams.

He had moments of clarity, of *knowing,* when he understood he'd broken, that survival had become irrevocably interwoven with the need to destroy. That he was no longer who he'd been, but some*thing* far more dangerous...to himself, to everyone else. That perhaps he should have died that night, if only to save his own soul. But those flashes of self-awareness could not compete with the hunger that gnawed at him, the ruthless appetite for carnage that had enabled his survival. They did not restore his sanity.

He was damaged and—in singular, terrifying moments—deranged. Unable to separate *then* from *now,* incapable of thinking past the blood, the pain, the incessant need to paint the world in living crimson. Everything he'd ever been—a son, a soldier, a decent human being—had bled away, leaving only a hollow, hateful husk driven solely by one goal: *vengeance.*

By any means necessary.

Cigarette smoke curled into the air around him. Outside his dingy motel room, footsteps sounded, and he tensed, his hand going to the Glock that sat on the bedside table. He moved to the window and looked through the narrow part in the worn, yellowed curtains. A man and child were climbing into a minivan parked a few feet from his door.

Will turned away, but retained the Glock. His security blanket, his talisman. The only thing left that he trusted.

He took another drag from his cigarette and sank into one of the chairs next to the table. His lung wheezed in protest, not yet fully healed, another thing he ignored. Another form of punishment. This, too, was something he recognized during those brief moments of cognizance, that as much hate as he held for those who had betrayed him, he hated himself more, knew he deserved the worst of fates for his failures. But now was not the time for that; it would come later.

After.

Light yawned through the curtains, but he didn't open them. He preferred the darkness, where he could fade into the shadows and simply be. Where his scars were hidden, and the only evidence of his ruin was the pain that throbbed in his hip, the damaged nerves that leapt and twisted in his arm, the rattle of his damaged lung. Where he could pretend, if only for a moment, that he had ceased to exist. *Finally.*

But the world would not let him fade, and as his cell phone suddenly lit, flooding the darkness with brilliant white light, he understood he would have to fight for that, too.

He reached for his phone, checked the number, and the adrenaline which had finally begun to subside surged through him like a geyser. He ground out his cigarette and answered it. "Blackheart."

"They cut you loose."

No. He'd cut himself loose. "It was time."

"Are you sure?"

Not of anything. Not anymore. "What have you got?"

Red Morrow hesitated, and Will's hand fisted, the singular point of tension he would allow himself. Red, Rye's twin brother, whose hunger for blood beat as strong as his own. Red the "hacktivist," who had taken a path opposite his partisan twin, a man wanted by no less than four of the world's largest governments for the disclosure of classified documents—including the one for whom Will had nearly bled out.

Red's collective of international, loosely organized hackers *the Unnamed* spent their days unmasking purported atrocity and injustice and plastering it across the worldwide web. Their mission statement was short and succinct: *no bad deed goes unpunished.* Every superpower on earth hated their guts.

Communicating with Red could raze Will's entire military career, but since he'd gone AWOL from Bethesda three days ago, he figured there wasn't anything left of that career to destroy. The service was singularly brutal toward its defectors, regardless of their intent. Of their damage. No, he would be painted with one broad, yellow stroke: deserter. And everything his team had died for, everything he'd killed for, would be expunged as though it had never existed.

As though *he* had never existed.

Walking away had gone deeply against everything Will stood for. Severing that tie had felt like hacking off a limb. Every second spent in boot camp hell, every mission he'd carried out, every life he'd saved, every fellow soldier he'd buried...*gone*. The foundation on which he'd built his life, his integrity, his *worth*, nothing but rubble. His entire definition, erased. *Replaced.*

By nothing good.

Surely his grandfather was spinning in his grave. Jake Blackstone had raised him better; *You ain't no quitter, boy. You fought your way into this world, and you earned your place. Now you gotta do somethin' with it.* And although Jake had dreamed of passing his cattle ranch on to his sole living heir, he'd accepted Will's decision to join the Navy with his typical blunt pragmatism. *Man's gut is the only path worth followin'.*

A veteran himself, Jake had instilled in Will a deep respect for his country and a profound love and appreciation for all that he'd been born into simply by virtue of geography. As far as Jake was concerned, knowing the difference between right and wrong was all the moral fortitude a man needed, and he'd spent every moment of their life together reinforcing that belief. He'd been a hard, complex man, one who was, by turns, both the kindest, most generous person Will had ever known—and the meanest, orneriest son of a bitch to ever walk upright. Will knew he had inherited both traits, although only one of them had crawled out of the desert that night.

Jake would not approve of his defection. He would expect Will to stay, to *fight*. He'd believed in structure, in hierarchy and the careful tiers upon which the military was built.

But there'd been little choice. They wanted Will shelved. They knew how fucked up he was, and they didn't want him anymore. Worse, they understood that, for him, it wasn't over. That he had plans, and they didn't include falling back in line like a good little soldier. Someone with bars on their chest had sent them into slaughter.

Someone he would find. Expose. *Kill.*

If that meant the sacrifice of all he'd worked for, *who he was*, so be it. It was far less a price than his men had paid. And that, Jake would understand. Still, Will was glad his grandfather was dead. His own shame was enough. Jake's would have been the final nail.

"Paris was a bust," Red said finally. "She definitely knew what she was doing. But I found something when I tracked her calls. Frankly, it was too easy, and I don't trust it, but right now, it's all I've got."

In the space of a heartbeat, Will was moving, pulling on his clothing, shrugging into his shoulder holster. "What?"

"Seven weeks ago she contacted an estate attorney in Milwaukee."

"So?"

"So she had him draw up a will—which leads me to believe she knew she'd been made. That, my friend, is what we call a *clue*."

Will only snorted. "Your point?"

"In the will she named a guardian for her minor child."

Will froze. "She had a kid? How the hell did you miss that?"

"I didn't. There's no record of him. I'm still looking for his birth certificate; she must have had him in Timbuk-fucking-to."

"Christ."

"I uploaded the guardian's name and background. *Most* intriguing."

Will's heart shuddered; he fought for breath. Clenched his fist again.

Tracking the theft of the crates to counter-intelligence hadn't taken long. The realization had come to him with sickening, piercing clarity as he'd dragged himself slowly through the sand, watering the barren, rocky desert with his blood. *What* he'd seen, *who* he'd seen. But it had taken three weeks staring at a water-stained hospital ceiling to put his brain in order, to reach past the meds and the pain, to separate memory from the ghosts and screams and phantom gunfire, to remember what he already knew.

Fucking spooks.

They would have had the intel. The means to intercept. Access to the airspace. And the chilling lack of moral and spiritual clarity required to butcher an entire SEAL team and commit the highest treason.

When Red called him the fourth week and vowed retribution for Rye's death, all Will had to do was point him in the right direction, and pull the trigger. Red had done the rest—because even the spooks could be hacked. And they'd unearthed their first name: CIA Officer Georgia Humboldt.

"She's booked on a ten a.m. flight out of Jackson Hole, Wyoming, tomorrow morning."

Will pinched the bridge of his nose. Grit his teeth. Made himself count every ragged, uneven breath as he struggled to rein himself in. "Who?"

"The guardian."

He blinked. His head pulsed like a heavy metal tribute. "Wyoming?"

"Random, I know. But she's our link."

"What's her connection?"

"Read the file."

"Just fucking tell me."

"Easy, brother. You sure you're up for this?"

Will would have laughed, if he'd known how. "Tell me."

"No," Red said, quiet. Final. "You need to read it."

"Why?"

"Trust me."

He said nothing. He trusted no one, not even Red. But he

wasn't going to argue; it was a goddamn waste of time. "Fine." He grabbed his keys and his pack. "Text me her flight number and description."

"There's a picture in the file. You'll know her when you see her."

CHAPTER THREE

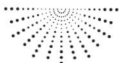

*H**ave u lost ur ℰ**$@!! mind?*
Cheyenne scowled down at the tiny letters on her touch screen. She hated texting. Well, she hated communicating. Texting just made it all the more loathsome.

Chuck's food is in pantry, she responded, snarling softly when the autocorrect turned *pantry* into *panty*.

"Yeah, because that's where I keep the dog food. In my *panties*," she muttered.

The elderly woman who sat beside her in row 12 of SkyWest flight 2311 offered a raised brow.

Don't forget treats, she continued, typing carefully. *Angus will feed Dexter ℰ Harry.*

Whoosh! And off it went. That, however, would not be the end of it. Because Whitney was currently on meltdown. Sirens-blaring, send out the troops, alert the media, freak-the-hell-out meltdown.

The hysteria was partly Cheyenne's fault—she supposed she really shouldn't have left the news that she was going to Wisconsin to pick up a kid on voicemail—but most of it was just Whitney and her penchant for drama. Everything was an Event.

U can't do this! CRAZY!

Well, there was no arguing with that—at least the whole "crazy" part. As for what she could and couldn't do—

Can too. AM. Chill out, woman. Will be fine.

Which is what Cheyenne had decided at 3:47 that morning. If she could just keep moving forward—and not look back—everything would be kosher. The Kid was ten. That left less than a decade until he belonged to himself.

Eight to ten years—max. She could do that.

Need to think about this! Is NOT Chuck!

"Duh," Cheyenne said.

But she understood. She knew The Kid wasn't the same as Chuck or Dexter or Harry. She knew he needed far more from her than they did. Better than anyone. That was the thing about Whitney—she failed to realize that everything she pointed out was something Cheyenne had already considered. Because in spite of Cheyenne's tendency to act on impulse, she wasn't careless, or thoughtless, or stupid.

She was prepared to do everything she could for Rafferty Humboldt. To embody the example she'd been given, and that would have to be good enough.

DECIDED. Whoosh!

Of course she had doubts. She'd sprung from crazy, been raised by apathy, graduated with honors in the transference of rage, and was—generally speaking—jaded, skeptical, and hopelessly annoyed by her fellow man. But she was also smart, perceptive, compassionate and loyal. Her knowledge was valuable. Worth teaching. And deep down, only one question drove her: *who would she be now if she'd never been saved?*

No one good or decent. Of that, she had no doubt.

Because Hank MacLean *had* saved her. Without him she

would have never known love. Trust. Her own value. That knowing him had come with devastating loss as well was just another life experience to be borne. She would not trade the day he'd discovered her jacking his pick-up truck for anything on earth, even if it hurt to remember.

No, this was right, what she was doing. Hank would approve.

Why r u doing this? Don't understand!

Why did people think she needed their understanding? Their approval?

"Get over yourself," she said.

The woman at her side smiled, but since she was thumbing through a *Ladies Home Journal*, Cheyenne wasn't sure if it was because of her own random self-talk or the magazine.

YOU WILL REGRET THIS!

Was it too much to ask for a little belief? Sure, she had a few issues, but she wasn't a freaking psychopath. *A sociopath* —which was what The Kid's mother had been. Seriously, how much worse could she do?

But Cheyenne wasn't going to argue. She never did. It was a goddamn waste of time.

Enough. Gotta fly (har!) Talk 2 u soon.

Whoosh!

"Everyone has an opinion," murmured the woman beside her. An accent shaped her words, something Slavic and guttural that spoke of a land far removed from the one in which they sat. "There was a time, sharing was considered rude. Now it is considered a right."

"So much for evolution," Cheyenne replied. She slid her phone away, sat back and tucked her "seat belt" discretely beneath her fleece. Hell if she was buckling the damn thing; it's not like it would *save* her if the flying boat she was on went down. Or exploded. Or lost cabin pressure. Or—

"I hate to fly," the woman continued conversationally. Her voice was rough and deep and spoke of a lifelong love affair with tobacco products. "I would rather eat dirt."

Cheyenne was not adept at small talk, so avoidance was her MO when it came to the general public and their inclination to yammer. But when the woman turned to look at her, the faded blue gaze that flitted over the waxy patch of scarred flesh that marred Cheyenne's left cheek didn't linger. Her eyelids didn't flicker, her smile didn't falter. She didn't even flinch.

Impressive. And unusual. Almost everyone looked away, as if it was somehow catching. Which prompted Cheyenne to respond, "This is my first time. Today is the popping of my aeronautical cherry."

A small smile turned the woman's mouth. "A bumpy, unpleasant ride that will leave you slightly nauseated. Is appropriate comparison."

If she only knew. "I thought the plane would be bigger."

"This leg is always small plane. No beverage." The woman scowled. "Cheap bastards."

"Less for more. Everyone's doing it now."

"Bah, is nothing new. Screwing people has always been in vogue." The woman offered her hand. "I am Olga."

Cheyenne hesitated a moment before accepting it. She rarely shook people's hands—her scars were one thing to look at, another to feel—but it seemed rude to refuse. "Cheyenne."

"A pleasure." Olga nodded, and her aged denim gaze took in Cheyenne's black cargo pants, fitted black fleece and YNP ball cap. "You dress like a boy."

Cheyenne stared at her. She didn't know whether to be amused or insulted, but she could appreciate the directness, so she only shrugged. "I like to fly under the radar."

"There is flying under the radar, and there is disappearing

from sight. You should not hide beneath a man's hat." Olga's eyes flickered to the scar on Cheyenne's cheek, and it prickled in awareness. "Or is that your purpose?"

Cheyenne tugged at her seat belt, annoyed. "People are dickheads. Dealing with it gets old."

"You let it be your problem when it should be theirs."

Cheyenne shook her head. This was *exactly* why she did not bother to talk to people.

"In my day, women looked like women," Olga continued. "We had breasts. Hips. We were not ashamed."

"I'm not ashamed," Cheyenne retorted. "I'm just not a billboard."

A grunt. "My son, he is engaged to a girl who wears plastic pants and ugly shoes. Her hair looks like Medusa. Rings in her nose, her lip, in her eyebrow! I just want to rip them all out."

A startled laugh caught in Cheyenne's throat. "Probably better resist that temptation."

"Yes," Olga agreed. "Until the wedding."

Which made Cheyenne feel for said future daughter-in-law. "Your son lives in the valley?"

"He is ski instructor. We send him to three ivy-league schools, and he wants only to play." A disgusted sound rumbled in Olga's throat.

"He's not alone, you know. This valley is full of that. I think it's generational."

"Is no excuse. You will be in big trouble when you are my age. They will leave you dying in the streets while they go to find pleasure." Olga looked out the small oval window next to her and squinted against the bright light reflecting off the plane's wing. Just beyond the wing, a man was pushing a cart of luggage across the tarmac. Behind him, the Grand Tetons rose to stunning grandeur. "Being mama is a thankless job."

Well. That was *great* news.

"At least he wants you to visit," Cheyenne pointed out.

Olga slid her a sideways scowl. "Is not his choice."

"Ah."

"He lives like American. But he is *Russian*. He must learn difference."

"A vast chasm, I'm sure."

"Like the hole in the desert."

For a moment, Cheyenne didn't understand. Then, "The Grand Canyon?"

"He thinks work should be *fun*. Is work! Is not meant to be fun."

"This is true."

The stewardess approached and eyed Cheyenne's lap.

"Please fasten your seat belt, ma'am." She phrased it as a request, but her wide smile was patently false, and her eyes were hard. *You're one of those, aren't you?* "We'll be taking off shortly."

Cheyenne met her gaze and wondered if the Bill of Rights covered aircraft seatbelts. Not that there was much left to the Bill of Rights. And there was probably an Air Marshal on board who would tackle her ass to the ground and cuff her if she refused. Which would be an interesting experiment…if she didn't really need to get to America's dairy land and collect an orphan. So she sighed and snapped the belt together.

"Thank you," the stewardess murmured. She stared for a long moment at the scar on Cheyenne's cheek—just long enough for the insult to sink in—before moving on.

Olga muttered something colorful and dark.

"Agreed," Cheyenne told her.

Around them, people settled into place, and the air stairs were removed. The door slammed shut with a rush of chilly air, and the steady hum of the engines turned into a low roar. A well-modulated, disembodied male voice suddenly crackled around them, welcoming them to the flight, announcing his name (*Bob!*), his title (*Captain!*), and then rattled off something about times, altitude and temperatures. Cheyenne didn't particularly care. As he signed off, the stewardess appeared in front of them and began a show-and-tell about airplane safety.

Then they began to move backward.

Cheyenne's stomach dipped. Since she didn't particularly believe her body needed to be at 30,000 feet—ever—and since she could totally see herself ending up an airline crash statistic, she wasn't looking forward to this flight. Or the one from Denver to Milwaukee, which would follow. There was a reason she drove everywhere. But time was of the essence —the Kid was in Haven.

House of fucking horrors.

So even though she really didn't want to be where she was—*like he did either*—she would deal. She would grit her teeth and sing *I Will Survive* in her head, and everything would be fine.

Buck up, little camper.

Beside her, Olga chortled. "You are afraid?"

"First time," Cheyenne retorted. "I reserve the right."

A snort. "You have lived through worse."

Again with the piercing stare at her scar. Cheyenne resisted the urge to rub it.

"Compared to that, this is nothing." Olga gave a wave of dismissal. Rings glittered on her fingers: rubies, emeralds and dark, glinting sapphires. She wore an expensive, boiled wool pantsuit in dark blue-gray plaid and low-heeled leather pumps that matched the slender black bag she cradled in her lap. Steel gray hair wound into an elegant twist at the back of her skull and pearls clipped to her earlobes; her lipstick was blood red. "If we go down, it will be quick." She shrugged. "Time to scream. That is all."

"Good to know," Cheyenne muttered.

The plane turned and rolled to a halt. The engines kicked abruptly into full gear, revving beneath them like NASCAR on steroids, and Cheyenne clenched her fingers around the armrests until they ached. The coil of power was almost painful, a stillness so full of motion her nerves shrieked in protest. And then, without warning, they were hurtling forward at a speed wholly unnatural to man. Just when she thought they were going to explode, the nose of the plane lifted, and suddenly they were aloft.

"See?" Olga said. "Nothing to worry you."

And then the plane shuddered and *clunked,* and Cheyenne glared at her in disbelief.

"The landing gear." Another dismissive wave. "Is normal."

It took a good two minutes for Cheyenne's heart to slide from her throat back into her chest cavity. Her fingers, however, preferred to cling to the armrests—as if they were any more capable of saving her than the flimsy nylon strap buckled around her waist.

"Fuck's sake," she said finally, forcing a breath in and then out.

"You are fine."

Well. She couldn't really argue that, so she just looked past the woman next to her, out the tiny window, and was immediately captivated by the sight of the mountains spread out below, a monstrous, twisted mass of granite and pine dotted by lingering snow fields, ebbing glaciers, and brilliant blue alpine lakes.

"Worth it," she said quietly, committing the sprawling scene to the eidetic memory she'd had since birth.

Because *this,* this was worth painting. This was the world reworked; so massive and wild it made mincemeat of the ego with which humans viewed their surroundings. If God existed, it was here, in this.

"Every time I see them, I miss home," Olga murmured.

For a long moment they sat in silence, undisturbed by the vibration of the propellers next to them, staring out at the untamed beauty of the granite spine that split the country from border to border. The crackling, disembodied male voice returned—*Captain Bob!*—and announced that they had reached their cruising altitude. Denver was less than an hour away, and oh boy, what a gorgeous day to fly.

Blech.

Olga turned away from the window. "Where are you going?"

Normally, Cheyenne's answer would have been vague and imprecise, but since her equilibrium was seriously disturbed at being thrust into the stratosphere—and since the paper barf bag was starting to look really appealing—she decided to share.

"I'm off to the dairy land to collect my inheritance," she replied. The *Fasten Seat Belt* light winked out and she unbuckled immediately. "He's ten."

"You inherited...a child?"

"Random, right?"

"I do not understand."

"Me either." Cheyenne shrugged. "His ma and I....we were *done.* And I mean—*finito*—but...well, he's me."

For a long moment, Olga only stared at her. "You are a strange girl."

"Takes one to know one."

Another small smile. "You are married?"

Cheyenne laughed. It was not something she did often, but when it rolled out of her, it was low and deep and vibrant. People turned to look. "Not in this lifetime."

"You do this alone?"

Cheyenne shrugged. "Alone is what I know."

"And this child's mother...you were not close?"

Cheyenne only snorted.

Olga sat back and eyed her shrewdly. "What is it that happened?"

Blood and terror and death.

"I know there's a purpose here," Cheyenne told her. "Some kind of machination—that's who she was—and I know the other shoe is coming. Probably right to the noggin. But a long time ago, I was where he is, and no one came for me." She paused, wondering why she was attempting to explain something she barely understood herself. "So I can't leave him there...no matter what lies in wait."

That faded blue gaze studied her with the same kind of frank assessment Hank had always watched her with, and Cheyenne found it oddly comforting. While she might not have a tactful bone in her body, she *was* honest. Assessment didn't faze her—she was who she was. Besides, not many people had the cajones to look her in the eye. It was always refreshing to meet one of the few.

"You do not know this child?" Olga asked. "You have not met?"

"Nope."

"But you believe you can care for him?"

"I know I can."

A moment of silence fell between them. "Confidence is good." Olga nodded slowly. "But there is something you are not considering."

"What's that?"

"You must forgive her."

The plane chose that moment to lurch like a drunk. Cheyenne grabbed onto the armrests and swore. *"Seriously?"*

"Is just turbulence," Olga scoffed. "We are not crashing."

"Well, you be sure and let me know if that changes," Cheyenne retorted.

A rough laugh broke from the woman next to her. "You would squeal like a pig. Why would I tell you?"

Captain Bob interrupted then. *"Just a little bit of turbulence, folks. We'll be turning the fasten seat belt sign back on, and it will remain on for the duration of the flight. We thank you for your cooperation. We should be landing in Denver in just under forty minutes."*

The stewardess moved slowly past, her eyes locked on Cheyenne's undone seat belt. Her mouth opened, but Cheyenne held out a hand and beat her.

"Yeah, yeah, I got it," she muttered. "Freaking seat belt police."

"Thank you," the woman replied coolly.

"My pleasure," Cheyenne told her.

Olga was smiling again. "I do like you."

"I'm a likeable girl."

A snort. "You think to distract me. But you know of what I spoke."

She was a sharp old bird. Just Cheyenne's luck. "Yeah, I heard you."

"Is important," Olga told her earnestly. "You cannot keep her child unless you forgive her. You must not punish him."

"I don't plan to."

"But you *will* if you do not let your anger go. It is…inevitable."

Which Cheyenne had not even considered. Her plan was to simply move forward and ignore what lay behind. But the past cast a long shadow—one she still stood within when her ire was stirred—so there was really no denying—or escaping—the truth she could see reflected in Olga's discerning blue gaze.

"Damn it," she said with a heavy sigh.

"Yes," Olga agreed.

You need to determine where this anger stems from, Cheyenne, and you need to exorcise it.

Exorcise this, Phil.

"Food for thought," Cheyenne said.

"You must do this," Olga urged quietly. "Is not fair to him if you cannot."

Perhaps. But leaving him where he was, *abandoning* him—that was worse. Because even if she could somehow summon the desire to forgive Georgia, Cheyenne wasn't at all certain she was capable of it. To forgive what she'd barely survived... not once had she ever considered it. Nor did she care to.

She was, however, perfectly capable of helping the child—in spite of the vicious, bloodied past. Of this, she was certain. Tangible, practical help: a home, a full belly, an education. Someone who gave a damn. It was more than she'd had at his age. And she knew the value of those few, simple things, so that's where she would start.

"Thank you," Cheyenne said. She met Olga's gaze. "I appreciate your words. I don't take them lightly."

Olga studied her for a long moment, that sharp, perceptive assessment flitting across her features once more. Then she nodded, briefly. "Remember them. And when you are ready, *use* them."

CHAPTER FOUR

Milwaukee County Police Department Report
Case # 160958J-3201
03/09/92 23:23

I responded at 21:02 to a call from dispatch regarding a domestic dispute in progress at 311 Brady Street. Upon arrival, resident Jonas Pettington approached me and advised that his neighbor, Abigail Elias, was threatening to harm her minor child. It was not known if anyone other than Ms. Elias and her minor child were inside the residence. I called for backup and approached the apartment complex.

Upon entering the building, I could smell smoke. I radioed into dispatch and requested the MCFD investigate the scene. With the aid of Mr. Pettington, we alerted residents to the possible fire and evacuated them.

As I approached Ms. Elias' residence, I could hear cries through the door and believed them to belong to the minor child, a girl named Cheyenne who Mr. Pettington stated was approximately 4 or 5 years of age. As I stood there, I realized the smoke was coming from Ms. Elias' residence.

I knocked on the door and identified myself as a police officer. I asked Ms. Elias to open the door and allow me into the residence. Ms. Elias did not respond. I knocked once more and demanded entrance. Again, she did not respond.

I forced my way into the residence and discovered the apartment dark and full of smoke. I could hear a child crying, but could not see her. When I located the light switch and turned it on, I discovered Abigail Elias on the floor of the main room of the residence, unconscious and bleeding from a stomach wound. I radioed into dispatch and requested paramedics.

Upon entering the apartment's sole bedroom, I located the minor child huddled in the corner, wrapped in a blanket. She had been badly burned on her left side. I identified myself as a police officer and attempted to get close enough to provide first aid.

I was approximately three feet from her when she brandished a bloody serrated knife (I believe it was a bread knife) and told me not to touch her. She grew more agitated when I identified myself, and she refused to allow me to get close. Mr. Pettington then entered the room and spoke to the child. Several minutes later, she agreed to give him the knife, and we were able to approach her and evaluate her condition.

Most of her clothing had melted to her skin, and the blanket that wrapped her was smoldering. She had what appeared to be third and fourth degree burns the entire length of her body on her left side and was unable to see with her left eye. I witnessed bruises to her face, blood from her nose and mouth, and her right arm appeared to be broken. I radioed into dispatch and requested a second ambulance be sent to the location.

Mr. Pettington asked Cheyenne what had occurred, but

she did not respond. I then asked what happened to her mother, and she began to cry, but would not provide a verbal response. At this time, the MCFD arrived and began an inspection of the premises. The initial ambulance immediately followed, and I directed the paramedics to Abigail Elias, who was still bleeding and unconscious. The second ambulance arrived immediately thereafter, and both were transported to St. Andrews Medical Center at 22:38.

The MCFD located a mason jar on the floor of the bedroom that contained approximately two ounces of kerosene. Fire Chief Ingalls believed this to be the accelerant used to ignite the fire. The wall behind the bed was smoldering, which was the sole remaining source of smoke they could locate. The curtains were burned, as was the bedding and the carpet. The residence was littered with dirty syringes and garbage.

Witness statements and Fire Chief Ingall's report are attached hereto. The case will be assigned to Detective Roberts for follow-up.

Officer: J. Keegan 289

∼

Cheyenne F. Elias Session #1
Case Manager: Connie Brock
07/02/1992

I met with Cheyenne today. She is a five-year-old female who was removed from her mother's home in March of this year. Cheyenne was discovered by the MPD in her mother's apartment with third and fourth degree burns covering 37% of her body. Her mother (Abigail) had suffered a knife wound to the abdomen and was unconscious when the MPD arrived. Because there were no eyewit-

nesses—and because neither Cheyenne nor her mother would speak of the events of that night—only the factual findings of Detective Ed Roberts' investigation could be entered into the record. Based on that physical evidence, Cheyenne was removed from the home, and her mother was sentenced to three years' incarceration at the Wausau Women's Correctional Facility for felony assault of a child.

I spoke to Detective Roberts at length before meeting with Cheyenne. While he would only reiterate his filed report with regard to his official findings, off the record he was quite candid. I include his thoughts in this case file only because it is the sole summary of events (as he believed they occurred) we have from that night.

I will preface his thoughts with the brief information I have gathered regarding Abigail Elias, who was a single mother at 17 and had a long history of drug use. She had been arrested for possession, distribution, prostitution, child endangerment, theft and various other misdemeanors by the time she was 19. According to neighbors, she was mentally unstable and often violent toward the people she encountered. She would regularly abuse Cheyenne both physically and verbally in public; at times no one would see the family for days, and the neighbors often worried for Cheyenne's safety.

We have no record of Cheyenne's father, who is listed as Alexander Stone on her birth certificate. When asked, Abigail refused to speak of him.

Based on his investigation, Detective Roberts believes that Abigail—upset that her boyfriend had been arrested for possession and therefore unable to supply her fix—flew into a violent rage. He believes Abigail set Cheyenne on fire.

A jar with kerosene was found at the scene and on what little remained of Cheyenne's clothing. A disposable lighter was discovered in Abigail's pocket, which was also covered in the accelerant, as were Abigail's hands and clothing. The Detective surmised, based on the Fire Chief's examination of the burn patterns on the carpet, wall and curtains, and the burns Cheyenne suffered, that Abigail poured the kerosene over Cheyenne's head and used the lighter to ignite the fire.

Even as I write these words, I cannot begin to fathom it.

Detective Roberts believes the only thing that saved Cheyenne was the knife she was holding when the responding officer arrived. It was matched to the abdominal wound suffered by Abigail. It is the Detective's supposition that Cheyenne stabbed her mother in self-defense and, somehow, managed to put out the flames.

Cheyenne spent three months at the Mendota Fire and Burn clinic in Madison, where she received multiple skin grafts. She arrived here just a week ago, still in bandages and an arm cast. Her eye has healed, and her hair is slowly growing back, but she is significantly damaged—both mentally and physically.

When I met with her, she would not speak to me. Someone had given her a sketchbook which she spent the hour bent over, scribbling. When I asked to see what she was drawing, she hissed at me. She is, oddly, both volatile and so silent I first feared her mute. Time will tell if she has inherited her mother's mental illness; Abigail was diagnosed a paranoid schizophrenic last month by the psychologist at Wausau. Her attorney has filed an appeal to change her plea to guilty by reason of mental insanity.

I've placed Cheyenne into the girls' ward and assigned her a bunk above that of another recent arrival, Georgia Humboldt. Both girls come from broken, inner-city homes with abusive, drug addicted mothers and absent fathers.

It is my hope they might befriend one another and benefit from their shared experiences.

The picture was taken from an obscure angle, as though the

photographer didn't want the subject aware of the lens trained upon them. It was dated October 1992.

The girl was no more than five or six. Too thin, all angles and edges, her bones frighteningly delicate. Scars marred her left side: her face, her neck, her arm. Presumably all of her left side, although Will couldn't see it. Red and angry and grafted together; a mottled patchwork of mismatched flesh. Hair the color of a copper penny hung thick around her face except for the edge of her left temple, where it was thin and short, curling against her skull.

Her features were broad, too wide for her narrow face, her cheekbones like blades, hollowing her jaw until she looked half-starved. Her chin was a sharp point kissed by a single dimple, and the wide bow of her mouth was turned down, a mark of sadness that stabbed something within him, like a bony, prodding finger pushing between his ribs. He couldn't see her eye color, only that they were too big in her small face, lined by thick lashes and turned up faintly at the corners. Above them, her brows were dark, slashing lines.

She stood in a line of girls, but it was apparent that she was *other*. Like a black mark on a smooth white page. She stood tense, as if waiting, but he saw no fear. He saw...readiness. Resignation. And such painful misery, that prodding finger turned hot and seared into him like a brand.

She had survived. But he knew that look.

He saw it every day in the mirror.

∼

Cheyenne F. Elias: Session #21
  Case Manager: Connie Brock
  10/05/1997

. . .

I met with Cheyenne this morning to discuss her recent behavior. Last night, she was discovered—along with her constant companion and cohort Georgia Humboldt—defacing the reading room walls with pornographic images. While they were not particularly detailed, they were wholly inappropriate and constitute vandalism. That she has rather astounding artistic talent does not excuse either her actions or her subject matter—in spite of her opinion to the contrary.

"It's art," she told me, quite self-righteously, in a tone I can only describe as exasperated and more than a little condescending.

I am certain it was Georgia who incited this behavior. My approval of the girls' friendship has begun to wane, and I am now beginning to question the wisdom of allowing them to cultivate the close relationship they've formed. Georgia has no boundaries, and she does not seem aware that there is a difference between right and wrong. I have witnessed such deliberate cruelty and manipulation in her that I sometimes fear for the safety of those around her. I cannot tell if it is simply the repercussions of her upbringing or if there is something more sinister at work. Her caseworker insists she is simply in pain and lashing out, as they all do. But my gut tells me there is more to it, and I worry about Cheyenne being in her constant company. Since the death of her mother, Cheyenne rarely strays from Georgia's side.

They have bonded, and I do not know how to undo it. Neither will conform, and both have been kicked out of every home that has fostered them. They return here, again and again, as though planned, and proceed to break every rule, even those in place to protect them. For Cheyenne, I believe it is rebellion. And pain. She lives in such stark, relentless pain, I find I can hardly blame her for bucking the system. And yet, as her caseworker, I cannot continue to allow such behavior. She needs discipline and guidance, and she must be made to understand that what Georgia considers "fun" is neither proper nor moral.

If I cannot find a good foster family for Cheyenne, I will lose her. Georgia has far too much influence over her, and I don't know that Cheyenne will ever see Georgia for who she is becoming. There is kindness in Cheyenne, courage and hope, and the promise of love. I see none of those things in Georgia. It is my greatest fear Georgia will turn Cheyenne into someone she is not, simply because she can—and because she does not want to be alone.

I have taken Cheyenne's sketchbook and art supplies and locked them away for ten days. This, in addition to dish detail in the cafeteria for the next month, is her punishment. Moving forward, I am going to schedule more regular sessions with her in hopes that I can somehow alter the path she seems to have chosen—and to create much needed distance between her and Georgia.

She is angry with me, but I can live with that. Someday she will understand.

In the second photo, she stared right at him.

There was no date, but she appeared to be fifteen, give or take. She had grown into those broad bones and that wide mouth, and the word *arresting* whispered to him as he studied her. She was not beautiful. But there was something alluring there, something that not even the scar that traced its way over the slope of her cheek and trickled down her jaw like melted wax could alter. Character and strength and determination.

She had decided to live.

Her eyes were green, lush, rich, earthy green, like the boughs of pine he'd grown up riding through. Freckles scattered across her nose and brushed her cheeks; her skin was the color of fresh cream, and her hair was a wild, untamed mane of fiery red.

What stirred within Will as he studied the photo was not something he would acknowledge. A recognition—*like me—*

too dangerous to concede; a tether woven of blood and pain and survival. He saw himself in her eyes. She was cold, closed, knowing. Life had nothing new to show her. She was not a child; she never had been.

Set on fire and left to burn...
Christ.

∼

Cheyenne F. Elias: Final Report
Case Manager: Connie Brock
1/13/2002

This is a follow up to the report filed 1/4/2002.

Cheyenne was reported missing by DFS on the morning of January 4, 2002. Although she disappeared twenty-four hours prior, Cheyenne has a history of running away and returning so the decision to allow her a twenty-four hour window within which to return was made.

As stated in the earlier report, Cheyenne was not alone when she left Haven. Georgia Humboldt accompanied her. However, Georgia returned to Haven at 4:30p.m. on the evening of the 4th. Cheyenne did not.

Although Georgia and Cheyenne have been best friends since they were children, Georgia would not speak of Cheyenne when she returned. She was cold and remote when asked, and even under threat of punishment refused to share where the girls had gone, what they'd done, or Cheyenne's whereabouts.

This evening, at 7:30 p.m., Cheyenne returned to Haven.

I was in the library, where Mr. Barns was reading I Am the Cheese. *Several of the older girls were there, including Georgia Humboldt. Everyone was sitting quietly, listening to Mr. Barns when Cheyenne entered the room. She went directly to Georgia, who immediately stood. They didn't speak.*

Before either Mr. Barns or I could react, Cheyenne pushed Georgia into the eastern wall. Georgia struck the wall with intense force; her nose broke instantly. She had no chance to defend herself. Cheyenne grabbed her by the hair and hit her, again and again, until I lost count. The blows were brutal; blood was everywhere. One of Georgia's front teeth was knocked out.

Georgia fell to the floor, and Mr. Barns moved to intercept. Cheyenne then pushed Mr. Barns into the wall and began to kick Georgia. She was pitiless. Some of the kids began to scream.

I'm ashamed to admit I just stood there, stunned and horrified.

When Mr. Barns again attempted to separate them, Cheyenne turned and head-butted him. She then said something to Georgia that I couldn't hear and immediately thereafter, fled. She somehow managed to avoid security and escaped the facility. As of this date, Cheyenne has not returned.

Georgia will not speak of that night. I can only speculate as to what destroyed these girls' relationship and why that break was so violent. While Cheyenne had a history of disciplinary problems and rule breaking—we were never able to place her permanently with any foster family—she never physically harmed anyone. Georgia, however, has an extensive history of physical assault. Personally, I believe something Georgia did was the catalyst for this event, but, again, that is only speculation.

I will continue to question Georgia, and the other children as well. The police have issued an APB, but I believe Cheyenne Elias has left Haven for the last time.

You'll know her when you see her.

Cheyenne Elias stood on the escalator, a leather pack

anchored over her shoulder, the brim of her hat pulled low over her eyes.

People milled throughout Mitchell International Airport as Will watched her, but he blended easily, moving against the slow crawl of the crowd like a fish swimming effortlessly upstream. His gaze locked onto her as she stepped off the moving track and made her way toward baggage claim.

She walked with a long-legged, confident stride: a city walk. Aggressive and uncompromising. She didn't go with the flow, she was the flow. Leading those too confused to lead themselves. She didn't smile; she didn't chat. She moved.

Will followed.

Awareness thrummed through him; anticipation licked at his nerves. If the girl in the photo had touched him, witnessing the woman in the flesh was like being struck by a bolt of fucking lightning. Instant and electric and goddamn painful. The allure was manifest: shocking and visceral, and something for which he was wholly unprepared. That tether of blood and pain and survival seeking to reel him in.

Like me.

But it was bullshit. She was nothing like him.

If his heart beat too fast, and his blood rushed too thick, it was just the promise she offered. The avenue she might yet present to his destination.

Means to an end. Nothing more.

Adrenaline surged through him as he stalked her through the crowd, only a few feet away. *Close enough to touch.* A stupid, dangerous thought that made the tension riding him tighten to the breaking point. But he was already broken. Nothing she could do—*or be*—would change that.

He followed as she made her way through the crowd and moved to the car rental counter, where she took a place in line. She stood patiently, one hand on the strap of her pack, the other tapping her leg in a rhythm that betrayed her calm veneer.

He should have retreated into the mix of bodies then, a phantom observer only. Learning her was his first priority, and that was best accomplished from afar, while she was unaware and unguarded. Her body language alone would tell him far more than any of her words. Truth, not lie. A foundation to build upon.

He stepped into line behind her anyway.

He couldn't have said why; in that moment, he wasn't asking. Instinct drove him, overriding his training, his experience, *common fucking sense*. Because she could be no one good. Even if part of him wanted to kiss her for beating Georgia Humboldt's ass into the ground; even if her pain had singed that part of his soul thought lost. She was the enemy, as proven by her presence. She was the guardian to Georgia's son. Whatever had passed, she and Georgia had survived. They'd been friends.

Conspirators.

And if everything within him rebelled against that idea, well...that was because he was fucked in the head. Plain and simple. He knew better than to believe.

Yet, he didn't move. Instead, he stepped closer. Called himself every name in the book and stood motionless as her scent washed over him.

Lemon and verbena and...turpentine?

She wore black cargo pants that clung, a black fitted fleece and a black ball cap. Scuffed, well-worn hiking boots covered her feet. He stared at the thick, tangled ponytail of fiery red hair she'd threaded through the back of her cap and wanted to wrap it in his fist. It hung nearly to the small of her back; it would provide an inescapable handhold. His hand clenched against temptation.

Sickened by the alien, unwanted *something* she touched within him, Will stood there, inhaling her.

For months there had been only fury, hungry and relentless, driving him forward, consuming everything in his path. He hadn't been burdened by any emotion outside the scope of his wrath. But reading that goddamn file, seeing those photos, the brutal slap of her existence…it threatened to make him *feel*. Beyond the fury. Beyond vengeance.

Illogical, inexplicable. And something he would not allow. *Enemy.*

The woman who stood in line beside them turned and glanced at Cheyenne. She flinched, looked away, and then turned back, as though helpless to resist. She eyed Cheyenne's scar, and distaste crawled across her features, as if she'd spotted something that preferred dark, damp corners and ate insects for dinner.

His hackles rose.

Damned fool. Some soldier you are. Distracted by the motherfucking enemy.

Cheyenne turned and stared at the woman, challenge and annoyance in her profile. She was a moment from speaking —he knew it, could feel it, which just spiraled him further into the chaos she'd produced—when the woman blushed and looked away.

Christ, it made him hard.

He was *fucked in the head.*

He told himself to step away. *You are the monster in the closet.* She had to fear him. Instead, he took another step forward, turmoil churning, pressing hot and sharp against his lungs.

So close. So easy, to just reach out…and touch.

CHAPTER FIVE

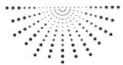

*G**oddamn humanity.*
Six hours and seventeen minutes of it was damn near all Cheyenne could take. And because she felt like a martini that had been quite violently shaken, any semblance of patience she'd had was gone. The crowd, the noise, the press of bodies—there was nothing about this place she had missed. Nothing at all.

And while she'd spent a fair amount of the last six hours mulling Olga's advice—and making mental lists of what The Kid might need—there had also been far too much time spent questioning her decision, second guessing her gut and replaying Whitney's freak out in her head.

YOU WILL REGRET THIS!

Christ, she hoped not. But standing there, trying to fake patience in the car rental line, she'd begun to wonder. She'd not expected to feel anything from this place, but she did. *She did.* Which only made her wonder if it could truly happen, if the new could fade away, bled out by the open wound of the old, until she was not who she'd become, but someone altogether different—*her*—that stupid, foolish, hopeless girl who had almost gotten them both killed.

And wouldn't that just be sucktastic?

But there was a choice to be made. She could either dick around in self-doubt and uncertainty, or she could stick to her guns and keep moving forward. She'd made a *commitment*. And even with her suddenly chilling feet, she would honor that. There was no turning tail now.

Movement stirred behind her, but she didn't turn. Her awareness levels were on full alert—*warning, warning, you are surrounded!*—and her nerves were so taut it was fortunate the airlines did not allow one to travel with firearms. Bad enough that she felt the eyes that touched her—flitting away and then returning again, as though the scene of a horrific accident played out across her flesh—worse was the feeling that it was personal, as though she'd been unknowingly tagged for a hunt.

Paranoia—not so uncommon when dealing with Georgia Humboldt. And not something to dismiss. Because that other goddamn shoe was going to drop. Cheyenne was certain of it.

But that was something she'd accepted. It was inevitable, like death and taxes, so she only squared her shoulders and gave the woman beside her—who was staring like an ignorant five-year-old—her darkest *You want some of this?* look.

As expected, the woman's gaze fell, and her cheeks bloomed bright pink, and Cheyenne sighed at the sad predictability of it all. Not everyone was Olga.

The line wasn't moving. She supposed she could give up and take a cab, but—

A nudge from behind, propelling her forward.

Annoyed, Cheyenne halted and turned to share her *What the fuck is your problem?* look. She stopped cold when she focused on the man who stood there.

He was tall and broad—two of her, at least—and roped with the kind of muscle that spoke of sunlight and sweat and raw, physical labor. Dressed in black jeans, a fitted, black soft shell jacket and black shit-kicker boots, he wore not a hint of color. That darkness was echoed in the thick, blue-black hair that was shorn close to his skull and matching, winged brows. But it was his eyes that captured her: chilling and pale, touched by only the faintest hint of blue, like the arctic glaciers she'd seen in photographs.

Dangerous eyes. And his expression...

All hands on deck! Death has entered the building.

Her response was instant, so instinctive she had to physically stop herself from taking a step back. Because she wouldn't give ground. Not even to someone who appeared...lethal.

Why had he touched her?

"Problem?" she asked.

That pale gaze went to her scar and studied it with leisure, seemingly unperturbed, before roaming over the rest of her features, ending with her mouth, which made her lips throb, and her heart beat too hard.

Some men got off on her scar. Some were repulsed. There were very few in between.

"No problem," the man said, and his voice was deep, a harsh, gritty rasp that rubbed everywhere the wrong way.

Goosebumps washed over her. Cheyenne wanted to turn away, but she didn't trust him enough to give him her back. The way he was looking at her...far too direct, too familiar—and completely unfazed by her disfigurement. Like he *knew* her.

Goddamn Georgia.

Of course. Death and taxes.

"Queen of fuckery," she muttered and forced herself to turn back around. Blood rushed through her like a freight train—*boom, boom, boom*—and her heart rattled unsteadily in her chest. Adrenaline spiked, and her hands clenched in effort to keep herself where she stood, calm and composed, when part of her wanted to run like hell.

Punch him in the face first.

Tension made her ache. She was so aware of him, she could feel the heat emanating off of him, touching her nape, the faint rush of his breath ruffling her hair. His scent had invaded her nostrils, something earthy and verdant, like the heart of a pine forest. His threat was no less grave for his silence, the utter stillness with which he stood behind her. She knew, if she turned, he would be standing too close. And she wanted to turn.

Punch him in the face.

But she was not that foolish, headstrong girl any longer. Now she thought before she acted. And there was the slimmest possibility she was jumping to conclusions. Maybe he just—

Another nudge, harder this time. Nails digging into her palms, Cheyenne slowly turned back around.

"Yes?" she asked, her smile feral.

One of his brows rose. "Sorry?"

She *was* going to punch him in the face.

"You touched me," she growled.

"I did," he agreed softly.

She stared at him for a long moment, but he only stared back. Her skin prickled. Awareness of a different sort rippled through her, and she inhaled sharply, unaccustomed to her body wrestling her brain for control.

A fine time for pheromones to fire. Thanks for nothing, libido.

"Why?" she demanded.

He shrugged, and she was made aware, once more, of his size. Like standing in the shadow of a mountain.

"Because I wanted to," he said.

Her breath tightened around the words that dammed in her throat as she glared at him.

"Miss? Excuse me, ma'am, but you're next."

Cheyenne knew the woman behind the counter was talking to her, but she didn't turn and acknowledge her. She couldn't. She was trapped in the pale gaze of the man who stood before her, her heart a violent drum-beat in her ears, an odd, unwanted slide of heat burning through her veins.

"Ma'am?"

His face was carved with such sublime perfection she wanted simultaneously to recreate it in oils and smash it into pulp, and when his mouth turned up, just a little, her palm itched furiously.

"You're next," he whispered.

It was far more than just an observation. Fury flashed in those arctic eyes, a jagged edge that sliced the façade of flirtation to ribbons. A warning.

A threat.

No matter his tone—hushed, intimate, just for her—no matter the slight smile that curved his well-made mouth. Cheyenne was no fool. She knew menace when she saw it.

All of her reacted. The new fell away, and the old resurfaced, vicious and hungry and far wiser. The crowd disappeared: the sounds, the scents, the press of humanity. Like white noise silenced by a sudden cessation of power, her surroundings winked out in an instant, leaving only the threat of him.

Cheyenne stepped close, so close they almost touched, and held those opaque eyes with a gaze that cut. The words she spoke were low, harsh. Angry. "Didn't she teach you not to show your hand?"

And then she hit him, one sharp, swift jab to his throat. He stared at her, stunned, gasped futilely for air, and then went down like a felled oak.

People scattered; someone screamed. The girl behind the counter picked up the phone. Chaos spread like a wave breaching a levee, until everyone around them was bleating in panic, bodies bolting, pandemonium in free-fall.

Cheyenne turned and walked away.

∼

A taxicab it was.

Cheyenne stared sightlessly out the window as the skyscrapers flew past, her heart a heavy, painful thud in her chest. Her knuckles ached, not from the hit she'd delivered, but from remembrance. An echo from the past awakened by the present. A brutal reminder.

She shouldn't have hit him. She should've turned away, rented a vehicle like a normal, reasonable, *ignorant* human being, and hauled ass once the keys were in hand.

Shoulda woulda coulda.

Your tendency to overreact is dangerous, Cheyenne. For everyone.

And your tendency to treat me like a child, Phil, is dangerous. For you.

So maybe she'd overreacted. Forgotten where she was. *Who* she'd become. But the threat was very real. She wasn't imagining things, reading something that wasn't there, caught in the throes of conspiracy. That encounter had not been spontaneous; his manner had not been innocent.

Try a stinking throw down.

Bad enough—but worse had been her corporeal response to him. A heretofore unknown, wholly physical reaction based solely on hormones. Something she'd heard about, read about, snickered over and often scoffed at, but never before experienced.

"Goddamn irony," she muttered.

"What's that?" the cabbie asked.

She only shook her head and focused on the first question that needed to be answered: who the hell was the man in black?

A gift from Georgia, to be sure.

The sound of that other shoe dropping was like a foghorn, but really, Cheyenne had only herself to blame. Death and taxes; she'd known it was coming. Georgia had been always been consistent. That was why Cheyenne had called Haven and verified The Kid's existence before she'd ever climbed onto that flying boat. Why she'd had the Cheesehead email her a copy of Georgia's will—not that she trusted anything so easily manufactured or even him, for that matter—but she'd recognized the neat, precise signature scrawled on the testator line immediately. She'd understood —with perfect clarity—that a stage was being set.

And now the players. Her, The Kid. The man in black....who was beautiful and dangerous and incredibly pissed off, apparently at *her*. Which made no sense, since she'd never laid eyes on him. But then, that was Georgia's special brand of magic: creating something from nothing. She'd always been exceptional at generating shitstorms.

But what was the goal? *Revenge?*

Cheyenne snorted. "Like she has any right."

"Huh?" the Cabbie wanted to know.

"Nothing." Fury licked at the edge of her calm, hissing and popping, hungry for full ignition. But now was not the time. Contrary to Phil's ignorant assumptions, Cheyenne knew when to pick her moments. And right now, she needed to *think*.

So...revenge. After all this time?

Cheyenne was a very successful artist; regardless of her refusal to attend showings and prostrate before the art world, she didn't exist within a vacuum. Nor did she hide.

Had Georgia wanted any kind of revenge, she could have attempted it long ago. Besides, how was tying Cheyenne to her child revenge? Was Georgia truly that far gone, that she would ante up her kid as part of the stratagem?

Hell, yes.

Because sociopaths didn't love, not like normal human beings. That The Kid was Georgia's blood wouldn't make any difference. That was fantasy. The cold, harsh reality was that he was just another pawn to be utilized, an opportunity, and Georgia never passed up an opportunity.

"Sick," Cheyenne whispered. Donning crazy shoes always made her skin crawl. But there was nothing to be done for it. *Someone* had to, because the game was afoot.

And if they wanted to survive, she had to understand it. That only came from crazy. From being able to *think* crazy with a rational point of view. Being born to a schizophrenic —and spending her childhood with a sociopath—had, apparently, not been for naught. "Yay me."

This time the Cabbie knew better than to respond.

So...here it was, whatever that meant. Part of Cheyenne was relieved. At least now it was tangible, real, something she could actively deal with—when she figured out what the hell it was she was dealing with.

In the meanwhile, she would go see the Cheesehead and collect her paperwork. She wanted to know how Georgia had died—and every other detail she could squeeze out of him—and she wanted to know about The Kid, too. Everything the Cheesehead hadn't shared, because she was certain there was more. There was always more.

Once armed with that, she would decide what was next. But first, they needed to make a stop.

"Hey," she said to the Cabbie.

He ignored her.

"Yo," she said again. He looked up and met her gaze in the

mirror. He was short and bald and spoke with a thick Middle-eastern accent, and he had no problem with her scar. He hadn't even blinked. *Two in one day. The Apocalypse must be near.* "You know a decent pawn shop on the way?"

He checked the address for the Cheesehead's office. "Yes, yes. Jenko's…it is only two blocks south."

"Groovy. Let's do that first, then. Thank you."

CHAPTER SIX

"No communications at all? You're sure?"

"Nothing electronic, brother. Snail mail, maybe. But no email, no IMs, nothing in their phone records. No social networking, nothing professional I could find." Red paused. "You read the file?"

Will rubbed his bruised throat, which burned and throbbed and hurt like a son of a bitch. "Yes."

"Quite the tale, no?"

He said nothing. Part of him wanted to strangle Cheyenne Elias until she turned blue. But the other part... *Christ.*

He should have seen that punch coming.

Fucking asshole.

The thoughts that had flooded into him as he'd stood in front of her, tempted by something he didn't even understand, betrayed every single one of the men he'd vowed to avenge. That anything—*anyone*—had the power to distract him from his mission incensed him. He was a soldier; he'd spent the last ten years of his life waging war. He knew how to fight, what it took to win.

How easy it was to lose.

He didn't care *why* or *how* or what the hell any of it meant. He knew only one thing: what he felt didn't matter. He was broken beyond repair. None of it could be trusted.

Means to an end.

No matter what his dick thought.

"You going to talk to her?"

He was going to do more than talk—and therein lay the danger. But he had no choice; she was all they had. Georgia Humboldt was dead, and whoever had pointed her at the cache of weapons his men had died for—whoever had helped her obtain them—was still a mystery. Because in spite of the short list of suspects, even Red, with all the intel he'd uncovered, couldn't find a connection between anyone on that list and Georgia Humboldt. And in order to act, they needed proof. *Incontrovertible evidence.* Nothing less would do, no matter how hungry they were for blood.

Which left only Cheyenne Elias and the kid she'd come to collect: they were the only way forward. And surely this anomalous *thing* he felt would fade. The hate had burned through everything: his pride, his integrity, everything he'd ever held valuable. Why not this, too?

"When I'm ready," he muttered.

"You tailing her?"

Not at the moment. Since she'd laid him out in front of the Hertz rental counter and disappeared—leaving him to deal with TSA and the local cops—tailing her had proven impossible. Instead he sat parked outside 268 Michigan Avenue, the building that housed the office of Georgia's attorney. Will knew Cheyenne would come here. She had to.

"I'm on it," he said briefly. "I'll touch base when I've made contact."

"Roger that, brother."

Red's blitheness grated, but Will bit back the words that

nipped at his throat. He knew Red was all in; Rye's loss had lit a fire no one was going to put out. Red just dealt with it his own way—from a dark room surrounded by computer monitors, where the world was just a stage for the acts of his international players. He wasn't a field man. Jesus, he'd end up dead if he tried. Betrayal and vengeance were just words to him…and the darkness came from without.

Not within.

"Don't be mean," Red told him. "We don't know that she's a player here."

"She's the kid's goddamn guardian," Will retorted. "There's no doubt she's part of it."

"Maybe. Maybe not. Could be she's just back-up for the boy, nothing more."

"No," Will said instantly. Because she *had* to be part of it. "She's here. She's part of it."

"If you say so. But…something happened there, brother. Something I can't find any evidence of them ever rectifying."

"Why would she come?" he demanded. "Why would she want him? The son of her enemy?"

"I don't know…decency?"

Will snarled.

"You read the file. She was the good twin. And you and I both know Georgia Humboldt was more than capable of doing something heinous enough to earn that beat-down and destroy a decade of friendship. Don't make any assumptions. Some people are led by doing what's right instead of what's easy."

"Not her."

"You don't know that. Look, I know she's our only lead. I'm just saying…tread lightly. Honey, brother, not vinegar."

Christ. Like he needed that thought in his head.

"I have to go," he growled.

"Be nice. Be the Will you were *before*."

He snarled again.

"She's a survivor," Red said softly. "Don't assume that came from any sacrifice other than her own."

Will disconnected and tossed his phone into the empty seat next to him. Red didn't understand. Cheyenne Elias was the *enemy*. To think of her as anything less was to underestimate her. To give her ammo that could take them all out—and enough people were already dead.

No one came halfway across the country to accept responsibility for the child of their enemy. No one. And that was assuming they'd even been enemies—which Will wasn't willing to do. He didn't give a shit what Red could or couldn't find. No one did that. No one.

She was part of this. Regardless of Red's fondness for fairy tales. Regardless of the words she'd spoken to him right before she'd put him down. Sharp and derisive and *angry*.

Didn't she teach you not to show your hand?

Followed by that hit...*goddamn*. For someone so small, Cheyenne Elias hit like a brick. And she'd known exactly what she was doing. He was nearly a foot taller and outweighed her by a good eighty pounds, minimum, but she'd known exactly how to put him down. No hesitation, no doubt. That came from experience.

What the hell had she meant?

He planned on asking. Not so nicely. Because even if Red was right—which Will didn't entirely discount—and she'd come only for the kid, why had she reacted so violently? She'd read the threat and responded instantly. Who the hell did that—if not someone who knew the stakes?

Someone who was set on fire and left to burn.

"Bullshit," he muttered.

Because her past didn't mean shit. Not here, not now. Nothing he'd read—in the lines or between them—could be counted on to tell him who she was, or what she wanted, or why she'd come. None of it made sense. Not her words. Not her actions.

Not his reaction to her.

What the fuck was his problem? He'd been *dead* inside. Nothing but rage and guilt and hate. And now this...whatever the hell it was. Betrayal. Distraction. Another fucking test.

Deep within, he could feel something stirring, as if part of him was reawakening, returning to the promise of the life he'd shed.

The one he no longer had a right to.

He didn't appreciate it. Black and white—that was how his world had reshaped itself. Right and wrong. Life and death. But with her had come color. Heat. *Temptation.* When he'd assumed himself immune. Hollow, an empty tomb gilded in ice. Vengeance had become his sole definition; his only fantasies embodied screams and pleas and blood that ran thick and black.

Nothing more.

And yet that brief, *violent* confrontation had touched him, marked him, had wrenched his focus past the immediacy of retribution. For one infinitesimal moment of time, it had made him *want.* Of course, it was nothing in the face of what drove him. What he'd become. But that one moment could have such power, could tempt him back into the land of the living...

He'd gone off the fucking rails. It was time to climb back on.

CHAPTER SEVEN

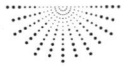

"What made you change your mind?"

Attorney Smith Jones was a born and bred Cheesehead. From his thick, vowel-pummeling Wisconsin accent and his stylish Green Bay Packer tie clip, to the small Miller Lite mirror—adorned by a healthy white tail buck—that hung behind his desk. He was a tall, narrow man, with a pleasant, mildly curious smile and a firm handshake. Unfortunately, his gaze continued to slide away from her scar, and for Cheyenne, this was always a deal breaker. There was so much worse in the world than a little mutilated flesh. That he didn't realize this truth—or had never experienced it—just made her write him off. *Clueless.*

Unfair, perhaps. But true.

"Been there, done that," she replied briefly.

"Ah...I see." His gaze fell to the small stack of paperwork in front of him. He was a tall, thin man, whose long, narrow jaw and sunken brown eyes made Cheyenne think of a sad bloodhound. His office was not much more than a hole in the wall covered in oak veneer and dotted by cheap furniture. Even the credentials that hung on the plastered wall behind him were framed in plastic. A dying ficus sat next to the only window. "Well. Let's begin with the will, shall we?"

"Go for it," Cheyenne told him. The expandable steel baton she'd purchased from Jenko's Pawn Palace dug into her thigh; she'd slid it into the side pocket of her cargoes, where it fit nicely, but now it poked rudely into her, so she adjusted herself until the pressure eased. It was one of her preferred weapons, although it required close contact, and Jenko had been willing to deal. It helped make up for his reluctance to sell her the Beretta she'd taken a liking to without the whole "background check" thing. There were other sources. She would just have to hunt them down.

Funny, she thought, how fast she was morphing back into the streetwise kid she'd once been. She could only hope she was melding then with now and not simply in free-fall. Still, survival was survival. She wasn't going to cry over what it took.

"As you know, Ms. Humboldt's will provides that you are to be named as Rafferty's guardian unless you are unwilling to fulfill that role, in which case his guardianship is awarded to the State. Since you are here, that won't be necessary." Another smile, eyes flitting over her left shoulder. "There is also a simple trust in place which holds Ms. Humboldt's assets until the boy is twenty-one. You are named as trustee of that trust. I didn't feel it was appropriate to share this information with you earlier, because if you didn't see fit to accept guardianship, the trustee powers would have been negated and—"

"Assets," Cheyenne interrupted. "What assets?"

"Er....well, there is an apartment in Paris, which is currently rented. A number of personal items—a vehicle, jewelry, artwork, that sort of thing—an account at Wellington First Financial and a condominium here in the city."

"Shiny," Cheyenne said. Clearly, Georgia had done well. "How'd she go?"

"I'm sorry?"

"How did she bite it?"

Mr. Jones blinked. "Ms. Humboldt was killed in the line of duty."

Um...what?

"Come again?" Cheyenne asked.

"Georgia was an operative with the Central Intelligence Agency. She was killed in the line of duty in Grozny, the capital city of the Chechen Republic."

For a long moment, Cheyenne only stared at him. Georgia had been...*CIA?* How the hell did a juvenile delinquent with a list of priors a mile long qualify for the freaking CIA?

By being a soulless strategist who excelled at manipulation. One with no fear of death and no moral compass. Gilded beauty that camouflaged a beast.

"True story," Cheyenne said.

"I'm sorry?"

She only shook her head, marveling. The CIA...she wouldn't have guessed. Not in a million years. To become an agent for one of the highest branches of national security... Who the hell had she blackmailed into that?

A pertinent and terrifying question. Just *who* was The Kid's father?

And who the hell was the man in black?

Cheyenne sat up straighter. Got poked by her baton. And realized her little stick wasn't going to cut it. A Beretta might not even be enough.

Try a grenade launcher.

This was the other stinking shoe. Holy balls.

"Shit on a stick," she said.

"Um...yes." Mr. Jones laughed nervously. "Apparently.

The Agency returned her to the states, where she was cremated, per her directive. Her remains are being held at the Rosemont Funeral Home over on 17th street. I assumed Rafferty would want them?"

He looked at her expectantly, but Cheyenne didn't respond. She couldn't. She was still turning it all over in her head, her heart pounding like a death knell in her chest.

The C-I-frigging-A.

It was insane. Ludicrous. A punch line.

Well played, you crazy bitch.

And here she sat, wholly embroiled, the patsy who'd followed her soft heart right down the rabbit hole. Just like Georgia knew she would.

Moron.

"Jesus," she said. Because while she knew better than to put anything past Georgia, and while she'd fully understood —and expected—something like this, she hadn't expected *this*. Something so alien and foreign that the implications reached far beyond any possible scope of her understanding.

Mind. Blown.

"I'm sorry this is such a shock," Jones said. "I truly am. It doesn't…it hasn't changed your plans to accept the guardianship, has it?"

A moot point. She was all in. Tagged, but not bagged. Not yet.

"No," she said. Even though—really—it might be doing The Kid a favor if she walked. To just let him get lost within the system. There was a good chance he would actually be safer if she left him the hell alone….

"Oh, good. That's good. He needs you."

Cheyenne narrowed her gaze. "Why?"

"I'm sorry?"

"Why does he need me?"

Jones shifted in his cheap chair. "There have been...issues. Minor things, really." An uneasy laugh. "Kid stuff."

"Meaning?"

He sighed, as if he'd hoped she wouldn't ask. As if he expected his response to send her running. But she rarely ran from anything, as proven by the spectacular shitstorm she was currently trying to navigate.

"He has a record. Truancy, vandalism, that sort of thing. Nothing serious. It's my understanding that he didn't live with Georgia. I believe—"

"Where did he live?"

A shuffle of the papers. "He lived...with a woman named Letitia Jones. I believe she cared for him while Ms. Humboldt was away, working."

No surprise there. Georgia had been as maternal as a concrete slab. If anything, the knowledge that she hadn't taken care of her child almost relieved Cheyenne. The less influence she'd had, the better.

Of course, that wasn't to say she would've left him with anyone good or decent. For Georgia, every decision had been shaped by one of two things: what was easy and/or what benefited her the most. If the two coincided, all the better. And if The Kid had a Juvie record, it was highly unlikely he'd had a stable, loving environment. That wasn't strictly true, of course, especially if he'd inherited his mother's mental dysfunction...

Balls. Well. She would just have to wait and see.

"Is that everything?" she asked Jones. Because her plan to squeeze him for details had evaporated, blown to smithereens by the CIA bomb he'd dropped. Every question she'd planned to ask had been muted by the sound of the explosion. She needed a dark, quiet place to digest. Time to think.

A goddamn drink.

Besides, the cabbie was waiting, which was undoubtedly going to cost an arm and a leg, but Cheyenne didn't care. She'd wanted a get-away car—and now that she'd learned who Georgia had been, it seemed all the more prudent. Because the man in black *had* known who she was—*overreacted, my ass*—and probably why she was there. Hell, odds were, he was parked on the street below, just watching and waiting and planning.

Cheyenne wondered how good the cabbie would be at ditching a tail.

"Not quite everything...there is also this." Mr. Jones shoved a fat, legal-sized yellow envelope toward her. "It contains her personal effects, keys, a copy of the will and trust, contact information for the renters in Paris, the bank account information, et cetera. I think you'll find it all in order, but if not, please don't hesitate to let me know. I've contacted Haven, and they understand you'll be collecting Rafferty. They have a copy of the will, and the paperwork transferring him to your custody has been filed. I will get you a copy when the Court signs off." Another nervous smile. A second, much smaller envelope was slid toward her. "Ms. Humboldt also asked that I give you this."

Cheyenne stared at it. "What is it?"

"I don't know."

This was something she'd known was coming, too. Because no way would Georgia set this in motion without having the last say.

Shred it. Burn it. Bury it.

Nothing good would come of reading it.

But Jones was watching her, waiting, and she was no coward. So she pulled the envelope toward her, ripped it open and forced herself to read the small piece of parchment within.

I knew you would come. Soft and stupid and weak. You'll always be her.

Good luck staying alive.

Fury flared. Fear turned to ash, obliterated by the wave of white-hot rage that whipped through her veins. It felt good. Cleansing. As if, with those final, hateful words, she'd been freed of any uncertainty that lingered. The words were a taunt meant to wound and weaken and return her to *then*, but Georgia had never truly understood her. What she wielded as a weapon Cheyenne used for fuel.

"Are you alright?"

Fan-fucking-tastic, thanks for asking.

"Is this it?" she asked calmly.

"Er...yes."

She shoved the letter into the large yellow envelope and hefted it into the crook of her arm. Then she stood. She was acutely aware of the baton in her pocket and the irrational desire to smash everything in the room with it. Instead, she turned and headed for the door.

"Please call me if you need anything," Mr. Jones called after her. "And...good luck."

Cheyenne offered him a smile over her shoulder, a baring of teeth she knew was less than pleasant. "I'm not the one who'll need it."

CHAPTER EIGHT

*A*s it turned out, the cabbie was from Lebanon—Beirut to be exact. And he had no trouble ditching a tail.

"Black Jeep," he told her. "Pretty good—but not as good as me."

Which she could only take at his word, seeing as how she spent most of the ride airborne, tossed wildly from side to side as he lived out his NASCAR dreams.

"That was very good," he declared when he dropped her at the Motel 6 that sat less than two miles from Haven—a seedy, derelict joint he'd protested was too dangerous for a "nice girl" like her—but Cheyenne was comfortable with seedy and derelict.

"You need anything, you call me—Yassir." He handed her a card, his tone stern. "I come right away."

She rented one of the rooms that faced the street—better to see them coming—and accepted the discount coupon for a large pepperoni pizza from the clerk. Between her pack, the envelope Jones had given to her, and the weight of the day, she felt laden as she trudged toward her room. Exhausted and strung out and struggling to get beyond: *Holy fucking shit. Now what?*

Behind her the sound of the freeway vibrated; somewhere far off, a woman laughed. The clamor of the city serenaded her, a song she hadn't missed. It made her head hurt.

The wind lifted, but the heat and humidity were suffocating, and it did little to cool her. She'd shed her fleece and her hat, but it wasn't enough; even her feet were sweating. Hot asphalt, exhaust and garbage scented the air. Memory threatened to stir, but she turned it aside, unable to face it on top of everything else. The last few hours had filled her plate to overflowing.

The blue paint on room 126's door was chipped and faded from the southern sun. Cheyenne stopped for a moment and looked carefully around before she entered. Only a few cars dotted the lot, older vehicles, the kind that still had windows that rolled up and cassette players. Across the street, a liquor store advertised a sale on PBR and Marlboros. Two kids stood just down from the store, playing around on skateboards. No black Jeep. No towering, pissed off man with icy eyes.

"One friggin' break," she said. "Just one."

She inserted her room key and sighed. *Just one.* But—

A large, heavy form slammed into her from behind. Tall, broad, as hard as granite, smashing her pack, shoving her into the door with brutal force. Hot breath touched her hair, her temple, her scar. Huge, scarred hands flattened themselves against the chipped paint. The scent of pine invaded her senses.

Man in black.

Her heart exploded. Adrenaline shot through her at the speed of light, and she reared back against him, but his weight and strength were pitiless, forcing her back against the door as though she weighed nothing. One of her hands was wrapped around the key, the other around the envelope; both were wedged against the door, trapped by the heavy pressure of his weight behind her. She couldn't reach her baton.

"Unlock the door," rasped that deep, gritty voice into her ear. "We need to talk."

Terror and rage flooded her. She fought, snapping her head back in effort to head butt him. She pulled at the motel room key, struggling to pull it from the lock. If he got her inside—

"Go fuck yourself," she snarled, bucking against him.

"Cheyenne," he growled into her ear, which only made her angrier, fight harder, because it disturbed her on the deepest level to hear him say her name. "Open the goddamn door. *Now.*"

Her hand tightened on the key, but one of those giant hands covered hers and crushed her fingers, turning it in the lock. The door swung inward and sent them both stumbling across the threshold.

Cheyenne dropped the envelope, the coupon, her pack and went for her baton, but the man in black was too damn fast, and arms like steel bands wrapped her rib cage from behind, trapped her arms in front of her and lifted her in a crushing hold that left her feet dangling helplessly above the dingy carpet. He lifted her easily, a wall of hard, hot, intractable human flesh surrounding her. His strength was terrifying.

He kicked the door shut behind them and carried her across the room, while she struggled and swore and drove her booted heels into his shins. Fists clenched, she bucked and squirmed and rammed her head back into the brick wall of his chest. It was like fighting the tide. He pushed her down, face first onto the bed and followed, smothering her with his weight until she was gasping for breath, and the muscle and sinew that roped him pressed against her like a second skin. Their combined weight made the worn bed springs groan in protest. His breath was at her cheek; his arms held her immobile, trapped, she couldn't move, couldn't reach her baton, couldn't *fight,* and for a moment, hysteria almost won.

Breathe. Just breathe.

But it was almost impossible. His weight was overwhelming. Heavy legs pushed into the backs of her thighs; his hips shoved her into the bedding. He was twice as big and ten times as strong. Fear like none she'd ever known threatened to undo her.

Blood and terror and death.

"Enough?" he grated into her ear.

"Get off," she demanded hoarsely, her throat burning with tears she refused to shed.

"We need to talk. Easy or hard is up to you."

A hint of the west shaped his words, a faint drawl that enraged her. It was a familiar sound, that drawl, reminding her of the most decent human being she'd ever known. It was wrong that they shared it. *So wrong.* "Bite me."

The arms around her tightened until her bones ached. Warm, moist breath washed over her scar, and every hair on her body stood up in awareness. "Don't temp me."

Rage bubbled in her throat, and she snarled like a trapped animal. She fought, even knowing it was a waste of precious strength, of energy, that nothing she could do would dislodge him. He only waited, his hold unbending, his heart slamming against the wall of her back like a hammer. Rough stubble brushed her scar, a place *no one* had ever touched, causing a riot of hate and heat to expand in her chest.

"Can't breathe!" she hissed. "Can't talk if I'm dead!"

His mouth whispered across her cheek, and a sudden, shocking streak of white fire lit through her and stole her breath. The sensation against her marred skin was stunning, too intimate, a privilege she'd never allowed anyone. That he simply took it—and that she felt it so deeply—enraged her.

"No screaming. And no punching." Sharp teeth nipped at her ear, making her start violently. "That hurt like hell."

"Good. You fucker."

His mouth twitched. Cheyenne felt it against her temple and wanted to rip his heart out. "Easy, now. I might start thinking you don't like me."

"Going to *kill* you."

"Such bloodlust."

A muffled roar was her only response.

He pressed his forehead to her temple, hard; their breaths mingled, washing across her skin. "Promise me you'll calm down, and I'll let you go."

Everything in her rebelled. "No negotiating with terrorists," she growled.

"Well. I guess we'll have to find something else to do while you rethink that." His hips pressed against her, pushing her down with a crude thrust, an implied threat that made her see red.

"Fucking kill you! Strip your flesh, crush your bones, feed you to fucking pigs!" She was yelling, totally losing her shit. But there was no stopping it. The threat he was making was *too real*. Too close to—

"Whoa, baby, easy. Take it easy." His voice changed, gentled—*liar!*—and he eased the pressure of his hold, lifting his weight just enough to allow her to take a deep, shuddering breath. "Just breathe."

She trembled violently, her teeth chattering, her blood a deafening roar in her head. "Get off."

"Promise, Cheyenne. Because I can stay here all night. Believe me."

She did. "Promise," she spat.

"Liar. You're gonna swing at me as soon as I get off you."

She said nothing. Damn right she was going to swing. But she wouldn't punish her fists with his hard head—that's what the baton was for.

"We can do it this way, too." Another tender press of his mouth against her cheek. A caress—there was no mistaking it for anything else. "Works for me."

"Fucker," she said again. "Lackey, flunky, stupid fucking pawn! Did she send you? Are you the cherry on top? The sequel? Part two of that stinking, shitty note? Go to hell, you cock—"

Those sharp teeth nipped at the corner of her mouth, and her words died a sudden, violent death.

"Shut up," he snarled, and in his voice she heard the same fury she'd seen in his eyes. His mouth brushed hers as he spoke, and her heart threatened to burst from her chest. "Just shut the fuck up."

Not an order she would have—ordinarily—obeyed. But something was happening inside her—something treacherous and unexpected and powerful—something she didn't recognize, didn't trust, didn't understand. Didn't *want*. And he was too still against her. When someone as big and dangerous as he was went that quiet and motionless, an explosion was sure to follow.

So she shut the fuck up.

"You think I'm hers?" he gritted, his tone a sharp juxtaposition against the tender press of his mouth. The difference was jarring. Because what she heard, and what she felt, were two different things. That they could coexist...was terrifying.

"She liked pretty," Cheyenne told him, hating the heat that

lashed through her when her mouth touched his. "And bullies."

A growl rumbled through him and vibrated against her back. "Not hers. Not ever."

"If you say so."

His hold tightened, threatened to break her in two. "Don't...*push*."

The words were broken, disjointed, and a violent tremor moved through him. Paradoxically, it both calmed and scared the shit out of her. Because he was clearly on the edge—an edge Georgia had been uniquely proficient at pushing people toward, herself included.

"How did you know?" His voice was rough, like gravel. "I haven't even said her name."

"I recognize her stench when I smell it." Cheyenne fought to breathe. "Fucking sulfur."

Another rumble.

"Crushing me," she hissed. "Passing out now."

His arms loosened, and she gulped in a deep, painful breath.

"You were her friend," he said.

"Once. No more."

"I don't believe you."

"I don't give a shit what you believe." Cheyenne struggled against him, enraged all over again. "Get *off* me, you—"

"Don't." His arms tightened in warning. His lips whispered against hers. "No more names."

Her teeth ground together. "Pretty please with sugar on top?"

"That's better."

She growled. "What the hell do you want from me?"

"The truth."

"About what?"

"Why are you here?"

She didn't want to answer. It was none of his damn business, why she was here. And who was he to ask? But he wasn't moving—and he wasn't going to—and Superman didn't exist, so she was SOL. She couldn't win this altercation. Not physically.

"The kid," she muttered.

"Of your enemy?"

"I prefer nemesis."

"Why?"

"Why not?"

"Don't fuck with me." Another tremor. "Just tell me."

"I can't. I don't know why. Just…that I couldn't leave him."

"Why not?"

She shook her head, and the stubble on his jaw stabbed her chin. She shuddered. *Too close.* Closer than she'd ever allowed anyone.

"Because he's me," she whispered. "Been there, done that. Abandoned, alone, totally screwed. That's why."

"Altruistic of you."

She bucked, but he didn't move. "I repeat: Go fuck yourself."

He nipped her bottom lip, and she started violently, hating him. Despising the flood of heat pooling in places she'd never paid much attention to. The irrational desire to turn her face just a little more, so that his mouth would press fully against hers.

Probably snap your fool neck trying. And you'd deserve it. Dumbass.

"How did she know you would come for him?"

Cheyenne stilled. Grew cold. And recognized then that she had no choice. *The truth.* It was all she had. No matter how personal, how private. How fucking painful.

"She knew," she said, her voice honed to a lethal edge.

The man above her stilled. "How?"

"I can't have children."

His arms tightened again, just a little, and Cheyenne realized she'd revealed far more than she'd intended with those words. "She knew that?"

"She made certain of it."

CHAPTER NINE

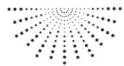

*C*heyenne was utterly still beneath him. *Finally.* But it wasn't a victory. And it wasn't surrender.

It was retreat. As if the fire had been encased in ice.

Will's rage churned, heightening with every round they went. Her words were frozen, but he heard fucking *pain*. Visceral. Fresh.

What did she do to you?

"Tell me," he rasped and rubbed his jaw against her scar. Like silk, no matter how ruined. He hadn't intended to touch her, not like this. But the temptation was too great and…it calmed him. When he teetered on that edge, the feel of her, the smell of her, eased the madness that threatened to unravel him. And it unnerved her. *Scared her.* He wanted her frightened. That it sent a stroke of pleasure down his own spine…well.

It wouldn't change anything.

Cheyenne was silent. No wiggling, no growls, no bucking against him. He particularly enjoyed the bucking.

"What happened?" He nuzzled her temple, her cheek, the

tempting lobe of her ear. He told himself to stop, but the reawakening he'd feared had seduced him, held him in a vice-like grip...and he didn't want to be free. Not yet. "Did she hurt you?"

Still, nothing. Shallow breaths, her eyes closed. Shut down entirely. So unlike the fierce, volatile woman who'd fought him, his rage grew.

"Tell me," he ordered.

"No." Cutting and sharp. Set in stone.

He kissed her, a hard press of his mouth against the corner of hers, and was rewarded by the faintest tremor. A sharp inhalation. Those deep green eyes flying open to glare at him.

"You will," he told her, certain of it. He would allow nothing less. But... "I can wait."

She only stared at him. There was no pretense there, nothing false; those eyes had the ability to strip him bare. *Dangerous.* In ways he'd never imagined.

"Who the fuck are you?" she demanded.

There was no reason not to tell her. He wasn't hiding in the shadows; he was barging in, both barrels firing. He wanted whoever had betrayed him to know he was coming. To understand he had nothing left to lose. To realize there was nowhere he would not go—*nothing he would not do*—to find them. That there was no escape—no matter who that person was revealed to be. If Cheyenne was part of it, there was no better messenger.

The kneejerk reaction in his gut said this woman was too raw, too real to be part of something shrouded in such cowardice and greed. She would not shoot a man in the back —her attack would come from the front. No less lethal, but unhidden.

Screaming like a goddamn banshee.

But Will didn't trust anyone or anything anymore—least of all his own gut.

"No screaming and no punching," he repeated, and helpless to resist, nipped her ear again. "Promise?"

She snarled. She was slight and round and delicate beneath him; that she fought with such strength and ruthlessness spoke volumes about where she'd come from. What she'd survived.

Fucking kill you! Strip your flesh, crush your bones, feed you to fucking pigs!

The darkness within him stirred at the memory, and he drowned out the words with her scent, pressing his lips to the silken skin of her throat. *He* had done that, awoken that terror, exploited it, and he hated who he'd become, a man for whom morality no longer trumped necessity. He feared it made him no different than those he hunted. It had not been intentional, merely another threat in his arsenal. That she'd reacted the way she had...*paint the world crimson.*

For her, too.

He wished they'd met in another time, another place. That they'd had a chance untainted by blood and darkness and hate.

But it was not meant to be.

"I'm going to kick your ass seven ways to Sunday," she grated.

His heart only beat harder. He was a man who'd always been attracted to quiet women, those who sat in thoughtful silence, who seduced him with stolen looks and shy smiles. It made no sense that he wanted nothing more than to strip bare the mouthy, angry, violent woman beneath him and fuck her until neither one of them could walk.

"Sweet nothings," he murmured and licked her cheek.

She shuddered. Her skin was hot, her cheeks flushed, and

he knew he wasn't alone in his physical reaction to their position. She was not immune to this anomalous thing that had risen between them. She was affected, too. He could see it. Hear it. *Feel it.* Which only fed his rising hunger.

"No screaming and no punching," she gritted. "Promise."

Will had no choice but to trust her. They had too much to talk about. And if he stayed on top of her, it wasn't words they were going to be exchanging. Still, every cell of his being screamed in protest as he slowly, carefully, lifted himself off her, off the bed entirely—because he didn't fucking trust himself—and moved to sit in one of the broken down chairs next to the cheap table that sat in front of the window, where the curtains hung partially open.

Cheyenne flew off the bed like a shot and faced him across it, her hands fisted, her hair a tangled cloud of fire trailing nearly to her hips. He didn't remember freeing it. Her breasts heaved, her nipples hard beneath the black, form-fitting t-shirt she wore. He stared at them for a long, motionless moment, his blood roaring in his head like freight train, his fingers twitching against the desire to reach out and—

"Don't look at me like that," she growled in a low, throaty voice that only made him want to push her back down onto the bed and take up where they'd left off.

"You taste good," he said.

"Save it for someone who's buying," she snarled.

"I don't trust you," he told her harshly. "But that doesn't mean I wouldn't love to fuck you."

He saw the tremor that went through her, the shock that shaped her unique, arresting features. She hid nothing.

"Noted," she said after a moment. "Now tell me who you are."

"Sit."

Her brows arched. She folded her arms over her breasts—and damn it, he almost protested—and stared him down. "Woof."

"I need you to relax," he said bluntly. "Your energy affects me."

She scowled. "You're the reason for my endorphin high—deal with it."

"Don't *push*," he said, and she blinked. She'd heard him the first time he'd said it—those infuriating, broken words, and she'd fucking *understood*. She did no less the second, nodding sharply and moving to sit on the far side of the bed, as far away as she could get against the headboard.

"I want an answer," she muttered.

Will took a deep breath and wished his heart would calm the hell down. His dick, too. She wasn't the only one on an adrenaline ride. "Will Blackheart."

"Blackheart." A sharp smile curved her mouth. "Because asshole was taken?"

He bit back a smile, something she'd almost made him do more than once. Something he no longer did. Something he no longer *wanted* to do. "Former U.S. Navy SEAL."

Her smile faded. "Former?"

"Recently retired." The acknowledgment of which made his wounds suddenly ache. "Four tours in Afghanistan, two in Iraq."

Which, for some unknown reason, sobered her.

"What do you want from me, soldier?"

He didn't like that. The distance created by her use of his now meaningless classification. *Compartmentalizing him.* "That's a loaded question, baby."

"Cheyenne," she bit out.

A smile flirted with his mouth. *Again.* "Tell me about the last time you saw Georgia Humboldt."

"Tell me why a former U.S. Navy SEAL gives a shit."

For a long moment, Will only watched her. Her gaze was steady, her wide mouth set in stubborn demand. No fidgeting, no looking away, no nerves other than the color that painted her cheeks a delicate rose.

"She hurt you," he said. "What did she do?"

"This is about *you*. Not me."

"This is about us."

She scoffed. "There is no us."

Which threatened to infuriate him. Christ, *so fucking lost*. "I want to trust you." Damn him to hell, it was true. "I can't do that if you don't tell me."

"Trust me with what?"

Another long moment of silence. He focused on breathing, in and out, in, out. Struggled to control the churning mix of all she stirred. He was broken, pieces held together by nothing more than hate and sheer force of will. If he shattered, he would hurt her.

"She slaughtered my team and left me to die in the Afghan desert," he said finally, and the madness that hunted him manifested in his voice, a living, breathing thing he could not pretend was illusion. "What did she do to you?"

Silence. Cheyenne stared at him, color leeching away, her legs curling up in front of her. She swallowed.

"I'm sorry," she said after a moment. "Georgia was capable of many things."

Which did not answer his question. The desire to throw the table he sat next to through the window gripped him, and he held very still in effort to combat it. He forced himself to remember her terror—those goddamn screams *feed you to fucking pigs!*—and understood it was something she would not share without trust, not even if he threatened her. Georgia had done something heinous to her. To them both.

Trust. He had no choice. Not even in this.

"We were readying a weapons cache for pick up," he

continued, his voice flat. "It was midnight. A sandstorm overtook us, and we couldn't see shit. When she flew in, we thought she was our retrieval unit. It wasn't until they started firing that we realized they weren't friendly."

Cheyenne studied him, frowning, and there was something in her eyes he hadn't expected: compassion. "What kind of weapons?"

"Nuclear."

"Georgia got her hands on nuclear weapons?"

"Two dozen dirty bombs."

"Holy shite." Cheyenne jerked violently, rolled off the bed and began to pace, volatility in motion. "Georgia had nuclear weapons? Jesus Christ. *Jesus Christ.*"

"Yes."

She swung to a halt and glared at him. "That girl was a sociopath when she was *seven goddamn years old*— how the hell did she get into the CIA? How—no—never mind. Fucking sociopathic bitch, could have sold sweaters to Satan."

He watched her begin to pace again. "Calm down, baby."

"Don't call me that," she snapped.

"You're agitating me," he growled, which, amazingly, stopped her in place.

She eyed him, her gaze narrow, hands on hips. "PTSD?"

A term Will despised. As if anyone could drown in blood and death and body parts and stay whole. "On good days."

For a long moment, she held his gaze, her eyes dark, glinting with something he couldn't read. Then she nodded, abruptly. "Meditation helps. Hokey, I know. But it works."

"Firsthand experience?" he asked softly and stilled as he waited for her to answer. She had to give him *something*.

"On good days," she replied with a sharp twist of her mouth. "How did you survive?"

"I shouldn't have." Which wasn't what he'd meant to say.

Another long, considering look. "But you did."

"They didn't." *Christ.* "Look—"

"There's no time for survivor's guilt," she told him, not unkindly. "Where are the weapons now?"

"That's what I came to ask you."

"Me?" A harsh laugh escaped her. "I haven't spoken to Georgia since I was fifteen years old. I don't have any clue where they are."

He only stared at her, unable to accept her at face value. He couldn't. She was all he had.

"Seriously?" she demanded. "You really think I'm stashing a semi-nuclear weapons cache in my barn?"

"Anything is possible."

"Not that. Sorry to disappoint, but I don't have them." She strode over to where her pack and the envelope she'd been carrying lay on the floor and picked up the envelope, ripped it open and emptied its contents onto the bed. "This is what Jones gave me." She began to rifle through it. "Keys, documents, blah-blah-blah…."

Will watched her, his pulse thrumming in his throat. She was white heat, warm, vibrant, outraged energy and goddamn him, he could see no ruse. No threat.

So fucked.

And then something she'd said came back to him. *Part two of that stinking, shitty note—*

"What note?" he demanded and stood.

"Note?" She frowned at him. "What note?"

"'That stinking, shitty note,'" he quoted softly and stepped toward her.

Something in his voice must have set her alarms off, because she hopped over the bed, to the other side, and her hand went to the pocket of her cargo pants.

"Down, boy," she said in a hard voice. "Don't make me hurt you."

Will smiled, but it was nothing pleasant or warm.

She leaned down to pick through the pile on the bed. She found a folded letter and thrust it at him.

"Go to goddamn town," she told him.

He pulled it from her hand. Scars streaked her fingers and twisted up her arm, a flow almost fluid in design. He hadn't even noticed them.

"Rude," she muttered.

He might have been properly chastised if the thoughts that flooded him didn't involve stripping her so he could inspect *all* of her scars. He said nothing and opened the letter.

I knew you would come. Soft and stupid and weak. You'll always be her.

Good luck staying alive.

"Can you hear her cackling?" Cheyenne snorted. "*I* can hear her cackling."

Will stared down at the neatly scripted words, and for a moment, rage held him motionless. Then he crushed the letter in his hand and looked up at her.

"The boy," he said. "The boy must know."

Cheyenne stared at him. She straightened slowly, squared her shoulders and took a stance he instantly recognized. It was the same one she'd taken that afternoon, before she'd laid him out in front of two-dozen people and three car rental agents. He opened his mouth, but she cut him off, energy radiating from her in electric pulses that speared through him like live current.

"Don't you even *think* about it," she warned in a low voice, her anger vibrating between them. "Not for an instant. You are *not* going to interrogate a ten-year-old boy for his mother's crimes."

"Nuclear weapons," he grated, tearing the paper he held into pieces. "If he knows—"

"*I* will find out what he does or does not know."

"Not good enough."

"Get out."

Will took a step, but she was amazingly fast. Before he could catch her, she was on top of the bed, snapping a steel baton to its full length and holding it before her in a grip that told him she knew exactly how to use it.

"Cheyenne—"

"Out. *Now.* We're done."

"No," he said instantly. "We aren't."

"I will beat the ever-loving *fuck* out of you if you make me," she told him, her voice steady, the look in her eye leaving no doubt she meant it. "You surprised me once. It won't happen again."

In that moment, all he wanted to do was break that damned baton, pull her beneath him, and ease both their furies.

Not meant to be.

"I'm not going anywhere," he warned. "I *have* to talk to him."

"He's ten—what can he know?"

"Everyone was her pawn. Even him."

She said nothing, because she couldn't. They both knew it was true.

"I won't hurt him," Will told her quietly. "I just want to talk to him."

"Get out," she said again. "*Now.*"

He watched her where she stood, armed and dangerous in the middle of the sagging mattress, her boots crushing the ugly blue bedspread, so tempted to go another round that his cock leapt at the thought.

"This isn't over," he told her softly, but he turned and strode toward the door. A good soldier knew when to bide his time and when to push on.

Patience. More fucking patience.

He wrenched open the door and shot her a smoldering look over his shoulder, taking one last look at the woman who was as much a warrior as anyone he'd ever met. "Until next time, baby."

CHAPTER TEN

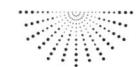

The kid on the bunk below him was bawling again.
Rafferty Humboldt flipped over and stared at the ceiling. It was patched and stained, dirty gray in the morning light. He wanted to lean over and tell the kid to shut the hell up, but he didn't. He knew all too well that sometimes tears were all you had.

They'd brought the kid in late last night. Young, maybe five, bruised and cut up. He cried himself to sleep while Rafe listened, unwilling to share his release. Rafe was done crying.

It's over.

For the most part, the realization relieved him. Because even here, in this dark, depressing, fucked up place some fool thought was a *Haven*, it was better than where he'd been. And so far, no more dangerous. At least he got three squares and a bed that didn't house a family of rats. No one screaming at him, chasing him, hitting him. At least, not yet.

He wondered how long they would keep him. He didn't think they'd send him back to Letitia's; the social worker who'd come for him had been pissed when she'd seen the place. Most of his stuff was there, but he didn't care. Hand-me-downs and broken shit. No loss. He had what he needed.

Where would they send him? Back to Juvie? To a foster home? Nowhere good—but compared to Letitia's, anywhere else was an improvement. Wasn't like he had a choice. He was part of the system now, for sure. An orphan. Like that little redhead in the movie—Annie. But he knew there would be no singing and dancing. No rich Daddy, no big house. No shaggy dog.

Just survival.

But Rafe was good at surviving. He'd been doing it for as long as he could remember, ever since his ma had started tossing him around like a bad penny. He couldn't remember the first people he'd stayed with—just the sound of dogs barking and the smell of sauerkraut—but the others he could list, one by one. Some of them he could even draw.

Most of them had been okay. They'd fed him, took him to school, put clothes on his back and shoes on his feet. Not like Letitia.

He'd never understood what he'd done to deserve her. He knew his ma hated him—she'd never made no bones about it—but he didn't get why she'd picked Letitia. What had he done wrong? Been born?

My little trump. Chump, maybe. Trump—whatever the hell that meant. He'd never understood.

Course he'd never understood anything. Why she didn't want him. Why she didn't like him. Why other people were raising him. Why she only showed up once in a blue moon and gave him dumbass shit he didn't want. Even the money she slipped him made no sense. At first, he'd spent it like a knucklehead. But then he'd realized he was on his own for real, and he'd started saving it. It was in his shoe, tucked under the sole, where he'd dug out a small hidey-hole for it. Forty-seven dollars.

Rafe knew it wasn't much, but it was better than nothing. Especially now that she was dead.

When the social worker told him, he hadn't known what to do. She'd hovered over him, flitting around like a bird and shoved a Kleenex into his hand. But he hadn't felt what he knew he was supposed to. He didn't feel sad. He felt...relief. Because his ma had always made him feel *wrong* somehow, like he was broken. He wasn't smart enough or tall enough or tough enough. He wasn't beautiful, like her. Her disappointment always hurt. And she'd let him know, over and over and over again, how much he displeased her.

You're nothing like me, little Trump. Too bad for you. And so very disappointing for me.

He didn't give a shit that she was dead. It was no loss. She didn't do what mothers were supposed to. Not ever. He watched the kids at school with their parents—he knew what it should be like. And it had never been that. She'd owned him, nothing more. Like he was a dog—worse, because at least dogs got pet. He'd only ever felt the back of her hand.

No. Rafe was *glad* she was dead. Because that meant he was free.

Sometimes he wondered about his father, who he'd never met and hadn't dared mention to his ma, but then he'd just put it away and turn the key. Didn't matter. Wasn't like his pop was around, like he'd coming swooping to the rescue like some masked X-Men character and save him—even if the reflection he saw when he looked in the mirror everyday made him wonder about the man who'd helped create him.

Rafe had never met anyone else who had two different colored eyes, like he did. One bright hazel, flecked with gold and green and odd bits of blue, and one black as night. Mosaicism, his teacher had called it, smiling at him like it was a *good* thing. But it just made him feel like a freak. He knew he must have gotten the black one from his ma, but the hazel one...that had to be from his pop.

"Big whoop," he told himself. A gazillion people probably had hazel eyes. Needle in a haystack.

Meaningless. *Turn the key.* He was on his own. He'd always been on his own. Nothing new there.

The social worker—he couldn't remember her name—said his ma died in an accident. He wondered what kind. A car accident? A plane crash? What?

Not that it mattered. He hadn't known anything about her life—not where she went when she left him, not what she did, not *who* she was—so what did it matter if he didn't know anything about her death?

It didn't. Because what little he had known, he hadn't liked. His ma had been *off.* Even as a little kid, he'd known that. Crazy in a way that scared him. She was sick in the head; she *had* to be. Or maybe it was just easier to tell himself that. Maybe *he* was the problem. Maybe everything she'd ever said about him was true.

He really didn't know. Truth was, he'd loved her. And he'd hated her. That's just how it was. Maybe someday he could forgive her for Letitia. For abandoning him. *Hurting him.*

But not today.

A brisk knock sounded on the door, and Tully stuck his head in and smiled at Rafe. Tall, stick thin, skin as black as coal, Tully walked like a 'banger but talked like a teacher. Rafe liked him.

"You're up, little man," he said to Rafe.

Rafe's heart leapt. He sat up in the bunk. "What do you mean?"

"I mean get your stuff together. Word is, you've been sprung."

But Rafe didn't move. "By who?"

"Your guardian."

"Guardian?" Panic shot through him. "I don't have a guardian."

"Apparently you do." Tully glanced at the kid on the bottom bunk. "You alright over there, little chicken?"

The kid just sniffled.

"Is it Letitia?" Rafe asked, terror crawling up his throat.

"I don't know, bud. They don't tell me that kind of stuff." Tully shook his head. "Pack your bag, and I'll be back in five."

Rafe wanted to refuse. If his ma had made Letitia his guardian... Fear threatened to paralyze him. He couldn't go back there. He couldn't.

He would end up *dead*.

"Five minutes," Tully repeated and disappeared.

Rafe shook himself. Looked out the window and wondered how far forty-seven dollars could get him. The train yard wasn't far from Letitia's. He could walk there in a day if he started early and stuck to the alleys. He could hop a train. People did that. As long as it was stopped...

He had a small army knife and forty-seven dollars. It would have to be enough.

Two dozen dirty bombs.

According to Wikipedia, a dirty bomb was a speculative radiological weapon that combined radioactive material with conventional explosives. The purpose of the weapon was to contaminate the area around the explosion with radioactive material. In contrast, a nuclear explosion, such as a fission bomb, released nuclear energy and produced blast effects far in excess of what was achievable by the use of conventional explosives.

So...no Nagasaki. Just a nice, slow, fatal simmer from the inside out.

If one survived the initial explosion, of course. And the shrapnel. And the bomb blast.

Fuck a duck.

Unfortunately, no matter how hard Cheyenne pinched herself, she was forced back to the same realization again and again: *I am awake.*

And this was real.

A goddamn semi-nuclear arsenal.

Sure, why not? Because the shitstorm bearing down on her wasn't enough. Oh, no, it had to go and turn into a freaking typhoon.

"What next?" she wondered. "Ebola?"

And, okay, she'd expected *something*. Something devious and nasty and uniquely Georgia. But not this. Never this.

"More fool you," she muttered.

She sat in the spunky red Subaru the car rental agent had dropped off at her motel room that morning, parked in the sea of cracked concrete that was Haven's parking lot. The aging brick building with its sagging chain link fence, small, barred windows and crumbling exterior sat only a handful of feet in front of her, the mortar and clay tomb of her childhood.

The sight of it had been like a bare fist to the belly, which she hadn't expected. Stupid, considering she'd spent nearly half her life within its plastered, hollow walls. Some things *didn't* fade, no matter how far you removed yourself from them, no matter how hard you willed yourself to forget. They simply *were*, like a virus that slumbered inside an oblivious host, harmless when asleep but fatal when awakened. None of the memories that stirred were pleasant, and if she liked to think she'd become someone different, they reminded her she was exactly the same.

You'll always be her.

An idea she'd always refused to accept, and had, in fact,

spent most of her life striving to disprove. But maybe it was the truth. Maybe it shouldn't be argued, but embraced. Everything she'd been through, every horrible, fucked up thing she'd both experienced *and* done were intrinsically part of who she was now. And Cheyenne liked who she was now. The entirety of her being was a tightly woven tapestry…and if she plucked out the threads she didn't like, it would just begin to unravel the whole.

So while she was in no hurry for a jog down memory lane…she was okay with it existing. No matter how unpleasant it might be. Besides, now was not the time to get sidetracked by her own slag. She had a ward to collect.

And a former Navy SEAL to shake.

Will Blackheart sat in a black Jeep two spaces back, hidden behind tinted windows and a pair of mirrored aviator sunglasses—which she'd watch him don this morning as he'd climbed into the Jeep, which was parked in front of *his* motel room, which was—*wait for it*—two doors down from her own.

Fucker.

That the memory of their clash the night before roused her heartbeat and other—far more disturbing—parts of her anatomy was not something she particularly wanted to dwell upon. Nor was the fact that he was the first man in the known universe to affect her on a sexual level.

"Big hairy deal," Cheyenne told herself.

But it *was* a big hairy deal. Because she'd always assumed she was immune to sexual need, that her past made it impossible, that she would go through life blessedly free of the sticky entanglements and emotional carnage that sex embodied. And she'd been A-Okay with that.

Now there was him. *Blackheart.* A man who had touched her with a terrifying kind of gentleness—surely a lie—and who, in spite of the profound lack of trust between them, apparently wouldn't mind fucking her. Frank, hungry, unapologetic lust.

The honesty of which she could appreciate. Because if she was honest, she would have to admit the same—a first, and a definite sign that the apocalypse was on the way. And an awakening part of her celebrated, to feel *whole*...even if it scared the shit out of her. Even if it was absent love or friendship or even any knowledge beyond a handful of basic facts.

Unbroken.

When she'd always considered herself a piecemeal creation. A revelation, and even delivered at the hands of a man she didn't trust any further than she could pick up and throw him, a gift. But she only took a deep breath and pushed it away, because she wouldn't give in and knew better than to dwell. He was the wrong man at the wrong time—but he'd taught her the right lesson.

Cheyenne was grateful, but she wasn't a fool. He was dangerous. Looking for revenge, not caring what it took to find it, capable of anything in his hunt. He would use her. Use The Kid. Everyone and everything he had to in order to avenge his dead.

The weapons were just a handy excuse, a cloak of legitimacy used to shroud his hunger for blood. She'd witnessed his damage first hand. Heard it in his words, felt it in his body, seen it in that pale gaze.

Nothing was beyond him. She should know. *Been there done that.* And she wasn't making a return trip. Not even for her newly risen libido.

Bad enough she'd made the admission she had...*I can't have children.* Not something she shared—ever. Something even Whitney didn't know. Let alone how or why...and yet, she'd spilled those beans, too. Even if it had been in the broadest of terms, the insinuation that Georgia had been responsible was an acknowledgment she'd never before stated to anyone.

That, however, was all he was going to get. Cheyenne refused to allow him to use that cataclysm as some kind of ridiculous evidence of her honor; as if her blood and horror and pain were currency with which trust could be purchased. As if their shared tragedies at Georgia's hand forged a link between them.

Tell me.

"Not in this lifetime," she muttered.

Fact was, none of it mattered. What mattered was extracting both herself and The Kid from whatever fucked up disaster Georgia had orchestrated. Two dozen dirty bombs which were, apparently, simply floating around like lost balloons.

The magnitude of the revelation continued to wash over her, and the list of questions she had was a mile long and growing. How had Georgia known about the bombs? She'd been CIA, not military. Or were the two organizations somehow intertwined? And who'd helped her steal them?

Ballsy of her, Cheyenne thought. True to form.

The one question there was no need to ask was why. For Georgia it would have come down to two things: cash and ego. The lure of both would have been irresistible, and the more blood, the better.

Good luck staying alive.

Such glee. Jesus. That sick, crazy, fucked up girl had turned into a sick, crazy, fucked up woman. One who'd set Cheyenne up. That taunt left no doubt. A manufactured construct involving her, The Kid, Blackheart...and how many others? One last hellish hurrah; Georgia's final calling card. But she was dead, which would not have been part of the plan. Which only led to a whole new host of unanswered questions.

How had she died? Who killed her? Why? And where the hell were those weapons?

Cheyenne was going to have to ask Blackheart, because there was no one else to ask. He was all she had—trust or not. Pheromone overload or not. *Cracked and on the precipice of breakdown or not.*

He was it. Him and The Kid.

Who would have to be questioned as well. But not by him. Cheyenne had been completely serious when she'd threatened to beat the ever-loving fuck out of him if he tried. She might not win, but he would bleed. On this, she wouldn't bend.

She was here to protect that boy, not betray him. And that's what she would do.

"So go do it," she told herself.

But she didn't move. For someone who had no problem belting a stranger in an airport, she was feeling annoyingly anxious about meeting The Kid. It made no sense. But kids were harder than adults—they saw through the bullshit immediately and had no problem calling you on it. Whitney's two girls—Sasha and Kendall—were the most direct, unflinching people Cheyenne knew. She loved them, but they unsettled the hell out of her.

And the idea of being anyone's guardian...who was she to think that'd been a good idea? It was *crazy*. Just like Whitney said. She wasn't fit to raise a child. In point of fact, she was pretty damn cracked herself, still the same reactionary hothead she'd been as a kid.

You'll always be her.

True story. And that was okay...for *her*. But maybe not so okay for him.

"A fine time for cold feet," she scoffed.

Indeed. The bottom line, however, had not changed. If anything, the whole dirty bomb thing only served to underline that the system could not—would not—protect him. Not like she would.

He'd get held—in Haven or Juvie—and then shipped off to foster care, where he would be vulnerable to anyone who came along. Be it a shitty foster family or some crazy-ass ex-Navy SEAL hungry for blood—or worse. Because God only knew who Georgia had been dealing with. And if Blackheart thought The Kid would have some answers, so might someone else.

She was all that stood between Rafferty Humboldt and the imminent threat his mother had brought to bear upon them all.

The only one.

Which made her cold feet—and all of the fears that had suddenly collided within her—moot. He had no one else. She was it. And abandoning him to whoever might be out there, waiting, was far worse that being a sub-par guardian.

So she climbed from the Subaru and went to collect her ward.

Rafferty Humboldt was short, skinny, and had two different colored eyes.

Cheyenne watched as he was led into the small, white-tiled room where she was seated, her heart trying to beat its way out of her chest.

He had his mother's delicate beauty: chiseled bones, dark mocha skin and full mouth. His hair was the color of dark chocolate and baby fine, falling into his eyes as he stared at her in bewilderment. One of those eyes was black as coal—his mother's—but the other was a glinting mixture of brown, green, gold and blue. The contrast was eerie and beautiful.

The smiling man who'd introduced himself as Tully winked at her. "He's all yours."

Outside, Haven looked the same. But inside it was modern and new, with shiny people and tiled floors and armed metal doors. Polyester filled furniture and copies of *People* on wooden tables. Fresh beige paint, pictures of happy, smiling families, flat screen computer monitors and healthy green plants. The only thing she recognized now was the smell.

Hopelessness and fear, something even the strongest air freshener couldn't kill.

Tully closed the door as he left.

"Who are you?" The Kid—*Rafferty*—demanded. His eyes went to her scar, which he studied with the ingenuousness of youth before meeting her gaze. "I don't know you."

Cheyenne stared at him, unable to respond. In that moment, he was suddenly, shockingly *real,* not just The Kid. But a living, breathing, sentient being who would—from that point forward—look to *her* for everything he needed.

"Balls," she muttered and tried not to hyperventilate.

"Huh?"

"Guardian," she rasped.

"Guardian?" he repeated. He stood tensely before her, his small hands fisted, clad in a faded Batman t-shirt, threadbare jeans and shoes that looked at least two sizes too small. He looked suspicious and terrified and ready to bolt.

Her heart squeezed so hard she almost fell out of her chair.

"Guardian," she said again.

"You already said that," he told her, frowning. "Who *are* you?"

A wild laugh caught in her throat. She wasn't prepared for this in the least, something she only realized when he stared at her as though she had horns. She hadn't thought about what she would tell him—or not tell him. She hadn't considered *his* fear. She hadn't even once contemplated this moment.

"I'm a moron," she announced.

Head tilted, he studied her, a look of confusion, anxiety, and what might have been hope shaping his features. "Come again?"

Cheyenne took a deep breath. "My name is Cheyenne Elias, and...I'm your guardian."

"Guardian?"

"A guardian is someone who is entrusted by law to be responsible for you."

"Why?"

"Because you're too young to be responsible for yourself."

He snorted at that. Cheyenne could relate.

"Why you?" he asked.

A good question, one for which she had no definitive answer. "I don't know. Your mom and I, we weren't...close. Not anymore. But a long time ago, we were friends, best friends. We loved each other. Well—I thought we loved each other." *Because you were a moron then, too.* "None of which matters, I guess. Bottom line, she named me as your guardian, and I've come here to...be that. So if you want to come with me, you can."

He only blinked. "Come with you?"

"To Wyoming. I have a ranch—well, not really a *ranch*, not by western standards—but I have a nice house, and a tack shed and a barn, and a three-legged dog and a one-eyed cat, and a goat who's kind of an asshole—*damn it.* Sorry."

"Is this...is it a joke?"

"Nope." She tried to smile. "Surprise!"

His hands clenched, unclenched, clenched again. "Letitia...Letitia didn't send you?"

His fear was heavy and thick, and Cheyenne decided she

would very much like five minutes alone with this Letitia Jones.

"No," she said. "No one sent me. I just came."

"But...you and my ma...you wasn't friends?"

"No."

"Then why did you come?"

A perfectly legitimate question, and one which deserved an answer. A simple answer. Which was *not* 'because your ma was a dirty CIA agent who killed a shitload of SEALs and stole their bombs.'

"Honestly, I don't really know. I can't have kids"—*might as well call the Times*, what the hell was her problem?—"and maybe that's part of it. But...I was raised here. In Haven. My mom died in prison, and this place was all I had and...I despised it. When I found out you were here...well. I just..." She shrugged, feeling herself shrink beneath the force of that bi-colored stare, as direct as a laser beam. "I couldn't leave you here. It wouldn't be right."

"That's...weird."

Another laugh, one that escaped. "Yeah. I know. I'm not what anyone would consider normal...so there is that." She sobered. "Truth be told, I'm kind of a freak. I don't play well with others. Sometimes things get out of hand. Sometimes... I punch them."

His mouth opened. And then closed.

"TMI, I know. You're just a kid. But, seriously, this is the lay of the land...and you deserve to know before you say yes."

"You...you *punch* them?"

"I know. Bad habit. But only if they're assholes—shit —sorry."

Going to have to work on that.

"I'm in anger management," she confessed. "The Judge ordered it so I could '*deal with my issues.*'"

"What...what did you do?"

"I jumped a guy. He was smacking his girlfriend around outside Loaf-n-Jug." Cheyenne met the kid's gaze, which was both fascinated and horrified. "He totally deserved it, but according to society it was *wrong*, so I got charged with a misdemeanor. Forty hours of community service and anger management." She made a face. "Yay."

Rafferty said nothing. Then, "You're kind of nuts."

"Yes," she told him honestly. "But not the kind of nuts your ma was."

His eyes widened. He looked down at his scuffed, overflowing shoes, at the seams that strained to contain his feet. Then he shook his head, as if lecturing himself internally, and looked up. "She was…"

"Scary," Cheyenne supplied when he faltered.

Those eerie eyes met hers. "Yeah."

"It's okay, Rafferty—"

"Rafe," he interrupted.

"Rafe," she said and nodded. "I'm a little crooked, but I'm not broken." *Not yet.* "But," she added, "you have to decide whether or not that's okay with you. Because I can't guarantee I'll change. Not even for you."

He seemed to consider that. "What happens if I stay here?"

An idea which, inexplicably, made panic rear within her. But her voice was calm when she replied, "Foster care."

"Yeah." He nodded. "That's what I figured. I gotta decide now?"

"Yeah." Which might not have been—strictly speaking—true, but considering the threat…well. No time like the present. "Sorry."

Cheyenne's heart pounded hard in her chest as she waited for him to decide, and she knew—even if he said no—she was going to take him with her. Even if it was against his will. Even if she had to hogtie him.

He glanced at her again, his eyes lingering on her scar, and she could see the questions building within him—and she understood she would have to answer them at some point—but he didn't give them voice. Instead, he scratched his head and said, "Okay."

"Okay?"

"Okay, I'll come with you."

Cheyenne stared at him, and something painful and hopeful and terrified swelled within her. The tears that burned the backs of her eyes were unexpected and unwelcome; she blinked against them. *Emotion.* That what she was feeling. Something other than fury.

"Cool beans," she said past the thrush in her throat. She looked at the small, tattered backpack he'd walked into the room holding. "Is that your stuff?"

"Yeah."

"Not all of it?"

He only shrugged.

"We can go get the rest," she told him.

His head was shaking before she'd even finished her sentence. "That's okay. I don't need it."

Cheyenne saw the fear that flickered in his gaze at the thought of returning to the place that housed his possessions. *Letitia Jones.* She wanted that five minutes. But that was *her* desire, not his. And she was going to have to start putting what she wanted on the back burner. He *had* to come first. She might not have ever had a parent who practiced that—or any parent at all, really—but she knew how it was *supposed* to be. And that was her bar. Still, she knew what it was to have nothing. No possessions, no home, no sense of place or purpose or belonging.

"We're not leaving your things behind," she said quietly.

"It just a bunch of junk," he insisted. "I don't want it."

"Rafe. It will be okay."

But he only shook his head again. "It's not worth it."

"Yeah, it is." Cheyenne stood. "We'll grab your stuff and then get some food. I could eat a Clydesdale."

He didn't move.

"Problem?" she asked carefully.

"That's it? I can just…go with you?"

"If you want to, yes."

He stared into her eyes with the same unflinching assessment Sasha and Kendall liked to subject her to. Cheyenne froze, fear that he would change his mind suddenly making her blood run cold, but whatever he saw—and she had to wonder—seemed to reassure him, and he went to pick up his pack. He slung it over his shoulder and turned to look at her

"Let's go," he said.

CHAPTER ELEVEN

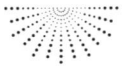

The Ghetto. Vandalism and graffiti. Streets littered with garbage. Buildings slowly disintegrating to the pavement; broken windows and black bars and burned out cars.

Will was following Cheyenne. She'd flipped him off when they'd pulled out of the Motel 6 parking lot that morning, but now seemed content to simply ignore him as she led him deeper into the armpit of the city. If he'd thought Haven was in a bad part of town, this shithole proved different.

Haven—where she'd sat unmoving in her rental car for nearly twenty minutes before finally going in. Haven, a monstrous brick building with barred widows and crumbling mortar; imposing and ugly, depressing as hell. It was as far from the sprawling ranch of Will's childhood as the moon, and just looking at it pissed him off.

Behind them, half a block back, another car followed, a sleek black sedan with Illinois plates and tinted windows that took care to stay hidden, but in this area of the city, stuck out like a dead man at a dinner party.

Will wondered who it contained. There were several

contenders: CIA, a jilted buyer, Georgia's informant, a minion for any of the three... He would confront them, but not yet. Not until Red got back to him about the plate registration, and he had some idea of who he was dealing with. Until then, let them follow. Hell, in this neighborhood, they'd be lucky to escape without being jacked.

Where are we going, baby?

Tailing her annoyed the hell out of him. He'd almost pounded on her motel room door and demanded she let him accompany her to pick up the kid, which was asinine considering her reaction to his suggestion that the boy needed to be questioned. Unless he wanted to get brained by that damn baton, he needed to keep his distance.

For now.

He would close the space between them soon enough. Because whether she'd been telling him the truth—or whether she'd been playing him like a chump—Cheyenne was the only lead he had, and he was going to stick to her like white on rice. If that thought appealed a little too much, that was too damned bad. There was nothing to be done for it; until this was over, they were stuck with each other.

But he wouldn't touch her again. No matter how tempted he might be, she was off limits. Last night had taught him he had no self-control where she was concerned, and the danger inherent in allowing that need free reign was wholly unacceptable—regardless of how good it felt. There was no room for distraction. No room for pleasure. He had a mission beyond retrieval of those weapons, and it didn't include falling in lust with a woman he couldn't afford to want. Or have.

No, last night had been an anomaly. A moment of weakness he would not allow himself to repeat. Everything that had driven him to this point—his determination for justice, the need to punish those responsible, the fear that the weapons would land in the hands of extremists—continued to push him relentlessly forward. Cheyenne's presence didn't change that, it only heightened the stakes, and if he let himself indulge, the price of failure would be catastrophic.

Not only because she and the kid were his sole clues in the clusterfuck Georgia Humboldt had left behind, but also because he was not the only one looking for those weapons—as proven by the black sedan following them.

Will was their first defense—their *only* defense—regardless of how capable Cheyenne was with that baton. Or her fists. And no one else was going to die for that cache. He would make certain.

So he was here to stay—until it was over. Being easy didn't enter into it.

Cheyenne turned again, down another ugly street lined with shacks, shanties and tall, narrow projects. There were no trees, too many loitering people, and enough crap in the gutter to fill a stadium.

Rafferty Humboldt sat beside her, staring out the window. He was short and skinny, with his mother's mocha skin, and dark hair that hung in his eyes. He and Cheyenne had left Haven side by side, but it was clear from their body language they were strangers, distanced by uncertainty and the unknown. The kid was small, far smaller than Will had expected. Just a boy.

A goddamn baby. One whose mother had anted him up on an altar of treason and blood.

Fucking sociopathic bitch, could have sold sweaters to Satan.

Which shouldn't have made him want to smile, but did.

Friend or foe, Cheyenne knew exactly who and what Georgia Humboldt had been. And right or wrong, Will had a hard time seeing her walk hand-in-hand with that kind of evil. He had a feeling she would kick his ass for even thinking it. And she would enjoy it.

You'd enjoy it, too. Asshole.

Cheyenne pulled into the gravel drive of one of the debilitated houses that lined the street, a narrow two story Victorian with peeling white paint and a sagging front porch.

Will parked next to the curb. He watched Cheyenne and Rafe climb from the Subaru and approach the front screen door that hung crookedly on its frame. Cheyenne halted halfway to the door and stared at the house, and Will recognized her stance: feet apart, hands clenched at her hips, shoulders back. She was pissed. She turned to the boy.

This place is a shithole.

They were only ten feet away; reading her lips was as easy as reading her expression.

The boy shrugged. He looked at the house, then back at her. *We can leave. We don't have to—*

No. She shook her head. *We're going to get your stuff.*

But the boy was hesitant, looking around as though he was afraid of who might suddenly appear. Will didn't blame him. The neighborhood was dangerous as hell and had the fine hair at his nape prickling in unease. He was glad he was armed.

The boy sighted the Jeep and stared at him. Cheyenne followed his gaze and made a face.

C'mon. She nudged the kid into motion. *Let's do this.*

They turned and headed toward the door. Rafe shot another look over his shoulder—glancing briefly at the Jeep, and then sweeping the street—before they entered the house and disappeared from view.

Will watched them go, knowing he should be with them. He wasn't at all surprised to find that this shithole was the closet where Georgia Humboldt had kept the skeleton that was her son. There was more than one way to go off the grid.

His phone beeped to life. The number was private, but he recognized it instantly. He thought about not answering, but he had questions, and even if he wouldn't be getting any answers, he was still going to ask them. "Blackheart."

"What the hell are you doing, William?"

Will supposed he should have appreciated the fact that his former Senior Chief, Ethan Scott, gave a shit, especially given how silent and idle Scott had sat while his men were buried, and the investigation into their deaths was deemed *concluded* by powers who had no desire for a war between U.S. counter-intelligence and the U.S. Navy. According to the information Red had found, he hadn't even argued when they'd closed the file—in spite of a dead SEAL team and twenty-four dirty bombs lost on his watch.

"Is there something I'm supposed to be doing?" Will asked, watching the door Cheyenne and the boy had disappeared through.

"Healing. Damn it, Will, you weren't cleared to leave Bethesda."

"I'm fine."

"You are *not* fine. You don't crawl out of the desert on your hands and knees with three bullets in you and end up *fine* eleven weeks later."

"You cut me loose," Will reminded him. "I'm no longer your responsibility. What do you want?"

The man on the other end of the connection snarled softly. "I had no choice! You've been through too much—"

"Others go through more, and you don't kick them out. Men fight with broken souls and prosthetic limbs, so save your speech. I know why you cut me."

"Will—"

"Have they found them yet?"

Silence. Then, "You know I can't discuss that with you."

"Yeah, I didn't think so." Will wondered if Ethan knew about Georgia Humboldt, or worse, if he was connected to her. Because only a handful of people had known their location that night—and one of them had been Ethan. Ethan, whom Will had always considered a decent man, if a little too fond of protocol. Structure was important to Ethan; he planned missions down to the last detail and ran them with an iron fist. He was predictable and unflappable and boring, which made Will doubt his involvement, but since no one was exempt from suspicion, he was still on the list.

"The spooks," he continued. "They don't like to share."

It was a calculated risk, a disclosure made simply to shake the tree to see what fell off. He hadn't shared anything with Ethan beyond what he'd told them in the debriefing he'd gone through at Bethesda, which wasn't much beyond a simple retelling of events. He certainly hadn't included any of his suspicions, not once he'd found out they were cutting him loose. They couched it in gratitude—thanks for your service, son—and insisted it had nothing to do with the two dozen dirty bombs that had been ripped out of hand by a treasonous faction within their own counter-intelligence community. Nothing to do with him witnessing that not-so-insignificant event. Nothing to do with those violent episodes the hospital staff had been documenting...or his bum leg, or his ruined arm, or his damaged lung.

A decade of his life, extinguished. A sooty, smoldering ruin. And they expected him to be *grateful.*

When what he felt was murderous.

So much so that when Red called, Will hadn't hesitated for an instant to spill it all. What happened, where, when, who he believed it had been. Why. And when Red had brought back a communication between one CIA agent and an anonymous source out of military ops...well. It wasn't rocket science. Followed by the abbreviated, defunct "investigation" into the mission—killed when counter-intelligence was connected to the bullet they'd pulled out of him—and the obvious reluctance of everyone around him to ask the hard questions…

They didn't want to know—or they knew, and didn't want *him* to know. Will didn't really give a shit which. He was his own army; he would do whatever had to be done. No politics involved.

"What makes you believe counter-intelligence was involved?" Ethan asked quietly. "What did you see that night?"

"Sand," Will replied. "Sand and spooks."

"Christ." Ethan sighed, and Will knew he was pinching the bridge of his hawkish nose. That's what Ethan did when he was exasperated, something Will had always been good at. "You didn't say anything."

"Nothing I said mattered."

Another moment of silence. "I'm sorry."

A harsh laugh caught in Will's throat. "Me too, boss. Me, too."

"You're going after them?"

Which meant they hadn't found them yet, either. "What do you think?"

"I think the assholes who left you to die in the desert will regret not finishing the job."

"Yes," Will said.

"Look…I'll do what I can."

"Careful, boss. We both know who's at the top of the food chain, and it ain't us grunts."

"I don't give a shit," Ethan said sharply. "I owe it to them."

Will thought about Hogan—father of three—Rye, recently engaged—Axel, a card-carrying member of Doctors without Borders—and Kent, just married and building his first house—and said, "Yeah, you do."

"I can get you a copy of the investigation file."

Which he already had, thanks to Red, but it would be interesting to compare the two.

"No need to take that risk, boss," Will told him. "I'll manage."

"Text me your email. I'll send it through a third party."

And the net widened. Red would have no trouble determining the identity of that third party…and they would have the official investigation file. Unexpected and perhaps a little too fortuitous.

But Will wasn't complaining.

Around him, all was quiet; no one had appeared at the house Cheyenne and the boy had disappeared into. The door was still shut. There was no noise filtering out from within, no screaming, no brawling. Problem was, Will's skin was beginning to crawl, and that only happened when something was brewing. His own personal portent—and he trusted it.

"I have to go," he said.

"I'll get you that file."

"Yeah, whatever, boss."

"Be careful, Will. This is bigger than you."

That was the problem with letting politicos head the hunt. Single people became factions which became legitimate organizations which then became countries, and pretty soon everyone was just standing around, shaking hands and agreeing it had all been just a big misunderstanding….

"Let me know what you find," Ethan said.

"Sure thing, boss," Will lied, smooth and easy, his sarcasm barely perceptible. Cheyenne would have heard it and called him on it. Ethan only said, "Good."

And hung up.

"How long have you lived here?"

Rafe looked up from the backpack he was stuffing with what little he could lay claim to and saw Cheyenne look around the filthy room he shared with Letitia's oldest son, Leon. He could tell she was pissed—she was easy to read, not like his ma had been—he just wasn't sure why.

Was it him? Had he done something?

"A while." He shrugged. "Since I was five."

Cheyenne muttered something he didn't catch, and his heart beat heavily in his chest. Even though they'd only met half an hour ago, he was terrified she might change her mind. The fact that she was a stranger didn't scare him half as much as the thought of staying with Letitia.

It didn't make any sense to him, why Cheyenne had come —because he knew who his ma had been and the kind of shit she'd liked to do to people, and he had a feeling she'd done something *bad* to Cheyenne, Jesus, he just hoped it didn't have anything to do with that wicked scar on her face—but he didn't *care*.

He just wanted to get his shit and get the hell out of Dodge.

He shot another look at her. Red haired and green eyed, she was clad in black cargos, a *Vote for Pedro* t-shirt and scarred hiking boots. And that scar.... *Damn.* It looked like a burn—he wasn't sure—but he knew for sure it had hurt like hell. The lady who'd checked him out of Haven had kept looking at it, but Cheyenne only stared her down like a pro, until the lady looked away and blushed.

Truth be told, I'm kind of a freak. I don't play well with others. Sometimes things get out of hand. Sometimes...I punch them.

Rafe still wasn't sure what that meant, but it was honest, and that was good enough for him. She'd looked him dead in the eye, and he'd seen her shame when she said, "Sometimes I punch them..." He knew all about shame.

Besides, she'd admitted she was nuts. He could deal with

that. Bottom line, she was all he had. And if she turned out to be dangerous, he still had forty-seven dollars and a small army knife. He could get away if he had to. And if it meant no more Letitia... No contest.

"Jesus Christ," Cheyenne said suddenly, and he followed her gaze to the large hole in the floor next to the wall. Bits of brown grass and bare ground were visible.

"Yeah," he replied and shrugged again. She wasn't going to tell him he couldn't come, was she? That this place had somehow changed her mind?

The thought scared the shit out of him, which only made him angry. He was tired of being afraid.

"I can stay," he offered, although his throat closed around the words. "You don't have to take me."

"No way." She met his gaze. "Even if you *wanted* to. I would tie your ass up and steal you."

There were lines around her mouth, and her scar was white. *Sometimes I punch them.* He could see it then.

"If your ma was still alive, I would kick her ass seven ways to Sunday." She looked over at Leon's bed, then back at his own thin mat shoved into one corner of the floor. The hierarchy in the room was clear. "This is total fucking *bullshit* —sorry."

"It's okay," he muttered. He went to Leon's bed and pulled the woolen blanket from it, balling it beneath his arm. The bright yellow and red woven coverlet was his, the last gift from his ma, the only one he'd ever bloodied himself in effort to keep. Leon had won that fight—like most of them—but it was Rafe's, and he was taking it with him. "That's it."

He heard the front door slam against its frame. Fear surged through him, and he pushed past Cheyenne to head off whoever it was.

"Rafe! When did you get back? Whose car is that?" Ruby, Letitia's six-year-old daughter and Rafe's only ally in the house appeared in the hallway. Her braided hair was escaping its weave, and the red shirt and pants she wore were grass stained. Her mother would be furious. She halted at the sight of Cheyenne behind him and eyed the backpack in his hands, the blanket beneath his arm. "Where...where are you going?"

Her voice wavered, and Rafe was suddenly aware that someone would miss him.

"I'm leaving. Cheyenne...she's my guardian." He still wasn't sure what that word meant exactly, but he knew it gave her more right than anyone else. More than Letitia. "We're going to Wyoming."

"Wyoming?" Ruby echoed, as though he'd named some distant planet. Her mouth trembled, and he could see the tears coming.

He pushed past her.

"But..." Ruby tugged on his shirt. "Wait!"

But he wasn't waiting. They needed to go, *now*, before anyone else—like Leon or Letitia—showed up. He'd only come to collect these things because Cheyenne insisted. He was grateful for that, but the longer they stayed, the worse it would be.

Letitia was big, ugly and mean. And Leon was his mother's son.

Ruby continued to tug on his shirt. "Rafe, *please.* Stop!"

He whirled around, aware that Cheyenne was watching. "Let go, Ruby. We have to *go.*"

He didn't want her to cry, to argue and plead with him. But she only threw her thin arms around him and hugged him tightly. He couldn't hug her back because his arms were full, but he laid his head beside hers. "I'm sorry," he whispered in her ear.

"Don't go," she said, and he could hear her grief. It was enough to make him whirl away again and head for the front door, weaving through the aisles of stacked magazines and old newspapers, stepping over the mountainous piles of clothing, around the trash.

"Wait!" Ruby said again.

Rafe didn't wait. He was almost to the door when Ruby raced up behind him and caught the waistband of his jeans. "Stop!" She pulled him sideways into the tiny bathroom that sat off the entry and shoved something he couldn't see into the front pocket of his pack. "This came last week," she said, her voice low. "I didn't want them to find it."

"Thanks," he muttered.

She stared at him with her soft brown eyes, tears webbing her lashes.

"You should go," she said softly. "Before they come."

He turned to leave, urgency beating at him once more. "Yeah."

"I love you," she said suddenly, as if she was afraid she'd never see him again.

He halted in the doorway, because he realized she was right. He met her gaze, which was blurred now by the tears that were streaming down her cheeks. He wished he could tell her the same, but he wasn't sure he loved anyone anymore.

"Take care of yourself," he said instead. "And be careful."

He looked back to find Cheyenne waiting patiently and said, "We can go now." Then he was out the front door.

Behind him, Cheyenne stopped and said something to Ruby he didn't hear. The black Jeep was still parked out front, ridiculously out of place, and he wondered who it was and what they wanted, but it didn't matter. His sole focus was escape. Down the porch steps, across the yellowed lawn, almost to the car—

The sound of a loud muffler and Fifty Cent suddenly filled the air, and his heart sank. He looked up to see a black

Monte Carlo pull into the driveway behind Cheyenne's car, and as it screeched to a halt, Letitia climbed out. She held a can of Diet Coke and a pack of Newport Lights in one hand, and a giant purple purse in the other. Her hair was freshly done. The Monte Carlo backed out and disappeared. Letitia looked at him, then at Cheyenne, and the expression that always made his hair stand on end settled across her face.

"I'll handle this," he told Cheyenne as Letitia stormed toward them.

Cheyenne arched her brows. "You sure about that?"

Hell, no. But compared to Letitia, Cheyenne was like a little stick figure. She wouldn't stand a chance. At least he knew how to handle Letitia…a little.

Ruby stared at him from the porch.

"Go inside," he told her sternly.

She opened her mouth to protest, but he shook his head and said it again. "Go inside, Ruby. Now."

She turned and obeyed, but slammed the screen door behind her. Then she scowled at him from behind the flimsy mesh, tears still staining her cheeks.

"Rafe," Cheyenne said quietly.

"I got this," he insisted.

Letitia kept coming, her face getting darker with every step. She was almost six foot, with big bones and big hands, at least two hundred and fifty pounds of pure mean. The only time Rafe had ever seen her smile was when Leon pummeled some poor fool to death and brought her the spoils. When she got close, she reached into her purse and pulled out the big wooden spoon she always carried. Her favorite weapon.

"Seriously," Cheyenne said.

Rafe didn't know what that meant, but he didn't respond because at the curb, the Jeep's driver's side door suddenly opened, and a man stepped out. A *gigantic* man. Tall and broad and built like a tank; his eyes were covered by mirrored sunglasses, and his hair was military short. *Cop or soldier*. Rafe hoped for the latter, because in his neighborhood a cop would just end up dead. The man wore a black t-shirt and a black shoulder holster, and the butt of his gun gleamed in the bright sunlight as he circled the Jeep. When he reached the front of the vehicle, he halted and leaned back against the hood, his arms crossed, one of his feet braced against the bumper—like he was settling in to watch the show.

But there was no time for him, because Letitia was suddenly there.

"Who the hell is this?" she demanded with an angry nod at Cheyenne.

"My guardian," Rafe told her. "She's taking me away."

"No, she ain't," Letitia snorted. "You ain't goin' nowhere, boy. Your ma owed me five hundred bucks, and I ain't lettin' you go 'til I get it." She looked at Cheyenne and waved the spoon. "You got a problem with that, scar face?"

Rafe's heart began to beat double-time, but Cheyenne only smiled. Not the same smile she'd given him; this one was cold and hard and *scary*. The difference made his skin prickle.

"I was going for civility," she said, her tone pleasant, not at all like the threat in her smile. "I really was." She turned and looked at Rafe. "Because you need that example—people setting aside their differences and working together toward a common good."

"Huh?" Letitia said.

"I know. Stupid." Cheyenne shook her head and stepped in front of Letitia, neatly cutting Rafe off. "No negotiating with terrorists. Only action."

Letitia shot Rafe a bewildered look. "What the hell is she talkin' about?"

"Shooting first," Cheyenne replied. She looked back at Rafe. "I tried to avoid this. You know that, right?"

Rafe blinked at her. "Shooting?"

Cheyenne turned to Letitia. "Let's do this."

Letitia actually took a small step back, but Rafe's heart pounded in panic. Cheyenne was like a tiny little doll next to Letitia; it was going to be a *bloodbath.*

What was she thinking?

"You're a crazy little white girl, but that won't stop me from bustin' your ass!" Letitia warned.

"I'm waiting," Cheyenne told her. "You go first."

"Oh shit," Rafe said.

Letitia glared at him. "Get your ass in the house."

Rafe didn't move. Letitia took a threatening step and lifted her spoon, but Cheyenne countered the move, until they stood toe to toe.

"Touch him and die," she said.

Looking at her, Rafe thought it might be the truth. Letitia must have thought so, too, because her gaze narrowed, and she eyed Cheyenne with far more consideration. Physically, it was no contest, but whatever she saw made her hesitate. Across the street, neighbors had collected on the front porch, watching with idle curiosity. The man at the Jeep watched, too.

"Still waiting," Cheyenne said coldly. "Go inside, Letitia. Drink your Diet Coke. Have a smoke. Because I don't want to hurt you. I'm trying to be a fucking *example.* But if you push me, I will push back. And it will leave a mark."

Letitia stared at her, and Rafe knew she was weighing her options.

"Five hundred bucks," she said and shrugged. "He's all yours."

"Not the sharpest knife in the drawer," Cheyenne replied. "Are you?"

Down went the purse, the cigarettes, the Diet Coke. Even the spoon. Letitia's fist was arcing through the air toward Cheyenne just as the soda bottle hit the ground, and Rafe felt his world tilt, because Letitia would *break Cheyenne in half*—

"Ow!" Letitia yelled. "*Owwwwwww! Oww-owwwww!* That hurts, let *goooo*—"

Cheyenne had caught that swinging fist with one hand and was slowly forcing Letitia to her knees by pressing her thumb into a spot just beneath Letitia's thick wrist. Rafe stared.

"This is the Nei Kuan pressure point," Cheyenne said conversationally as Letitia collapsed, slow-motion-style in front of her. "It's very effective against people who are dumb enough to think size matters and will, in fact, leave your arm partially paralyzed for a brief period."

"Owwwwww!" Letitia cried.

"Perhaps you should use that time to consider the wisdom of picking on people your own size," Cheyenne continued. "Now, we're going to go. I wish I could say it's been a pleasure, but—clearly—that would be a lie. And since I am trying to be a fucking *example*, I won't lie and say it's been fun. Because it hasn't. You suck, Letitia. Your home isn't fit for pigs. As I'm sure the DFS will agree."

Cheyenne let her go, and Rafe tensed, ready for Letitia to lunge at them like an angry Rottweiler. But she only sat back on her haunches and cradled her wrist. Fat tears trickled down her cheeks.

"Are you ready?" Cheyenne asked him, cool as a cucumber, and Rafe reached down and pinched himself hard, certain he was dreaming.

Ouch. Nope. Wide awake.

"I'm ready," he said, and if his voice was a little higher than normal, she didn't notice. His gaze flickered to the man at the Jeep who watched them with a small smile. "That a friend of yours?"

Cheyenne followed his gaze and snorted. "Not in this lifetime." She stepped around Letitia and headed for the car. "Let's go. Bullies burn calories."

Rafe hurried after her. He glanced back at Ruby and waved, but she didn't wave back. He looked at Letitia, who stared after them with hate and fear and tears still tracking down her cheeks.

"Damn," he whispered.

And for the first time *ever* he felt...hope.

CHAPTER TWELVE

"That was tits," Rafe announced. "For *real*."

They sat in a dark green booth at *Denny's*. Cheyenne was contemplating the menu, weighing the Cobb salad against the chicken fried steak. She needed gravy like she needed a hole in the head, but she *had* expended important energy on that Nei Kuan pressure point—never mind the wrestling match with Blackheart the night before—which—*seriously*—was perfectly adequate justification for ordering what equated to an entire day's worth of fat and calories in one meal.

"'Tits' is not a proper adjective for someone your age," she replied.

"Technically, it's a noun."

She glanced up at him. "So is smartass."

He grinned, and she blinked, taken aback by the happiness that lit his features. Had she ever looked like that? *Ever?*

"The look on her *face*." He sighed, and it was a sound of bliss. "Wish I had a picture."

"I should have handled it differently," Cheyenne

conceded, voicing the worry that had begun to gnaw at her. "There was no need for it to get physical. That's *not* how to handle things."

No matter that she'd *always* handled things like that. It was time to change the program. No more fisticuffs—not unless absolutely necessary.

Define absolutely.

"Nah. That was how it was gonna happen." Rafe shook his head. "That's who she is."

Who I am, too. He just didn't realize it.

"You really gonna call family services?" he wanted to know.

"I don't know. They'll probably take Ruby away if I do."

He sobered. "Yeah."

The waitress chose that moment to return. She was short and round, with freshly dyed honey-colored hair, bright pink lipstick and reading glasses that threatened to slide off the tip of her nose. She smiled widely at Rafe and blinked at Cheyenne's scar and scowled down at the small handheld computer she carried.

"Stupid thing." She poked it a few times. "I hate technology."

"We should form a club," Cheyenne told her.

"It's supposed to go back to the main screen, but it always gets stuck on the á la cart dinner menu, when I didn't even *enter* á la cart because it's eleven in the morning and—no, no, no, you stupid thing—"

She muttered under her breath and continued to poke angrily at the device's touch screen.

"Can I help?" Rafe asked, watching her.

The woman glanced up at him. "Do you think you could?"

He held out a hand, and she gave it over with a sigh of relief.

"Thank God," she said.

Three deft touches later, he handed it back to her. "I minimized the á la carte menu and put it down in the right hand corner. You can just pull it up if you need to."

"Hallelujah!" she said and sighed. "I'm too old for this techno-crap."

"You and me both, sister," Cheyenne said.

"It's not that hard," Rafe told them. "You just gotta play with it."

"Hmph," the waitress said. "Now, young man, what can I get you?"

Cheyenne looked at Rafe. "You're up."

He hesitated, and Cheyenne scowled at him.

"Eat," she ordered. "Whatever you want. Or I'll order one of everything, and we'll be eating hash browns until next Tuesday."

"Bacon cheeseburger," he said.

"You want fries with that, honey?"

He looked at Cheyenne.

"Whatever you want," she repeated.

"Yes, please," he said.

"You want regular or sweet potato?"

He looked confused by the question. It was obvious he was unfamiliar with the whole dining out experience. He'd perused the menu as though it was the first one he'd ever laid eyes on and ordering was clearly a novelty.

Holy shite. If Georgia wasn't already dead, Cheyenne would have killed her.

"I like the sweet potato," the waitress told him. "But sugar is my crack, so." She shrugged. "The regular are good, too."

Another look at Cheyenne.

"Let's go with regular for now," she said.

"And to drink?" the waitress prompted.

"Um...milk?"

"Good boy." She looked at Cheyenne. "And for you?"

Screw it. "Chicken fried steak and eggs, over medium, potatoes, no toast. Coffee and a large milk." Cheyenne handed her their menus. "Thank you."

"You bet. I'll be right back with your milk and coffee."

Then she was gone. Rafe looked around, studied the other diners, glanced out the window next to them where the sun was struggling to break through the mass of gray slowly churning toward Lake Michigan, and then turned sharply when a crash came from the kitchen, followed by a noisy stream of Spanish.

"Have you never been to a restaurant before?" Cheyenne asked him.

Color flooded his cheeks. He shrugged. "McDonalds."

"Your mom didn't take you out?"

"Nah. We went to a museum once, when I was seven. But that's it."

"How often did you see her?"

"Almost every summer."

"Did you live with her during the summer?"

He picked up his silverware and unwrapped the napkin that secured it. "No. She just came to visit."

"Did you ever live with her?"

"No."

"Why not?"

Those dual-colored eyes met hers, and Cheyenne was struck again by how unique and beautiful they were. "She didn't like me much."

The fury which had remained quiet for the last few hours stirred within her. "She was…sick. You know that, right?"

He smoothed the napkin, pressed out the wrinkles. "She was my ma."

Yes, and wasn't that the crux of it all?

"Mine was touched, too," Cheyenne told him. "I can relate."

His gaze lingered on the scar that marred her cheek. "Did she do that?"

So much for only moving forward. But Cheyenne had known better, no matter how much she liked to pretend different. "Yes."

She braced herself for the next question, but he only said, "Who was the guy with the Jeep?"

And she knew that eventually she would have to tell him what had happened to her that night, but not here. Not now.

Not yet.

"He looked like a cop," Rafe added. "Or a soldier."

Cheyenne nodded, impressed—and more than a little dismayed. For a ten year old, the kid was astute as hell. Bad enough that Blackheart felt the need to trail after her like a bad theme song, but it hadn't occurred to her Rafe might spot him. Which only made her an idiot, because at Rafe's age, she would have spotted him, too. And although she was still wrestling with how much she should tell him, she knew she wouldn't lie. He deserved the truth.

"Navy SEAL," she said. "Retired."

"Why's he hanging around?" Rafe's gaze narrowed. "Is it because of her?"

Well, there would be no fooling this kid. So much for the Tooth Fairy.

Cheyenne sat back. "Did you know she was CIA?"

"CIA?" His eyes grew so big they looked like they might drop out of his head. "*CIA?*"

His voice rose, and Cheyenne put a hand on his arm and squeezed. It was a strange thing to do—to touch someone of her own accord—but it felt appropriate, and it seemed to calm him.

"Are you kidding?" he demanded.

"No."

"That's crazy."

Cheyenne had to agree. "Yes."

"CIA," he said again. "Holy shit."

Which she didn't reprimand him for, even though she probably should have. The stunned look on his face made it impossible.

"So…" He shook his head. "Maybe that was it."

"Was what?"

That eerie, beautiful gaze met hers. "Why she didn't want me."

Cheyenne's heart fluttered in her chest. "What do you mean?"

"Maybe she had a reason. Maybe…maybe it wasn't safe."

Oh, guaranteed. But Cheyenne doubted it was Rafe whom Georgia had been protecting. She would not, however, point that out. Let him believe what he wanted; a dead woman was not going to argue.

"CIA," he said for a third time. *"Damn."*

"You're impressed?"

He seemed to think about that. "She was a good liar. That probably made her a good spy. But…it doesn't change anything, I guess. I still got the shaft, and she got…whatever she wanted."

Very astute. Son of a nutcracker.

"What does that have to do with a Navy SEAL?" he asked.

For a long moment, Cheyenne said nothing. This was the tricky part, because while Rafe deserved the truth, she didn't want to scare the bejesus out of him. Those damn bombs were Blackheart's problem—she would not let them become Rafe's problem.

"Your mom took something from him," she said finally. "And he wants it back."

"What?"

Cheyenne stared at him, and he stared back. Before she could summon an appropriate non-lie that wouldn't freak him out, Will Blackheart suddenly materialized and said, "A weapons cache."

He stood next to the table, free of his shoulder holster but still monochromatic in all black. His arms crossed his massive chest, and his legs were braced like a fighter's. His folded sunglasses hung from the collar of his tee. He looked grim and tense and dangerous, and at the sight of him, Rafe paled.

"You're a jackass," Cheyenne told him.

He turned that pale gaze on her, and she cursed the color that immediately flushed her cheeks. "Because I told him the truth?"

"Because you're a jackass." She looked at Rafe. "Don't worry. He's all bark."

"Am I now?"

She heard the taunt in those words—her cheeks were on *fire*—but she didn't deign to look at him. "Like one of those little purse dogs. All yap."

Rafe appeared skeptical. "He looks like a wolf."

"Woof," Will said. When Cheyenne looked at him, she found him staring at Rafe with an intensity she didn't at all appreciate.

"I warned you about this," she said softly.

He looked at her. "Tick-tock," he replied, equally softly.

"This is *not* how this is going to happen," she growled.

When she moved to stand, his hand shot out and cupped her shoulder.

"Relax," he admonished, his massive hand squeezing with deceptive gentleness as he pushed her back down; such effortless, casual strength. Good thing she didn't break easily…but the bolt of awareness that shot through her was another matter entirely. Violence she knew and understood. But sex…

How ruinous it had the potential to be. No wonder it had built and destroyed empires.

Because she was pissed off and just getting angrier, and Rafe was looking at her with fear in his eyes—she should *not* feel anything other than the need to run Will Blackheart through with something serrated and sharp. And yet—

"We're on the same side," he told Rafe, who wisely continued to look skeptical. "She's just used to being the lone gunman."

"Jackass," she repeated and tried to shrug him off.

"I told you, no more names." He released her shoulder only to lean down and cup her hip. "Sets a bad example."

Then he slid her bodily along the bench of the booth, until he could slide in next to her, and before she could protest—or pull her baton from her pocket and smack him with it—he was seated next to her, a warm, immoveable wall of pine-scented man. His thigh pressed against hers, and she scooted over, only to have him follow until there was no escape. He leaned back and laid an arm along the top of the booth behind her.

Territorial bastard.

Or perhaps just intimidation. He was capable of either. *Both.*

"You—" Cheyenne began, but the waitress chose that moment to return with the milk and coffee.

"Here we go," she said and put Rafe's milk down in front of him. Cheyenne's milk followed, then coffee. She had another set of silverware and a second coffee cup on her tray, both of which were placed before Will. Cheyenne silently cursed her efficiency.

"Will you be eating?" she asked him pleasantly, menu in hand.

"Yes, ma'am, I'd like that." He gave her a wide smile, and

Cheyenne blinked at the dimples that suddenly creased his cheeks. "Thank you."

Stinking dimples!

"My pleasure," the waitress said, smiling in return as she handed him the menu.

"What's your favorite?" he asked her, and Cheyenne watched in bemusement as the older woman flushed with pleasure at the attention.

"Well, the waffles are good—and Jose is the best omelet maker around. You can just chose the ingredients you'd like, and Jose will make it special for you."

"Well, now, that sounds mighty tempting." He gave her another smile, dimples winking. "I might have to try that."

Cheyenne stared at him, instantly recognizing the smooth, good-old-boy charm that shaped his manner, the easy-going charisma and warm, appreciative courtesy. Another echo of Hank she did not care to witness. He hadn't even *tried* to use those dimples on her. No, it had been all intimidation and aggression and brute goddamn force.

Real. He'd been real. Damaged and angry and honest.

"And that's supposed to mean something?" she muttered.

"What's that?" the waitress asked.

"Nothing."

Rafe sipped his milk and watched her with a worried expression. Cheyenne told herself beating Will with her baton would only get her arrested.

"I'll take the Denver omelet, a side of bacon, a side of sausage, potatoes, toast, a side of waffles, OJ and coffee." He handed the menu back. "Thank you, ma'am."

"You're very welcome." She winked at him. "And thank you for your service to our country! It's good to see you home."

Then she filled his coffee cup and whirled away.

"How did she know that?" Cheyenne demanded.

"The tat," Rafe said.

"Tat?" she repeated blankly.

"That one." He pointed to the small tattoo on the inside of Blackheart's left forearm—a three-pronged spear, like the kind Neptune was always depicted holding. A tattoo that sat at the base of a massive, ugly twist of what looked like fresh scar tissue and made an uncomfortable ripple of awareness move through Cheyenne.

She slaughtered my team and left me to die in the Afghan desert.

"You've seen this before?" Will asked Rafe, touching the tattoo.

Rafe shrugged. "One of the guys in the 'hood had one. But he didn't fight no more. Said he got hit by a...IBD?"

"IED. Improvised explosive device."

"Yeah. Couldn't hear after that. Said they didn't want him no more."

A dark smile touched Will's mouth. "Sounds about right."

Cheyenne sat up and took a sip of her coffee. She knew bitterness when she heard it. Clearly, she wasn't going to halt this conversation—but she could learn from it.

"It's a trident," Will continued. "He was probably a SEAL."

"Like you," Rafe said, watching him closely.

"Yes." Will offered Rafe his hand. "Will Blackheart, former U.S. Navy SEAL. It's good to meet you, Rafferty."

"Rafe." Rafe shook his hand and eyed him with a surprisingly hard look of assessment. "Former?"

Another dark, faint smile. "They don't want me anymore, either."

For a long moment, Rafe only watched him. Then, "What kind?"

"What kind of what?"

"What kind of weapons?"

The brevity with which he asked made Cheyenne reach

out and touch his arm again, but he only stared at Will, waiting.

"Dirty bombs," Will replied.

Rafe blinked in confusion.

"Dirty bombs are conventional explosives with a disbursement of radioactive material attached," Cheyenne explained. "Like smoke bombs...an explosive component, but instead of smoke, they're filled with something radioactive."

"Radioactive," he repeated. His voice wavered. "Like...nuclear?"

"Similar," she said, matter of fact. "But not the same. Nuclear explosions are much larger in scale."

"But...a bomb is a bomb," he said.

"Yes," Will said.

"Jesus Christ," he said. He sat back, closed his eyes and swallowed. Cheyenne squeezed his arm and tried to ignore the unexpected tightness threatening to close her throat.

"It's okay," she whispered. "It's not your fault."

Because she knew exactly what it was to feel responsible for your crazy mother and her crazy actions. Inexplicable, illogical, irrational—*wrong*—but dogged and unswayed by reason. As if there was something that could have been done to prevent that moment of madness.

Just one thing. Something you should have *known.*

It was a relentless haunting, one Cheyenne still experienced. And seeing it in Rafe only made her hate Georgia more.

You must forgive her.

When pigs fucking flew.

Rafe opened his eyes and looked at Will with the gaze of an old man. "What did she do?"

For a long moment there was only silence. Part of Cheyenne wanted to know everything, but another part wanted to cover Rafe's ears—and her own—to protect them from the ugliness, because she knew it would be ugly. Malevolent and vile.

"She stole them," Will replied finally.

"No," Rafe snarled. *"What did she do?"*

Tears burned Cheyenne's throat, but she didn't interfere. Rafe's arm was thin and fragile, his skin cool beneath her hand.

"She slaughtered my team, took the cache and left me for dead."

"Did she shoot you?"

"Her or someone with her." Will shrugged. "It was dark, and we were in the middle of a sandstorm. It's hard to say who fired the rounds."

"Is that what happened to your arm?" Rafe's chin trembled, but his gaze didn't waver. He held Will's pale blue stare without flinching.

"My arm, my hip, and my left lung," Will said.

"Balls," Cheyenne muttered.

"But you survived," Rafe said.

"I had no choice," Will told him. "I had to sound the alarm."

Cheyenne knew better than to try to envision what that meant, but her imagination made the attempt anyway and drew her gaze back to the mass of scar tissue that covered over half of his forearm. His leg and lung, too. What had he done—crawled back to his base? Jesus. He was fit enough.

And stubborn enough.

Damn it, she didn't want to like him. But she was beginning to respect him.

"Cheyenne said she worked for the CIA," Rafe said, but it was clear he was asking for confirmation, which Cheyenne tried not to take personally.

"Yes," Will said.

"Are the CIA and the military connected?" she asked him, curious.

"Everything is connected."

"So the CIA is privy to operations being carried out by US Navy SEAL teams?"

"If it's a response to a threat made to national security, yes."

"The interpretation of which can be nice and fluid."

Will's gaze met hers. "Yes."

"How did you connect it to her?"

He sipped his coffee. "An email communication to her CIA address transmitting the GPS coordinates of the cache location was uncovered."

"Uncovered by whom?"

Will only looked at her.

"I see," Cheyenne said. "What about the source of the email—who contacted her?"

"The message bounced off a hundred different servers, worldwide. It was impossible to trace."

"But you have suspects?"

Another unblinking look.

"Besides me, I mean," Cheyenne said sarcastically.

"How did she die?"

Rafe's quiet question sliced between them like a clean, lethal blade, and Cheyenne's heart fluttered again.

Will met her gaze, and for a moment she saw the man who lived within the machine: bleak, battered, steeped in guilt. Painful and raw. She wanted to look away, because it was so much safer if he stayed a jackass. But she didn't. It wasn't in her to run.

Even when she should.

"Did you kill her?" Rafe asked bluntly, and Cheyenne wanted to hug him, even though it was not something with which she'd ever been comfortable. Instead, she held her breath, because she wanted to know, too.

"No," Will said. "She was killed in Grozny, in the Chechen Republic. The official record states she was killed in the line of duty by pro-Russian dissenters, who presumably believed her to be an American spy."

Cheyenne arched a brow. "And the unofficial record?"

"She brokered at least three deals for the weapons—one to a Columbian cartel, one to a jihadist movement out of Pakistan, and one to a Chechen rebel faction. She sent all three bogus coordinates. My guess is the Chechens discovered the double-cross in Grozny and took her out of play."

"Why was she in Grozny—officially?"

"She wasn't. Not officially. But if I were to hazard a guess, I would assume her mission had something to do with an exchange of intelligence between the CIA and the Chechens—a convenient time to meet with the rebels and offer them a couple of dozen dirty bombs without any suspicions being raised."

"How do you know they don't have the cache?"

"I don't. Not for sure. But chatter leads me to believe she hadn't delivered the weapons—or their true location—to anyone. I think they're still sitting where she left them after she stole them."

"How do you know all this?" Rafe asked with a frown.

Will only blinked at him.

"Because you don't look like no hacker," he continued. "And that's what you're talking about. I know, 'cause I got a friend who's into that big time. Intercepting communications and tracing them back—that takes backdoors, and a shitload of servers, and someone who knows how to get in and out without getting caught. In and out of the CIA." He shook his head. "That ain't wolf territory. That takes a fox."

Cheyenne began to laugh. She couldn't help it; she was really beginning to dig Rafferty Humboldt.

"Yes," she added. "Do tell."

But the waitress arrived at that moment with a tray overflowing with plates, and they were silent as she set them all out on the table. Blackheart had so many there was hardly any table left.

"There's butter, ketchup, mustard, hot sauce and maple syrup. I think that's everything. Can I get you folks anything else?"

Just looking at it all made Cheyenne's stomach hurt.

"I hope not," she said.

"No, ma'am, thank you. Looks wonderful." Will used his dimples again, and the waitress preened as she refilled his coffee cup before walking away. He looked down at Cheyenne's chicken fried steak and said, "That looks good, too."

"Seriously," she snorted. "You have one of everything."

That pale, glinting gaze met hers. "I'll share mine if you share yours."

Which, inexplicably, made her blush. She shoved a forkful of steak into her mouth, and ignored him and watched as Rafe dug into his burger with relish, something she took as a sign that their conversation hadn't scarred him for life. They'd just begun to eat when Will's phone beeped.

He pulled it from his pants pocket, checked the number, and then put it back.

"Your fox?" Cheyenne asked sweetly. "Maybe you should return home to the den."

Will only shook his head. "Sassy pants."

She'd show him sassy—

"You think I know where they're at," Rafe said abruptly. "Don't you? That's why you're here. 'Cuz you ain't found them—even though you hacked her email and probably her phone, too."

Will took his time, cutting his waffles into neat little squares and drowning them in syrup before responding. "Your mother was brilliant, Rafe, and she'd been in the game for a long time. She knew how to play without getting caught. That's why I came to you. You were…a surprise."

Cheyenne pushed her plate away, regretting the food that was beginning to solidify in her belly. Pain flitted across Rafe's face. One by one he pushed his French fries into the lake of ketchup he'd poured onto his plate, as if burying them at sea.

"Do you…" He hesitated. "Do you know who my pop is?"

Beside her Will stilled, and every alarm bell in Cheyenne's head began to clang obnoxiously.

"No," he said softly. "I don't. I'm sorry."

And she knew it was a lie.

She tensed instantly, anger turning her slow boil at his unhidden interrogation into a hot, steady simmer, but Will slid his hand beneath the table, wrapped it around her thigh and squeezed. She started at the intimate hold, and the unexpected lash of heat that arrowed through her veins stole her breath and infuriated her. His touch was heavy and warm and urged caution—*fucking calming her*—and she didn't appreciate it, not one bit.

"Easy," he murmured in a low voice, just for her. His thumb stroked the outside of her thigh, slow and easy, and for a moment every part of her focused on that touch, one that seemed to spread far beyond its limited reach, streaking along every vein until she felt it brush her pulse, her lips, the hollow of her spine.

"I will stab you through the heart with my butter knife," she muttered under her breath. "I swear to God."

"Such bloodlust." His eyes went to her mouth, where they lingered.

Her breath locked in her throat. Her mouth throbbed beneath that look, and other parts of her were stirring, too, damn him.

"Heart, stab, *knife*," she repeated.

But his hand only tightened on her, his long fingers digging into her flesh, pressing against the seam of her cargos where it traced her inner thigh, and deep within, every part of her responded. She grew warm and damp and *ready*. A wholly physical response, without concern for time or place or circumstance.

Just desire, adamant and piercing and totally foreign.

Will turned away abruptly, and his hand closed into a fist atop her thigh, his knuckles pressing hard into her. Cheyenne felt her heart pound in the back of her throat, in her temples, at the notch of her thighs.

"When was the last time you saw your mom?" he asked Rafe, his voice rough. He removed his hand, picked up his fork, and stabbed a piece of waffle.

"Last August," Rafe replied, watching him with narrow eyes.

"That long ago?"

"She didn't like me."

Will's fork scraped his plate. "What do you mean?"

Rafe looked at Cheyenne. "He didn't know her."

Such weariness in that gaze. It hurt to look at. "No," she said.

"She didn't like you?" Will repeated, frowning.

"She didn't like anyone," Cheyenne said.

"Not even her own child?"

"You saw where she left me," Rafe muttered.

Will's hand tightened on his fork until his knuckles pressed white. He stabbed another piece of waffle. "She didn't email you? Send you letters? Communicate in any way?"

"I don't have email," Rafe told him. "And I told you: *she didn't like me.*"

A painful moment of silence punctuated that statement.

"Who else is looking for them?" Cheyenne asked. "Are the Chechens, the cartel and the jihadists going to come knocking, too?"

"You won't have to deal with them," Will said.

"Why not?"

"Because I will."

CHAPTER THIRTEEN

"We don't need a *goddamn* babysitter!"

Will watched Cheyenne stride away from him and told himself it was okay to look. She had a fine ass; he was a healthy heterosexual man. There was nothing wrong with *looking*.

It was the touching he had to curb. Wrapping his hand around her firm, sleekly muscled thigh had been *bad*. He'd only meant to soothe her, to douse the spark before it caught flame and burned him—and damn it, it had *worked*—but the sense of possession that gripped him was dangerous.

She didn't belong to him. She never would.

No matter how much he was growing to like her. Last night might have left him aching and hard and furious with loss, but it changed nothing. They were not meant to be.

He'd gone to Cheyenne with the assumption she was Georgia's collaborator, but their confrontation had shattered that certainty, and Will wasn't sure what to think. Which left him with one of two choices: take at face value what Cheyenne told him or assume it was all lies. His gut told him she spoke the truth—her pain had been raw, as palpable as the ache in his lung—but he no longer trusted that judgment. So it was a roll of the dice, another fucking risk: to *trust*. But he had little choice.

She and the boy were his sole lead. Truth or lie, they were the only way forward. And he couldn't walk away from them —not considering the identity of Rafe's father. Standing before the boy, Will had realized instantly who'd fathered him. He hadn't seen it from afar, but looking into that odd, bi-colored gaze, it was obvious. Two important pieces of the puzzle had clicked together.

And Cheyenne, damn her, had seen it. So he'd touched her. When he shouldn't have.

"I'm an *adult*!" she continued furiously. "I don't need you sticking around—"

"Like white on rice, baby," he said.

"Don't call me that."

Above them, thunder rumbled. The Denny's parking lot was beginning to fill with lunch diners, and Cheyenne wove in and out of the parked cars as she made her way to the Subaru. Rafe followed, far more subdued.

"We aren't helpless," she snarled. "We don't need you standing sentinel. Go find those goddamn bombs. If someone comes—"

"Someone *will* come," Will interrupted, annoyed. While the view from behind was nice, it was everything he could do to stop himself from wrapping his hands around her and forcing her to stop, to listen, to turn around and *look* at him. "And I won't leave you to deal with it alone."

"I'm not alone!" she yelled.

"No," he said. "I'm here."

Which finally made her stop and turn to face him. "Last night, you thought I was her co-conspirator. Now you want to protect me? Go fuck yourself."

Will walked up to her, not stopping until she had to tilt

her head back in order to hold his gaze. *Lemon and verbena.* But no turpentine. Her eyes flashed; color bloomed in her cheeks. Her hair was pulled back in a ponytail, and his hand itched to free it. No woman had ever affected him so quickly, so deeply; none had ever pushed back like she did, and goddamn it, *he liked it.*

"I'm *trusting* you," he growled.

"Well. Be still my heart."

"I'm not going anywhere until this is over."

"Define 'over.'"

"Those weapons, delivered safe and sound, to the US military."

"Then you'd better get on that—*tick tock, tick tock.* Because this is just a time sink. We don't *need* you, Will."

His hands curled into impotent fists in an effort to prevent himself from reaching for her. He couldn't walk away. Not just because of the weapons, but because the identity of Rafe's father made it impossible. It made the boy a target. No wonder Georgia had hid him; he wore bull's-eye painted by his own damn DNA.

Cheyenne would have to be told. But not here, not now... not when Rafe stood beside them, absorbing it all like a sponge.

"What do you think?" Will asked him. "You want someone between you and them? Someone besides her?"

Cheyenne bristled and opened her mouth, but Rafe nodded and said, "Hell, yeah," and her mouth snapped shut.

"I can protect us," she told him after a moment.

"I know." But it was Will's gaze he sought. "But you're all I have. If something happens to you..."

She scowled. "You're playing me."

"No." The boy looked down at his shoes, which were old and scuffed and clearly too small. "Well, maybe. A little. I like the idea of a bodyguard."

"We're not rock stars," Cheyenne muttered. "We don't need a bodyguard."

But Rafe only looked up at her, his gaze solemn, his face far too serious for the kid he was, and Will watched her protest die in her throat.

"Fine," she bit out. "But he's going to be a pain in our ass."

Rafe glanced at Will with a look that said, *see? That's how it's done.* And Will realized she was right: she *had* been played.

"Like white on rice, my ass," she snorted and turned away to continue her walk to the car. "I've been had."

Rafe looked up at him as they followed her. "You'll watch out for her, right?"

"Yes," Will told him. "And for you, too."

The boy studied him with a direct, unflinching look that made Will fear, for a moment, what he might see. *Rage and hate and deep bloody cracks.* But Rafe only nodded, as if satisfied with what he found.

"My ma…she was crazy," he said in a low voice. "She liked to hurt people. I don't want her to hurt Cheyenne."

Will's heart beat with painful intensity. He laid a hand on Rafe's shoulder, painfully aware of the boy's fragility. "She's dead, Rafe. I promise."

But a dark, twisted smile curved Rafe's mouth. "You didn't know her," he said with a shake of his head. "Being dead don't mean a thing."

"Ambassador Andrew Malik. He's the connection."

"Have you been calling the psychic hotline again, brother? Or did something happen I don't know about?"

Will eyed the black sedan in his rearview. Cheyenne was in front of him, weaving in and out of the freeway traffic like a Daytona 500 competitor, and the sky was darkening as the storm that had hovered just on the horizon for most of the morning descended.

He didn't know where they were going. Cheyenne had snarled at him when he'd asked.

"Can you hack his system?" he asked, instead of answering Red's question.

"Of course. If I know *why* I should. What happened?" A long moment of silence. "You met the kid today. Jesus Christ. Don't tell me the kid is his?"

Will wasn't surprised. Red was no dummy, and it wasn't rocket science.

"Holy shit," Red breathed. *"Holy shit."*

Yes. Because Ambassador Malik had been wed to the middle daughter of the Saudi royal family for the last twelve years. They had three beautiful daughters, and the disclosure of his illegitimate son—with a treasonous CIA agent, no less—would not just be a scandal.

It would be an international incident.

"He's the link," Will said, certain of it. "He had access. Opportunity. Motive."

"Motive?"

"Blackmail's a bitch."

"Christ, she was a piece of shit." Red's voice was harsh and furious, and for a moment Will was surprised. Red rarely let his true feelings surface; he was dark and droll and deadpan. But he'd lost his brother—his *twin*—to Georgia's treachery, and occasionally that rage bled through. Frankly, Will was glad to hear it. It made him feel a hell of a lot more human.

"We need to know who reached out to her," Will said, "and told her there were two dozen dirty bombs up for grabs in the Afghan desert."

"Malik and Ethan Scott are both West Point grads. They've been friends for two decades. I know that makes your gut ache, brother, but I've said it from the beginning:

Scott has to be involved. Other than you and your boys, he's the only one who knew about the cache and its location, and he and Malik were both stationed in Kabul at the time. Two and two equals four, my friend. No matter how you shake it out."

Except for Will's gut, which instantly rejected the connection. Scott was married to the daughter of a United States Senator and had been part of the military establishment for the last twenty-three years. He'd been a rumored contender for the Secretary of Defense under the previous administration. It made no sense that he would seek those weapons out for any reason, let alone aid in the massacre of his own troops and get into bed with a crazy, treasonous CIA agent to do so.

Georgia had been good; but had she been *that* good?

Will didn't buy it, but he wasn't going to argue. "Let's start with Malik."

"On it." Red hesitated. "This complicates things."

"Yes," Will said.

"If you found the kid..."

"So will he."

"Do you think Malik is capable..."

"Of killing his own kid to protect his ass?" The darkness stirred. It had bled past the deaths of his men, the stolen weapons, the threat of dirty bombs to the civilized world, and escaped the boundaries he'd set. *Useless lines.* As if he'd any control. And now he found it wasn't just himself he would fight for. Not just his own interests he would protect. As soon as he'd recognized Rafe, he'd understood protecting the boy was *his*, too. And Cheyenne, as well. Whether she liked it or not. *Mine to keep safe.* And while he understood that was not quite right—that the certainty was born within the ruined part of him—he didn't give a damn. Because it felt like fucking *hope*. And right or wrong, he held tight. "The bastard committed treason to protect his secret. What do you think?"

"The only way to protect him is to go public," Red said. "Right now."

Cheyenne would carve his heart out and feed it to him. "No."

"Have you thought about the fact that Georgia might have arranged for the boy's existence to surface if anything happened to her? That destroying Malik from beyond the grave would hold infinite appeal for her?"

"Jesus," Will snarled. "What a mess."

"And getting messier," Red warned.

He hadn't expected this. Not the kid. Not Cheyenne.

Nothing beyond simple greed and murder with a little treason thrown in for kicks. But it was changing shape around him, finding dimension. Making him think and feel and *want*. Making him fight for something other than death.

He wasn't sure that was a good thing.

"Brother?"

Will shook his head. Tried to order his thoughts. In front of him, Cheyenne took the Michigan Avenue exit, and he followed. "What about the tags on the sedan?"

"Rental tags. Name on the contract is John Doe."

"Of course it is." Will scowled.

"You get a look at them yet?"

"Not yet." But soon. Very soon. "Check out Malik. Find out what you can and call me."

"What about the boy?"

"You let me worry about the boy."

"Alrighty then." Red paused, grew serious again. "We finally have a living, breathing suspect. Good work, brother."

Will terminated the connection and tossed his phone down. He followed Cheyenne down Michigan Avenue to

Lake Shore, then turned left onto Iris Lane. He wondered where the hell they were going.

Cheyenne was furious, but that was okay. Will liked her mad. And when she learned why he was sticking to them like glue, some of that temper would ebb. But only some. Because there were hard choices to be made, and she was going to have to make them.

Nothing was simple anymore. Not for any of them.

CHAPTER FOURTEEN

There were wrought iron fences and neatly trimmed hedges; ivory white sidewalks and towering oak trees. A bed of profusely flowering lilies edged the road, giving way to a field of lush green grass as far as the eye could see, and a row of two-story wooden buildings sat within that incredible field of grass, each with its own small, neatly fenced yard and stone patio, each shrouded by hanging planters filled with blooming flowers, each looking out onto the sandy beach below, where Lake Michigan lapped leisurely at the shoreline.

Rafe stared at the scene in astounded silence. When Cheyenne had told him they were going to his ma's condo, he'd thought she was joking.

His ma didn't have a condo. His ma didn't live in the city. His ma...*didn't exist.*

But here was proof that she had. Perfectly, happily. And without him.

"Here we are," Cheyenne said and looked at him sideways. He could tell she was worried about him blowing a gasket. But he was fine.

Because it didn't matter. Not any of it. Even if was beautiful. *Fucking* beautiful.

This is where she lived.

While he was at Letitia's.

Finding Cheyenne had given Rafe hope. For the first time...*ever*. And he was grateful she sat beside him, chewing at her lip, her eyes filled with worry. Because he felt... numb. To see this...it *shouldn't* have mattered. It didn't change anything. He had no illusions to destroy, not anymore.

But anger simmered. So pure and hot and *real* he couldn't deny it.

They pulled into one of the asphalt driveways and parked. Rain began to patter against the roof, big drops that hit the windshield and rolled down like fat tears. Cheyenne was still looking at him, but he couldn't tear his gaze from the perfection spread out around him.

"Rafe?"

"I'm okay," he muttered.

"Bullshit," she said. "You're mad as hell."

He turned to meet her gaze. "Yeah."

She nodded. "You should be."

"I don't want to be," he said.

"Of course not. It fucking hurts." She looked at the condo, with its warm wooden planking, the screened in front porch, the silver numbers above the door. "Grief is that way. Like you're drowning. All you can do is keep swimming." She shook her head. "You *have* to keep swimming. Because it's the only way out."

"I been swimming a long time," he said quietly.

Cheyenne looked back at him. "I know you have."

"I'm tired."

She only reached out and touched his head, lightly. She wasn't good at touching, but he thought it was more from lack of experience than lack of wanting. She'd always been alone; he could tell, because he'd always been alone, too.

In some ways, they were the same. Which was the only thing that gave him the courage to reach for the door handle.

"Let's get this over with," he said.

As they climbed out of the car, Will turned into the driveway behind them and parked.

"Pain in my ass," Cheyenne muttered.

Which almost made Rafe smile. He liked her. She was funny and smart and real. He never would have imagined his mother would leave him something like *her*. But he knew better than to think she didn't come with strings.

Like terrorists and dirty bombs.

But those were his strings. Not hers.

"You ready?" she asked him over the roof of the Subaru.

No.

Chilly rain pelted him and made goose bumps rush along his arms, but he didn't move.

"This is where she lived?" he clarified, his voice a rasp of sound against the pressure building in his chest, pressing against his lungs until they hurt.

"Presumably," Cheyenne said. "The lawyer said she had an apartment in Paris and this condo. I assume that when she was in the states, she lived here."

He stared at her for a long moment through the rain, his heart pounding in his ears. "Paris?"

"I know," she told him. "I fucking know, Rafe. *I'm sorry.*"

He only shook his head, aware that Will had come to stand behind him, and wished he was alone so he could punch something.

"If it's any consolation," Cheyenne told him. "It's all yours now. This and the place in Paris."

He met her gaze. "It's not."

"Yeah. Didn't think so."

He looked around and felt sick: manicured lawns and picnic tables and trees shaped like bowling pins. "Jesus Christ."

It was crazy.

Crazy.

"Rafe."

"No," he said, aware that his voice had gotten louder. The pressure was in his throat, blurring his eyes. *"Fuck."*

Cheyenne said nothing.

"I knew she hated me. But this…"

"She didn't hate you. She wasn't capable of hate. For her, everything was a game. This included." Cheyenne turned and strode up the front steps. "C'mon. Let's get out of the rain."

Rafe followed reluctantly. He didn't want to see any more. He just wanted to get back into the Subaru and go to Wyoming or wherever and forget he'd ever laid eyes on this place.

But Cheyenne stood next to the screen door with keys in her hand, waiting. And Rafe didn't want her to think badly of him. Even though he was pretty sure—if he asked—she would take him away from here. He didn't think she would force him to do something he didn't want to do. She wasn't his ma. But he wasn't *weak*. And he didn't want her to think he was.

So he walked up to the porch, aware of Will at his back—another stranger he shouldn't trust but kind of did, just like Cheyenne—and tried hard to swallow the pressure down, to blink away the blur of tears that threatened, to breathe against the painful band that crushed his lungs. His heart beat so hard it hurt.

Cheyenne said nothing. She only unlocked the screen door and stepped onto the porch. Surveyed the huge wooden swing that hung there, overflowing with bright orange and yellow cushions, and then moved to the second door and unlocked it as well.

The entry was tall and filled with light. The walls were steel gray, the floors black marble. It was clean and sparse, with dark furniture and blood red rugs and gleaming silver appliances. Pictures hung here and there, but there were none of him. Some of them were landscapes, others were filled with people he didn't know. There were paintings and bookshelves overflowing with books, and a huge rock fireplace with no wood in it.

As they walked slowly through the condo, Rafe took note of everything. Every piece of art—statues, sculptures, carvings—every painting, every photograph—prints where his ma was smiling, surrounded by strangers—every piece of delicate pottery, every useless, priceless thing she'd owned.

By the time they climbed the stairs to the second floor and entered the master bedroom, he felt ill. The cheeseburger he'd eaten churned in his belly, and he thought it might be appropriate to just chuck it up, right there, in the middle of his ma's giant black bed.

There were no pictures of him in here, either. Just a tall grandfather clock and a large painting of a little girl that hung next to the bed. Cheyenne had been silent on their walk through, but now she moved to stand in front of the painting and stared at it.

Rafe put his hand on his belly. "What?"

She shook her head and reached up to brush the canvas with her fingertips. "I didn't expect to find this here."

"What?" he repeated.

"This painting. It's the first one I ever sold." She stepped back. "And it totally creeps me out that she had it."

"You did that?" he asked, staring at the painting. "That's…amazing."

It was an oil painting, which he recognized from art class.

A little girl stood in a field of knee high grass and white daisies, leaning over a fallen log to peer down at a small fox that was curled just beneath the log. The sky was bright, clear blue, and the expression on the girl's face made him take another look at Cheyenne.

"Really?" he said. "You did that?"

"Really." Cheyenne reached up and removed the painting. "This will be coming with us."

He watched her turn it into the light and study it, and he thought of all of his scribbled drawings, every character he'd brought to life, every story he'd tried to tell, that world he horded and gorged on and escaped to when he couldn't take the real one anymore—

She would understand.

Because she went there, too.

And suddenly, it all welled up, ready to blow.

Rafe turned and stepped around Will, who'd followed them soundlessly through the place and now stood next to the window, watching Cheyenne, and quickly headed back downstairs.

Going to destroy it all...

He knew it was wrong. He didn't care. It was his to destroy. This place—this *palace*—had only confirmed every dark thought that had ever occurred to him, every twisted truth, every relentless fact.

She lived here, like a fucking princess. *While he was in hell.*

Furious, he walked into the living room and swiped the tall blown-glass heron from its bronze stand and watched as it shattered against the floor. It felt *awesome*. The pictures were next, flung against the floor and stomped for good measure. Then the porcelain lamp, *wham!* The crystal bowl filled with dusty potpourri, *crash!* The old wooden butter churn, which splintered when he kicked it, *crack!* The white horsehair vase—

"Rafe." Cheyenne stood at the foot of the stairs, her painting in hand. Staring at him. *"Stop."*

He didn't want to; he was going to obliterate it *all*. But when he looked into her eyes—filled with pain and *knowing*—the pressure in his chest seemed to swell until his ribs groaned for mercy, and when he opened his mouth only a harsh, rasping sound emerged.

"I hate her," he grated and kicked the vase. *"I fucking hate her guts!"*

It crashed against the stone fireplace and shattered, and he stared down at it, his heart beating furiously, his vision blurred by tears.

"I hate her," he repeated, choking, his voice breaking.

Cheyenne said nothing.

"Did you hear me?" he yelled. *"I hate her!"*

He focused on the biggest statue, a large, stone horse with legs too big for its body and eyes of inlaid jade, and he charged it, determined to push it over, to *destroy it*—

Arms like steel bands lifted him from the ground, halting him in his fury nearly three feet above the floor.

Will.

"Let me go," Rafe snarled. "It's *mine*."

He struggled and wiggled and wormed, but there was no escaping. He slammed his head against Will's chest, kicked back with his heels, pounded his fists against Will's thighs. Will only waited, his hold unrelenting, his hands gentle.

"Screw you," Rafe said and sagged against him, exhausted from the fight. Tears clogged his throat. "Let me go."

"Not until you calm down and man the fuck up." Will's voice was harsh in his ear. "You're acting like an asshole, and you're scaring Cheyenne, and that's *pissing me off*."

Rafe stilled. He looked over at Cheyenne, who stared at him with pale cheeks and dark eyes, her scar ugly and stark in the light, and felt horror and terror crash through him in equal parts.

Oh God. No. No, no, no. Not now, not when he'd been given something important, someone who gave a shit, someone who might learn to love him—

"I'm sorry," he cried, and the tears fell, rolling down his cheeks, dripping from his chin. "I'm sorry, I didn't mean to be an ass-asshole, I'm sorry, Cheyenne, please don't be mad, I'm sorry, Will—"

His shoulders were shaking, and sobs were choking him. Will turned him in his embrace and hugged him tight, and Rafe bawled like a baby, unable to stop, filled with shame and fear and such overwhelming pain he thought he just might die.

"Goddamn it," Cheyenne said brokenly, and suddenly she was there too, hugging him from behind, and they stood like that for a long moment, the three of them, his sobs shattering the silence. Will slid his arm around Cheyenne and rocked them both, and Rafe knew she was crying, too. The scent of pine and lemon surrounded him, and he thought those must be the best smells in the whole world.

The storm was violent, and when the last shuddered breath escaped Rafe, his throat was raw, Will's shirt was soaked with tears. Cheyenne was beside him, her head next to his against Will's chest, her hand under his shirt, warm against his bare back.

"I'm sorry," he whispered.

Cheyenne only shook her head and hushed him, and they rocked.

CHAPTER FIFTEEN

Cheyenne stared at the gleaming red Audi A6 that sat in Georgia's garage and let the rage wash over her. Like cheap, toxic moonshine, fire in her veins, making her knees weak and her fingertips tingle.

The urge to take a baseball bat to the car was overwhelming. But Rafe had already taken that road, and there was nothing to be gained by following him. If anything, his journey had forced her to consider her own.

And what she discovered was not comforting.

For years, she'd been the one freaking out. Angry, impatient, unwilling to follow the rules. Creating chaos because she'd *felt* chaotic, never recognizing the repercussions for that chaos, never aware of the fallout others experienced from her anarchy. Never the one who stood and watched, helpless, as the world came undone around her.

"It *sucks*," she said, her voice echoing around her. The garage was empty except for the costly SUV and a yellow snow shovel. She'd left Rafe eating pizza and watching *Supernatural* with Will.

Because she needed a moment.

Watching Rafe lose his shit had affected her. She'd known something would happen—once she'd seen the crapfest where the kid lived, it was unavoidable—but she'd been too busy being pissed off at Will and his slick bullshit maneuvering to focus on what was headed toward them. Toward Rafe.

Reality. One he'd never known existed. One where he was a dirty, ugly secret kept hidden from existence. Where his mother lived like a queen while he was punished for breathing.

If it had been her, Cheyenne would have burned the fucking place to the ground.

"Goddamn stupid," she growled.

But worse. Bad enough she'd lost the ball, and it had smacked her in the face. Worse was being forced to witness an act she'd always before perpetrated. To know fear and anxiety and sadness, to be still within the fury, powerless to do anything but *watch*. To understand what it was to clean up the mess.

Jesus Christ.

She'd spent her life making other people clean up her messes, thinking she was one step ahead, smarter, *better,* when really...she'd just been making a goddamn mess. Making things worse. Like an angry child: destroying instead of building.

Just like Georgia.

Only...different.

Tears burned her nose, her throat; her eyes stung. It hurt to see it so clearly. To rewind and remember and know she should have done differently. How lost she'd been, how smug and self-righteous and *wrong.*

I suspect you know this isn't the best way to handle what you feel, Cheyenne. Don't you agree?

Fuck off and die, Phil.

A sob caught in her throat, and she covered her mouth, horrified by the sound of it. She couldn't afford to lose it. Not here, not now. Rafe needed her to be his shelter—strong, unwavering, willing to put him first, no matter the personal cost. She'd assumed herself capable of that, but she'd spent her life putting herself first—doing what she wanted, when she wanted, regardless of the repercussions.

Regardless of the fallout.

"I'm an *asshole*," she muttered, aghast at the realization.

"No, you're not," Will said quietly.

She didn't turn and look at him. Instead she leaned on the car and buried her head in her hands, drained of fury.

"Yes, I am," she said, her voice muffled.

"No, baby, you aren't."

"Don't call me that," she mumbled.

Bastard had held her, held Rafe, rocked them like children. And it had felt so *right*...he'd known precisely what to do, while she'd stared, horrified and helpless and paralyzed by the meltdown of a ten-year-old boy.

"Should have *known*," she whispered.

"Don't." Closer, as if he stood right next to her. Pine and heat. He moved soundlessly, as lithe and fleet as a cat, in spite of his size. "Today was hard, was always going to be hard. Nothing to be done for that except survive it."

Stinking bastard with his perfect words. Except he wasn't a bastard. Watching him hug Rafe—*the exact right thing*—feeling his arm pull her into the embrace, the kiss he'd pressed to her head as he rocked them—*there was decency in him.* A morality she wanted to overlook. His methods infuriated her, but his motives...they appeared to be pure.

Except for the blood that steeped them.

But Cheyenne didn't hold that against him. He deserved his revenge.

That revenge, however, was dangerous. To Rafe. To *her*. They would bear witness; they would be the fallout. Left to clean up the mess...

No.

Regardless of decency or morality. Will Blackheart had too many secrets—no doubt his fox had uncovered every document ever written about Rafe, about *her*, a realization which sickened and infuriated her—and the carnage he dreamed of would destroy them all.

No. He would have to travel that road alone. Even if he was a man to whom she was deeply, disturbingly attracted. One she kind of understood. One she was beginning to *like*.

An unprecedented occurrence, in and of itself, foreign territory where she didn't trust herself. Or him. *Twenty-four hours*. Hardly enough time to test someone's mettle, to know their heart, to *accept* them.

"Crazy bullshit," she said and tears slid from the corners of her eyes.

"Everything, all the time," Will murmured. Fingers tangled in her ponytail and tugged gently. So careful.

So many little things coalescing into a whole she dare not believe.

"You're doing good," he told her softly, tucking a stray lock of hair behind her ear. He stood on her left side; her scar prickled when his warm breath touched it. She should have felt self-conscious and turned away. That she didn't...*bending too far*. When she never bent for anyone. "Look at me, Cheyenne."

She didn't want to. She wanted to hide and lick her wounds. Weep for the woman she'd believed herself to be; rage against the one she'd discovered she *was*.

Figure out how the hell to live with them both.

But this was not her time, no matter the personal

epiphany that had just crapped all over her. This was about Rafe, a boy who had no one but her to count on, to protect him.

To love him. Something she'd been afraid she might be incapable of. And yet—

"Twelve hours," she murmured and looked up at Will. Tears blurred his image, and she blinked. They slipped down her cheeks. "How is that possible?"

"Life happens fast, baby." A small smile, a flash of dimple. The tender sweep of his palm over her hair. "That's why you have to hold on tight, and enjoy the ride."

It wasn't fair, that he should know just what to tell her. Ammunition she didn't have and didn't even know where to get.

"Is that what you're doing?" she asked. "Enjoying the ride?"

His smile faded. His hand dropped.

"We need to talk," he said.

His tone made her spine stiffen. She swiped at her tears and pushed off of the SUV, stepping back to put some distance between them. *Distance.* An imperative, something she *had* to remember. He wasn't the enemy. But he wasn't a friend, either.

"Go ahead," she said with a sigh. "Make my day."

"Rafe's father is the American Ambassador to Afghanistan."

Cheyenne did a double-take. She stared at Will, opened her mouth, closed it, and stared at him some more.

"His name is Andrew Malik."

She shook herself. "And you know this because…?"

"Because I've met the Ambassador. Rafe looks just like him." Will pulled a photograph from the front pocket of his tee and held it out to her. "He's the one right behind her."

The picture was creased, one corner torn and bearing the faint imprint of shoe tread. It was one of the ones Rafe had trashed. Georgia stood within a circle of men on a white balcony; palm trees and a crystal blue sea were visible in the background. The men wore moneyed casual wear; she was in a sari. The man to whom Will referred was tall and well-built, with dark, steel-gray hair and bright hazel eyes. As soon as Cheyenne focused on him, she saw the resemblance.

"Son of a bitch," she whispered. She looked up at Will. "Why did you lie?"

"Because Malik is married to a Saudi royal. He has three daughters and everything to lose if his illegitimate child with a treasonous CIA agent pops out of the woodwork."

Cheyenne smacked her forehead with her palm. She stared down at the picture. "Goddamn *it*."

"It gets worse."

"Of course it does."

"I think he was the one who supplied Georgia with the location of my team."

"He had it?"

"He could get it."

"Why?"

"Because if he wanted to keep his secret, he had no choice."

Lead filled Cheyenne's belly. For a long moment, she said nothing. Then she turned and kicked the driver's side door panel of the SUV, a violent but practiced blow that left a deep dent.

"Bitch," she growled.

"Rafe was the perfect leverage. But that leverage is now moot. Which either protects him or—"

"Screws him." Cheyenne's gaze narrowed on Will. Apparently he had a pair of crazy shoes, too. "You think she's going to out big daddy from beyond the grave?"

"Quite possibly."

"Hell, yes, she is." Cheyenne slid the picture into her pocket, turned and began to pace the length of the SUV. "Nothing left for her to lose—fill the lion's den, and let the slaughter begin. Leaving a bloodbath in her wake is the perfect goddamn eulogy."

Will said nothing, his pale eyes glinting in the light, and Cheyenne saw the man who lived within watching her from the shadows. Two identities, so close yet so far; who he was, who he needed to be. Two halves linked by blood and violence and purpose.

She could relate. But that tie did not bind them.

"You think he's in danger from Malik?" she asked.

"The Ambassador has everything to lose. That's why she hid him so deep."

"Does the kid ever catch a break? Ever?"

Will stepped into her path, halting her. "You have to decide."

"Decide what?"

"How to handle it."

Cheyenne stepped around him, continued to pace. "If we announce to the world he's Malik's bastard son, it will bring on a shitstorm that will blow his life apart."

"It also removes the danger that the Ambassador might decide to make him disappear before his existence becomes a problem."

"*Motherfucker!*" she snarled.

"If you wait," Will said, "and Georgia has something planned, you lose any control you might otherwise have over how it's done."

"Fuckity, fuck, fuck!" Cheyenne stopped and kicked the back quarter panel of the SUV. Another dent. "How do I tell him? *How?*"

"I don't know," Will said, as quiet as she was loud.

It tempered her. "It's not fair," she said, and when a tear streaked her cheek, she let it fall. She turned and resumed pacing. "I know how trite that sounds—but seriously. What the hell did he do to deserve this? Be born? He's just a *little boy*. He's *innocent*. Not like she was. Crazy, murderous bitch—"

Hard hands caught her hips from behind and halted her pacing frenzy. Cheyenne stiffened and tugged against the hold, unwilling to step back into a fire that would only burn and scar and leave nothing but ash in its wake.

"No," she said.

Hands tightening, Will dragged her back against him. "You need to calm down."

"Is that what you're doing?" A sharp laugh caught in her throat. "Calming me down?"

Strong arms slid around her waist and locked her to him; instant heat, tensile muscle that flexed and stretched around her, the steady beat of his heart against her back. "Someone has to."

"Not you," she said instantly, stiff in his hold. She hated it that he made her feel...*safe*. When no one had ever made her feel safe.

Beyond stupid. An illusion that could, quite possibly, be fatal. Even if his heat seeped into her bones, and awareness rippled across her flesh like the stroke of a rough tongue.

"Why not me?" he demanded, his voice like gravel.

"You dream of vengeance," she told him. "Of painting the world in flesh and blood and bone. Nothing more." Her breath snagged when he nipped her throat, and heat forked through her like live current. Such a visceral, mindless response...as though she were animal alone. "I can see it. It's eating you up...and there won't be anything left. You can't have us both."

He stilled, silent. His heart pounded against her like a jackhammer.

"Let me go," she said.

But his arms tightened, until the hold became something to break.

"I can't *choose*," he grated, his breath hot in her ear.

"No," she agreed. Goosebumps washed across her flesh. "Let me go, Will."

A violent tremor moved through him; his hands flexed in their hold. "I don't want to."

"Do it anyway."

But he didn't. Instead, he rubbed his bristled chin against her scar, and she shuddered, her hands gripping the thick muscle of his scarred forearm.

"I dream of being inside you," he whispered. "So deep I'm all you know, and you're crying my name, begging me to make you come..."

A flash of brilliant white heat arrowed to the hollow place between her thighs, and a low sound whispered from her. His hands moved restlessly, stroking her: curving along her abdomen, up her belly, tracing the rigid curve of her ribs, a hairsbreadth from her breasts. She knew she should step away, *stop him*. But she didn't. No. Instead, she waited, breathless, blood a distant roar in her ears as his touch slid further north, his blunt, rough fingertips a whisper against the tender underside of her breasts, tracing her shape, and she pressed back against him, unable to help herself. The line of his cock was startling, brutally hard, and she was tempted to—

"Cheyenne?"

Rafe's muffled voice penetrated her consciousness—*from the other side of the door*—and Cheyenne reared in Will's arms and pushed against him in utter panic, her legs flailing, her nails digging into his arm.

"Easy," he growled, his arms tight, and for a moment she feared he really wouldn't let her go, that she would have to fight—

And then she was free, and he was turning away. Her knees were so weak she had to reach out and brace herself against the SUV for support.

The garage door opened. Rafe appeared, every line of his body filled with uncertainty. He'd apologized a hundred times for his meltdown; Cheyenne was sure he was going to apologize a hundred more.

She fought for breath. Her cheeks were on fire.

Holy shite.

"Sorry," he said awkwardly, his gaze flitting between them.

"No worries," she croaked. "You okay?"

"Yeah. I just...you were gone a long time."

She nodded. Tried to catch her breath. Willed strength into her knees.

"I have to go," Will said.

"Go?" Rafe repeated, his voice raising.

"I'll be back."

Cheyenne turned to look at him. "Go where?"

She didn't appreciate the panic she'd heard in Rafe's voice —not when she felt its echo ripple through her. She didn't rely on anyone; she never had. She would *not* start with a man she didn't know from a hole in the ground.

No matter how he made her feel; his interests were *not* her own.

"I'll be back," he repeated, his tone cold. When Cheyenne met his gaze, he only stared back at her, his blue eyes as pale and opaque as the glaciers they resembled. He looked nothing like the man who'd confessed his dreams and nearly seduced her into them.

I can't choose.

"Don't bother," she told him.

Then she went to Rafe, put her shaking hands on his thin shoulders and turned him back toward the house. "C'mon, sweet pea. I think I saw some unopened ice cream in the freezer. God willing, it's mint chocolate chip."

CHAPTER SIXTEEN

*R*ain pounded the roof like steel pennies.

Night had fallen, and wind buffeted the black sedan Will sat within, awaiting his prey. The man who'd been tailing them all day had been gone for two minutes and forty-five seconds. A piss break, taken behind one of the cone-shaped juniper shrubs that lined the opposite side of the street. *Stupid.*

A proficient tail never left its mark.

Getting into the sedan had been child's play; it was left unlocked. Will wondered who this clown was—CIA, presumably—and how a well-trained spook could be so ridiculously inept. He was either too green to know better, too lazy to care, or too arrogant to worry about it. Will put his money on arrogant. Spooks were notoriously hubristic.

Adrenaline shimmered in his veins. Part of it was the hunt; the wait for his prey, the knowledge that he would *finally* be able to work out some fucking angst. But mostly it was just thwarted lust.

Shouldn't have touched her.

No matter how many times he told himself *never again*, no matter his discipline, his judgment, his intent, regardless that it was stupid and dangerous—to them both—he reached for her. Put his hands on her, put his *mouth* on her. And it wasn't enough.

Not nearly enough.

God help him, he *did* dream of her.

Denying temptation—even need—wasn't the issue; he was a soldier. Doing without was part of the job. It was the denial of his gut that sheared him in two; a dual existence where what he wanted, and what his instincts told him *should* be, opposed the certainty that what he wanted could *never* be. And it was his gut that continued to reach for her, overriding his every good intention, ignoring the line he'd drawn, making a mockery of his self-control.

Worse, the blame was solely his own. She did not try to entice him. There were no sly looks, no unnecessary touches, no come-hither smiles.

She was just…Cheyenne. Tough and brave and funny; too smart for her own good. For his.

A survivor.

Like him.

Watching her take down Letitia Jones had beguiled him, and her manner with the boy was frank and uncertain, and so earnest he knew it was genuine. She was doing her best, and Will respected that. Another conflict within him; another hurdle, because he didn't want to feel anything for her: she was a tool. A stone upon which to step. Her only value had been in her connection to Georgia, something he'd condemned her for. *Punished her for.* But her worth was growing beyond that tenuous link. And that could not be. Not for either of them—a truth he returned to, again and again.

Because it remained unchanged.

You can't have us both.

No. And he shouldn't want both. The hunt was all he had; a justification for his continued existence. The only clear path was the trail he followed—the same one he'd been following since he'd woken broken and scarred and *changed*—and even if that trail led him to the unexpected, he had to follow it to the end. There was no veering off course, no short cuts, no side trips.

There was only one destination—and that did not include a crazy, mouthy woman who'd awoken him to all that would never be his. It did not include a boy who looked at him with such painful, hopeful trust it felt like a fucking knife in the chest.

He would protect them from anyone who threatened them. He understood that was part of the responsibility, part of making his failure less damning, but that was all he would do. Being their friend, helping them navigate each other, giving of *himself*—those were things he would not do. Could not do.

Because part of him greatly resented their presence, and the awakening they'd provoked. The distraction they'd created, prying him from the darkness, tempering his blood-lust, offsetting the hate by expanding his world beyond the narrow confines of the path he followed, those were things for which he was not at all grateful. That disruption had born temptation and *need*, neither of which he wanted to feel. Neither of which he'd believed himself capable of. The knowledge that he was susceptible to such weakness could be utilized in only one manner: shoring himself against it. Refocusing on the endgame, removing all interference, moving forward, single-minded, until his goal was met.

He was getting closer; Malik was an important piece of

the puzzle. He would lead to another. And another. It was inevitable. Eventually the whole would materialize, and Will would know who. Why. How. He would locate the weapons and secure them. *Punish those responsible.*

After that…well. It hadn't occurred to him there might be an *after.* There was only *now.*

And it was better that way—for everyone involved.

The sedan's driver's side door opened abruptly, and the car rocked slightly as a tall, narrow man with thick red hair and black-framed eyeglasses slid in. His face was freckled and pitted by acne scars in the reflection of the street light overhead. He smelled of wet wool and stale coffee.

As he pulled the door shut, Will slid his forearm around the man's throat from behind. His Glock kissed the man's temple.

The man stilled. He didn't tense, and his voice was calm. "What do you want?"

"Let's start simple," Will murmured. "Who are you?"

The man said nothing. The sound of rain pounding the sedan's roof filled the silence.

Will gave him ten seconds, then tightened his hold against the man's carotid artery. "I can't hear you."

A tremor moved through the man, but he didn't panic. He swallowed, and his Adam's apple bobbed beneath Will's forearm. "Frank James."

Georgia's CIA partner. He looked different than the black and white photo Will had seen. According to Red's research, James and Georgia had hated each other's guts. "What are you doing here, Frank?"

"I suspect I'm doing the same thing you are…Lieutenant."

"And what's that, Frank?"

A moment of silence. Will watched in the rearview mirror while the agent weighed his words, but didn't rush him. Considering the file he'd read, he hadn't expected James to appear. More fool him.

Such a tangled, sticky web.

James met Will's gaze in the mirror. "If I don't find them, I'll be indicted for treason."

Will only raised a brow. "Are you a traitor, Frank?"

A sharp laugh broke the air, but there was nothing humorous in the sound. "She was good. I'll give her that. I should have killed her when I had the chance."

"You and everyone whoever knew her."

"Isn't that the truth."

Will pressed his Glock against the pale, vulnerable flesh of Frank's temple. "You'd best explain yourself, Frank. It's been a long fucking day."

"She laid a trail straight to me. I found it three days ago. A string of emails from an untraceable source in the State Department—the time and date and location of the planned operation for retrieval. Emails from a known merc out of Beirut confirming a team assembly, a flight schedule, meeting time and place. Christ, there's even a record of the sale—to the *Chechens*. As if I'd ever sell anything to those crazy bastards."

Will said nothing for a long moment. The sound of the rain was almost deafening.

"You have to believe me," Frank continued, his voice tight, his eyes unwavering. Desperation etched in darkness and polished glass. "I would not jeopardize twenty-two years of service for a handful of Russian bottle rockets."

"She sold them for half a million, Frank. Three times over. Pretty good for a handful of bottle rockets."

"My reputation is worth far more than anything she could've sold them for." Frank's eyes narrowed behind the lenses of his glasses. "Just like yours."

"Meaning?"

"They know you're on the hunt, Lieutenant. That you walked out of Bethesda—and out of your service—because you know one of them betrayed you. It's no secret that you've made it your mission to find that person—and to punish them."

"What's your point, Frank?"

"You crawled out of the Afghan desert on your hands and knees—the sole survivor of an attack that butchered your team and loosed a small, semi-nuclear arsenal on the world. You didn't do that because you were a good soldier. You did that for *them*. Because they were *yours*. Because, to you, that loss far surpasses the bottle rockets—and that is the loss you're concerned with. The weapons are merely an incidental. You seek those who committed this crime because you want vengeance."

Will's finger flexed on the trigger of the Glock. "Spare me the psych eval, Frank, and hurry this along. The rain is making me sleepy."

"I value my reputation as much as you valued your men. Our goal is the same: to recover the weapons, and to make those who perpetrated this crime *pay*."

The tremor in Frank's voice went a lot further than his words. That he was pissed was written all over his face. And the record reflected his enmity toward Georgia; they'd filed several official complaints against one another.

"How did you know it was her?" Will asked him. Because it had taken Red four days—and unrestricted access to the CIA's heavily encrypted system—to pinpoint her name.

"She's the only one who would choose to frame me. Believe it or not, I have a rather good working relationship with the majority of my colleagues." Frank sighed. "My contact was unable to trace the planted emails to the original source, but I have no doubt it was her. I imagine the only reason she never moved forward was because she was killed before the orchestration was complete."

"Killed in Grozny."

"Yes. Such a shame."

"In the line of duty."

"So I heard. I was in Venice, by the way. In case you're wondering."

He was. "And you're sitting here because..."

"Because, like you, the boy and the guardian are the only lead I have."

Will didn't particularly care for that comparison. "Who led you to them?"

"The Agency. I simply inquired who received Ms. Humboldt's possessions when she died. Those items were sent to an attorney out of Milwaukee: Smith Jones. Who, as I'm sure you know, drafted a will and trust for our friend. It was not difficult to uncover the rest. I must admit, the child surprised me. I was her partner for three years; I had no idea she had a son." Frank paused. "I wonder who his father is."

Will ignored the implied question. For all he knew, James was well aware who Rafe's father was; the agent had spent plenty of time overseas. He would know exactly who Malik was. If he hadn't recognized the connection it was only because he hadn't focused closely enough on Rafe, and eventually he would. "You think the boy will lead you to the cache?"

"The boy or the guardian." Frank's eyes narrowed in the mirror. "Interesting story there, don't you think? I do wonder what happened. You've read the file, I presume? I could find no link between those ladies, not in all the years since. So *odd* that she would come for him. The son of her enemy."

I prefer nemesis.

Cheyenne's voice echoed in Will's head. He didn't like

James talking about her, even though he'd had the exact same thought—and voiced it. He didn't like the speculation on James' face or in his voice; he didn't like it that a spook was watching them, armed with the same information he had, using that information for the same purpose, determined to use them in order to solve the mystery.

Just like he was. Which only made him a hypocrite, but he didn't give a shit.

"How did *you* find them, Lieutenant? Somehow I doubt you reached out to the Agency...."

Will only stared at him coldly. "Did she screw you over, Frank? Did she take the weapons and sell them out from under you? Is that what happened?"

Frank's face closed. "You insult me at your own peril."

"You were her partner, Frank. I'm supposed to believe you didn't know she was playing both sides of the deck?"

"She was a faithless, conniving bitch, who got more than one of my assets killed. I knew she was for sale to the highest bidder, but she was very good at hiding her true face. Ask your Senior Chief. I hear they were quite...*close.*"

Will ground his teeth together. First Red and now Frank. Christ.

"You do realize it had to be one of yours who reached out to her, don't you? Your senior chief, one of your men—"

His words ended when Will's arm flexed around his throat and cut off his oxygen.

"Thin ice, Frank. Very thin ice."

Frank stilled. That he didn't simply pull his own weapon and fire through the seat behind him told Will he just might be telling the truth. So Will let him breathe.

"Crazy bastard," Frank muttered. "I heard you'd lost it."

"Yes," Will said, eyes glittering, smile feral in the mirror.

"We have to find them."

"Yes."

"How do you know they haven't been sold?"

"I don't. Money was exchanged, but delivery was never confirmed."

Frank eyed him thoughtfully. "I would not have imagined you would have such…efficient resources."

Will only blinked at him.

"And the boy…?"

"Knows *nothing*," Will said coldly, hackles rising.

"God forbid I ask about the guardian—"

Will cocked the Glock.

"Jesus, man. You are reactionary."

"Don't forget," Will advised him.

"Why are you wasting time with them if they have nothing for us?"

He didn't like the use of that word "us." But Will didn't correct him. If Frank really did want to find those weapons—if he really did have something to lose, and having Red check that out would be no problem at all—well, Will would make use of him. The more people with an ear to the ground, the better. Spook or not.

"Don't worry about me, Frank. Worry about yourself." Will slid his Glock back into his holster. "Quit tailing us—and make use of those assets you're so fond of, and find out if the bottle rockets were delivered to anyone. Let me know. Then we'll talk again."

Frank looked less that thrilled with the prospect. "And if you discover anything, you'll let me know?"

Will smiled, all teeth. "Sure, Frank. First thing."

"We need to work together, Lieutenant. We have different strengths and together—"

"She made you her bitch. That's a sinking ship."

"I had nothing to do with—"

"So you say." Will shrugged. "Time will tell."

"Which means I'm on my own?"

THE BEQUEST

"We're all on our own, Frank."

Will was soaking wet by the time he slipped through the back door of the condo, courtesy of the keys he'd snagged from the kitchen counter where Cheyenne left them. Only one lamp lit the darkened unit, and the TV flickered with flames and screams.

Supernatural was still on.

Rafe lay on one end of one of the large couches that dominated the open room that was the condo's main living space. Cheyenne lay on the other end. Will was surprised to find them both sound asleep. Then he looked at his watch and realized it was after eleven.

He secured the condo, locking every door and window tight. He called Red, who didn't pick up, and left a message about Frank James. Then he went through the condo, top to bottom, and searched every nook and cranny he could find.

Because the condo had been a surprise.

Presumably it was titled in either Rafe's name or the name of the trust the lawyer had drawn up, and that's why Red hadn't caught it. Either way, when they'd arrived that afternoon—led by Cheyenne, who'd had keys in hand—Will had stood there like an asshole with his pants down, his heart beating like a drum at the thought that they'd missed the place—and wondering what, if anything, it might contain.

There were two important items they hadn't been able to locate: Georgia's phone and her laptop. Both would be treasure troves of information. And both seemed to have fallen off the face of the earth.

Searching the condo yielded nothing—until Will reached Georgia's bedroom, where in the farthest reaches of her closet, a small wall safe hung behind a false front of shoe shelving. The sight of it sent anticipation spearing through him, and for a long moment, he stood there and stared at it, knowing it couldn't be that simple, that Georgia Humboldt had enjoyed playing puppeteer far too much to let it end there.

Nevertheless, he screwed his silencer onto his Glock, wrapped one of her thousand dollar suit coats around it, and fired twice. Had the safe been made out of high-grade steel with a combination mechanism, his ammo never would have penetrated it. But Georgia had been arrogant, which often equated to careless, and the safe was cheap, the locking mechanism a small keyhole that his bullets tore wide open.

The sole occupant of the safe was a well-worn leather-bound book. Will pulled it out and opened it, almost dizzy with the rush of his blood, but when he focused on it, he found only…gibberish. Page after page of nonsensical garbage. No words, just a crazy mix of letters and numbers and symbols. Line after line after line.

He stared down at it, infuriated and flummoxed and despising Georgia Humboldt with every fiber of his being. The need to smash everything Rafe had missed gripped him, the desire so strong, his hands fisted around the book and tore several pages in half. The rage rose like a tidal wave, and for long moments, Will was awash in fury and pain and the struggle to just *be*. To let it ebb again and return to the vast place where it slept fitfully within him.

To regain control.

Minutes passed, and Will knew he was going to have to decide. Whether to allow the rage free reign to continue, to rise within him like a spark catching flame, and to let it to burn until nothing was left. Or whether to douse the flames, to exert himself and take back all that it laid claim to…the life he no longer felt he deserved.

But not yet.

He stared down at the book and fought to marshal his thoughts.

Red. Red would be able to decipher it, but that would take time.

Tick-tock.

What about Rafe? Maybe he and his mother had had some sort of code...or Cheyenne. She'd known Georgia a long time. She might be able to help.

He would have to share it. He had no choice, because he sure as hell didn't know what he was looking at. Maybe it actually held what he was looking for...but he wouldn't know until someone could make sense of it.

Intensely disappointed, Will fought the urge to wake both Rafe and Cheyenne so he could thrust the book at them and demand they decipher it. Tomorrow would come soon enough; they needed their sleep. Besides, there was no guarantee it would make any more sense to them than it did to him...

He closed the safe, replaced the shelving and left the closet as he'd found it.

Cheyenne's painting sat in the downstairs hallway, and he paused in front of it. The scene was incredibly life-like, from the blades of grass the girl stood within, to the fine, silky fur that covered the fox. As if he could reach out and stroke that thick fur. And the look of wonderment on the girl's face... Will hadn't paid much attention to the information in Cheyenne's file about her artwork. He should have. Anyone who could do this would have no need to steal and sell dirty bombs. He'd known she was solvent—Red had been thorough—but staring at that painting made him realize she was far beyond flush.

Stupid asshole.

In the living room, he found another photograph of Malik and Georgia on the mantle, but nothing else. No stashed GPS coordinates. No hidden letter to Rafe. Nothing at all to lead him in the right direction.

No less than he'd expected.

So he took a long, hot shower, sprawled out on the free couch, and fell asleep to demons and hellhounds and men who changed shape beneath the bright light of the moon.

CHAPTER SEVENTEEN

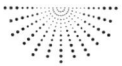

"What do you think?"

Rafe stared at the elaborate display of cremation urns. There was a silver one, a black one, a gold one, a wooden one, and a porcelain one with butterflies plastered all over it. Some were round, some were square, one was even shaped like a sleeping cat.

None of them made him think of his ma.

"Maybe we should just use a Big Gulp cup," he suggested.

"Economical but weak." Cheyenne shot him a small smile. "I'd hate to end up wearing her."

"Yuck." He rubbed his arms, creeped out by the thought. And even more by their surroundings.

The Rosemont Funeral Home was a huge, sprawling Victorian home with dark woodwork and plastered walls. Huge wooden caskets dotted the interior like ships set adrift. Several worn, sagging couches were placed in corners along with uncomfortable looking chairs, and the place smelled old and musty, like Letitia's attic.

Rafe had never been in a funeral home. Hell, he'd never even been to a funeral. When Cheyenne had asked him if he wanted to have one for his ma, he wasn't sure what to say. It seemed wrong, to not have a funeral. But he didn't see the point in having one, either.

His ma hadn't been anyone good. No one would miss her. Not even him.

Oh, he wanted to. He wanted to pretend all kinds of crazy shit about her: that she was good, that she loved him, that she'd died protecting him… But he knew better than to let fantasy overwrite reality. She was who she was.

He felt no sadness at her passing.

So he told Cheyenne he didn't want a funeral. They decided to get her "to go" as Cheyenne had put it and were now tasked with the job of choosing a final resting urn. As far as Rafe was concerned, his Big Gulp cup was a good choice.

"Let's go with simple." Cheyenne reached out and stroked a finger down the grain of the wooden one. "This is nice."

"She didn't deserve nice," he said.

"This isn't for her," Cheyenne replied. "It's for us."

Which he only partially understood. But he didn't care, so he only shrugged and looked over at Will, who stood before the thick glass double doors, staring out at the rain. Something had changed. Today, Will was quiet and…apart, somehow. Different than he'd been yesterday.

Rafe wondered if it was his fault. He hadn't meant to freak out.

At least Cheyenne wasn't mad. Even while they'd cleaned up the spectacular mess he'd made, she just kept saying, "It's fine. No worries. I've done worse—believe me." And Rafe was pretty sure she meant it. But Will…he seemed *cold*.

"Have you decided?"

Rafe jumped, startled by the silent approach of the funeral director. He was a short, gray-haired man with thick eyeglasses and soft hands—which Rafe knew, because he'd shook Rafe's hand, his second handshake ever after Will's the day before. It was weird to shake someone's hand, but Rafe kind of liked it. It made him feel like an adult—like they saw through his skinny legs and small head to the person underneath...the one who wasn't a kid.

Who'd never been a kid.

"Yes," Cheyenne said and pointed to the wooden urn. "We like that one."

"Very good." The man smiled kindly at Rafe. "Would you like to wait or would you rather return this afternoon?"

"We'll wait," Cheyenne said.

"Very good," he repeated. "It shouldn't take too long. Please feel free to help yourself to some coffee while you wait."

"Thanks."

Rafe glanced back at Will as the funeral director walked away. "Is Will mad at me?"

Cheyenne eyed Will for a long, silent moment, and he turned to look at her, as if he felt the weight of her gaze. His brow arched, but Cheyenne only shook her head, and he turned away again.

"He isn't mad at you," she said. "He's obsessed with his mission, and we're getting in the way of that."

"But he came to us," Rafe said, confused.

Another moment of silence, and Rafe's heart beat a little harder in his chest. Cheyenne eyed him thoughtfully, and he demanded, "What?" because he knew a secret when he saw one.

"C'mon," she said and led him to one of the faded blue couches. They sat down, and his stomach began to churn because even though he'd demanded to know, he didn't want to. *No more bad.* He'd had enough in the last three days to last the rest of his life. But he'd asked...and Cheyenne would tell him.

So suck it up.

"Just tell me," he told her.

"Okay. Your father is a man named Andrew Mailk."

Rafe stared at her, poleaxed. A dull roar filled his ears. "What?"

"He's the current Ambassador to Afghanistan. He's married to a Saudi national, and they have three daughters."

Rafe's fingers tingled. He felt his cheeks burn, but his skin was cold, and he rubbed at his heart where it hammered in his chest. "I don't understand."

"Will recognized you. He's met Malik, and you look a lot like him."

Rafe looked over at Will, but didn't really see him. Thoughts whirled in his head. He hadn't expected this. "Why didn't he tell me?"

Silence. Then, "Because being Malik's son puts you in danger."

Rafe's heart leapt; his gaze flew back to her. "What does that mean?"

"Malik is married to someone who has power," Cheyenne said. "Someone who will be very angry when they learn he had an affair with your mom. And even angrier when they find out about—"

"Me." *My little trump.* Was that what his ma had meant? That he was her...ace in the hole? "That's why she had me. So she could use me."

Cheyenne said nothing. He wished she would—but he knew it would be lies made up to make him feel better. Useless and stupid. But—"Does he know about me?"

"Will thinks so, yes."

Rafe nodded. The pressure he'd released yesterday rebuilt in an instant and pressed against his lungs until they ached. Tears burned the backs of his eyes. "But he doesn't want me."

Cheyenne reached over and wrapped her hand around his. "You're mine. He can't have you."

He clung to her. He didn't want to. He was stronger than that—hell, he figured he'd never even know who his pop was, let alone his name or anything else, so what did it matter if he was a scumbag who cheated on his wife and kids? Who would never, ever want him, no matter what? But it did. And he wished he could rewind, go back to be being in the dark. It was a much nicer place.

"We have to make a decision," Cheyenne told him quietly.

"What?" he asked dully.

"Will is afraid Malik might try to...do something so his wife will never find out."

Rafe started and lifted his gaze to meet hers. "You mean... like, kill me?"

"I didn't want to tell you. You shouldn't have to know this. But if he approaches you and I'm not around..." Cheyenne squeezed his hand. Her eyes shimmered, and her scar was white. "You need to know. It's safer that way. I'm sorry."

He nodded, but he didn't understand. Not really. Not any of it.

"If we go public, it will protect you," she continued. "Once everyone knows, the threat is gone. But it will turn your life into a three-ring-circus. I can help protect you from that, but it will always—*always*—be something you have to deal with. Forever."

Cheyenne watched him with her worried look. Rafe didn't want to admit that he didn't understand what "going public" meant, or why anyone would care who he was, or how that would protect him...it was important, but he didn't care. Maybe someday. But at that moment all he knew was that his father was man he didn't want to know —*no different than his ma*—a man who might actually hurt

Rafe to protect himself—*just like his ma*—and Cheyenne was all he had, so whatever she thought he should do, he would do.

"Whatever," he muttered.

For a long moment, Cheyenne stared at him, her eyes dark, her hand tight around his. "I'm sorry, sweet pea. If lies could protect you from this, I would lie. But the truth is all we have. Solid ground in a shifting world. And if we have to use it, we will."

He nodded again. The pain in his chest was sharper, piercing, and he felt...lost. A small bottle in a big sea whose message would float aimlessly around the planet, forever unread. He'd always known he didn't *matter*. But he hadn't imagined someone might want him *dead*. Especially not his pop.

An asshole. Just like his ma.

Tears wedged in his throat, but he refused to let them fall. He was done crying. *Suck it up.* He looked at Will again. "Is that why Will's mad at me? Because of my pop?"

"Will is not mad at you," Cheyenne insisted. "He's pissed off at a lot of things: fate, circumstance, whatever power put him in the desert that night. Me, even. But not you. *Never you, Rafe.* I promise."

Rafe met her gaze and searched it. He was good at seeing lies—even his ma hadn't been able to pull one over on him, and she'd believed most of her own lies. But he saw only truth in Cheyenne's eyes, and he hoped she was right. Because he didn't want Will angry with him.

Shouldn't care. He's a stranger. Who gives a shit what he thinks?

But Rafe did.

"Ah, here you are." The funeral director was back. In his hands was the wooden urn Cheyenne had chosen, and Rafe stared at it, unable to believe it contained the craziness that had been his ma. It seemed too small, too...benign. As if it should carry a warning—like a skull and crossbones.

That would be appropriate.

"Thank you." Cheyenne stood and accepted the urn. "You'll put it on my card?"

"Yes, yes. It's all taken care of. Thank you for using Rosemont, and again, I am very sorry for your loss."

Rafe watched him walk away. "He's the only one who's sorry."

"True story," Cheyenne said. "You ready to beat feet?"

Rafe didn't need to be asked twice. He stood and headed for the door.

Are u there? WHAT'S HAPPENING???
Raining here (Gray, gray go away!!) *SIGH*
Dexter ate Angus' hat. He says you owe him a new one.
So...what's the kid like? Are you really keeping him?
Sorry wasn't supportive. STILL THINK CRAZY.
But love u. Will love him, 2.
CALL ME!!!!!!!!!!!!

Cheyenne smiled down at Whitney's text.

All is well, she responded, *be home soon. Tell Angus will bring him Green Bay hat.*

Which, as a stalwart Denver Broncos fan, he would despise.

Across from her, Rafe sat quietly eating his chicken fingers. He'd been subdued since the funeral home, and that worried her: she shouldn't have told him about Malik. But if Malik—or one of his flunkies—approached Rafe when she wasn't around and spun him a fantasy, she would lose him. Maybe forever. Because in spite of how horrific a thought it was, she did not doubt Malik was capable of murdering his child to save his own skin. It was quite probable that he'd willingly sacrificed an entire SEAL team—and countless unknown victims should those bombs be detonated—in order to cover his ass. What was one more life? One he'd never tried to find or protect or care for.

"Son of a bitch," she muttered.

Will glanced at her from his position against the wall. They sat at the food court of the Mayfield Mall, surrounded by packages, their table filled with all manner of fried and ludicrously unhealthy food options, but he hadn't eaten anything. Instead he sat still as a statue, staring at the people who came and went in waves, his arms crossed against his broad chest, his expression the epitome of *badass*.

He was distant today. Cold. Even with Rafe, he was brusque—which she was going to take him to task for when they had a minute alone, because a ten-year-old didn't deserve that shit—and he'd barely said two words to her since they'd awoken.

Which she didn't understand. He was the one who'd disappeared last night without explanation. The one who blew hot then cold. The one who kept crossing lines. She should be the moody, pissed off one in this picture. She was *always* the moody, pissed off one.

Goddamn irony.

"Thanks for all the stuff," Rafe said.

But there was little excitement in him. The only gleam of interest he'd shown was when they'd walked into the Apple store, and she'd told him to pick out a laptop, which he had—but only after asking the clerk a hundred and fifty questions, the intricacy of which made Cheyenne feel like a complete and utter moron, and also made her realize the kid was far more intelligent than she'd comprehended. She'd bought him clothes, shoes, a new backpack, the laptop and a new phone—she'd gone a little crazy, and she knew it but didn't care because she understood what it was to not have anything of one's own—but Rafe had been reserved and diffident—if grateful—in his reception.

Her fault and she knew it. She'd upended his world—*again*—and utterly destroyed any illusions he may have retained about his parentage.

"You're welcome," she told him as she put her phone away. "Is there anything we missed?"

A dark, surprisingly bitter smile turned his mouth. "Someone who gives a shit?"

"Hey," Will chastised sharply.

"I give a shit," Cheyenne said.

Color touched Rafe's cheeks. "I know. Sorry."

Cheyenne stared at him thoughtfully. When she'd decided to accept responsibility for him—to keep him—she hadn't understood that it was something which would take all of her. Not just the parts she'd polished to perfection in the last decade, but *every piece* of who she was. Every bad memory, every hard won lesson, every wrong she'd ever committed. Not just the good. Because it was the bad which had shaped and molded her into who she was, and that was…okay. She'd come out *alright*. Not perfect, but not *bad*, either—and not someone who believed others should share her pain.

The bad had made her strong, resilient. It had made her *better*. So being ashamed of it meant being ashamed of who she'd become. And she liked who she'd become.

Mostly.

"I was five when they took me away from my mom," she said into the silence that had fallen. She felt Will's gaze touch her, but ignored him. "Permanently away, I mean. They'd taken me from her a couple times before that, but always put me back. When I was five…that was it. Because she did this." Her hand lifted, and her fingers smoothed over the uneven flesh that marred her left cheek, a light, sweeping motion, one she'd repeated endlessly after it first happened. They'd had to tie her hands down because she'd done it so often it bled. "It was the first day of spring. I remember because it was the first time I'd played outside since Halloween, and Mr. Pettington was excited that his daffodils were coming up. Until my mother came for me, it was a beautiful day."

Rafe sat frozen, staring at her with stricken eyes, but Cheyenne didn't stop.

"Years later, I learned that she'd been diagnosed paranoid schizophrenic, but that night..." Cheyenne shook her head, remembering. "I thought she was the devil."

"You don't have to—" Rafe began, but she cut him off.

"Yes," she said. "I do."

"Cheyenne," Will said softly, but she only ignored him.

"I'm not sure why she had me; she didn't want me. I have no idea who my father was. I'm not sure *she* knew who he was." Cheyenne rubbed her scar again, the feel of it almost comforting. "I used to think he would suddenly appear and save me from her. But he never did. And in the end, I had to save myself."

She sipped her iced tea. Will's stare burned into her, as palpable as a touch, but she didn't turn to look at him. "When she came for me, everyone ran. She scared the hell out of the entire neighborhood; no one interfered when she dragged me inside—except Mr. Pettington. He tried to calm her down, but she swung at him and threatened to cut his balls off. She was always colorful in her threats. Must be where I get it from." *And isn't that a kick in the face?* "We went upstairs, and she sat me down on a kitchen chair. Very theatrical, my mother; she liked an audience. So I gave it to her and just watched, quiet and still, like a mouse. She ranted and raved and screamed like the lunatic she was...and to this day, I still don't know why." A bitter smile. "I waited, and I prayed. Sometimes she just made a lot of noise, but sometimes...

sometimes she beat the hell out of me. There was never any way to predict it. But that night, she was different. I must have known that, because when she went into the bedroom to get her belt, I grabbed a knife off the counter and hid it under my leg."

Another sip. "My memories aren't clear. I remember her rage. She was so *angry*. I remember her telling me to go to my room and being relieved, because I thought it was over... but then she followed me." Cheyenne rubbed her scar again. "She made use of that belt. Her fists, her feet... She wore these sharp-heeled cowboy boots, and she liked to kick. When she stomped on my right arm, it snapped like a twig. I'd never felt pain like that. It made me crazy. I'd held onto that knife through it all—even when she punched me in the face, I didn't use it—but when my arm broke...I stabbed her. I buried that knife in her belly and wished it was her heart."

Rafe inhaled sharply, his eyes as big as saucers, but Cheyenne couldn't stop. It was like a dam bursting, and there was no halting the flow. "Of course, that just enraged her more. I remember her screaming as she ran from the room; it was like a horror movie. I couldn't see, and I was mindless with pain and terrified I might have killed her. But then she came back." A deep, steadying breath. "She told me I was the spawn of Satan, that she was going to send me back to hell. Then she poured kerosene over my head and lit me on fire."

Around them, people murmured and laughed. Children played, babies cried. The sizzle of food frying was a constant hiss in the background. Cheyenne heard none of it. Instead, she heard the echo of her own screams, the crackle of fire, the roar of her blood, her mother's insane laughter.

"So much pain," she murmured. "I wanted to die. But I remembered what they taught us at school, and I rolled, trying to put myself out. I begged her for water. I didn't know that would have been the worst thing for me...I just knew water put out fire. But she left and never came back. Then Mr. Pettington was there with the police, and it was over."

Over. Yeah, right. As if.

"After I got out of the hospital, they put me in Haven. That's where I met your mom." Cheyenne met Rafe's gaze. "I didn't tell you this to scare you or make you feel bad. I told you to make you understand it can always be *worse*."

His mouth opened, then closed.

"It's okay," she told him. "You don't have to say anything. I just...needed to share it."

Will was silent, but she realized he'd moved closer, that beneath the table, his leg pressed against the length of hers. Firm, warm, generous solace. He might have been a terse bastard all morning long, but he didn't waver when it came to offering comfort.

Cheyenne moved away. The temptation to turn to him was far too strong; she'd never needed *anyone.* Never wanted anyone. That he held such allure both shocked and scared her. Especially when he was in the middle of his own personal war, as proven by his secretive disappearance last night. She was still pissed about that, especially since it had occurred right after he'd had his hands on her. He wanted her to rip out her guts and give them to him—her deepest, darkest secrets—while he guarded his own, unwilling to share any of what he demanded she give.

Jackass.

Worse. Because she'd begun to trust him...and last night was just further evidence that she shouldn't.

No, she had no business thinking about him in any context. The safety he made her feel was illusion, born of nothing more than potent sexual chemistry. It wasn't real. And just because she felt vulnerable didn't make it real. Having him with them today had been—she could admit it

—*nice.* But they didn't need him, and clearly his presence was just going to screw with her head. A distraction she couldn't afford, because she had Rafe to think about. Their future to put first. And a man who kept secrets was not safe.

Will strove toward only one conclusion, and that resolution had little, if anything, to do with her or Rafe. Will's reasons for "protecting" them were all aimed at accomplishing his own goals and did not exist outside of those objectives. There was nothing selfless or noble in his actions —they were merely a means to an end.

Stupid of her, to lose sight of that. She wouldn't forget again.

CHAPTER EIGHTEEN

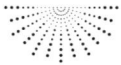

"We need to talk, Will. There's been a development. Call me."

Will hadn't decided what—if anything—he was going to report to Ethan Scott. More and more fingers were pointing in his direction, and regardless of what Will's gut said, he couldn't afford to ignore the growing number of voices who claimed Scott was suspect. Especially considering that the official investigation file Ethan promised him had never materialized.

Like Malik, Ethan had knowledge. Unlike Malik, he hadn't had motive—at least, none Will could figure out. Hell, he didn't even know if Georgia had known Ethan. But judging by the photographs in her condo, it was possible. Most of the faces in those pictures were ones he recognized —diplomats, ambassadors, men with the DOD and the State Department.

Powerful men. Which meant no one was exempt from the list of suspects—including Ethan Scott.

Will deleted the message. Still nothing from Red. Agent James, too, had disappeared, and Will wasn't certain what to make of that, but it made him nervous. He preferred to keep the players where he could see them.

"I can fly!" Rafe's gleeful cry echoed around him, followed by the call of a gull. "Look!"

The kite soared high into the air, riding the currents that rose from the lake. Shaped like an eagle, its wings lifted and fell as Rafe ran along the beach with it, his laughter trailing behind him like a song. Cheyenne watched him from a picnic table that sat at the edge of the sand, sketchbook in hand as the sun sank slowly behind her and turned her hair into a halo of red flame.

Will walked toward her, Georgia's book in hand. He'd taped the torn pages together and waited all day, impatient to see if she could make some sense of it. His plans to demand she decipher it first thing had been foiled by her announcement that Georgia's ashes awaited pick up—and Rafe's stricken look in response. Then the funeral home, the mall… and, finally, the tale Cheyenne had shared.

I told you to make you understand it can always be worse.

Will had read the police reports, the caseworkers' accounts, even some of her medical records, but he hadn't allowed himself to fill in the blanks. Any speculation he might have indulged in was forbidden; not because he didn't want to know, but because it had simply served to muddy the waters. What she'd experienced simply didn't matter. Those details were nothing more than white noise, a useless distraction and utterly meaningless to his goals. They were not something he had allowed himself to think about.

Fucking asshole.

Those details had everything to do with the woman Cheyenne Elias had become. Everything to do with *who* she was and *why*—both important factors when determining the level of her involvement in a treasonous scheme to sell semi-nuclear weapons to the scum of the international world.

Everything to do with understanding her friendship—or lack thereof—with a woman like Georgia Humboldt.

He could tell himself it had been those *meaningless* details he'd ignored, but in reality, it was her he'd shied from. The harsh reality of her pain; the hollow eyes and distant gaze and thick, twisted scar tissue. A vision of himself in a child he was afraid to know.

Will was not proud of the realization, but it was a valuable lesson, and one he could not afford to forget. That he felt connected to Cheyenne was neither right nor wrong. It simply was. Denying it only confused things—and made him a liar. Neither of which moved him forward.

And now she was angry with him. Will knew the signs. He wondered if it was because he'd spent the entire day trying to put distance between them. To stay within the parameters of his mission; to be nothing more than a shadow in the periphery of her vision. It had worked...until she'd shared that night with them. Until the picture she'd drawn in stark lines of horror and pain had shattered his reserve. And when she'd pulled away from him—

Christ.

He wanted her to look at him, to acknowledge that what she'd shared hadn't just been about Rafe, but about him, too. It was unreasonable, and he was kicking his own ass for it, but that's what he wanted from her.

Sooner rather than later.

She was drawing the lighthouse that sat on the small peninsula just north of the shoreline. Will looked over her shoulder at it for a long moment, still astounded by her skill, awash in her scent.

"Can I help you?" she asked coldly.

Definitely pissed off, and he wanted to know why. So he put a hand down on either side of her and leaned over, caging her with his body. She stiffened immediately. Her hair lifted on the breeze to kiss his skin.

"Yes," he said and placed the book in front of her.

She made no move to take it. "What's this?"

"I was hoping you could tell me."

For a long moment she did nothing. Will could feel her unwillingness, the anger she felt. She nearly vibrated with it. Then she flipped the book open and stared down at the jumbled mix of letters, numbers and symbols.

"I found it in the condo," he murmured into her ear. "But I don't know what it is. Do you?"

She shifted away from him and bent over the book. "Not without deciphering it."

"Can you?"

She said nothing.

"Please," he said.

She turned to look at him, so close he could see the flecks of gold that speared her iris. Close enough to kiss—something he'd been thinking too damn much about in the last twenty-four hours. He'd dreamt of her again: dark, hungry dreams where he woke drenched in sweat, hard as stone, aching and furious she wasn't there.

She would never be there.

"I can decipher it," she said, staring up at him. "But then I want you to leave."

His heart shuddered, as if he'd taken a killing blow. "What?"

"I want you gone," she told him. "We don't need you."

Blood was a dull roar in his ears. "I'm not leaving. It's too dangerous."

"I can take care of us."

Will stared down at her, and panic licked at his nerves. "No."

"If we find out where the cache is, I'll let you know. I promise. But you need to go."

His hands fisted atop the table. "Why?"

"Because I don't want you here."

He flinched. "*Why not?*"

She only shook her head. "Do we have a deal?"

"I'm not leaving," he repeated.

"Then we will." She closed the book. "And you can figure this out for yourself."

He stood frozen as the wind lifted her hair around him, and it caught in the stubble of his beard. Her scent teased him; her heat beckoned. He wanted to lean down and press his mouth to hers, to thrust his tongue into her mouth the same way he dreamt of thrusting his cock into her, to swallow and diffuse the words she'd spoken, which lashed so deep.

"You can't just take what you want," she whispered, her gaze dark on his. "And leave the rest."

One hand lifted from the table and tangled itself in her hair; he couldn't stop it. Perched on the knife's edge every moment he was near her; denying himself, punishing himself, hating himself for feeling anything other than the hate that drove him. She was everything he would never have. The life he'd lost; the future he didn't deserve. A symbol of what had been stolen from *all of them*.

And he couldn't let her go.

Fucking asshole.

"Cheyenne! Will! *Look!*"

Rafe's cry sliced between them like a blade. Will looked over at the boy to see him headed into the surf, the kite abandoned on the sand. He was running toward him a heartbeat later, Cheyenne on his heels.

"No!" Rafe protested when Will lifted him from the water

and turned back toward shore. He pointed out at the water. "Look!"

Will followed his hand to where a small outcropping of rock broke the surface of the water. On the center rock a small dog sat shivering violently.

"We can't leave him there," Rafe said, wiggling furiously. "*We can't.* Please—"

"I'll get him," Cheyenne said leaned down to untie her boots.

"The hell you will," Will snarled and shoved Rafe at her. He pulled off his t-shirt and toed off his boots and headed into the surf. "Stay here."

The water was cold. As he dove in, the undertow licked at his heels, and he swam hard against it, the thought of Cheyenne or Rafe fighting that current waking fear in his heart. He glanced back at the shore, relieved to see their forms haloed by the setting sun, and kicked himself into gear. By the time he reached the rock—ragged and sharp and covered in slippery algae—his heart was throbbing in the back of his throat. He was out of shape; it had been too long since he'd made his heart work. He could feel the weakness in his left lung where the bullet had punctured it; breathing hurt like hell.

When he surfaced, the dog leapt to its feet and began to bark. Just a pup, with a nasty scar on its face, a golden retriever mix of some sort. The animal growled and yapped and circled nervously on its small plateau of rock.

"Hey, girl, how'd you get out here?" Will moved carefully to avoid the razor-sharp edge of the rock and not startle the dog into leaping back into the water. "Somebody dump you? Is that what happened?"

The pup eyed him, tail wagging hesitantly, small growls bursting from her throat.

"C'mon, sweetheart." He reached out and grabbed the

pup; the animal was skin and bones and trembled violently. A soft whine escaped her, and claws dug into Will's bare chest. "Easy, girl. Just take it easy."

Will rolled onto his back, keeping the dog above the surface of the water by placing her on his chest. He stroked back with his right arm, pulling them smoothly through the water toward shore. The pup whined, but stayed where Will held her, and by the time they were at the point where Will's feet touched the lake bottom, the pup was nestled quietly against him, her tail thumping Will's chest steadily as they got closer to shore.

Will's heart beat with painful intensity; his lungs ached, and his right arm felt like spaghetti. The rush of his blood in his head made glints of light swim across his vision. A wet tongue licked at his chin and everything around him whirled, turned, morphed—a fraction of a second that took him *back* —and he could do nothing to stop it—

Heart going to burst; so much blood. A river in his wake; hands slippery with it. Left lung deflated, a leaden weight in his chest. Wheezing, burning, suffocating. Arm broken, bone piercing skin. Hip wrong. Can't go anymore. So fucking cold. Can't do it. Done. Over.

DEAD—

A wet tongue, the scent of dog, a furry, warm body circling him—

A soft whine, wetness at his ear, a sharp bark, and then voices arguing—he knows those words—and hands, pushing, prodding, lifting him, and the pain shears him in two, makes him scream like a child, and then—

Nothing.

"Will?"

A hand touched him, warm and strong. He knew that voice; he wanted something from that voice, but he wasn't sure—

"Will."

He stumbled back and slapped the hand away with such force, Cheyenne staggered.

He was on the beach with no memory of how he'd gotten there. Cold water streamed down his back, over his belly, into his eyes; his jeans were heavy, sodden and cold. The animal in his arms squirmed and whined, and Rafe watched him with big eyes.

Will put the pup down, his heart beating so hard he thought it might bust his damn ribcage.

"Will," Cheyenne said again, softly, and she looked at him as though she knew exactly what had just happened to him.

Fucking pity.

"Decipher the book," he told her harshly. "And then I'm gone."

He picked up his shirt and his boots and left them standing on the beach, staring after him.

CHAPTER NINETEEN

Rafe had never imagined a world in which he had a dog.

He was the stray—abandoned, alone, dependent entirely on others—and he'd never allowed himself to think beyond that. Wanting never got him anywhere. It was hard enough to get what he needed—clothes, shoes, school stuff—forget having anything extra.

Anything of his *own*.

So when Cheyenne picked up the pup Will had rescued and said, "So what are you going to name her?" Rafe had been dumbstruck.

"She's a golden," Cheyenne continued. "Look at that scar. Somebody hurt you, didn't they, baby?" She brought the animal to her and nuzzled her. "Pew. Stinky. She needs a bath. And a good meal. Shots, too. A flea bath, a brushing..."

Rafe only stared at her, afraid he'd misunderstood.

"You've got your work cut out for you." Cheyenne held the dog out to him. "We'll have to get her some food. And a collar. And a leash. Chuck is going to love her."

Rafe accepted the little dog, which thumped its tail against him and licked his face. "Chuck?"

"My heeler. Thinks he's a ladies' man. C'mon. Let's go before it gets dark."

And she'd walked away, leaving him standing there with a warm, wet, furry body in his arms, his heart huge and painful in his chest. The pup stared up at him with dark, caramel colored eyes, and Rafe could see the same fragile hope that had taken root within him only a day earlier.

"It's okay," he told her. "We'll take care of you."

When he got to the condo, Cheyenne was already in the car. But the Jeep—and Will—were both gone.

"Is he going to come back?" Rafe asked, afraid he already knew the answer.

"I don't know," Cheyenne said, her eyes dark.

They found a pet store and bought food, a collar, a leash, flea and tick shampoo, a book on training, a rawhide bone, bacon flavored treats and a stuffed hedgehog. Then they'd picked up fried chicken from the local grocery store and eaten it at the picnic table on the beach while the pup growled and attempted to dismember her hedgehog.

Will didn't return.

After dinner, Rafe bathed the pup (and ended up more wet than she was) and put on her new red collar. Then he fed her and paged through the book on training while Cheyenne worked on deciphering some crazy code his ma had left (which Cheyenne had shown him but he didn't recognize). He watched four more episodes of *Supernatural* and tried to decide what to name his new friend.

Will still didn't return.

At ten, Rafe took the pup out, urged her to pee and looked down the street for the Jeep.

Nothing.

He didn't really understand what had happened earlier,

when Will had come out of the water with the pup, his eyes blank. *Flashback,* Cheyenne had said. *A bad memory. It's not your fault.* But that meant little to Rafe. All he knew was that the empty look on Will's face had scared him—like he wasn't really *there*—and he hadn't responded to anything they'd said. Then, when Will shoved Cheyenne away, Rafe had realized he *wasn't* there, but was somewhere else, somewhere in his own head. Somewhere bad.

Rafe knew about PTSD. He'd gone to school with plenty of kids whose parents had fought in the wars, and they'd come home all messed up. His friend Tommy wouldn't go anywhere with his Uncle Joe, because every time a car backfired, the guy freaked out to the point someone always called the cops. Rafe wondered if Will ever freaked out that bad.

Not that Rafe blamed him. He couldn't even begin to imagine war. And he knew Cheyenne didn't blame Will, either. Rafe figured it was because she might get flashbacks, too. Considering what her ma had done, how could she not?

Set on fire. That was *fucked up.*

But he didn't think about it too closely, because it scared him.

So he went back inside and curled up in front of *Supernatural*, the pup secure in his arms, while Cheyenne fell asleep, and he waited for Will to return. It was nearly eleven by the time Will came in, so quiet at first Rafe got scared until he heard the telltale sound of Will's boots. But even after Will laid down on the other couch, and his breathing grew steady and even, Rafe couldn't fall asleep.

His brain was too busy. Thinking about his ma and all of her secrets, about the revelation of his pop...who probably wanted him dead...about this three half-sisters, who he would probably never meet, and who would probably hate him anyway...about Cheyenne's ma and her scar and Haven and Will...about the animal nestled in his arms, a life he was now responsible for...

It was overwhelming. So much had happened in such a short period of time...his whole life turned inside out. But he was... *hopeful*. His ma was dead, and his pop might try to kill him, and he was in the care of total strangers—*again*—but he was optimistic. The darkness that tainted everything had lifted and he could see...possibilities.

Hope.

It was crazy. He should be scared—and he was, of his pop, of those bombs, of whatever fucked up thing his ma had left behind because there had to be *something*, because that's who she was—but the freedom he felt made him brave. Cheyenne gave him courage. And Will...he liked Will. Respected him. And really, really wanted to believe in him.

But only time would tell if he was worthy.

They were leaving for Wyoming in the morning. Cheyenne had shown him the map and marked out the route they were going to take—Rafe had hoped they would fly, because he'd never flown before—but Cheyenne said hell would freeze over before she got on another "flying boat" and besides, she didn't trust the airlines with the pup, so they were going to grab some camping gear and make a road trip out of it. She had ticked off several intriguing places as they'd poured over the map.

"There's the Corn Palace, Wall Drug, Pipestone National Monument, the Badlands, the Black Hills, Devil's Tower..."

He was going to look those places up on his Mac—his unbelievably sweet new Mac (life was *good*)—tomorrow morning. It was exciting, the thought of going somewhere new—anywhere that wasn't here—and seeing something he'd never seen and—

A deep, harsh sound broke through the quiet murmur of the TV, and Rafe froze. It took him a heart-pounding moment to realize it had come from Will. That Will was dreaming.

"Go...." Will growled softly, and Rafe looked over to see him jerk on the couch, a low sound—like pain—rasping from him. "Goddamn it, fucking *run.*"

Rafe's heart beat heavily against his ribs. Against him, the pup lifted her head, and a soft whine escaped her.

"Shhh," Rafe whispered. "It's okay."

"No! Just go," Will snarled. He sounded...tormented, and Rafe didn't move, trapped by fear and uncertainty. "Too late to stop it...Hogan! Kent! Get the fuck down!" Another loud, harsh groan rippled into the air, and Cheyenne stirred on the other end of the couch. She sat up, blinking, and looked at Rafe.

"No, no, no, no, no..." A painful sound murmured in Will's throat; grief and rage and something there was no words for. Rafe felt his own throat swell in response.

Cheyenne pushed up from the couch and moved toward Will. She was hesitant, but then reached out and touched him, placing her hand on his shoulder.

"Will," she said softly. "Wake u—"

A horrible, enraged roar shook the condo, and Rafe cried out. The pup began to bark, and Cheyenne squealed as Will grabbed her by both shoulders and pulled her down, rolling off the couch to land on top of her on the floor. "Damn you," he muttered, his voice broken and harsh, and so alien it terrified Rafe. "You fucking *bitch.*"

He crushed Cheyenne beneath him and grabbed her neck, and the sight of his big hands wrapping around her slender throat broke Rafe's paralysis. He flew up off the couch while the pup barked hysterically, and Cheyenne bucked and tried to throw Will off.

Rafe flung himself at Will's back, wrapped his arms

around Will's neck and pulled desperately, yelling, "Wake up, Will! Please wake up! No, Will, *stop*...."

Terror made his limbs weak, but he pulled and pulled, even though it was like trying to stop a giant, even though Will was huge and strong, his body hard as stone, even though he shook so violently, Rafe could hardly hold on, even though that horrible blank look was back, and he continued to mutter like a crazy person in that scary-ass voice—

Cheyenne punched Will—hard—right in the nose, once, twice, and the third time, Will woke up. Blood burst from his nostrils, and he blinked, and for one, brief moment, he froze. Then he seemed to realize what was happening, and he scrambled back—dislodging Rafe, who fell to his side and squished the pup, who cried out—and stared at Cheyenne in shock and horror as she reached up to grab her throat, raw, harsh gasps breaking from her as she tried to breathe.

"I'm sorry," Will grated, and his hands lifted toward her, but Cheyenne flinched and shook her head, and he froze again. "*Fuck*. Are you okay?"

Rafe pushed himself off the floor and gathered the pup in his arms and tried to calm her. "I'm okay," he said, although his heart was beating so hard in his throat he could hardly swallow. But the look on Will's face made Rafe want to reassure him, even as he reached out a hand to touch Cheyenne's shoulder to make sure she was okay, too.

Will met his gaze, and his pale eyes were so anguished, Rafe felt his throat tighten. "I'm sorry, Rafe."

"I'm okay," Rafe repeated.

Cheyenne inhaled raggedly, and Will reached for her again, but she said, "No," in a harsh, painful rasp that made Will flinch. Then she slid away from him.

"*Fuck*," Will said again, staring at her in horror. "I never meant to—" He broke off and stood, swaying unsteadily above them. "I'm sorry."

And then he turned and walked out.

Rafe dropped to his knees beside Cheyenne.

"Are you okay?" he asked anxiously.

She nodded, rubbing her throat.

"Are you sure?"

The pup yipped softly, as if echoing him.

"I'm okay," she whispered.

Rafe looked at the door Will had disappeared through.

"He didn't mean to hurt you," Rafe said.

"I know," she said.

"He was dreaming."

"I know."

Rafe looked between her and the door, unsure what to do.

"Should I go talk to him?" he asked her, rubbing her arm to reassure himself she was okay.

"No."

"But…." He hesitated and then wrapped his arms around her and hugged her tight. He wasn't good at hugging; he didn't have much practice. But she jerked against him and slid her arms around him and held on like she was dying. For a long moment, they just held each other, the pup worming her way between them, the TV casting them in flickering light.

"We can't leave him alone," Rafe whispered.

Cheyenne didn't say anything, and his heart squeezed painfully in his chest. He felt desperate to make her understand, although he couldn't have said why. Just that it was important. "He *needs* us, Cheyenne."

She shuddered, and her arms squeezed him so tight he couldn't breathe, but then she let go.

"I'll go talk to him," she said and patted the pup on the head before pushing to her feet.

"I'll come, too," Rafe offered.

But she shook her head. "No. I'll go. Stay here and take care of little Miss. She's probably pretty freaked out."

Rafe looked down at the pup, who watched Cheyenne with big, frightened eyes, a faint tremor in her limbs. He picked her up and held her close. "Okay. But if you need me…"

"I'll let you know."

"Promise?"

Cheyenne turned and met his gaze. "Promise."

Then she went to see Will.

CHAPTER TWENTY

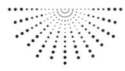

*C*igarette smoke curled through the screened-in porch, and Cheyenne inhaled deeply, even though it hurt her throat. She'd smoked once, long ago, and still missed it; for her, the scent was tantalizing, like the lure of freshly ground coffee or baking bread. She'd long ago accepted it would always smell good. And it would always tempt her.

That was the thing about addiction: it never went away.

Moonlight streamed into the small room. She could see Will seated on the wooden porch swing, his elbows on his knees, the coal of his cigarette glowing like an unearthly jewel in the darkness. He was shirtless; the plane of his muscled back was washed white by the moonlight, and her gaze was drawn to the brutal scar on his left side, a thick, ridged rupture of uneven tissue in the shape of a sunburst. She remembered how it had looked that afternoon in the bright sunlight. He had marks all over him—knife wounds, bullet wounds, even a burn scar not unlike her own—and a large, black tribal tattoo around one bicep. A scorpion on the back of his neck and a round, intricate symbol she didn't recognize stamped on the carved muscle of his belly. His left nipple was pierced with a slender silver bar.

Seeing him like that had affected her. Witnessing his scars had made her own *less*, somehow, and freed something within her. Something wild and reckless.

Something she didn't trust.

Her throat hurt, and for a long moment she stood motionless, rubbing what would be a ring of dark, ugly bruises in the morning. She knew Will hadn't meant to damn near break her neck—knew better than anyone—but she wasn't dumb. She had a strong sense of self preservation, and it was in four alarm—*are you fucking stupid?*—mode at the moment, and she had to stop herself from turning tail.

But she couldn't run. Circles were closing—*irony and karma and goddamn fate*—and she understood her place within them—for once—and she was beginning to understand that paying something forward was a process, not an event, not a person, not merely one moment in time. It was a tapestry woven of past meeting present, and a conscious weaving of the future. It required diligence and sacrifice.

Again and again and again.

So she didn't run. Because this was not her first trip down bad memory lane—it was just her first time on the receiving end.

"I'll be gone by morning," Will said harshly, rocking the swing back and forth, a jerky, agitated motion that made the chains which anchored it to the ceiling creak in protest.

Cheyenne walked along the back of the swing, circled it, and when it swung toward her, caught the chain in hand and halted it. Then she sat down beside Will and drew her knees to her chest.

"I'm sorry," he whispered, and the pain and regret and fear she heard made her chest ache.

"When I was seventeen," she told him quietly. "I stabbed a man. A good man. A man I never, ever wanted to hurt."

Beside her, Will froze. The swing halted.

"It wasn't intentional," she continued. "Like you, I was dreaming and bringing down the house, and he was trying to wake me up. I never should have touched you—that was *my* fault."

Will shook his head but she kept talking.

"Hank took me in. Gave me a job, a home, a family. I didn't really know what it was to belong to something bigger than myself. He gave me that. So when I hurt him…I felt like a monster. Like my mother." She hugged her knees tight and drew the words from the dark, quiet place she kept them, painfully aware of the faint tremor in her voice, the fine tremble in her limbs. "He knew it was an accident, that I hadn't meant to hurt him. He blamed himself, not me. But I blamed me. I knew I was dangerous. It wasn't the first time something like that had happened, but I wanted what he gave so badly, I took the chance. And he paid the price."

The wind lifted, and somewhere far off, a wind chime sounded.

Cheyenne paused and took a deep breath and listened. The sound of the waves lapping at the shore below them soothed, made it easier somehow. "I wanted to run, but Hank wouldn't let me. Luckily, it was a minor wound—all I had was a tiny Swiss Army knife—and I hit him in the arm, so it didn't do anything but leave a small scar. He had me bind the wound, and while I did, he told me about his time in Vietnam. About the jungle and the Vietcong, about the napalm and the dead children and coming home to a country that despised him. About how he still woke screaming in the night, and how the sound of a helicopter flying overhead took him right back to that jungle. About how he'd almost killed his son when they were elk hunting, because the rifle firing made him go crazy. It was the first time I understood what happened to me in those moments, that I realized I wasn't alone." She turned and met Will's pale gaze, almost otherworldly gilded in moonlight, watching her with an intensity she would have—at any other time—shied from. "It happened for a long time after I first got to Haven, but eventually it stopped. After my mother died, and I knew I was safe. But what I did to Hank...what I did to Hank was because of what Georgia did to me."

Hank was the only person she'd ever told. Now there would be another. But if it helped Will...it was little enough.

No matter how painful the telling.

"Baby," Will said, a whisper of sound, and she almost faltered.

But she had decided. *Jumped*. And was already falling.

"Two months before I left Haven," she continued. "Georgia and I snuck out and went to a frat party. I won't bore you with the details—suffice to say, there was a lot of alcohol, a lot of drugs and way too many horny frat boys. I got shit-faced drunk—which I would like to blame Georgia for, but can't because I liked cheap beer and whiskey shots—and ended up getting cornered by a very large football player who had a thing for—as he put it—'damaged goods.'"

Will snarled softly. Cheyenne only shook her head. "If I was sober, I could have handled him—I knew how to fight—but I was too drunk. He pushed me down, right there in the hallway, and put his knee in my back. When he tore my shirt off, I started to scream." She paused again, her heartbeat a hollow throb in the back of her throat. Her stomach churned, and she didn't look at Will, doing her best to ignore the heat of his body, the scent of pine that marked him. *Too tempting.* Because he would let her seek comfort, let her touch. "I fought like someone possessed. Head butted him and made his nose bleed, elbowed him, kicked him. But then he slammed my head into the floor and knocked me silly. I was in and out of consciousness. Finally, Georgia came. I thought she would get him off me. I thought she would *help*. I was a fucking idiot. She just egged him on. Told me I should enjoy it, that it was the only kind of fuck a freak like me was ever going to get. And then she watched while he raped me."

A rumble broke from the man beside her, but Cheyenne only stared sightlessly out into the moonlit night, remembering. "I don't have clear memories of it. Just flashes, moments when I realized what was happening and then…nothing. Like a fucked up, horrific dream. I blacked out afterward. If it hadn't been for the pain and the bruises afterward, I probably *would* have assumed it was just a dream. Georgia acted like nothing had happened; for two days I wasn't sure it *did* happen. I didn't know what to do. She was all I had. I couldn't understand why she would do what she did…and when I asked her, she told me it was for my own good. She was toughening me up—and the asshole gave her fifty bucks, so as far as she was concerned, it was a bang-up deal."

"I can find him."

The menace Cheyenne heard was both terrifying and sweet. She turned and looked at Will, who watched her with predatory stillness.

"No," she told him softly.

"I'll kill him for you."

She should not have been turned on by that offer, but she was.

"No," she said again. She hugged her knees tighter. "Six weeks after the party, I realized I was pregnant. I didn't want a kid—I *was* a kid—and…I didn't trust myself. I was afraid I would be my mother. I was still trying to decide what to do when Georgia caught me puking up my breakfast for the third day in a row and figured it out. She cleaned me up and told me she would help, that she knew just what to do, that everything would be okay. And I believed her."

Another deep breath. *Almost done.* "Three days later we snuck out again and got on a city bus. Georgia told me we were going to Planned Parenthood, that they would help me. Instead, we got off downtown, and she led me into a blind alley where the boy who raped me ambushed me. Shoved a chloroform rag in my face and threw me in a white van. I passed out...and when I came to, I wasn't pregnant anymore."

Will was suddenly right beside her, his size—once so intimidating—now comforting, the length of his body warm and solid and real, a hairsbreadth from hers, but not touching. He didn't speak, didn't interrupt, and Cheyenne was grateful.

"There was blood gushing down my legs and the pain was...." She shook her head. "I was dying. They dumped me in the street and drove away. I remember sitting on the curb, watching my blood flow down the sewer drain and screaming until my voice broke. Flashing lights, sirens...then nothing. I woke up in the hospital three days later, alive but permanently damaged. An infection and too much scar tissue, they said, and I was lucky to have survived." A dark smile. "I didn't feel lucky."

The swing swung gently, back and forth. Moonlight kissed the surface of the water below them, a scene so peaceful and earthy, it helped smooth the jagged edges of memory. "I stayed for another two days, ducking questions and lying about who I was and what had happened, but then the doc let slip that the cops were on their way, and I snuck out. I stayed another five days at a local shelter. Spent the entire time talking myself out of stealing a gun and killing her. A knife, a club, a tire iron. The things I fantasized about would have made my mother proud. Instead, I went back to

Haven and collected the money I had stashed and beat the fuck out of her. It wasn't enough. It was *never* enough, but it was all I got." A long shuddering sigh. "After, I went to the bus station. Cheyenne was the one of the destinations, and I took it as a sign. Of course, I was dead broke by the time I got there, and being the juvenile delinquent I was, I tried to jack an old Chevy truck. The guy who owned it caught me, tore a strip a mile wide off me, and gave me two choices: work off the damage at his ranch or get up close and personal with the local sheriff. Obviously, I chose to work. And then, one night while dreaming of blood and terror and death, I stabbed that same man with my pocket knife."

And so the circle closed. The wind chime sounded again, and Cheyenne sighed once more. It had come easier this time, but she really hoped she never had to tell anyone else. Some things were best left in the hole in which you buried them.

"Fuck," Will said and grabbed her, hauling her into his lap, where he wrapped his arms around her and held tight, his forehead pressed into the hollow where her pulse leapt unsteadily. "I'm sorry."

For a moment Cheyenne didn't move; her heart pounded with painful intensity, and her throat ached, but not from the bruises. Her eyes burned. Emotion rose and scalded her, and she wanted to push him away and run, but it felt so good—*he* felt so good—that she slid her arms around him instead and clung, even when one of those violent tremors shook him, even when his hold tightened, and his lips pressed gently against her throat.

"I hurt you," he grated.

"Yes," she said, unwilling to lie.

"I thought you were *her.*"

"A dream," Cheyenne said. "Just a dream."

"Fucking nightmare." His arms tightened. "I can't protect you from *me*."

"I can protect myself. That's why you're bleeding."

A rough sound escaped him. For long, silent moments they simply rocked, her arms stretched around him, his mouth tender against her bruised flesh, his fingers digging into the swell of her hips.

"Tell me what happened," she whispered. "Purge. It will help."

Will said nothing, his hands flexing against her, his chin rasping the sensitive skin of her throat. He was so hot against her he felt feverish, his body hard and tense, like supple hardwood, and she dug her nails into his shoulders in effort to hold him to her.

Just when she thought he wouldn't tell her, he began to speak.

"We shouldn't have even been there." His voice was vibrant with pain and rage and frustration. "The team who was supposed to pack the cache out got hit by enemy fire in Kandahar, and we were sent instead. Middle of goddamn nowhere: sand and scrub and dunes as tall as trees. No shelter, no cover, nowhere to hide. Hell on earth."

She raised a hand, hesitated, and then gave in and ran it through the coal black hair at Will's temple, thick and lush, like silk in her palm, and he made a low sound of pleasure and turned his head, like a cat seeking another stroke.

"We went in early, before the heat could cook us to death, and set up at the ridgeline. The weapons were stashed in a cave halfway up the rock face. A couple of kids from one of the local villages found them and reported them in exchange for food rations and medicine. They told us to look for the poppy field."

Silence fell, and Cheyenne continued to stroke her hand

through Will's hair. It was an intimate act—far more so than she would have imagined—but it seemed to soothe him.

"The poppies were easy to find. They stuck out like a beacon." He shook his head. "I don't know how the hell they were even alive. Hogan said it was proof that miracles existed, and I laughed, but I don't think he was kidding. Not a lick of water for a hundred miles, and there they were, a blanket of blooms in the shadow of the ridgeline, like a red flag waving in the breeze. They were beautiful."

Silence fell once more, and Cheyenne realized Will had not told anyone what he was sharing. The words came haltingly, pieces he was putting into place as he spoke them. She continued to run her hand through his hair—because she enjoyed it, too, more than a little intoxicated by the freedom to touch him—and waited.

"We brought the crates down with a winch system. It took hours. By the time we had them on the ground, the sun was sinking, and the wind was rising. Retrieval was supposed to be 2100. We grabbed some grub, confirmed we were a go with command, and waited."

The gentle rocking of the swing halted abruptly, and Will grew still, as if locked into immobility by the images flipping through his head.

"When we heard the Apache approach, Hogan knew. *He fucking knew*. Retrieval was early, and his gut was rotten, and he knew it was going bad. But I didn't listen, and he didn't argue. He just did his goddamn job. And he died for it. They all died for it." A violent shudder moved through Will, and sweat beaded beneath her fingertips, and his heart pounded like a hammer against her, but she only stroked him calmly and listened. "The sand rose, and we couldn't see shit. I told them to stand down, to get to the ridgeline because I realized Hogan was right, but it was too late. The Apache landed, and a team disembarked, but it wasn't ours. They opened fire as soon as they hit the ground." His body jerked in her hands, as if he was reliving the bullets that had torn into him. His voice grew harsh, and the hands that held her to him tightened to bruising strength. "They slaughtered us like animals while she laughed. *She fucking laughed.* One by one, we fell. And then they were gone. They should've never known—not about the cache, not our location, not a single *thing* about that mission. Hell, the sand storm should have brought the copter down. Everything was against us. Everything. Even the goddamn weather."

Will was shaking, but Cheyenne didn't think he noticed. He stared into the distance, half a world away, trapped in a time and place he hadn't come to terms with, locked in a loop of memory he couldn't yet escape. "After they were gone, I had to decide."

"Decide?"

He lifted his head and looked at her, his gaze so desolate it made her heart hurt. "To live or die. *I should have gone first.* That was my job, my sole responsibility. None of them should have gone before me. But every single one of them had. *Every one.* I might as well have killed them myself."

"No," she said softly.

"I wanted to die. It would have been so easy. My lung was collapsed, my arm was shattered, and my leg was hanging from my hip socket. I *should* have died; the doctors all agreed. But I wanted *blood.* 'Blood and flesh and bone,'" he quoted her softly. "'A world littered with body parts and gray matter. Death and destruction like no one has ever seen.'"

"Yes," she said. "Until the rivers run red."

Those pale eyes searched hers, but she couldn't read them, didn't understand what he was seeking.

"What?" she asked.

"You understand."

"Of course."

He shook his head. "No one understands."

"Some do. Like me. But if everyone did…the world would be mad."

"Isn't it?"

Cheyenne cupped his face, her heart beating hard. Tears built in her throat, an overwhelming swell that threatened to burst from her like a geyser. "It is what we make it."

"You give me hope," he said. "And part of me hates you for that."

She stared at him. "Because part of you still wants to die."

"Yes."

"But you lived."

"I had to." Will pulled from her touch and turned away. "I couldn't let it be for nothing. So I crawled through the desert for hours and hoped like hell I was going in the right direction. I heard the second copter pass over me—the retrieval unit sent by my senior chief—but there was no way to signal them. I just kept going…until one of the dogs from the local village found me."

Light dawned. "Is that what happened today…was it because of the dog?"

"She licked me. Took me right back to that moment. The smell, the sound of her whine…the voices, the pain. I was so *cold.*"

Cheyenne slid her arms around him again and held tight. "I'll keep you warm."

He shuddered, and his hands clenched around her. "I woke up in Bethesda two weeks later, my head even more fucked up than my body."

The wind chime sounded, and Will began to rock them again, slow and steady. He was rigid against her, his turmoil a palpable force she wanted to ease.

"One of the bullets they dug out of me came from a 9mm issued by the CIA. But the investigation found 'no legitimate or proven connection' to the Agency so they discounted the link. They buried my men, and my senior chief sat on his fucking hands while they closed the investigation and wrote us all off."

"They closed the investigation?"

"Oh, they're still looking for their bombs. Can't have those falling into the wrong hands...but my men, they're negligible. Collateral damage. And when I raised hell, I was told I either accepted the honorable discharge they had lined up, or face a dishonorable discharge for the loss of the cache."

"God Bless America," Cheyenne muttered.

"Bad apples. Rotten to the core. My whole life—my whole goddamn career—gone. My men unavenged—abandoned by the country they died for—and the treasonous bastards who killed them are being protected by the system I spent most of my life upholding. Makes me sick to my soul."

Cheyenne, too. "I'm sorry."

"When Red called me, I jumped at the chance to hunt them down."

"Red?"

"My fox." Will paused. He looked up at her and lifted a hand to tuck a strand of her unruly hair behind her ear, his thumb lingering to stroke her scar. A slight shudder moved through her; she still wasn't used to him touching it. To anyone touching it. "The twin of one of my men. A hacker who found the connection to Georgia and who's checking on Malik, but I haven't heard back."

Cheyenne sat up a little straighter. "And last night?"

Against her, Will stilled. "What about last night?"

"Where did you go?"

He only watched her, his gaze lidded.

"No more secrets," she told him, her voice hard. "We're in this, we're in it together—or not at all."

For long moments they stared at each other, and

Cheyenne was suddenly aware of the fact that she wore only a pair of thin cotton Snoopy pajama bottoms and a red t-shirt she was braless beneath. Will seemed huge in comparison and as warm as a furnace. Hard and broad and tall; too strong to fight and win.

"Together," he repeated, and something in his tone made the hair at her nape prickle.

"Or not at all. I mean it, Will. No more half measures. If you can't do that—just go."

He stared at her, his eyes glinting with something she couldn't name, but which alarmed her, and she moved to scramble from his lap, but his arms became iron bands, and he trapped her easily, with hardly any effort.

"Knock it off," she demanded. Heat crawled into her cheeks. She was sprawled in his lap; somehow she hadn't realized how intimate a position it really was. His thighs were solid beneath her, and she could feel his—

"All or nothing," he said and leaned in to flick his tongue against the hollow of her pulse.

She inhaled sharply and dug her nails into his shoulders. "Yes." But he made it sound—

"Everything," he said, and she wanted to agree—in theory—but the way he said it—

"No secrets," she told him as he rubbed his bristled chin against her neck and pulled her closer, until her breasts flattened against the hard wall of his chest. He made a deep sound in his throat at the connection, and that vibration made her nipples hard, and when he rubbed her against him, her breath locked in her throat. A shudder of pleasure made her grip him tighter.

"Oh," she said, surprised.

"You like that?" he murmured and did it again. The drag of her nipples against his hard chest made white heat arrow from her breasts to the flesh at her core.

She inhaled sharply. *"Oh."*

"I'll take that as a yes." Sharp teeth nipped at her throat, and his hands glided from her hips up beneath her t-shirt. The rasp of his hot, hard hands on her bare skin made her go still.

"Easy," he whispered. "I just want to feel you."

Rough, callused, huge; those hands should have frightened her. Instead, she remembered how they had felt stroking up her belly, and she wondered how they would feel—

"Oh," she whispered when his thumbs traced the underside of her breasts, his palms cupping her ribs, his tongue flickering against her earlobe.

"More?" he asked softly.

She made a low, humming sound in the back of her throat. Some part of her brain knew this was stupid—they'd been having an important conversation—but the newly awoken awareness of her own sexuality and the flood of hormones this man produced managed to drown out every sound but that of her own heartbeat.

Thump-thump, thump-thump, thump-thump.

"Yes," she told him. "Please."

A rasping laugh touched her ear, and that pleased her, and then he swept his thumbs higher, brushing her nipples with a tantalizing touch that made her breath catch sharply. But it wasn't enough. Her back arched and she shifted in his lap, aching and damp and impatient.

"More," she said, pressing her thigh into the hard line of his cock behind the zipper of his jeans, and when he shuddered, she pressed harder, because she liked that reaction, liked it that she could affect him, and he was giving her pleasure.

She wanted him to feel pleasure, too.

"Like this?" The rough pads of his thumbs dragged across her nipples and she shuddered.

"More," she whispered. A strong steady pulse beat at the notch of her thighs, and she wanted to turn so she could straddle him—

He pinched her, a searing streak to her groin; prickling pleasure and a slight bite of pain. She moaned helplessly.

"Look at me." His voice was harsh, and Cheyenne looked down at him, and the sight of his face—that beautiful, finely carved face—taut with lust made her shiver.

"Kiss me," he said.

But she hesitated. She'd never kissed anyone. And then he said, "Kiss me and I'll put my mouth on you," and she thought about that and decided it was worth looking like a novice if he would use those sharp teeth and that rough tongue on her. So she leaned down, shuddering when he pinched her again, lightly, and pressed her lips to his.

Will made a low, rough sound, and his tongue slid along hers, deep into the cavern of her mouth, a carnal sensation that stroked between her legs and made her moan again. He nibbled and suckled and rubbed the roof of her mouth with the tip of his tongue and thoroughly seduced her. She mimicked what he did, and he groaned and slid a hand up to her jaw, tilting her head, adjusting her so he could plunder at will. He twisted her nipples and tugged, and she rose against him, her fingers spearing into his hair, and—

Without warning, he pulled away. Slid his hands to her waist and stopped her from following, smoothing her hair and hushing her when she protested.

He pressed a hard kiss to her lips. "Rafe."

"Rafe?" she repeated stupidly, and then the door was opening, and over Will's shoulder Rafe's small face appeared, wreathed in moonlight and lined with worry.

"Is everything okay?" he asked apprehensively.

Cheyenne slid sideways, but Will stopped her and held her tight for one brief, breathless moment. His gaze burned into hers.

"All or nothing," he said.

She pushed against him.

"*Together*," he stressed, and she stared at him. Alarm prickled through her, but before she could respond, he set her down beside him gently and turned to look at Rafe. "I'm sorry. I didn't mean to scare you."

Rafe walked onto the porch, and Cheyenne scrambled to straighten her clothing, to fold her arms over her braless breasts. To cool her blood and *not* look like a horny sixteen year old.

Together.

Christ. She didn't even want to think about that. Couldn't a girl indulge in a little hanky panky with no strings attached?

"I'm okay," Rafe told him. "Are you?"

"Yes." Will smiled at her, dimples and all. "Cheyenne made me feel much better."

Her cheeks burned. "Jackass."

But he only laughed, and Rafe blinked at him in wonder. Cheyenne stared too, because she'd never seen him laugh. He could have graced the pages of a fashion magazine. Or been sculpted from stone.

He was that beautiful.

"Oh, stuff a sock in it," she snarled.

But he only laughed harder.

One kiss.

Her first and only.

And she'd created a monster.

CHAPTER TWENTY-ONE

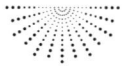

"It's a ledger."

Will looked up from the map he was studying and found Cheyenne standing in the kitchen doorway. She wore a pair of worn blue jeans and a Samcro t-shirt, and her hair was wet, a wave of dark fire against her creamy skin.

His fingers twitched, and his gut tightened, and the memory of her filling his hands threatened to render him immobile. And that kiss.... *Christ.* "What?"

"The book. It's a ledger. A compilation of favors owed. Almost seven years' worth." Cheyenne walked toward him. Her feet were bare. "Senators, diplomats, NSA, FBI, military officers. Each of whom owed Georgia a favor. Why they owed her is vague, but the scale of value is pretty clear. One, two, or three. One being something small—paperwork, a phone call, a meeting—two being something a little more intricate—like operational involvement in whatever scheme she was schilling—and three, three was an active risk. Three was life and limb and professional suicide—if she so chose."

Will leaned back against the counter and stared at the bruises he could see peeking out from beneath the collar of

Cheyenne's t-shirt. The sight of them sickened him. *Shamed him.* And he wanted to sink to his knees before her and beg forgiveness.

Forgiveness he didn't deserve. Because no matter what he told himself—or her—there was no guarantee he wouldn't lose himself and do it again. Even if—in his waking moments—he would put a bullet in himself first, he could make no promises about those moments he spent disoriented and adrift, susceptible to every violent, fucked up thing he felt.

That she understood—and accepted—the danger both exhilarated and infuriated him. Because she saw what no one else did…and that made him feel accepted, human, almost *normal*…but only because she knew hell as intimately as he, only because she had crawled through the darkness and blood and terror and *survived*.

He wanted to kill the piece of shit who'd raped her, who'd butchered her and left her to die in the street. *Snap his neck like a fucking twig. Skin him like an animal and hang him from his entrails. Break every bone, one at a time, and fill his lungs with holes, so he drowns slowly, suffocating in his own blood.*

And worse.

It was profoundly unfair that Georgia Humboldt was already dead. She deserved the most colorful—painful, torturous, excruciating—of deaths.

But it was too late.

Will knew, because he'd seen the photos of her body, courtesy of the Agency file Red had hacked. She'd been dead for no more than thirty six hours when they found her, and whoever had killed her had made it personal. Her bones had been broken, her beautiful face carved into mush, and she'd been nude, as if whoever had taken her life wanted her left humiliated and stripped bare of her machinations. The Agency had assumed it was the Chechen rebels, but Will wasn't so certain.

She'd been too damaged. Whoever killed her had hated her enough to leave her defiled and almost unrecognizable. That was more than just a deal gone bad.

"Hello?" Cheyenne said, her brows arched. "Are you hearing me?"

Will's gaze traveled over her again, and every muscle that lined his frame pulled exquisitely taut.

Stupid selfish bastard. He should have left. To stay only put her—and Rafe—in danger from himself. No matter what she knew or understood; no matter how hard she hit.

But he was not the only danger. *The worst danger.* And goddamn it, he wanted to keep her.

"I heard you," he said and forced himself to look away, back at the map. "Are you sure?"

"Yes. I have an eidetic memory. The code is one we used at Haven. She knew I would be able to read it. Doesn't that make you nervous?"

"It's a clue," he said, his chest tightening. "Are you finished?"

"Not yet. Halfway. You think whoever tipped her is in it?"

"Possibly." He stared at the map without seeing it.

Keep her.

Fucking stupid. Ludicrous. *Impossible.*

"Earth to Will," Cheyenne said. "A lead has landed. What's your problem?"

Keeping her...he didn't deserve to even consider it. He'd done nothing to earn her. He'd failed his men, his country, and last night he'd failed *her.* Spectacularly. So what the fuck was he thinking? And who said she would get on board with that kind of craziness? She might like his hands on her, but that didn't mean she wanted to be tied to him. That didn't mean she thought he was good enough.

Because he wasn't. Damaged and angry; the frog, not the Prince.

"Hey, Blackheart, where's your Glock?"

His hand went to his holster automatically and landed on the smooth butt of his gun.

"Yeah," Cheyenne said. "That's what I thought."

He looked up at her, and in that single space of breath, let himself imagine it.

Together.

"Why are you looking at me like that?" she demanded. Color bloomed in her cheeks, and the temptation to touch her made his hands curl into impotent fists. Impatience snapped within him, fed by the prowling, restless hunger she'd awoken, and he understood then that only part of him was still fighting.

The rest had surrendered. Had staked its claim. Had only two goals left: to woo her, because she deserved to be wooed, and to take her.

Because he was going to lose his fucking mind if he didn't.

And that part of him didn't give a shit about his mission, or the weapons, or the men whose hands were steeped in blood. About the bitch who'd slaughtered his team, or the traitor who'd betrayed him, or the bastard who might very well try to kill his own kid to protect himself.

Selfish, stupid, ignorant bastard.

"I never answered you," he said.

She blinked. "What?"

"Yesterday you asked where I went the night we got here, but we got…distracted."

Color bloomed in her cheeks, and it pleased him. Her physical response to him was immediate, powerful, and he would use it. He would use every weapon he had, without compunction.

"So where did you go?" she asked, her gaze steady, a warm flush kissing her skin.

"Frank James."

"Who?"

"Georgia's CIA partner. He was tailing us. So I went and had a little…chat with him."

"That you didn't feel the need to mention?" Her brows arched, anger a whip in her voice, but Will only watched her and accepted it.

"I didn't want to worry you," he said.

"Bullshit." She shook her head sharply. "You don't trust me."

"You're the only one I trust," he replied, his voice hard.

Again, she blinked. Her mouth opened, then closed. She watched him with dark, narrow eyes, and he could tell she wasn't sure if she should believe him, which shouldn't have been a surprise. Still, he was disappointed.

"No more secrets," he told her quietly.

She stared at him for a long, silent moment. Then, "What did Mr. James have to say?"

"Frank said Georgia set him up. Laid a false trail right to him. Said he's looking for the cache to prove his innocence."

"Did you believe him?"

Will shrugged. "They hated each other, so it's possible."

"But why follow us?"

"Because you and Rafe are the only trail she left."

"Awesome." Cheyenne scowled. "So he's just going to tail us?"

"No. He's gone now."

"Because of you?"

"I might have…discouraged him."

"Mmm-hmm," Cheyenne said, her gaze narrow. "First you, now Frank. Who's next?"

Will didn't appreciate being lumped in with Frank James, but he said nothing. He couldn't argue.

"I'm coming with you," he said.

"Coming with me where?"

"To Wyoming. We'll take my Jeep. Rafe said you wanted to camp along the way and stop at a few places."

She leaned back against the counter and arched a brow. "Don't you have a weapons cache to locate?"

"You're working on my only lead. Red is working on others. Right now, there's nowhere else to be."

"Flatterer," she told him. "You know how to make a girl feel adequate."

"Just adequate?"

Those rich green eyes glittered. "I can email you the transcript of the book as soon as I get it done. You don't have to hang around for that. I know you have plans."

Will met her gaze. "Getting you and Rafe safely to Wyoming is the only plan on the table."

She shook her head. "Not your problem."

"We go together or not at all."

Cheyenne scowled and folded her arms beneath her breasts. Her stance widened, and her mouth pursed, and his heart beat heavy in his chest, because he recognized that look.

"You," she told him, "are not sailing this ship. Oh, we've let you climb aboard and paddle, but that's doesn't mean you're captain. We don't need you to take care of us. I'm armed and aware, Rafe is armed and aware—that's as good as it ever gets. We'll be fine."

"Rafe is armed?"

"Personal Taser and a handy little butterfly knife. Don't worry—I didn't go commando." She tilted her head. "It's okay, Will. Really. I know you're on a mission. I know you don't appreciate the distraction. And we're not your responsibility."

He stared at her, not at all liking the sound of his own thoughts being voiced by her. Moot, now, anyway. He could pretend it was a struggle all he wanted, but somewhere between last night and this morning, he'd decided. And no argument on earth was going to sway him.

Not even his own.

"Together," he told her softly, and the awareness that flared in her gaze sent a lash of heat down his spine. "Remember?"

"I wasn't talking about…whatever the hell *you're* talking about."

Which made him laugh. But the panic that flashed through her was not lost on him, so he only looked back down at the map.

"I talked to Red," he told her. "Malik hasn't been seen for almost a week."

"Which means what?"

"I don't know. But I'm not going anywhere." Will wasn't going to argue with her. "We're keeping the pup?"

"Stop changing the subject. I'm trying to set you free."

Will gave her a hard look. "I don't want to be free." He glanced back down at the map. "Pipestone is first. I've never been there."

"Will."

The way she said his name sent a spike of something dark and hungry through him, and he was helpless not to meet that verdant green gaze, lined by lush, startlingly black lashes. A small beauty mark kissed the skin beneath her right eye. And her mouth…

He looked away again, back at the map.

"I'm coming with you," he said, because it was the truth. "I would prefer it be at your side, but I'll tail you in the Jeep if I have to."

Cheyenne watched him, her gaze assessing. He felt a piercing moment of self-awareness and knew she saw every fucked up thing in him. But she didn't look away.

"You don't have to save us," she told him quietly. "I don't expect that."

Will wasn't sure what that meant, but he didn't care. "I'm not going anywhere."

She said nothing. Then, "You dream of blood and vengeance and justice. We *can't* be part of that."

He stared at her. "Do you think I expect you to?"

"I don't know," she replied. "We have different goals. I want to get Rafe home safe and sound, preferably in one piece and free of this shitstorm. You want to sail right into that storm."

"No," he said.

"Yes," she argued. "We're a means to an end for you. Nothing more. And we will not go down with the ship."

Anger seared him, but he wasn't sure who he was angry with. Her for reading him so accurately and calling him on it…or himself, for ever thinking it.

"You're right," he told her bluntly. "I want blood. Justice. Goddamn payback. And my failures are immeasurable: *look at your fucking throat.*"

"Will—"

"But I will never, *ever* sacrifice you or Rafe on the altar of my vengeance. I would die first."

Cheyenne stared at him, and he let her. Let her see it all… the pain, the darkness, the profound damage he couldn't seem to mend. Pretending was useless and a lie, and he wanted nothing but truth between them. Bad or good, he didn't give a shit.

As long as it was real.

"I'll get you home," he said. "Whether you like it or not. Beside you or behind you. And I won't leave until you're safe —that means Malik dealt with, one way or another. *Together.* That's what you said. That's what I'm doing."

Her mouth opened, then closed. "I didn't mean to make you feel obligated…"

"You didn't. It just is."

"What does that mean?"

That you're mine to take care of. "It means I'm not leaving, no matter how hard you push."

For a long moment she just studied him, her gaze troubled and uncertain, and Will's heart beat like a drum at the thought she would turn him away, that he would be relegated to following, untrusted and unwelcome.

That he gave a damn was something he would have seen —just a day ago—as weakness, but today he didn't care. He was tired of punishing himself for feeling things beyond his control. He felt enough guilt and self-hate to fill a goddamn canyon. He would get Cheyenne and Rafe home. Deal with Malik. Find that damn cache and cut the throat of the bastard who'd betrayed him.

And then…Well.

That was a whole different bridge.

"I can handle whatever you dish out," Cheyenne told him finally. "But Rafe…he's been through enough. If you make a promise, you need to keep it."

"I will," he told her, his tone cold. That she would think he would let Rafe, or her, down infuriated him. But he couldn't blame her. All she knew—all she'd seen—was the damage and the darkness. He was more than those things. Much more.

Then get a fucking grip and show her.

"Alright," she said finally and nodded, but her eyes glinted with promised retribution should he fail. "Together…until it's over."

Will only blinked at her. He wasn't putting qualifiers on anything.

"If you want to camp," he said. "We need supplies."

"I know." She sighed and rubbed at the back of her neck,

and as Will watched the tension ease out of her, his eased as well. "I didn't bring any gear. We can stop in Madison, I think there's a *Gander Mountain* there."

"Are you almost ready?"

"Yes."

Rafe came through the door then, the pup leading the way. She wore her collar, her feet were too big for her body, and joy glowed from her when Rafe reached down and swiped her into his arms. He rubbed her ears, and she groaned loudly and wiggled against him.

Cheyenne laughed softly, and Will eased a little more.

"I'm ready," Rafe said. "Let's blow this joint."

"Did you get everything you want to keep?" Cheyenne asked him. "You should do a walk-through and make sure, because we're going to have to figure out what to do with the rest of it. We can take it or sell it or donate it—"

"Donate it." Rafe said. "I don't want it."

"What about the condo itself? Keep it or sell it?"

Rafe looked around. "I hate it."

"Then we sell it."

"But it's really sweet. The lake is right there…."

"And its value will only grow. It's a good investment. But there's no need to decide today. We have time."

Rafe put Lucky down and hefted his backpack over his shoulder. "We're going to the Badlands," he told Will. "You ever been to the Badlands?"

"Once," Will replied. "When I was a kid."

"You were a kid?" Cheyenne asked, shocked.

Rafe giggled.

"I was a very smart, very naughty kid," Will told them.

A small snort escaped her. "No doubt."

Rafe eyed him in consideration. "Where'd you live?"

Cheyenne frowned, as if realizing she didn't know the answer to that question.

"Montana," Will said. "My grandfather's ranch in Whitefish."

"You didn't live with your parents?" Rafe asked. Cheyenne said, "Rafe—" but Will only said, "No. They were killed by a drunk when I was seven."

"I'm sorry," Cheyenne said.

"What was your granddad like?" Rafe asked.

"He was a good man. I was lucky."

"So…Montana. Does that make you, like…a cowboy?" Rafe's eyes grew big as they studied him. "Can you ride a horse?"

Will caught Cheyenne's eye and winked at her. "Horses, bulls, camels. I'm versatile. How about you, Cheyenne? You ride?"

"Well, I wouldn't call myself a horsewoman, but I can stay in my saddle." She smiled, warm, wry, and Will wanted to touch her. "Generally speaking."

"Can you teach me?" Rafe asked, turning to look at Will.

"Sure."

Cheyenne straightened. "We need to get moving. We're burning daylight."

She was right, and Will knew it. But he wanted to linger; she wasn't at all certain of him, no matter what he'd told her. He could see it in her body language, hear it in her voice. She wasn't convinced.

He needed to fix that. To reassure them both, but he wasn't certain how.

Time.

Something he was in short supply of.

"I'll get the Jeep ready," he said.

Then he made himself turn and walk out.

CHAPTER TWENTY-TWO

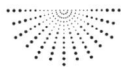

Screw it. "Are you gonna leave?"

Will turned to look at him. They stood in the *Gander Mountain* parking lot, watching the pup investigate the lone strip of grass that lined the lot while Cheyenne picked out their camping gear. The rain had finally quit, and the sun was warm and humid overhead.

"'Decipher the book and then I'm gone,'" Rafe continued. "That's what you said. Is it true? When Cheyenne's done, are you out?"

Will wore all black, and his Glock was tucked away, hidden by his coat, but Rafe knew he was armed. He seemed *there* in a way he hadn't before. And more relaxed. But after last night—

Rafe wasn't sure what to think.

"I'm not going anywhere." Will held his gaze. "I promised you I would stay, and I will. Yesterday was a bad day. I'm sorry for that."

Rafe shrugged. "You didn't mean it."

"But it happened. I don't have a lot of control over it, but that's no excuse. I hurt Cheyenne, and I scared you, and I'm more sorry for that than I can say. I'd like to tell you it won't happen again, but that would probably make me a liar. So I won't tell you that. But...you have to know, Rafe, I would never hurt her. Not intentionally."

Rafe knew that. He saw how Will looked at Cheyenne; he wasn't *stupid.*

"I don't care about what happened yesterday," Rafe told him bluntly. "I care about you taking off. You said you wouldn't let anything happen to us, but then...then you said you was leaving." Rafe's stomach churned as he held Will's pale gaze. He liked Will...but he needed to be able to *count* on him. "That's okay. You don't gotta take care of us. But if you're gonna go...do it now."

Will didn't move. He stared at Rafe, and Rafe's heart shuddered in his chest, but he held that pale, eerie gaze with everything he had. He wasn't used to protecting anyone—except maybe Ruby—but he felt the need to protect Cheyenne. To *try*. She was as much his as he was hers, and they had to work together if they were going to survive this craziness and come out on top. And Rafe knew that Will's presence would greatly enhance those odds.

But only if he was in it to win it. Only if he gave a damn. And if he didn't...Rafe didn't want him.

"She told me about my...Malik," he added. "So there's him. And I know you're looking for the bombs, and you want revenge and stuff, and we're kind of in the way of all that. You don't have to stay. We'll be okay."

Will only watched him. "Do you want me to go?"

"No!" Rafe shook his head. "I'm just saying...if you want to go, then go. But if you're gonna stay...then you gotta *stay.*"

For a long moment, there was only silence and the sound of Rafe's blood rushing through his head. He wasn't trying to push or make threats, but he wanted cards on the table. He wanted to know who was in and who wasn't. The Taser and the knife Cheyenne had gifted him with were cool, but they weren't going to stop an asshole who wanted him dead. He wasn't even sure Will could stop him, and Rafe was pretty sure Will was capable of almost anything. Will was like the characters in Rafe's comic books—bleak and damaged and kind of fucked up, but inherently good. Someone who survived something horrible and went on to help others, someone who gave everything they were to everyone else.

But Rafe also accepted that people had limits; he'd seen Will's limits. What happened last night had scared the piss out of him. Will was too big and too strong—they couldn't stop him when he got like that. Not unless they hurt him.

So maybe it was better if he was just…gone.

Still, Rafe didn't want that. He was selfish and scared, and he wanted Will by his side. By *their* side. And he knew, deep down, that Will needed them, too. But things didn't always work out. People were—

"You have no reason to trust my word on this, but it's all I have to give," Will said quietly, his features solemn. "I'm here until it's done, Rafe. The cache, Malik—whatever it means."

Rafe looked into that pale gaze and wanted to believe. But no matter what, it was a risk. A leap of faith. And for someone who'd spent most of his life not relying on anyone, that was hard. Will wasn't Cheyenne. Cheyenne was there because she wanted to be there. But Will…Will had plans.

"Cheyenne thinks you're just a means to an end for me," Will continued. "But you're not."

Rafe only blinked at him.

"When I came here, all I could see was blood…no one but me, nothing but my mission. And then Cheyenne knocked me on my ass and turned the world upside down."

"She's good at that," Rafe said.

A small, sharp smile. "Yes."

"I didn't know she knocked you on your ass," Rafe said, wishing he'd seen it.

"She punched me in the throat while we stood in the car rental line. Put me down with one hit." Will shook his head. "I didn't even see it coming."

"I don't think anyone ever sees her coming." Rafe paused. "Why did she hit you?"

"Because I threatened her."

Which made Rafe hold Lucky a little tighter. "Why did you threaten her?"

"Because I thought she was part of it."

He nodded, silent.

"I won't lie to you," Will told him. "The cache is important. I have to find it. But you come first."

"What about your revenge?"

Will met his gaze. "It can wait."

"You sure?"

"Absolutely," Will said.

Rafe only stared at him for a long, quiet moment. "Do you know my father?"

"No. I met him once when he visited the base I was stationed at, but that's it." Will put his hand on Rafe's shoulder. "I'm sorry I didn't tell you when you asked me."

"I understand." Kind of. "You really think he might…try to kill me?"

"He might try. He won't succeed."

Will's tone made Rafe shiver. Still… "But he might try?"

"I don't know."

Rafe sighed. "I liked it better when I was just an orphan."

Will squeezed his shoulder. "Cheyenne will take good care of you."

"I know." Rafe smoothed his cheek along the pup's silky

head. "She let me keep Lucky. I didn't even have to ask. She said Chuck will love her."

"Chuck?"

"Her dog. She said he's a ladies man."

"Yeah?"

"Yeah. She has a goat and a cat, too."

"See, it's not all bad. You're getting siblings."

Which made Rafe smile. "I always wanted a brother."

"Well, there you go." Will looked up as a horn sounded. Cheyenne was headed toward them, wrestling with a large, overflowing cart.

"I bet she bought one of everything," Will said.

Rafe looked at the cart. "She totally did."

"Our girl likes to be prepared."

They watched her fight with the wayward wheels on the cart, all of her weight pitched behind the handle. She made two cars wait for her to cross in front of them and then flipped off some guy in a pick-up who honked and roared past her.

"She's different," Rafe said, watching her.

"Yes," Will said, and he was watching her, too. "How do you think a man would go about pursuing a woman like her, Rafe?"

Startled by the question, Rafe glanced at Will. "I don't know."

"Me either."

"I can Google it," Rafe offered, and Will laughed softly.

"That's okay," Will said. "I'll figure it out."

Another horn; another single-fingered salute. Will shook his head and headed toward Cheyenne. Rafe put Lucky down and followed.

The pup barked at Cheyenne, her tail wagging furiously. She liked Cheyenne. She liked, Will, too. Rafe had decided to name her Lucky because it fit—she'd survived whatever left that scar, and she'd made it to the rock in the middle of the lake, and she'd found *them*—besides, he figured they could all use a little more luck. Especially since people were probably after them.

People. Malik. A tall, handsome man with the hazel half of Rafe's eyes and a familiar smile. He didn't look like the kind of guy who would kill his own kid, but what did that look like? Rafe didn't know. And while he was still pissed that both his mom and his pop were assholes—he would give *anything* to be a damn orphan—he really couldn't complain, not with what Cheyenne had shared about her own ma. Oh, he wanted to, but she was right: it *could* be worse. And it might get worse before it was over.

He really hoped Will kept his word. Because they needed Will. Cheyenne was tough; after the Letitia showdown, there could be no doubt she would hold her own. But Rafe still worried. Missing bombs were bad enough, but when you added Malik and whatever craziness his ma had been involved in—spies and codes and killing SEALS—nothing good could come of it. And now he had Lucky to take care of. They were headed out west, a foreign place he knew nothing about, and they were going to camp—something he'd *never* done—and he felt very unprepared.

At least in the city he knew where to hide. How to get away.

But he wasn't alone anymore. He couldn't just run and leave Cheyenne and Will and Lucky behind. They were…a unit. They had to stick together.

Rafe wasn't used to being part of a unit. He was apart. But he knew they had to work together. He knew they had to talk to each other and listen to each other and help each other.

He could do that. But would it be enough to keep them safe?

Enough to beat his ma. Because that's what this was: a game. Them against her. Rafe knew that much was true. And she'd been smart. Really, really smart.

Which scared him. It meant no one was safe.

Him least of all.

CHAPTER TWENTY-THREE

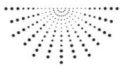

"Building a fire is like wooing a woman. You start small and go slow, building layer by layer by layer until it's strong enough to take anything you throw at it. But you gotta make sure that flame can breathe. That's critical. Otherwise it will just turn to ash and die."

Cheyenne wanted to snort in derision, but when Will glanced up and winked at her a blush turned her cheeks into burning coals.

"You start with a ball of tinder—dried grass or moss or crushed leaves—and small, dry twigs." Will arranged a pile of moss in the middle of the steel campfire ring that was the centerpiece of their campsite. Rafe and Lucky sat next to him, watching curiously. "Then you build. Most folks use a teepee. Simple but strong and it allows the fire to breathe, which makes it stronger. Here's your tinder, then you add your twigs like this, one by one, feeding it thicker and thicker kindling until you have a nice little bed of coals that can handle bigger wood."

"You used a lighter," Cheyenne pointed out. "That's cheating."

Will arched a brow at her. "I should've used a bow drill?"

"That's true survival," she said. "No lighter fluid necessary."

She was trying to poke him, but he only smiled at her, dimples and all. "You're right. We'll try a bow drill tomorrow. You can demonstrate how it works."

Backfire! Damn it.

Bow drills were a shitload of work.

Smoke curled into the air and filled Cheyenne's lungs, and the scent was so sweet she breathed deep. It had been too long since she'd sat around a crackling fire, staring into the flames while the stars glittered overhead.

"Cool," Rafe said. "Nobody ever taught me that."

"You can build tomorrow's fire," Will told him. "After Cheyenne gets it started with her bow drill."

Still smiling, his pale eyes glinting.

Gorgeous bastard.

Rafe grinned at her, one hand rubbing Lucky's head. Then he bent over and began to help Will add kindling.

Cheyenne watched them, Will so big, Rafe so small, heads bent close together as they spoke about the fire and worked to build it, and felt something prickle in the region of her heart.

Indigestion.

"Just need a Tums," she told herself.

Even though she hadn't eaten since Madison, and they were now stopped and set up at Blue Mound State Park in southern Minnesota, seven hours later. In point of fact, she was starving. Rafe had begged for hotdogs on the fire, and since the kid had never had the pleasure of cooking a hotdog over a campfire, she'd been unable to refuse. But now she had to wait for them to get done before she could lodge a dog on one of the narrow metal skewers she'd bought at *Gander Mountain* and fry it to a crisp.

"Fire isn't something you should ever take for granted," Will said. "It can get away from you in a heartbeat, spread in the blink of an eye, and it will destroy absolutely everything. Fire can keep you alive or it can kill you. It should be respected." He stood. "We'll let that burn down, and then we should be ready for some hotdogs."

"Sweet." Rafe picked up the pup and pushed to his feet. "I'm gonna throw the ball for Lucky until it's ready. That was a long ride."

"You ain't seen nothing yet," Cheyenne told him.

She watched him lead the pup into the field next to them and marveled at how decent and kind a human being he was; nothing at all like his mother. Smart, too, and witty—something Georgia had never mastered. He didn't act like a ten year old, but Cheyenne hadn't expected him to. Only when it came to the things he'd never done—and had never expected to do—did she see the little boy who lived within. Camping, cooking hotdogs over a fire, having a dog...how silly she felt, mentally listing all of the things she wanted to introduce him to simply for the pleasure of seeing that boy. But silly was okay. She was still going to do it.

"He's a good kid," Will said, as if reading her thoughts. He sank into the camp chair next to her, his long legs stretched out before him. He'd set up the tent, unpacked the sleeping bags and the food, and started the fire; she hadn't had to do diddly squat. Now he sat beside her, more relaxed than she'd ever seen him, which considering the events of the previous night, perplexed her. Because she was hyperaware of both what she'd shared and what had passed between them afterward—neither of which she was particularly happy about.

Stupid soft heart. Always leading her astray. And that kiss....

She'd spent the morning kicking her own ass—mostly because she didn't regret it. But it couldn't happen again.

Emotions were stirring—rusty and unused—and allowing herself to feel *anything* for Will was profoundly stupid. That she already did—at least a little—was shocking and horrifying and utterly unacceptable. Which was why she'd tried her best to push him out the door this morning.

Only to have him dig in his heels.

He had to know she and Rafe were only a decoy. Neither one of them had any knowledge of the cache or the people who'd stolen it or its current location. They had nothing—other than her translation of the ledger—to give him. And while she appreciated his concern for their safety, she didn't understand it.

Why put himself in front?

The question had gnawed at her since he'd declared his refusal to leave them. It made no sense to her, especially when he had such grand plans. And while the idea of his protecting them from the (possible) criminal collective looking for the cache—and Rafe's (possibly) murderous father—was incredibly noble, it was also...curious.

What were his motives, really?

A cynical question, but what could she say? She was a cynical gal.

Maybe he thought the location of the cache would appear to Rafe through osmosis. Or maybe he just didn't want his only lead to get dead.

Winner, winner, chicken dinner!

The true test would be his response to the book that sat in her lap. The ledger was filled with names, people she didn't recognize but who Will might—people who could very well be the ones he sought. Seventeen brand new leads...

"What are you thinking about?" Will asked quietly, pinning her with his pale gaze.

Cheyenne looked down at the book. She'd finished it halfway through Minnesota and had spent the other half wondering what he would do. *Stay or go.* If he found a smoking gun among the list of names—regardless of what he'd said—she expected him to go.

"Here." She handed it to him. "Merry Christmas."

He took the book, opened it and scanned the first page. She'd written the translation above the code, the name, date and numbered value. "You're done?"

"Malik is in there," she told him. "Number three."

Will nodded. Then he closed the book and tossed it on top of the picnic table next to him.

"You aren't going to read it?" Cheyenne demanded, frowning.

"Later," he said. "Tell me what's wrong."

She only stared at him. "You're not going to see if someone you know is in there?"

"Later," he repeated and reached out to capture a lock of her hair where it trailed over the slope of her breast. He wound it around his index finger, stroking the texture with his thumb, and as she watched the unhidden pleasure he took in the act, everything within her went tight. "So spill it."

She ignored him. That was all that was left to her: pretending he didn't exist. Because he clearly wasn't going to stop looking at her like that, he wasn't going to stop touching her as though it was his right, he wasn't going to stop calling her "baby" in that rough, possessive tone which should have infuriated her but just made her wet. All the damn man had to do was *look* at her, and she was ready.

It was lunacy. And it had gone beyond sexual awakening. *Beyond harmless.*

Anything that happened from here on out was going to leave a mark. And Cheyenne—for all her fearlessness—had no desire to bear any more scars.

He tugged at the strand of hair he held. "Talk to me."

"We made good time," she said. "Traffic was light."

"Don't bullshit me, baby."

Cheyenne said nothing. Then, because honesty was her way, she said, "What happened last night…it can't happen again."

Next to her, Will went still. "I didn't mean to hurt you."

"Not that." She shook her head. "I meant…us." Her cheeks burned, but she met his gaze and held it. "It was…nice, but—"

"Nice?" He laughed and shook his head, and she scowled at how beautiful he was. "That wasn't nice, baby. Nice is… ordinary." His smile faded. "Average. That was fucking incredible."

His seriousness made her heart beat hard in her chest. Cheyenne cleared her throat. "If you say so, but—"

"You wouldn't say so?"

Cheyenne blinked at him. He was frowning at her, but there was a glint in his pale eyes she didn't recognize, almost as if he were *teasing* her. He leaned close and cast her in shadow; the scent of pine invaded her nostrils, and his heat pressed against the bare skin of her arm, making awareness hum within her.

"You don't want to do it again?" he murmured, his gaze falling to her mouth, tracing its shape, and she could feel his lips against hers, the rough stroke of his tongue claiming her. Her breath grew short, and her lips tingled, and she remembered how it felt to have his hands on her, that biting pleasure-pain when he'd—

"Rafe is my priority," she said, struggling to focus, her hands fisted in her lap to keep from reaching for him. "Not sex."

Will snarled softly. "It's not just sex."

Cheyenne's heart jerked in her chest. "Then what is it?"

"More."

The definition of which baffled her. And scared her.

Contemplating sex was bad enough; what the hell did he mean by *more?*

She could only shake her head. "I'm not that girl."

"For me, you are."

Cheyenne wanted to look away, but couldn't. His certainty shook her. There was no question in him. No doubt. *No fear.* And he was right.

For him she *was* someone she'd never been. Someone she hadn't imagined existed. Still...she was *not* that girl. She never had been, never would be.

Alone is what I know.

Sex was one thing: physical, unadorned by morality or emotion. Simply a response to stimuli. But *more* was...

Dangerous. And something she'd not—in a million years—envisioned.

"A lot is happening," Will continued. "I know. And Rafe... he's important. But so is this."

Panic was a mad flutter in her chest, as though a bird had gotten trapped in the fragile framework of her ribcage. "There is no 'this.' No us. No we. Just because we strike sparks—"

"Don't," he said.

"Don't what?"

"Don't denigrate it."

Cheyenne blinked at him.

"At the fucking least, we're friends. Don't make it less because it scares you."

She inhaled sharply. But she couldn't argue. Because it *did* scare her. This was an area of life she knew absolutely zero about—and hadn't planned on learning. And damn him for making her think about it. With Rafe, she'd jumped. But with Will....

"You know I'm right," he said.

He didn't budge, watching her with a perception and

understanding that sent her mentally fleeing for cover. When had this morphed into...*more?* Jesus. She wasn't 'significant other' material; she was barely *friend* material.

"I don't know how to do this," she told him.

"I know. That's okay. There's no rush, baby. But I want us on the same page."

Cheyenne looked at him, nonplussed, the rush of her blood a dull roar in her ears. Will only looked back, intense and unwavering, and she didn't know what to make of him.

"Smile for the camera." Rafe stood before them suddenly, holding his phone out. "Say hi."

Cheyenne scowled blackly.

"*Smile,* Cheyenne."

"What in Hades are you doing?" she asked.

"I'm going to make a movie of our trip. Maybe I can send it to Ruby." He hesitated. "Is that okay?"

God help me.

"Of course," she said and smiled through her teeth. "Cheese."

Will laughed softly.

"Yuck it up," she told him. "You Tube likes pretty. You'll be very popular."

"This is Cheyenne. She's my guardian. And this is Will. He's...." Rafe halted his narration and looked at Will. "What are you?"

"I can answer that," Cheyenne said.

Will tugged on her hair. "Careful."

"He's...our friend," Rafe said, his gaze meeting Will's. When Will nodded, Cheyenne wanted to smack him. And scream. And do everything she could to regain control of this out of control situation.

Yeah. Good luck with that.

"Chaos bites," she muttered.

"We're at Blue Mound State Park in Minnesota," Rafe

continued as he panned around their campsite and focused on the quartzite cliff that rose from the prairie like a jagged tooth. "Tomorrow we're going to Pipestone Monument and the Badlands." He panned back to the fire he and Will had built. "This is our fire. Tomorrow I'll teach you how to make one. And now, we're going to cook hotdogs and roast marshmallows."

Cheyenne's stomach rumbled. "About freaking time." She yanked at the strand of hair Will held. "Let go. It's time to eat."

He only smiled at her. Dared her.

"Getting between a woman and her weenie is dangerous," she warned. Rafe giggled.

"I would never," Will said and let her hair slide through his hand. "A hungry woman is a dangerous woman."

"Don't you forget it."

CHAPTER TWENTY-FOUR

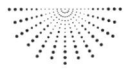

*A*lexander Wentworth, FL Congressman, 3.
      Ethan Scott, Navy, 3.
Andrew Malik, Ambassador, 3*.
General Robert Forsyth, Army, 3.
Alan Phillips, Special Agent, FBI, 3.

This list went on and on, names Will recognized, powerful men from every facet of the American government.

Including his Senior Chief.

The sight of Ethan's name was a vicious punch to the gut. Will returned to it again and again, wondering what the hell Ethan had received from Georgia Humboldt that'd earned him the highest debt marker in her ledger.

What the fuck had been going on?

Something. Something bigger than he'd ever realized.

"What?" Cheyenne asked from her place beside him in the Jeep's driver's seat. Rafe sat in the back seat, filming the rolling hills, excited over the gradual change in the landscape.

"This is tits," he'd declared, more than once.

Will didn't respond to her. Instead he reached over and took her free hand, twining his fingers through hers.

"What?" she asked again, watching him. She tugged against his hold but he only tightened it, and she sighed. "Someone you know?"

"Several." She expected him to leave. Hell, after yesterday Will realized she *wanted* him to leave. Because she was scared shitless—of him, of *them*. Although she might not run from a fight, she was more than willing to run from him.

And that was not acceptable.

"It reads like a Who's Who list of federal law enforcement, counter-intelligence and military brass." He met her gaze. "My Senior Chief is in here."

"I'm sorry," she said and squeezed his hand. "Your smoking gun?"

"I don't know." He continued to peruse the list, trying to imagine what the hell had happened to put that many of the country's elite in the debt of a woman like Georgia Humboldt. "Makes no sense."

"Par for the course," Cheyenne muttered.

"Hey, can we stop at Wall Drug?" Rafe asked. "There's, like, a bazillion signs for the place."

"Sure."

"Cool. How much farther?"

"Hours and hours."

Rafe groaned, and Lucky echoed it. Cheyenne grinned at him in the mirror. "Poor baby."

"I'm bored."

"Boredom is a state of mind," she told him.

"Let's play twenty questions," he suggested.

"Let's not and say we did," she replied.

"C'mon, Cheyenne. Please?"

"Fine." She slid a look at Will. "I didn't used to be such a sucker."

He only lifted her hand and pressed a gentle kiss to the back of it, enjoying the flush that colored her cheeks.

"I'll go first," Rafe said. "Okay, Cheyenne…what's your favorite color?"

"I like them all," Cheyenne said.

Rafe looked at Will.

"Green," Will said.

Cheyenne glanced at him. "Really?"

"Why does that surprise you?"

For a moment, he didn't think she would respond. Then, "Because it's a color of rebirth. And your focus seems to be endings, not beginnings."

Will stared at her, a hard knot of something caustic and…*angry* throbbing within him.

"Mine's orange," Rafe said. "How about food? What's your favorite food?"

"Too many to choose from," Cheyenne said.

"Okay—just one."

"Raspberries."

"Will?"

But he was still staring at Cheyenne, turning her response over in his head.

Fucking asshole.

No wonder she was fighting him. Not only was he broken, the darkness was obvious, a living, breathing thing she could see. The endgame was all he'd thought about since he'd awakened. As if he could expect her to choose a man who saw only death in his future.

I can't choose…

But if he wanted to keep her, he was going to have to.

"Will?" Rafe pressed.

He shook his head and tried to remember the question.

"Food," Cheyenne prompted.

"Pecan pie," he said.

She sighed. "Yum."

"They make pie outta nuts?" Rafe asked skeptically.

Cheyenne only shook her head. "Guess I know what I'm baking when we get home."

"You can cook?" Rafe asked, his excitement palpable.

"You can't?"

"PB&J," he said.

She laughed. "That doesn't count. So—one more thing you get to learn how to do."

His excitement waned. "I have to learn?"

"Everyone should know how to feed themselves."

He sighed heavily. "Damn it."

"You never know—you might actually like it."

Rafe's look was skeptical. In spite of the turmoil Will felt, he smiled. And he wondered when smiling had stopped feeling like a betrayal. The raw, open wound he'd worn like a badge of honor still bled and throbbed and screamed for justice…but it was beginning to heal. And no matter how guilty he felt for that, he knew his men would not begrudge him *her*. Hell, every one of them would have liked her. And they would be pissed to know he used them as an excuse not to live.

Perhaps that was also betrayal.

"I got another one," Rafe said. "What's your favorite animal?"

"I love all critters," Cheyenne replied. "Well, except sewer rats. And mosquitos. And ticks. And those bastard horseflies."

"Will?"

His phone chose that moment to vibrate, and he held up a finger as he answered it. "Blackheart."

"I found something," Red said without preamble, his voice tense.

Will tightened his hold on Cheyenne, and she glanced at him in question.

"What?" he asked.

"You'll have to see it to believe it. Let's just say…it widens the pool."

"Meaning?"

"You'll see. I'm sending it now." The click of a mouse. "There. Fair warning—don't play it while the kid's around."

Which made Will curious. "Okay. Where did you find it?"

"On Malik's server. He's still AWOL. But I found something else."

"That being?"

"One of his wife's half-brothers is Ahmed Asfour. According to my sources, he's a very high-ranking member of El Hashen."

El Hashen.…the Pakistani jihadists to whom Georgia had brokered the cache.

"And the circle closes."

"Yes."

But there was still the ledger. Still Ethan Scott—and an entire assortment of Feds, military and politicians. Any of whom could be involved.

"They arrested Frank James," Red said.

"When?"

"Yesterday."

"Charges?"

"Word is treason."

"They found the trail she laid."

"You don't think he was involved?"

"Maybe." But Will didn't think so.

"Anything new on the location?"

"No."

"And you're still there because…?"

Because the job wasn't done. Because Rafe wasn't safe.

Because he didn't want to leave them.

"I found something at her place," he said. "A book. I'm still going through it."

"What kind of book?"

"A ledger of some kind."

"Who's in it?"

Fucking everyone.

"I'm still going through it," Will repeated.

"Can you send me a copy?"

Not until he figured out what the hell it meant. "When I get a chance."

"Where are you?"

"Halfway between Sioux Falls and Rapid City."

"What?"

"I'll look at what you sent and call you back."

"Wait—I thought you were in Milwaukee."

"I was. I'm not anymore."

"Cryptic bastard. Alright, take a look and call me. It's a doozy."

"Will do."

He hung up. Rafe stared at him in the mirror.

"That was about her, huh?"

"Yes."

"Your fox?" Cheyenne added.

"Yes."

She tilted her head and slid him a look. "*Red*...is this a vixen we're talking about?"

For a moment, Will didn't understand. Then he smiled, and the knot within him dissolved. "No."

She looked away, that lovely color painting her cheeks.

"You still don't know where the bombs are?" Rafe asked pensively.

"No. But we'll find them."

The boy nodded, but the worry and tension that lined his

face made Will want to punch someone. Cheyenne shook her head, and he knew she felt the same way. But she didn't address it. Instead, she looked at him and said, "Favorite animal? Let me guess…koala bear?"

A small smile curved Rafe's mouth.

"Too cute," Will said.

"Sloth?"

"Too slow."

"Hagfish?"

Rafe giggled.

"Have you seen the hagfish?" Will demanded. He pretended to shudder.

"I bet it's the Blue-footed Booby."

"No way," Rafe said. "That's not real."

"Cross my heart," Cheyenne told him. She smiled knowingly at Will. "It's the Booby, isn't it?"

And he laughed, unable to help himself. He lifted her hand and pressed another kiss to it. "Definitely the Booby."

CHAPTER TWENTY-FIVE

The Blue-footed Booby (Sula nebouxii) is a marine bird in the family Sulidae, which includes ten species of long-winged seabirds. Blue-footed boobies belong to the genus Sula, which comprises six species of boobies. It is easily recognizable by its distinctive bright blue feet.

Rafe eyed the photo which accompanied Wikipedia's description of the Blue-footed Booby and thought he might like to see one someday. According to the website, they lived along the continental coasts of the eastern Pacific Ocean from California to the Galapagos Islands. He'd learned about Galapagos in school and thought he'd like to go there, too.

He'd always figured he'd never get the chance to go anywhere, least not until he was grown. But with Cheyenne…with Cheyenne, anything was possible.

He closed his laptop and looked out the window. Once they'd crossed the Missouri River the landscape had begun to morph, a distinct change Cheyenne called "east turning to west." The hills grew in size, and in the distance, jagged, colorful mountains kissed the horizon. The skies above were such pure, clear blue they hurt his eyes.

Cheyenne promised only an hour more, but he wasn't sure he believed her. His butt was asleep, his t-shirt was covered in dog drool, and he had to pee. He'd never spent so long in a car before—it was hard. The sun beat down with relentless intensity, slowly creeping from one side of the Jeep to the other, and they kept losing internet service.

Twenty Questions had lasted for an hour, and Rafe learned that Cheyenne was old school when it came to pretty much everything, and that she didn't like to answer questions. Will was more dialed-in and easy going and, oddly enough, had way more in common with Rafe than he would have guessed. That Cheyenne could cook—even if she made him learn—was the best news *ever*.

To Letitia, "cooking" had consisted of spaghetti O's and chicken ramen.

Rafe didn't miss her.

In fact, even though it had only been a few days, she felt far away, as though that part of his life had already begun to fade. Considering how hard it had been to live through, that seemed wrong somehow, like he shouldn't forget that easily —because things could change in a heartbeat. And often did.

There were some things you *should* remember. Even if they were ugly—*because* they were ugly.

Letitia was one of them.

Rafe was worried about Ruby; he really hoped she was okay. He didn't know if she would ever get to see the movie he was making, but he hoped so. He wanted her to know that, even though he wasn't there anymore, she wasn't alone, and he wouldn't forget about her. That was important. They were still friends, no matter how far away he was.

And it was *far*. They weren't even in Wyoming yet, and it felt like they'd been driving forever. The sky was huge, and he could see for miles. The sun seemed bigger, brighter, and the further west they got, the fewer cars they saw. It amazed him that here was all this space and yet...no people.

Why cram so many into one place and have none in others? It didn't make any sense to him. But he liked it.

South Dakota was different. Halfway through the state, in the middle of a random field, there'd been a skeleton made of steel leading a giant dinosaur on a leash. Damnedest thing Rafe ever saw—luckily, he'd gotten footage of it—and it made him wonder how many other random, wonderful things there were to see in the world. More than he could count, probably.

The idea that he might actually get to *see* some of them....it was more than he'd ever dared hope for.

Cheyenne was singing *Hotel California* off-key. Will watched her, smiling a little, and Rafe wondered if what he saw between them would turn into something. The thought that Cheyenne *and* Will might be part of his life going forward was too good to be true, and he knew better than to wish for something that felt too good. That they liked each other was obvious, but adults were weird, driven by things he didn't understand and couldn't predict.

Who knew why they did anything?

Still, Rafe hoped Will would stick around. There was a hell of a lot he could learn from Will. Men had been scarce in his life—especially decent ones—and Rafe really wanted to be a good one...that was important to him.

Rafe was not his mother—or his father.

He was going to be *better.*

Better than both of them combined.

Anyone who would kill a bunch of SEALs was someone he didn't want to know—let alone be related to. And he wished he could stop thinking about those bombs. Sometimes he dreamt of them, of his ma standing on a dark street with the bombs all around her, and he couldn't get to them or to her before they started to go off, one by one, and when he awoke he was wet with sweat, and he could still hear them, *tick-tick-tick,* in his head. Fear would swell like a giant bubble in his chest, panic would crawl into his throat, and his heart would beat so hard he could taste it. He hated how helpless, how *responsible,* he felt. As if he should have been able to do something—anything—to stop her.

But even in his dreams, he was powerless. Because, really, what could he have done? He was just a kid. Even if he *had* known, he couldn't have stopped her.

She wouldn't have let him.

In his lap, Lucky twitched and whimpered in her sleep. He stroked a hand down her hindquarter, and she calmed.

"Rest stop?" Will asked. He was driving. "Next one is—"

"Hell, yeah," Cheyenne said, and Rafe breathed a sigh of relief.

They took the exit with the bright blue sign and pulled into the front lot, parking next to a green pickup truck. Back behind the rest stop, a colorful row of tractor trailers sat parked, their chrome gleaming with blinding brightness in the sun. A woman was walking her Chihuahua on the grass, and a man stood studying the map of South Dakota that hung on the outside wall, protected from the weather by a pane of scratched Plexiglas.

Rafe got out, his legs protesting as he stretched them. Lucky whined at him but Will reached in and grabbed her, clipping on her leash.

"I'm good," he told Rafe. "I'll walk her."

Lucky wagged her tail and licked his chin.

"C'mon." Cheyenne shut the Jeep's passenger side door and slid her arm around Rafe's shoulders. "Here's to hoping this one smells better."

They used the facilities, and when they came out, the man and woman and green pickup were gone. Down at the end of the parking lot, an aging white Camaro sat at an odd angle, and a man and a woman stood beside it, arguing. Rafe glanced at them and then looked toward Will, who stood in the grass, Lucky sniffing around his feet.

Will was watching the couple.

"You want to sit up front for the last leg?" Cheyenne asked him, but she, too, had eyes on the man and woman.

The man was big and hairy and wore a stained yellow t-shirt and jeans. The woman wore a short denim skirt and a red and white halter-top. She was skinny as a rail...and young. Really young. Her hair was dark, almost black, long and thin, and dark bruises dotted each of her arms like ugly tattoos. Her legs, too, were bruised, and when the wind lifted her hair, Rafe could see raised red marks on her back. The man had one beefy hand wrapped around her forearm, and the other was fisted at his side. Both of his arms were covered in sleeve tats.

"Sure," Rafe said, but he didn't move to climb into the Jeep, didn't look away. In his belly, unease hardened into a thick knot. The man's voice carried toward them, low, angry, and the woman—no, she was a *girl*—sounded like she was crying.

"Get in the fucking car," the man snarled, and with his free hand, he wrenched open the passenger door of the Camaro. The girl shook her head and backed away, even though there was no way she was breaking his grip, he was way too big—

"Here." Will suddenly stood there, holding out Lucky's leash. Rafe took it and reached down to lift the pup into his arms; she was warm and solid and felt good pressed against him.

"Call 911," Will told Cheyenne.

"Why?"

"Because that dickhead is going to need an ambulance."

Then he turned and walked toward the couple, his hands

curled loosely at his sides, his stride aggressive. Rafe watched with bated breath, suddenly seeing the warrior in Will so clearly his heart lurched. Confident and fearless and bold; not at all worried about losing.

He's going to cream that guy.

"Kick his stinking *ass*," Cheyenne said softly, watching Will as she pulled her phone from her back pocket.

"Don't ever do this," she added to Rafe, dialing.

He snorted.

"Yeah," she said. "I know."

Will didn't try to talk the guy down. He didn't say anything at all. He just walked right up to them and got into the guy's face, breaking the man's hold on the girl by sheer force of presence. Suddenly free, the girl stumbled back.

"I'm at the rest area just outside of Wasta, mile marker 98," Cheyenne said into her phone. "There's a man here trying to force a young woman into his car."

The man roared, loud, enraged, and the sound made Rafe flinch. Next to him, Cheyenne went very still, watching Will, the man, the woman.

"Who the fuck—" the man began, but Will only stepped toe-to-toe with him and said something they couldn't hear. The look on Will's face—mean and hard and unforgiving—made goose bumps wash across Rafe's skin. He *really* wished he could hear what was being said. Will was broad and lean where the man was stout and thick, but they were the same height, almost nose-to-nose as the girl backed slowly away.

"This ain't none of your fucking business!" the man yelled, but he was backing up as he said it, Will advancing on him like a hungry wolf. "She's *mine*. Go find your own cunt to—"

Will hit him. Lightning fast—Rafe didn't even see it coming—a vicious connection so straight and perfect, the man's nose burst like a balloon. Blood sprayed into the air, across the sloped back window of the Camaro, onto the pavement, on Will.

"*Damn*," Rafe whispered.

"You son of a bitch!" the man snarled. He swung, but Will ducked, and when he came up, it was with another brutal punch Rafe was sure broke the guy's jaw. More blood fountained into the air. The man fell back onto the trunk of the Camaro and then slid down the quarter-panel like a limp noodle, landing in a heap next to the back tire.

Once he was down, Will was on him, shoving him facefirst to the pavement, one knee digging into the guy's spine. When he tried to rear up, Will clocked him in the side of the head, another pitiless blow that knocked him cold.

"Hell, yeah," Cheyenne said.

And that quickly, it was over.

"Put Lucky in the car, and get that rope I bought," Cheyenne told him and began to walk toward the Camaro, her phone still at her ear.

Rafe stuck Lucky in the backseat and hurried to the back of the Jeep, his heart beating like a jackhammer. The rope was there, tucked next to the sleeping bags, and he gathered it with shaking hands. He closed the back of the Jeep and ran toward Will.

Cheyenne was crouched before the girl, who sat on the curb of the sidewalk halfway between the Jeep and the Camaro. She was talking to her, one hand on the girl's shoulder.

"Good man," Will said when he got close and held out the rope. Will took it and pulled his Leatherman from his belt. He flipped the knife out and sliced a two-foot length of rope from the rest and handed it back to Rafe.

Beneath him, the man was still as death.

"Did you kill him?" Rafe wondered.

"He's too mean to die that easily." Will wrapped the man's

hands in the rope and efficiently tied them together. He looked up at Rafe. "Don't ever do this."

"That's what Cheyenne said," Rafe told him. "But she's done it. You're doing it. Don't seem fair to tell me *not* to do it."

"She's done it?"

"Sure. She didn't tell you?"

Will glanced over at Cheyenne, who sat next to the girl. She gave them a thumbs up, and a smile touched his mouth. "She did not."

"Yeah. She popped some guy in the mouth at a gas station because he was smacking his girlfriend around."

"That's our girl." Will glanced up at him, his smile widening into a grin. "How did you find that out?"

"She told me."

The man beneath Will began to stir.

"Stay," Will told him.

Far off, sirens suddenly sounded.

"Cops," Rafe said.

"Troopers, probably." Will leaned harder on the man when he began to stir. Blood leaked from the guy's nose and mouth and streamed down the concrete in miniature red rivers.

"Motherfucker," the man muttered. "You're gonna regret this—"

Will hit him again. The sight of the hit—and the sound—at such close range, made Rafe flinch again, violently.

"Sorry," Will said.

The sirens grew closer. Cheyenne left the girl talking on her phone and approached them. She slid an arm around Rafe's shoulders and pulled him close.

"Her name's Amanda," Cheyenne said. "She's fifteen. Met him online. An Amber Alert went out this morning."

Will looked down at the man. "Wish I'd known that."

Rafe shivered at his tone.

Cheyenne reached out and touched Will's arm. "You did enough." She looked at Rafe. "Can you go sit with her for a minute?"

Rafe looked over at the girl. She was still on the phone.

"Please," Cheyenne added.

"Sure."

He stuck the rope under his arm and went over to where Amanda sat on the curb. He sat down beside her.

"I'm still here," she said into the phone, her voice thick with tears. Rafe looked at the bruises on her face, on her arms, on her legs, and part of him wished Will had killed the asshat.

He deserved it.

Amanda noticed him then, and looked away, down at the ground, and Rafe could see her shame. It made him angry. She had nothing to be ashamed of—she was just a kid. Like him. It wasn't fair, that the world was nothing like they said it was. All those stupid movies, painting it golden and filling it with love and kindness, when nothing could be further from the truth. Some people were good. But a lot of them were ugly and mean and not at all good. And it was damn hard, most of the time, to tell the difference.

Amanda looked over at Cheyenne, who stood beside Will, their heads bent close together. "The operator wants to talk to your mom again," she told Rafe.

Mom. The word jolted through him. He blinked at her stupidly.

"Can you get her?"

He looked over at Cheyenne and thought about using that word. *Mom.* Wondered how she would react. He couldn't imagine it—not today. But maybe…someday.

He lifted an arm and waved her over.

"What's up?" she asked when she got close.

Amanda held out the phone. "She wants to talk to you."

Cheyenne took the phone and stepped away from them. The wind picked up, and a wave of sand and dirt blew over them. Amanda shivered.

Rafe looked over at Will, where he stood guard over the man and thought about what he would do. Then he took off the fleece coat Cheyenne had bought him and laid it over the girl's lap. "Here."

She tucked it beneath her legs. "Thanks."

Silence fell. In the distance, the sirens grew closer.

"You okay?" Rafe asked.

"Yeah," she said, but tears leaked from the corners of her eyes in a steady stream, and her nose was running. She looked over at Will. "Is that your dad?"

"Nah," Rafe said. "That's Will. He's my friend."

"He saved me," Amanda whispered.

"Yeah, he's good at that."

She hiccupped. "I was so s-scared. I thought I was going to *die*."

"You're safe now," Rafe told her. He watched her for a long moment and then, hesitantly, slid his arm around her. "No one's gonna hurt you again."

He thought she would shrug him off or pull away. Instead, she bent her head to his shoulder and cried.

CHAPTER TWENTY-SIX

Rafe's soft snores filtered through the thin wall of the tent, seconded by Lucky's sighs and snorts, and between the two of them, they sounded like a couple of content piglets. Cheyenne stood staring into the dying campfire, smiling as she listened to them.

The worry that she might not be capable of being what Rafe needed—that she might not *feel* what she should—had died an abrupt death somewhere along the line, although she couldn't have pinpointed when or where. Maybe it happened when he'd lost it in Georgia's condo and trashed the place; perhaps it was simply the moment she realized what a great little person he was.

She didn't know, and she didn't care. He was *hers*.

Today, when he'd sat next to that young, brutalized girl and comforted her, Cheyenne had almost starting *bawling*.

He'd talked to Amanda, given her his coat, and held her while she cried. Cheyenne had watched, knowing he was better than she would ever be, knowing she didn't deserve him—not really—and so freaking proud of him, tears had filled her throat until she could hardly respond to the 911 operator's endless stream of questions. When she'd glanced over at Will to find him watching Rafe with that same pride stamped across his features, her chest had gone tight and she'd realized—*finally*—that she was totally, hopelessly screwed.

Because every time she looked at the man, she had to tell herself *no*. Bad idea. *Hormones do not happiness make.* But what he'd done today...well.

The war was over. And it was not reason or logic that prevailed. *Lust.*

Something which astounded her...but Will was right. It wasn't just sex. When he'd gone after that hairy SOB, her entire world had tilted. Shifted. *Opened.* And as she'd watched him unleash the darkness he held in such tight check, every one of her nerve endings stood to attention, an electric, almost painful sense of such heightened awareness, it made her skin prickle. If it hadn't been for the kids and the cops and the curious onlookers, she feared she would have pushed him to the pavement, right then and there, and had her way with him.

Even now, just looking at him where he stood at the mouth of their campsite, staring out at the risen moon, his body taut with tension, made the darkness in her rise, stretch, and reach for him. It wanted to *take*.

And to hell with the consequences.

The depth and power of that desire scared her. Intimidated her—when nothing intimidated her. That what she felt only continued to grow was both daunting and inexplicable. Her need had spilled far beyond the physical to permeate every barrier she'd ever constructed, until she wanted everything he was, all of the pieces, broken or not.

Which was, in all honestly, mildly terrifying.

Because this was a choice she was making. Something she would own—win or lose. But the thought of standing idly by out of fear was wholly unacceptable. She'd never allowed it before; why would she start now, with him?

Because it would hurt when he left?

Yes.

"Big hairy deal," she told herself.

Life hurt.

And to not take what she could—this gift that had brought her an awareness of herself she'd never expected—seemed wrong, somehow. A betrayal of something rare and precious.

Something that may never come again.

So while now was not the time and this was not the place, and in spite of the trepidation she felt, she'd decided she was going to grab this bull by the horns.

And ride him.

Yee haw!

"Nice," she muttered. "Classy."

But she was who she was...and Will seemed okay with that.

He'd been quiet after the rest stop. Wound tight and pensive—part of it was adrenaline residue, which she'd experienced herself, but there was something more going on, and she wondered if it had to do with finding his Senior Chief's name in Georgia's ledger. Or maybe the call he'd received from his fox. Both.

They'd forgone Wall Drug in favor of fast food, and the sun had been sinking in the western sky by the time they'd gotten to Badlands and picked out their campsite. The park had only a handful of people in it—the time of year was definitely on their side—and the only other folks in the campground were on the other side, a young couple in an old VW van who'd waved at them when they'd driven through.

They were quiet neighbors, and the only sounds were the rustle of the wind and the crackle of the dying fire. The air was cool and dry and reminded her so much of home, part of her ached. Cheyenne hadn't realized how much she loved the place she'd settled until she left it.

This trip had taught her far more than she'd expected. More than she'd ever realized she had left to learn.

An ignorant presumption—that she knew anything at all.

She strode over to Will and halted next to him. He was looking up at the Milky Way, his mouth a hard line as he took in the glittering twist of galaxy that pulsed and grew more vibrant as the sun faded beyond the horizon.

She leaned close and gave him a nudge. "You okay?"

He shook his head, silent.

"What?" she asked.

For a long moment, Cheyenne thought he wouldn't tell her. Then, "I wanted to kill him."

It took a second to understand. "And that's bad?"

"The beating used to be enough." He turned to look at her. "It isn't anymore."

"Well. It was never enough for me. But…I get it."

He watched her, his pale eyes glinting luminescent in the moonlight. "Do you?"

"Sure." She shrugged. "Your patience is gone."

"Meaning?"

"Meaning you have no more tolerance for the predatory assholes who inhabit this world. No more belief in the possibility of redemption, and no desire to turn the other cheek. You're done thinking they'll magically get *better*. They're like rabid dogs—so you just want to put them down."

"Christ," he said, staring at her.

"Judge, jury and executioner."

He lifted a hand and touched her scar gently, and she let him. "And that's okay? To be the one who decides?"

"Sometimes."

He shook his head again. "That goes against everything I've ever fought for."

"You fought because someone else decided. At least now you'll be doing the deciding."

Silence fell, and far off, a pack of coyotes yipped and snarled at the moon.

"It scares me," he said softly. "How clearly you see."

"Only what doesn't touch me."

His hand slid around her nape, warm, heavy, possessive. "Thank you."

She should have been accustomed to the flare of white heat that arrowed through her veins, the hollow ache that bloomed between her thighs, but she wasn't. It continued to steal her breath. To lash at her nerve endings and jump start her heart. "For what?"

When he slid the hand at her nape around her shoulders and pulled her into the hard plane of his body, she followed. "For being you."

Heat washed into her cheeks. He felt good, solid and warm against her. "Bloodthirsty and angry?"

He smiled down at her. He was a different man with that slashing curve; the darkness withdrew, leaving only grace in its wake. She wondered—not for the first time—which would win him.

"Human," he murmured. "When sometimes I feel more animal than man."

"Same coin," she said and shrugged. "No choice in that."

Will's hand curled tight around her shoulders, and he tugged her closer, until she pressed against him from breast to thigh, her cheek nestled against the muscle that padded his chest. His scent flooded her, and for a moment, she felt almost drunk on him, intoxicated by his heat and strength and the visceral response he drew with nothing more than his presence. His lips whispered over her hair, and his fingers stroked her arm, and she moved closer and wrapped her arms around his waist. For a long moment they stood like that, silent, staring out at the glittering sky as shadows pooled around them, and the creatures for whom dusk was dawn stirred in the undergrowth. It was nice, standing there in his arms, allowing herself to be sheltered. Giving what comfort she could. Dangerous, too. Far more so than the lust she'd been fighting.

This was...*intimacy*. A shared moment that had the power to create far stronger ties than sex. This, she suddenly understood, was the true danger inherent in following her libido. This...place where they collided and came to understand one another. Where they...*bonded.*

Which made her step back and tug from his hold, her heart suddenly pounding with sickening force. Will watched her with an intent gaze, his mouth hardening, as if he saw her struggle, but when she pulled away, he let her go.

"I need Rafe's laptop," he said as his warmth faded from her.

"Why?"

"Red sent me something I can't open on my phone."

Cheyenne nodded, grateful for the distraction. She went to the Jeep and retrieved Rafe's computer, carrying it over to the picnic table. When she opened it and turned it on, the light was jarring and alien in the darkness, its whirl and click as it loaded abnormally loud. Will sat down in front of it and reached up to tug Cheyenne down next to him. She went without argument, watching as he pulled up an email account and hit the link Red had sent.

Without warning, the screen filled with naked, writhing bodies. Moans and cries and *Oh God*s filled the air, and as Will hurriedly hit the mute button, Cheyenne giggled, in spite of the woman who dominated the screen.

Georgia Humboldt.

Engaged in an orgy of epic proportions. She rode one man—Malik—while another bent her over and prepared to mount her from behind—someone Cheyenne didn't recognize, but who Will *clearly* did. A bevy of men surrounded them, watching avidly, some touching themselves, some touching each other. Behind them, more bodies indulged in various sexual acts; whips and bondage and ball gags galore.

"Goodness," Cheyenne said into the silence. She might not have been experienced, but she was no prude—still, she was glad it was dark.

Because her cheeks were on freaking fire.

"Fuck," Will said softly, viciously.

"Clearly," she said. "I take it you recognize contestant number two?"

"Fuck," he said again.

"I'm sorry."

They watched in silence. Every so often, Georgia would look at the camera and smile, a wide, Cheshire grin that had nothing to do with sexual pleasure, while the men grunted and moaned and got off on each other as much as they were getting off on her. When Cheyenne snuck a look at Will, she found him staring at the screen with a look of utter disgust.

When he shut the video down and closed the laptop, she put a hand on his forearm before he could stand.

"Talk to me," she demanded.

He was tense, the muscle that roped him like steel beneath her touch. "Contestant number two is my fucking senior chief."

"And the reason he's in the book."

"Fuck."

"I should have guessed," Cheyenne said. "Sex was her weapon of choice. Where did this come from?"

"Malik's server."

"Your fox is good. Why would Malik keep this?"

Will turned to look at her. "I don't know. I assumed she was blackmailing him because of Rafe, but maybe they were partners. Malik's brother-in-law is El Hashen—the Pakistani Jihadists Georgia contacted to broker the cache."

"The ones she screwed over?"

"I didn't say it made sense."

"None of it makes sense." Cheyenne shook her head. "Why would Malik risk everything for her? His Ambassadorship, his marriage, his whole life… He has everything to lose. If he did this…it was about ideology. Because there is no upside. What about your senior chief?"

"That asshole."

"People have secrets, Will. Sex is often one of them. That doesn't mean he's the one who put you in firing range."

"Don't defend him."

"You feel betrayed because he screwed her?"

"Yes, I fucking do."

"Well, get over it. This isn't about you. This is about that cache and whoever reached out to her. Your senior chief… until now, you refused to believe he was involved—even when you found him in her book."

Will shook his head. "He's married to a Senator's daughter; they have four little kids. He's the most logical, level-headed man I've ever met. That he was a part of this makes me question everything I thought I knew about him."

Cheyenne squeezed Will's arm, thinking. "Who else knew about the weapons? You said kids found them…surely they told someone besides the US military?"

"Undoubtedly. I'm sure they told their families, their friends…but there's no connection to Georgia. She wasn't stationed in Afghanistan. And once the intel had been brought in, it went from the Rear Admiral to my Senior Chief, to my team. No one else knew."

"You're sure?"

"There's no way to be sure. But the only connection we found to *her* was Malik. And now...Ethan Scott."

The pain in him made Cheyenne slide her hand down his arm to spear her fingers through his and hold tight. "I'm sorry."

"Back to square one."

"No. The picture is filling in." She paused. "You should talk to him."

"I'd like to do more than talk."

She squeezed his hand. "Start with words."

Will's hand turned over and swallowed hers. His palm was rough and callused, and the rasp of it against hers made awareness prickle through her. It never ebbed, that bristling, steady hum of energy between them. Every move he made, his heat, his scent, the strength he wore so easily, all of it made her hyperaware of his proximity, of her attraction to him. Of the desire to have him *closer*.

"They arrested Frank James," he said.

"Her CIA partner? What for?"

"Treason."

"Her patsy."

"Yes." Will lifted her hand and pressed a gentle, lingering kiss against it. "Poor, stupid bastard."

It was ridiculous, how good he made her feel. That such a simple touch could send an arrow of blistering white heat through her and make her want to crawl into his lap.

Hopelessly, utterly screwed. No doubt about it.

"I want something from you," he said quietly.

Alarm prickled through her. "What?"

"A promise."

"Which is?"

His gaze met hers. "No more going it alone."

Cheyenne stiffened and tugged at her hand. "I don't need you to fight my battles."

"We fight together, baby. That's how this works."

Cheyenne stared at him, her heart beating furiously, the awareness that had prickled to life earlier flaring in alarm. Being alone was all she knew; she relied on *no one* and never had—not even Hank. The knowledge that she could fight any battle had been the only belief in herself she'd had for most of her life. To act together instead of alone…to trust him to be there to help…

Was she even capable of that? She didn't know.

For a long moment, she said nothing, and Will waited, patient, his eyes glinting in the moonlight, his hand warm and strong around hers.

"I will if you will," she said finally.

"Done," he said.

CHAPTER TWENTY-SEVEN

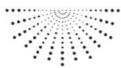

The Badlands creation began 69 million years ago, when an ancient sea covered what is today the Great American Plains. The buttes, pinnacles and spires of the Badlands were created by sediments left when the sea retreated, and with the further succession of rivers and floods across the land which deposited more sediment, the geologic formations continued to grow in size. While the sediment accumulation halted approximately 28 million years ago, the erosion which shapes the Badlands did not begin until 500,000 years ago. Erosion continues steadily today and ultimately, the Badlands will wear away entirely.

That thought struck Rafe as he stood before one of the large buttes with its striations of pale pink, dusky orange and violet touched by gray. His gaze traced the lines as they stretched along the row of formations, and he tried to imagine what the land looked like before the erosion began, how big this odd mix of rock and prairie had once truly been. Last year in science class, he'd learned that the planet was always changing, that there was no such thing as "forever" when it came to the Earth. Once upon a time, it had been covered in nothing but ice. At another, all of the continents had been one. Everything had, at some point, morphed into something else. What was now desert had been rainforest; what had been ocean was now desert. And on and on it went.

The idea of it fascinated him. Nothing stayed the same—not even the planet. Things were *meant* to change. Evolution didn't stop just because everyone walked upright. Nothing stopped—ever.

Energy can be neither created nor destroyed.

It simply was; constant, continuous, everlasting.

He liked the idea, and as he adjusted the screen on his phone in effort to film all of the formations without losing their grandeur, he thought it was comforting to know that change was *normal*. That things weren't supposed to be written in stone, because eventually that stone would wither away just like the buttes before him. Nothing was permanent.

The sun was just above the horizon, and the colors in the formations were brilliant where they were hit by the golden rays. In the shadow of the western faces, they were dark and muted. He tried to film both and do them justice, but knew he failed.

There were some things you just had to see to believe. He had a feeling this was one of them.

"You about ready, Mr. Spielberg?" Will asked from behind him.

Rafe looked at him over his shoulder. "Almost."

Will walked over and halted beside him. "Pretty spectacular."

Yes. Rafe had woken early and crept quietly from the tent. He'd watched the sun rise while Lucky explored their campsite. The chill of night had gradually been replaced by the creeping warmth of the sun, and as it slowly crawled across the land, the critters had come alive, birds singing, insects buzzing. More than one prairie dog had stood up from a safe distance and checked him out.

"What you did yesterday," he said to Will, because he'd been thinking about it ever since, "was the coolest thing I've ever seen anyone do."

Will only shrugged.

"No, really," Rafe said. "Most people just keep on walking. But you didn't. You *saved* her, Will. Changed her life. That's a big deal."

Will looked down at him. "It was the right thing to do."

Rafe shook his head. "I wouldn't have been that brave."

"You are that brave."

"No, I'm not."

Will crouched down to pet Lucky. Sunlight reflected off the lenses of the mirrored sunglasses he wore, but Rafe knew he was looking at him. "That night, when I was dreaming and I grabbed Cheyenne, you acted. You weren't thinking about yourself, you were thinking about *her*. That's what bravery is, Rafe. Putting yourself out in front of someone else. Nothing more."

Rafe thought about that. "That's different."

"Why?"

"Because…I didn't think you would hurt me."

"But I could have. You knew that."

Rafe shrugged.

"Don't sell yourself short, Rafe. There are enough folks out there who will do that for you. Besides, you were pretty awesome yourself."

"I was?"

"You gave that girl comfort in a way Cheyenne and I couldn't."

"What do you mean?"

"We're adults," Will said simply. "Like he was. But with

you, she could be the scared kid she was, and you didn't hold it against her. She felt safe with you, Rafe."

He stared at Will. Amanda hadn't moved, not until the cops put her into their car. She'd sat beside him on the curb, huddled under his coat, her head on his shoulder. His t-shirt had grown wet, and his arm had begun to ache where he held her, but he didn't protest, didn't move. Not a muscle. Because he knew she needed it. And it was little enough if it made her feel better.

"Not everyone would do what you did," Will told him seriously. "Not everyone could. Be proud of that, Rafe. I'm proud of you for it."

Rafe's chest tightened as he looked up at Will. "Yeah?"

"Absolutely."

Rafe nodded. He wanted to ask Will if he was going to stick around, if he and Cheyenne were going to be…*together*, but he didn't. Mostly because it wasn't his business. That, and he wasn't sure he wanted an answer. He liked Will. He wanted to *keep* Will. But that wasn't his call, and thinking about it just made him want it more, which pretty much guaranteed it wasn't going to happen.

So he just turned off his phone and stuck it in his pocket. He reached down to pick Lucky up. She licked his chin and snuggled closer and smiled at Will, who scratched her ears and made her groan.

"She's a sweetheart," Will said. "She's going to be a great dog."

Rafe hugged her tight. "Yeah."

"I need coffee," Cheyenne yelled suddenly, from where she stood next to the Jeep. "Or I won't be held responsible for my actions."

Will grinned at him. "At least she warned us."

Rafe took one last, lingering look at the Badlands and told himself it wouldn't be the last time he saw them. Then he turned to go. Will fell into step beside him and put a hand on his shoulder, something that made Rafe feel...safe. Cared for.

Will was his friend. With any luck, he would *always* be a friend. That didn't have to change.

No matter what happened.

"I have two words for you, boss: Georgia Humboldt." Will tilted his head back and stared into the blanket of stars that hovered above Devil's Tower. He didn't see them. Instead, he was imagining the look on his senior chief's face. "Care to explain?"

It was only because he'd always respected Ethan Scott that he was even presenting this opportunity. The sight of Ethan in that video had knocked Will down. Flummoxed him.

Infuriated him.

"Jesus Christ," Ethan muttered, and Will could almost see him, pinching the bridge of his nose, eyes closed, mouth tight. "How the hell did you find out?"

"You're very good," Will told him. "Straight-As-An-Arrow-Scott." A rough, ugly laugh. "I wouldn't have believed it if I hadn't seen it with my own eyes."

"Fuck," Ethan whispered.

"In Technicolor."

"That *bitch*."

"You get into bed with dogs, boss, you get fleas."

"She was blackmailing us."

"Us?"

"Everyone who was...involved."

"Is that why you told her about the cache?"

Silence. The wind lifted, and the scent of sage and pine and faint wood smoke filled Will's nostrils. He could see

Cheyenne through the trees, Rafe's shadow in the tent, the flicker of their fire against its metal enclosure. Next to him, the stark, arresting tower of phonolite porphyry that was Devil's Tower rose from the Wyoming landscape, alien and powerful even in the moonlight. The campground had only two other vehicles in it, a couple of Winnebagos parked on the other end, lightless and silent.

"It shames me," Ethan replied finally. "That you think I would betray my people like that."

"Didn't you?"

"No. I fucking did not."

Outrage quivered in Ethan's voice, more emotion than Will had ever heard from the man. It meant little. "Then who did? Because it was her in that desert, boss. Her and a team of mercs who knew exactly where we were—when we didn't even know until we got there—and her smoking bullet they pulled out of me...but you already know that. Don't you?"

"Yes. Will, there was nothing I could do without—"

"Exposure. I know. I get it. My career for yours."

"I never meant—"

"Save it." Will shook his head. "I don't give a shit."

"I do."

Will ground his teeth together. The rage that had flared to life the night before as he'd sat watching Georgia Humboldt's homemade porno caught flame, turning the calm that had settled over him in the last few days into ash. He wanted to smash something—preferably Ethan Scott's bland face. Earlier, he and Red had argued about having this conversation, Red being afraid it would somehow tip the scale, but Will didn't care. This man was someone he'd trusted. Someone he'd *believed* in. He wasn't going to pretend.

"Have you found the cache?" he asked, just for kicks.

"No."

"And the investigation file?" That he'd never delivered. "You lose that, too?"

"The file has been heavily redacted. It's useless. I didn't want to waste your time."

The darkness stirred, impatient and angry. "And your last message, the one that indicated you'd found something 'important'?"

"Yes. Georgia and Malik...they had a child."

Will stiffened. "I know."

"You do?"

He looked over at Rafe's slight shadow. "Yes."

"I'm afraid that could be a problem."

"For Malik," Will said coldly.

"And for the child."

Fury licked at the periphery of his vision. "He touches that child, he's a dead man."

"Malik isn't someone to make an idle threat against, Will."

"I don't do 'idle', boss."

"Damn it—"

"You knew. He knew. Who else knew? Another one of your fuck buddies?"

"Will—"

"She's going to bury you. You know that, right?"

"It doesn't have to happen that way."

Another raw, angry laugh. "Even dead, she's still playing—and winning."

Ethan swore softly. "Where are you?"

For a long moment, Will said nothing. The thought that Ethan had thrown them all under the bus because of an indiscriminate fuck enraged him. Even if he hadn't been the one to contact Georgia about the cache, he'd sat on his hands while the investigation was aborted and buried his men in treasonous silence. He'd *protected* her in order to protect himself. And was still doing so.

"What a fucking disappointment you are," he said.

He hung up and fought the urge to smash his phone against the asphalt beneath his feet. Blood chugged through his veins; in his ears, the drumbeat of his heart pounded with violent force.

Memory flickered. *Whoosh, whoosh, whoosh.* A spattering of gunfire. Screams.

Pain.

And he wanted blood. Violence. *Death.*

"Hey," Cheyenne said softly from behind him, and Will turned on her, the phone falling to the ground as his hands lifted to wrap her arms even as he knew he shouldn't touch her, knew he should run in the other goddamn direction as fast as he could. She didn't deserve his wrath, his damage, his pain; he didn't deserve *her.*

But it didn't matter. Control wavered, a mirage in the far distance. *Illusion.*

Will lifted her from the pavement and stepped from the walking trail into a cluster of lodge pole pines, where there was darkness and silence, nothing but her heat and her scent and the cacophony in his head. She made a sound—of consent or protest he didn't know—but her hands curled around his shoulders and held tight. She didn't fight as he pushed her against one of the rough tree trunks and took her mouth. When he freed her arms, she thrust her hands into his hair and held him tight as he slaked his thirst for blood with her taste, her heat, her sweet, eager welcome. She moaned into his mouth, and the endless hunger that lived within him overtook his need for carnage, turning it into another animal, one just as starved, but less bloody. He wrapped his arms around her in a hold she couldn't escape and squeezed her ass and hissed when she wrapped her legs around him and arched against his cock, a hot, wild feminine demand that threatened to undo him.

Blood roared in his head; he told himself to ease up, to cage the beast.

Give, not take.

But that only inflamed him, that idea, and the need to give back what she shared so selflessly consumed him. He ran his hand up her side, shoving up the t-shirt she wore, only vaguely aware of the ridged scars that rippled beneath his palm. Her bra annoyed him, but it only took a moment to destroy the small clip at the front that kept her from him, and then he held her perfect, beautiful breast in his hand. Such soft, succulent weight; he wanted her in his mouth.

Yes.

"Oh," she said, and he fucking loved it, because she always sounded so surprised, like she'd never before felt what he made her feel, like it was always an awakening.

He thumbed her nipple, tugged and twisted and then pinched, just a tiny bite, because he knew she liked that, and she hissed into his mouth and clenched him tighter, digging her fingers into his scalp. He felt the exquisite pull of it in his cock. She rose against him, her mouth a raw, wet demand, and sounds purred from her throat into his. He knew, if she let him, he could take her right there and pound them both into mindless, excruciating pleasure.

Fucking ecstasy.

But now was not the time; he wanted more from her than a quick, furious mating. No matter how tempting, how damn good it would be.

He tore his mouth from hers and lifted her higher, until he could see the filtered moonlight gilding her in pale silver, fingers of light that laced her breasts and tipped her nipples and shown white against the faint scars that traced the slope of her left breast. The sight of those scars made him ache, and he touched his mouth to them, a gentle, reverent press that made her tremble against him.

"Will," she whispered, and the sound of his name on her lips only made him hungrier, more determined to give her something she wouldn't want to be without.

He licked her nipple, flicked it with his tongue. A broken cry murmured from her.

"Rafe," she said raggedly.

"You can see him," Will muttered and suckled her.

"*Oh!*" she exclaimed and arched sharply, an offering he could not refuse, and he moved to her other breast and nipped her there, too, rubbing her with his tongue, sucking her deep into his mouth with strong pulls that made her gyrate against him in a rhythm that almost made him come.

He plucked at her free nipple, enjoying the wetness left by his mouth, awash in her scent, the song of her cries, the burning heat of her cradling his cock. The bite of her nails into his scalp streaked down his spine like live current; he pulsed and swelled and fought off release with gritted teeth.

"Will," she said again, a broken cry, but he slid his hand down and cupped between her legs, and she was so hot he shuddered. He scraped his teeth over her nipple and pressed his palm against her clit, hard, rough circles that made another *Oh!* echo sharply into the air.

"That's...that's *incredible*," she whispered into his ear, hot, damp approval that made his cock throb. "*Oh.* Don't stop. Please, don't stop."

He couldn't. Even if he tried.

Instead, he tore open the button of her cargos and slid his hand inside, a smooth glide that tucked his fingers beneath the sturdy band of her underwear, and then she was in his hand, her curls an erotic rasp against his palm and then just burning silken skin: slippery, delicate flesh that made his mouth water.

"So wet." He was deeply satisfied by the knowledge and kissed her again, swallowing the hungry sounds she made, sliding his fingers through the weeping, needy flesh that melted beneath his hand. He pushed his rough palm against her clit, more of those tight circles that made her shudder and grow tense against him. She responded fiercely to his kiss, as passionate, demanding and impatient as he felt. The muscles of her thighs quivered where she gripped him, and the scent of her filled the air, ratcheting his need until every muscle was like steel, and he clung desperately to control.

More.

One hand at her throat, gentle as he separated their mouths, her cry of protest a lash that burned him. He pushed her legs from his waist, down to the ground. Then he went to his knees before her. He yanked her pants and underwear down in a sweeping rush and left them tangled between her ankles, locking her into place, and wedged his shoulders between the strong, silky length of her thighs, nudging them wide apart. He steadied her with possessive hands shaping the ripe, bare curve of her hips as her hands went to his shoulders, where she held him with strong fingers that tangled in his shirt and dug into him.

"You smell so fucking good," he said roughly against her belly, flicking his tongue against the gentle swell, lingering on the small smattering of scars that trailed down her like a dusting of fine silver sand. "I want to taste you."

"We can't..." Her voice was thick, a deep rasp that licked at his nerve endings like live flame. He lifted her higher, nipped at the tender flesh above her mons. She shook in his hold, her breath surging from her in uneven bursts. *"Will."*

"Yes," he grated and put his mouth on her.

She whimpered.

Will slid his tongue into her sweltering, hot flesh, and the taste of her—spicy and sweet—exploded on his tongue, slid down his throat, and rooted deep. The sound he made was low and deep and rumbled in his chest, and she answered with a helpless moan of pleasure.

He delved with his tongue, holding her still for his exploration, and she shuddered violently beneath his hands, wild, hungry sounds breaking from her, making his cock twitch and surge in response. He stroked her tender opening, flicked her clit and nibbled on her succulent, vulnerable flesh as though it was the sweetest delicacy.

"I can't..." She gasped, and her nails scored him through his shirt. His hold tightened.

Fear in that cry.

He lifted his head and looked at her. Color filled her cheeks; even in the shadowed moonlight, he could see the flush that painted her skin. She was panting, her eyes closed, her mouth open and wet; her hair was a dark, wild cloud that clung to them both.

"Look at me," he murmured, squeezing her hips, holding her still.

Her lashes fluttered, and that dark, lush green gaze met his, pleasure and fear a palpable sheen in the pale light.

"I want you to come," he told her, his voice raw, his cock surging at the thought.

"It's stealing me," she said, her voice hushed. "I'm...afraid."

Something he never would have imagined: her, afraid. Of anything. But he understood. And that she would admit such a thing, here and now, to him...

Keeping her.

"You have to trust me, baby." He held her gaze and leaned in to flick his tongue against her clit. She jolted in his hold, her eyes rapt on him. When her tongue slid along her bottom lip, his cock threatened to burst, and he held very, very still in effort to maintain what little control he still had. "There's nothing to fear here. Just you and me and pleasure."

"So much pleasure," she whispered in open awe.

Everything within him tightened. "Yes."

And then he put his mouth back on her clit and suckled. Hard.

She came with a sharp, lush cry, the tremors that shook her nearly inciting his own orgasm. But he wanted more. He took every sweet drop she offered up, and when she finally stopped shaking, he started anew.

"That's...*oh*...too much. I'm..." And she shook her head, but she gripped him hard, and when he slid his thumb along the entrance to her body, dipping just the tip into the thick, wet moisture gathered there, she moaned, low and deep.

"Again," he said.

CHAPTER TWENTY-EIGHT

"That's a *bad* girl. Bad, bad, bad." Rafe wagged his finger at Lucky, who looked away guiltily and whined. "You go pee *outside*."

She hung her head, and he had to check the urge to rub it. Will warned him about that.

"You pet her, she thinks it's a reward. You discipline her, and let it settle in. Then you can pet her."

But it was hard. She was dang cute. And she looked devastated by the scolding.

Still, she couldn't just go around peeing everywhere. She'd whizzed all over the blanket from his ma this morning, and now here he was, rinsing it out in ice cold water at the camp spigot, his hands freezing, the smell of wet wool almost as bad as the smell of pee. On the far side of the campground, Cheyenne and Will were breaking camp and packing up the Jeep. They'd been oddly quiet this morning, but Rafe had seen Will touch her more than once—her hand, her scar—so he wasn't worried.

The blanket was heavy. He'd gotten it more wet than he'd meant to, and he'd gotten himself soaked. The bottom edge of the bright red and yellow creation was muddy from the puddle he was making, and he hefted it higher in effort to get it off the ground.

He hadn't planned on washing it, but Cheyenne told him she wasn't riding in a car for ten hours with a blanket covered in dog pee. He tried to bargain by offering to strap it to the roof of the Jeep, but Will just laughed, and Cheyenne ordered him to get scrubbing.

So he was scrubbing.

He'd gotten most of the pee out—he thought—so he stood, staggered a little beneath the weight and went to the road, where he laid it out so he could fold it. He figured he could try to squeeze out the extra water once he had it folded, because it wasn't manageable all spread out. He was folding it in half when Lucky suddenly barked.

Later, he wondered how he let it happen. He was a city boy who was—probably—being hunted by the man who'd fathered him, and his mother had stolen a butt load of bombs more than one person was looking for. No one should have been able to get the jump on him. But as he folded, he was staring up at the huge rock protrusion of Devil's Tower, watching the sunrise slowly creep up the ridged eastern face, and by the time Lucky warned him, and he turned around, it was too late. The man was already grabbing him.

Strong arms lifted him from the road and trapped his arms at his sides; a big, rough, dark hand that stank of cigarettes covered his nose and his mouth. He gulped, but there was no air, and he squealed and kicked and fought to breathe while Lucky raised holy hell.

The man said something to her in a language Rafe didn't recognize, and terror for her shot through him like a bullet. When the man lifted a booted foot and gave her a good kick, Rafe felt himself jerk, and heat burst through him in a dizzying rush. Fury exploded, and red bled into his vision, and he kicked back as hard as he could, desperately hoping he hit the guy's balls. The hand over his mouth loosened for a split second, and Rafe screamed for all he was worth.

"Wiiiiilllll!"

But then the hand was back, and the man was muttering, and they were turning toward a large black car. The trunk was swinging open, and Rafe understood then that was where he was headed.

He fought viciously, screams trapped in his throat, adrenaline surging through him, kicking, hitting, wiggling, but it was useless, like a leaf fighting the wind, and they grew closer and closer to the trunk as he fought to get free.

Just as the man bent over to dump him into the dark hole of the trunk, Rafe heard Lucky growling and snarling over the deafening beat of his heart, and Cheyenne yelled his name and then—

Darkness.

Cheyenne was running as soon she heard Lucky bark. The pup rarely made any noise. If she was barking, there was trouble.

The sight of the large black Caddy and the equally large black man who held Rafe made her heart lurch into her throat. Fear burst within every cell of her being, a terror unlike any other, and she ran as fast and hard as she could, half hysterical with the thought she wouldn't reach him in time.

That she wouldn't save him.

Rafe fought like a child possessed, but he was no match for the son of a bitch who lifted his foot and kicked Lucky aside, making the pup cry out sharply and sending her sprawling into the grass.

Kill. Him.

Cheyenne was halfway to him when Rafe screamed Will's name. A shadow streaked past her—Will, his huge strides eating up twice the ground of hers—and she was glad for it, because two against one was far better odds. And Will was armed.

Almost there—but the man was turning, and the trunk was opening and he was tossing Rafe inside. Cheyenne yelled at him, furious, terrified, and Lucky scrambled to her feet and went after the man as he slammed the trunk shut, clamping her sharp puppy teeth around his left ankle. He snarled at her and tried to kick her off, but she clung tenaciously, her growls savage. When he pulled a gun from the interior of his coat and aimed it at the pup, Cheyenne felt her world stop, but before he could fire, Will was plowing into him with such force they both went airborne.

Lucky let go and ducked; the men landed nearly five feet away, a tangle of brutal fists and kicking feet, sending a cloud of Wyoming dust into the air as they rolled across the ground. Cheyenne hurried to the trunk of the Caddy, and Rafe's desperate banging and muffled screams made something deep and dark and primitive rise within her.

Something that wanted blood. She had felt such things before, but not like this.

Never like this.

Because she could handle being fair game; that was life. But Rafe was off limits. He was fucking *sacred*. And anyone who threatened him would die.

"It's okay," she yelled and pounded on the trunk with her palm. "I'm here. I'll get you out. Just hold on!"

The Caddy's driver's side door was open, but the keys weren't in the ignition so she climbed in and rooted around for the trunk release—there had to be one—but it wasn't obvious. She went around the front of the car and strode to where Will and the man were fighting. Although Will was bleeding—from his lip, his nose, a deep, ugly cut above his eye—he was on top, straddling the man and pounding the crap out of him. But at that moment, the tables turned, and the black man rose from beneath Will with a loud roar and flipped Will to the ground, his own huge fist slamming into Will's jaw with a loud *thud* that made Cheyenne flinch.

She pulled her baton out of her pocket and snapped it to length. The men paid no attention to her. It was a simple matter to walk around behind them, set her stance and swing the baton for all she was worth into the back of the black man's skull.

Crack.

Just like a Louisville Slugger. The force reverberated in her bones, and as he fell over sideways, she kicked him for good measure. And then again, because it felt good.

Will was on him instantly, rolling the man face down into the dirt, climbing on top of him. One of his arms slid around the man's throat, and there was suddenly a knife in his hand, big and serrated, the ten inch blade glinting with a freshly honed sheen in the morning light.

Cheyenne stared at it, her breath frosty as it shuddered in and out, her heart threatening to shatter her ribs. For a moment she thought Will was simply going to slice the man's jugular and let him bleed out right there, at the foot of Devil's Tower while she watched. He adjusted his grip on the knife once, twice; he was sweating, a fine tremor shaking his limbs, and as his blood dripped down to streak his opponent's cheek, she could feel his struggle for control, the war he waged to in effort to deny himself the carnage he so clearly wanted.

Cheyenne stepped up beside him and laid her hand gently on his shoulder and squeezed. Because she wanted the asshole dead, too, she said nothing, acutely aware of Rafe's cries permeating the air, the thud of his fists against the trunk. Lucky whined softly from where she sat, just beneath the Caddy's license plate.

"I'm okay," Will grated. "Get him out of there."

"I need keys," she replied. "I can't find the release."

But before Will could search the man, the guy stirred beneath him, grunting and moving to push himself up until the tip of Will's blade nicked his Adam's apple. Then he went still. Very, very still.

"Who sent you?" Will asked him softly.

The man spat a word, something harsh and foreign, and Cheyenne kicked him again. When Will replied in the same guttural language, she blinked in surprise. The knife went deeper, until a little stream began to trickle down the man's neck, and although Cheyenne couldn't understand the words they spoke, she could tell Will was conveying his intent to gut the guy like a fish if he didn't talk.

Violence always translated. Another flurry of words from the man, all but one of which went in one ear and out the other.

Malik.

"Motherfucker." Cheyenne kicked him again, hard.

"The next one of you will be sent back in pieces," Will said in English, and his voice was so cold, so brutal, Cheyenne looked at him. "Including the Ambassador himself."

"I was only to take the boy, not harm him," the man muttered. "I don't kill children."

"Just their pets," Cheyenne growled.

"This is the only warning you'll get," Will told him. "Make sure he knows." And then he hit the man, a short, powerful blow to the temple that rendered the man unconscious. A moment later, he handed her the keys to the Caddy.

She ran to the trunk and opened it. Rafe's cries died, and

he stared up at her, blinking in the bright sunlight, his face awash in terror and tears.

"Is Lucky okay?" he whispered.

Cheyenne leaned over and scooped him up, staggering beneath his not inconsequential weight, and crushed him to her. "She's fine, sweet pea. Just fine."

Rafe clung to her and burst into huge, shuddering sobs that made him shake, and tears coalesced like acid in her throat, stung her eyes, trickled down her cheeks in salty streams.

Will was there then, carrying the black man in a fireman's hold, and he dumped him into the trunk of the Caddy, which bounced beneath the weight. He slammed the trunk shut, and Lucky barked, as if in approval. His arms surrounded her and Rafe a heartbeat later, and he held them tight as Rafe's sobs quieted. Cheyenne shook, furious and sick with adrenaline, her arms locked so tight around the boy she didn't know that she *could* let him go.

Will pressed a kiss to her head. "I took his phone, but someone probably heard that. We need to go."

Yes. Rafe's scream had sliced through the morning like the death cry of a fallen animal; guaranteed the echo had traveled for miles, and even though there were very few people at the monument, someone would have heard him. A Ranger wouldn't be far away.

Cheyenne nodded and pulled back. She set Rafe down and ran her hands down his arms, up his legs, making sure he was whole.

"I'm okay," he muttered, a huge shudder making him quake. "He didn't hurt me."

Rage licked at her calm, and she said nothing, not trusting herself. She didn't want to make it worse—because the urge to grab Will's knife and plant it deep into the black man's belly was tempting. So dangerously tempting.

Split him open like a—

"Cheyenne," Rafe said, his hands capturing hers. "I'm okay."

She met that dual-colored gaze and nodded, aware of the tears that continued to course her cheeks. Will's hand wrapped her nape, warm and strong, and squeezed, silent, powerful reassurance she absorbed like a sponge.

Falling into a weepy heap wasn't what she was worried about. Creating a bloody one was.

Will turned and went to retrieve Rafe's blanket, and Cheyenne forced herself to release the boy and step away. He immediately scooped Lucky into his arms, and she slathered him in puppy kisses and slobber.

"He kicked her," Rafe said, running his hands over her flanks.

"She's okay," Cheyenne told him. "She went after him, you know."

"Good girl," Rafe murmured to the pup, who thumped him with her tail.

Cheyenne reached out and rubbed her silky head. "She deserves a treat."

"*Rafe.*"

They both turned at the sound of Will's voice. He stood staring down at Rafe's blanket.

"What?" Rafe asked.

"Come here."

Something in his tone made the hair at Cheyenne's nape bristle. He stood motionless, fists clenched at his sides, his entire being so tense it made her spine ache. Dread blossomed, thorned and toxic in her belly. But Rafe didn't hesitate, and she was forced to follow him, until they both stood beside Will, staring down at the blanket.

"What?" Rafe asked again.

Will's gaze didn't waver, and Cheyenne tried to figure out

what he was looking at. The blanket was actually quite beautiful with neat rows of yellow and red squares. The border was a deeper red and along the bottom of one edge there was a tag sewn onto the blanket, a narrow ribbon of black satin with a line of golden embroidery—

"Where did you get this?"

The softness of Will's voice made her stiffen. Rafe looked up at him, his eyes widening. "My...my ma sent it to me."

"When?"

Cheyenne's heart began to beat hard and strong, and an ominous feeling of portent washed over her. She knelt down next to the blanket to get a better look.

"For my birthday," Rafe whispered. "Last month. Why?"

Because the glinting gold thread on the tag wasn't the name of the weaver. Or the weave. Or even washing instructions.

It was a set of GPS coordinates.

"Holy shite," she said.

CHAPTER TWENTY-NINE

*W*ill's brain knew immediately. It was his mind that needed a minute to make sense of what he was looking at. *What he was seeing.*

And then—

Here the whole fucking time. You stupid son of a bitch.

Will knew those coordinates. He's spent too many years in Afghanistan not to recognize the latitude and longitude instantly. Further east than Kabul, close to Pakistan.

Jalalabad.

"Are those what I think they are?" Cheyenne asked and looked up at him, her cheeks stained with dried tears, her eyes as dark as the forest behind them.

"Yes," he said.

"They were here all along."

"Yes."

"I…I don't understand," Rafe said, his voice trembling.

"We need to go," Will said again. Adrenaline was surging through him; the blows he'd taken throbbed, and his nose was bleeding. The hair at his nape was doing its *get the fuck outta here* dance. He'd known when he'd awoken that something was coming. And his skin was still itching.

This wasn't over.

He pulled out his knife and kneeled next to Cheyenne. Her scent washed over him, and the taste of her filled his mouth, and his heart threatened to pound its way out of his chest. Blood roared in his head.

Gunfire and screams and sand scouring every pore.

He fought viciously for control. Too much stimuli; memory bleeding over reality, every goddamn thing he felt swelling, a monstrous wave that would carry him from this place, this moment, and drown them all.

Cheyenne took his knife from him, and he watched while she cut the tag from the blanket and held it out to him. His hand shook as he accepted it, and he didn't argue when she leaned over and slid his knife back into the sheath he wore strapped to his belt.

"I don't understand," Rafe said again, and Will could hear his anger and fear, the borderline hysteria that rode him.

Almost getting kidnapped and being thrown into a trunk could do that to a kid.

"There are GPS coordinates on the tag," Cheyenne told him and stood. She reached out and wrapped an arm around his shoulders. The other she laid on Will's shoulder, and the tensile comfort of that touch brought his pulse down a notch.

"You mean…." Rafe looked at Will, and what little color he'd had, fled. He turned pale, and he swayed, and Cheyenne gripped him harder. "That's…that's where the bombs are?"

"Maybe," Will said, but that was bullshit, because he *knew* that's where they were. Every instinct he had was singing out, a fucking four-alarm choir of certainty.

"She put it on my blanket?" Rafe voice rose. He stared

down at the bright coverlet and squeezed Lucky so tight, she whined softly. "Why would she do that?"

"Easy," Cheyenne told him.

"I didn't know." His gaze flew to Will. Tears leaked from the corners of his eyes, and his voice grew panicked. "I swear, I didn't know, Will. It came in the mail and...*I didn't know.*"

Will's chest went tight, and he reached for the boy, pulling him into a fierce hug. "It's okay. I know."

So damn fragile. Nothing more than skin and bones; so easily broken. His heart had stopped at the sound of Rafe's scream, and the sight of that huge, ugly asshole swinging the boy into the trunk had sent terror shearing through him. The rage he held barely contained had surged to the surface and led the charge. If it hadn't been for Rafe, Will would have killed him.

"We should go," Cheyenne echoed his words, her voice urgent. Her hand squeezed his shoulder, and Will stood, carrying both Rafe and the pup. Cheyenne grabbed the blanket, and as they strode toward their camp, Will kept a sharp eye and ear out. For a Ranger, for anyone watching, for another one of Malik's people. The phone he'd taken from the asshole who'd tossed Rafe into his trunk was in his pocket, but it was a burner, and when he'd dialed the only recent number on the phone, a code had been required to connect. A code he didn't have.

He will send another, the man had warned. *He wants his son. I am only the first.*

Which was great fucking news.

The knowledge that he finally—*finally*—had the location of the cache was like a drumbeat in Will's skull. Every nerve prickled; every muscle was tense, waiting, ready to act. He had a location. A motherfucking location. All he had to do was find it. Retrieve the cache. Get it somewhere safe.

"I'm sorry," Rafe whispered, his head tucked beneath Will's chin.

"Don't be," Will told him. "How could you know?"

"I should have figured it out."

A harsh laugh caught in Will's throat. "I didn't figure it out. Cheyenne didn't figure it out. Why would you?"

"Because she was *my ma*. I should have known—" Rafe went tense in his arms and looked up at him so quickly, he nearly smacked Will in the jaw with his head. "Holy shit!"

He began to wiggle in Will's arms, and Lucky yipped, and Cheyenne said, "What?"

"Ruby!" he yelled, pushing against Will's hold. "Put me down. I gotta get something!"

"Huh?" Cheyenne said.

Will put him down, and Rafe raced toward the Jeep without responding. They quickly followed, and Will grabbed the bag with the tent in it and both sleeping bags as Cheyenne picked up the camp chairs, and they tossed everything in the back of the Jeep while Rafe dug through the backseat. Lucky looked on curiously.

"Is that everything?" Cheyenne asked.

She was pale and strained, her eyes dark in her face. Unlike that morning, when her cheeks had been flush with color every time she looked at him, her manner almost bashful, something which had surprised Will. But she hadn't shied from him, hadn't denied his touch, and when he'd pulled her behind the Jeep and put his mouth on hers, she'd wrapped herself around him and made him forget what day it was. There was nothing of that shared, secret pleasure left. Just reality.

Fear.

Will reached for her and pulled her into his arms. Her arms came around him and held on for dear life, and he realized she was shaking. He wanted to tell her it would all be okay, that nothing else bad would happen, but he knew it would be a lie. And she would know it, too. So he said nothing and just held her, swaying a little, and pressed a kiss to her hair.

"We have to go," she muttered, rubbing her cheek against him, and his heart squeezed tight in his chest, because in that moment, he understood how important she and Rafe had become.

Everything.

"I found it!" Rafe cried, startling them both. He opened the Jeep door and spilled out. In his hand, he held a greeting card sized envelope. "When we went to Letitia's, Ruby put this in my pack. She said it came for me, and she kept it because she didn't want her ma to get it, and so she stuck it in the outside pocket of my backpack when she pulled me into the bathroom!" Rafe took a breath, his words falling over each other as he tore the envelope open. "But I forgot about it, and then I got a new pack, and I didn't even remember she'd put it there and—it's a key!"

A key.

Will's hold on Cheyenne tightened.

Here the whole goddamn time.

Rafe held out the key, which was taped to a piece of plain white cardboard. There was nothing to go along with it: no hint of what it might unlock, no clues to where it fit, no words of any kind. Just a plain silver key taped to a piece of white board.

Will took it and slid it into his pocket. He could hear a vehicle approaching.

"Get in," he told Rafe.

"But—" Rafe said.

"Now," Cheyenne said and opened the door and pushed him in.

They climbed in after him, and within a minute they were

headed out of the monument, driving along the winding road that led back out to the freeway, the hills lit into deep red and orange by the rising sun. Silence permeated the Jeep.

"The key...that's important, right?" Rafe asked hesitantly. He sat forward, one hand on the back of Cheyenne's seat, one on Will's.

"Definitely," Will said.

"The location and a key," Cheyenne said. "My guess is you have what you need."

Everything within Will went still. "I'm not going anywhere," he told her softly, furious she would think—

"Will. You *have* to."

His hands gripped the steering wheel so tight, it groaned in protest. "I'm not leaving you."

"They're *bombs.*"

"I made you a fucking promise."

"Can't you call somebody?" Rafe asked, his face solemn in the rearview mirror. "Have them do it?"

"No one I trust," Will replied grimly.

Sad but true.

"You have to go get them," Cheyenne said quietly, her voice intense.

"No," he said shortly.

"We'll be okay—"

"Were you paying attention back there?" he demanded. "Because that wasn't about the cache. That was about Malik. *I'm not going anywhere.*"

"But the cache—"

"Fuck the cache."

Silence. The morning was golden, streams of light filtering through the pines as the sun continued to rise. The hills were covered in sage and pine and scrub brush, and high above, a hawk circled in search of breakfast. So calm and serene and beautiful; the antithesis of what he felt.

"You gotta go," Rafe said finally. "If those bombs go off and kill people...I don't wanna live with that."

"Me either," Cheyenne said.

"You aren't safe," Will bit out. "That asshole is only the beginning."

Next to him, Cheyenne went still. "Is that what he told you?"

"Yes."

"Shit," Rafe said.

Cheyenne shook her head sharply. "It doesn't matter. You still have to go."

"Christ," Will snarled.

"Seriously," she said. "We're almost home."

"And what then?" Will asked her. "Your army will defend you?"

She reached over, curled her hand over his thigh and squeezed. "If necessary."

"Army?" Rafe repeated.

"You have someone there?" Will asked, startled. *Someone else.* Something he hadn't even considered; something they'd never spoken of. He looked at her, and the ground shifted beneath him. "Who?"

"I can make some calls, if necessary," she replied calmly.

"Are they armed?"

"It's Wyoming. Everyone's armed."

"Who?" he asked again, unsettled by the thought.

"Angus has an entire crew of ranch hands. If I need them, they'll come."

"Who's Angus?" he wanted to know.

"A friend."

"What kind of friend?"

Cheyenne smiled at him, clearly amused. "An old one."

Will wondered what the hell that meant, but she only shook her head, her smile fading. "I mean it, Will. You need to deal with this. We can stop in Gillette and rent a car. You can take the Jeep to Denver—it's probably five, five and a half hours—and Denver has an international airport. You could be on your way by tonight."

He should have leapt at the chance. Half of his goal was within reach. But he wanted Malik's head on a pike, and everything within him rebelled at the thought of leaving them unguarded. He didn't give a shit about some yahoo named Angus and his collection of cowboys—*no one* would protect Cheyenne and Rafe like he would. He didn't trust anyone else to do the job. And his instincts were telling him that job was far from done.

"No," he repeated, his tone harsh with finality.

"Goddamn it," Cheyenne said and smacked him in the thigh. "Don't be a jackass about this. This is more important that we are."

Will looked at her. "Nothing is more important than you are."

She stared at him for a long moment, color slowly filling her cheeks. "Thank you for that. But you know I'm right. We'll go through Yellowstone. There will be people everywhere, and I know those roads like the back of my hand."

"Like there were people at the Badlands? At the Tower?"

"It's *Yellowstone*. There are always people. We'll be okay. And once we get home, we have the advantage. I have weapons. And friends. You have to trust me."

Son of a bitch.

She was right. That cache was bigger than all of them; no soldier would sacrifice an entire unit for the safety of a few. He knew better. But the thought of walking away from them —especially after what just happened—went against every cell of his being. It felt like betrayal, even though she was telling him to go. Another fucking failure.

"It's okay, Will," Rafe said, his gaze grave in the mirror.

The boy's eyes always struck him anew, their difference in color, their seriousness. The old man who looked back at him. "You have to go. Just...come back."

For a long moment, Will didn't say anything. It felt wrong, to leave them. Deep in his gut, wrenchingly *wrong*. But leaving that cache sitting anywhere unprotected was just as wrong. If it was even still there. Because there was no guarantee someone hadn't found it. Georgia hadn't been working alone. Malik, Ethan, Frank James...any one of the men in the book, in the video...just because the enemy was still faceless didn't make them any less of an enemy. And while he had friends in Afghanistan, there was no one he could send the key to and have them search out the cache. No one he trusted that much. He would have to go, see for himself. And then—if the cache was there—get it someplace safe.

"Fuck," he said.

And Cheyenne sighed, as if she'd heard his capitulation. "Stubborn man. Just like a mule."

"You have to go straight home," he told her, his voice tight, his stomach heavy with dread. "No more side trips, no more sightseeing. You go home and stay there."

"Cross my heart," she replied.

"I mean it, baby. No fucking around." His voice was harsh; fear for them filled his throat. "You get home, and you shoot at anything that moves until I get there."

"We'll be okay," she said again. "We're not the ones going into a war zone."

"I'll be fine."

She pinched his thigh, hard. "You'd better be."

CHAPTER THIRTY

*R*afe stared at the shimmering mass of Yellowstone Lake and wondered if he would ever see Will again. When they'd parted in Gillette, Will had hugged Rafe hard and told him he'd be back soon. But Rafe wasn't so sure. Because Will finally had what he'd been looking for all along: the location of the cache. So there wasn't really any reason for him to come back. And he wanted revenge, too; maybe when he found the bombs, he would figure out who Rafe's ma had been working with. Maybe he'd just go for blood and forget all about them.

It could happen.

Even though before Will left, he'd kissed Cheyenne —*really* kissed her—and told her to be careful, that he would see her in a few days. Even though he'd given her the wicked looking knife he carried and his gun.

Big hairy deal, because even Rafe knew you couldn't fly with weapons. It meant nothing that he'd left them with her. That he'd kissed her didn't even mean anything: lots of people kissed each other. It didn't tie them together. Will could have just as easily been kissing her goodbye.

It wasn't that Rafe didn't trust Will, that he thought Will was *lying*...he just knew things could change. That those bombs were bigger than him and way more important. And who knew what might happen when Will went to get them? Because Cheyenne was right, Afghanistan *was* a war zone, and SEAL or not, war was dangerous. Anything could happen.

So Rafe wasn't going to count on seeing him again.

On being rescued by him again.

The kidnapping attempt had scared the shit out of him. He hadn't had his taser or his knife—both of which were now in his pocket where they would live for the rest of his life—and hell, he hadn't even been paying attention. He'd been folding that damn blanket, totally assuming he was safe, which was just about the dumbest thing he'd ever done. No one was ever safe. Life didn't work like that. Shit, he *knew* he was a target; there was no excuse for his stupidity. Except that Cheyenne and Will made him feel safe. And in the end, they'd kept him that way. Still, he knew better.

The memory of that guy grabbing him replayed again and again in his head. He could feel the man's strength crushing him, smell the stink of his hand, remember how the carpet that lined the trunk felt pressed against his skin. And even though he now sat beside Cheyenne, Lucky in his lap, his heart still beat hard and fierce in his chest as the memory washed over him; his stomach still churned.

Rafe knew eventually that would fade. He'd had other messed up things happen; they always grew dimmer as time passed. But this...this might well happen again. And next time, he might not get away. He trusted Cheyenne to try to keep him safe, but she was just one person. One tiny—if ferocious—little person. Armed or not. Just one. And Will had said...

That asshole is only the beginning.

THE BEQUEST

Which was what Rafe was afraid of. So he tried to be hyperaware as they drove through Yellowstone National Park toward Cheyenne's home, of the tourists and their giant, house-sized campers as they jammed the roads to get a look at a grizzly, of the people who lingered outside the restrooms, of anyone who even looked at him sideways.

It was exhausting.

He hadn't gotten any video of Devil's Tower, but Cheyenne said they could go back. He hadn't gotten much video of Yellowstone, either, even though it was filled with wolves and grizzlies and giant, shaggy buffalo that lingered everywhere. Elk stood in clusters, grazing, and they'd seen a small black bear in a tree. There were bubbling mud pots and steaming pools and geysers that would suddenly shoot skyward as they passed.

According to the brochure they'd gotten at the east entrance, Yellowstone was a super volcano—the largest in the work. The Yellowstone Caldera was thirty-four by forty-five miles and was filled with magma. The Park was active, with several hundred earthquakes happening on a daily basis, and half of the world's geothermal features were located within its borders.

"There's no place like it on earth," Cheyenne told him.

It was massive and alien and beautiful. Even Yellowstone Lake was different than anything he'd ever seen. It wasn't as big as Lake Michigan, but it was surrounded by mountains and pine trees, and it had a weird feel to it, not bad, just... odd. Otherworldly, almost, as if they'd driven through some invisible barrier where everything was touched by magic. A fanciful thought, but it stuck with him. And, he thought, everything else aside, this was a place he would like to learn.

"You're very quiet," Cheyenne said as he pulled his phone out and began to take video of the lake.

Rafe only shrugged.

"I'm sorry about your blanket."

He looked at her. "What do you mean?"

"The coordinates." Cheyenne shook her head. "Your mom shouldn't have done that; none of this should have touched you. It was her final gift to you, and I'm sorry even that was tainted."

"Ain't your fault," he told her. "It was the nicest thing she ever gave me. I should've known something was up."

"That's just sad."

Yeah. It was. "I can't believe it was there the whole time."

"Right? It's almost funny."

He sighed. "I should have seen it. But Leon took it when it came, so I never really looked at it."

"Leon?"

"Ruby's brother. He's a dick."

"He took it from you?"

"Letitia gave it to him. Said my ma owed it to her."

"I should have kicked her ass."

Rafe smiled. "You did."

Cheyenne only shook her head.

"I only grabbed it, because he wasn't there," Rafe added. "I almost didn't."

"That's why Ruby hid the key? Because she knew they would take it?"

Ruby. Rafe's heart squeezed. "Yeah. She's a good kid."

"You miss her?"

He shrugged. "How much farther are we going?"

"A couple of hours, give or take."

In Rafe's lap, Lucky yawned and stretched, her little legs quivering. He swept a hand down her back, and she sighed and settled again. "You think Will is gonna be okay?"

"I don't know," Cheyenne said. "I hope so."

Rafe did, too.

"I think he's a tough SOB," she added. "And he has a better chance than most."

"What about us? You think we'll be okay?" Rafe waited for her answer, his chest tight. He hadn't meant to ask; he knew she couldn't predict the future. But she always told him the truth, and he *needed* the truth.

"Yes," she said.

"How?" he whispered.

"Because we're not helpless, sweet pea. We're not at their mercy. We decide. Not them."

"I feel helpless."

She looked at him then, her eyes serious. "Then we do something to make that feeling go away."

"Like what?"

"Whatever it takes."

Will was just north of Denver when his phone rang. He tensed, half expecting to see Cheyenne's name, terrified chaos had descended the moment he'd left them, but the display read "UNKNOWN."

Red.

"You rang?" Red asked.

"I found it."

"Define 'it.'"

"The location."

Silence. Will wondered if he'd lost him. Then, "Holy shit. *Holy shit!* Way to go, William. Where are they?"

"Afghanistan."

"Where in Afghanistan?"

Something in Red's tone made Will's skin tighten. A little too sharp. Too impatient. But who could blame him? They'd waited far too long.

"I'm on my way to collect them," Will said.

"You don't trust me?"

"I don't trust anyone."

A sigh. "Did you get any closer to discovering who reached out to her?"

"Your guess is as good as mine." Will paused as he changed lanes. "Malik went after Rafe this morning."

"Unsuccessfully, I presume?"

"You presume correctly."

"Did you have to kill anyone?"

"Not today. Not yet."

A soft laugh. "Where are you?"

"Just outside Denver."

"And the boy?"

"On his way home."

"With the guardian?"

Will didn't particularly care for Red's questions, even though they weren't unreasonable. Where Rafe and Cheyenne were was none of Red's business. And never would be.

"There were GPS coordinates," Will said. "And a key."

"Where?"

"Somewhere I should have seen them."

"Did the boy have them?"

Will only shook his head. "I'll let you know when I land in Kabul."

"You can't do this alone," Red told him. "You *shouldn't* do it alone. Tell me where they are. I can meet you."

"I'll handle it."

"Will—"

"*This is mine.*"

Another silence. "Alright, brother, you win. At least GPS is more exact than some random poppy field. I'll talk to you when you land."

The line disconnected, but Will sat frozen, phone in hand, and drove right past the exit for DIA. Red's words played and replayed in his head until they were a relentless, unending stream. Until the truth bled through and settled over him, as distinctive as a fingerprint. As irrefutable as DNA. A handful of thoughtless words that were, in effect, an admission.

An ingenuous confession.

Some random poppy field.

But there had been nothing random about that patch of poppies; someone had planted those blooms deliberately. A field of blossoms so vibrant it had glistened like scattered rubies among the desert scrub; "X" marking the spot. Something only his team—and Cheyenne—had known. Because Will had never mentioned it to anyone else. Not even Ethan. And sure as hell not Red. Ergo, Red would only know if Cheyenne had told him...

Or if Rye had.

"Son of a bitch," Will said.

He'd patently refused to believe any of his men were involved. He'd been *certain*. They'd all died—brutally, violently—and while Will knew double-cross was the name of the game when it came to the spooks, he'd *chosen* to believe in his men's innocence. He'd witnessed no subterfuge; none of them had shied from the battle which had ultimately killed them. There was no reason for him to believe any of them were involved...except, now, this.

But if Rye had reached out and told his brother about the weapons and—goddamn it—planned their theft and the execution of the team, why had he, too, ended up dead? Was it possible Red would murder his own brother for a handful of dirty bombs? Red, whose every move was—purportedly—about serving his own brand of justice to those he considered humanity's worst transgressors...a group he had clearly joined. And what connection could there possibly be between Red, Rye and Georgia? How had those paths crossed? Had Georgia betrayed them both?

How the hell did it all fit together?

Will didn't know. Because every single piece of information he had was supplied by Red. Every fact, every detail, every photo and file. He had only Red's word that it was someone with military ops who'd reached out to Georgia; only Red's insinuation that Malik or Ethan had been that someone. It was possible that connection didn't even exist, that Red had fabricated almost everything he'd told Will simply to steer Will exactly where Red wanted him to go.

Except for the video. No Photoshop was that good—and Ethan had copped to it.

But what had been left out? A picture could appear to be many different things when only half painted. What hadn't he seen? What didn't he know?

Will needed to think. He needed to sit down and *think*. Before he acted.

Red. Rye. And Georgia Humboldt.

"Fuck," he muttered.

He took the next exit and merged onto a ramp that would lead him to the airport. He dialed Cheyenne, but got her voicemail, and when he checked his watch realized she would be in the Park, where she'd warned there would be no service. He left her a brief, brusque message and put his phone away. His mind continued to churn.

Why go after the weapons?

Because Rye would have been jeopardizing his entire career—and Will knew Rye had valued that career. You didn't go into a war with a man and not come out knowing exactly who and what he was. And Rye had been a damn fine man, one Will had trusted, more than once, with his life.

So what the fuck was going on?

That Red had no clue what he'd inadvertently revealed

was the only upside—that and the fact that Will hadn't disclosed the location of the cache.

Sometimes it paid to be fucking paranoid.

But the only way Will was going to come out on top of this was by utilizing that slip—that and Red's massive ego. He already had bait. He simply needed a trap. An airtight, windowless trap—one with steel teeth and a snap powerful enough to break bone.

One from which the leader of the *Unnamed* could not escape.

Red was right about one thing: Will couldn't do it alone. The crates would take at least two men to move; there was no way he was going to get it done by himself. And he couldn't bring in anyone who knew anything about them, anyone who might—in any way, shape or form—be connected to them.

Will thought about the handful of men he called friends, those who wouldn't bat an eye at walking into this situation, one they were not necessarily guaranteed to walk back out of. Who were fearless and courageous and believed in purpose. Who were trustworthy. And a little nuts.

He slowed down as he approached the airport and picked up his phone, scrolled through his contacts and dialed.

Brodie McAllister answered immediately. "Blackheart, you crazy bastard. What's goin' on, hoss?"

"You bored yet?" Will asked, knowing Brodie had been stateside for the past six months.

"Hell yeah. Why? You got something cooking?"

"How fast can you get to Denver?"

CHAPTER THIRTY-ONE

Red's involved. He knows who you are, and where you're going. Call me as soon as you get home. And be fucking careful, baby.

"Fan-freaking-tastic," Cheyenne muttered as she slid her phone into her pocket.

Next to her, Rafe snored softly, slumped against the passenger side window, his breath fogging the glass. Poor kid. He was beat.

She was, too. The adventure that had played out over the last week had kicked her sideways, and nothing sounded better than her own bed and a cold beer.

She'd left Whitney a message and asked her to drop Chuck off at the house; she also needed to talk to Angus, but that was better done in person. Because after what had happened that morning, Cheyenne wasn't going it alone unless she had to, and Angus was well armed and mean. He also had a passel of wranglers who were young enough and tough enough not to shy from the situation at hand.

Will's reaction to the knowledge that she wasn't alone in the world—that she had friends who would help her—had been somewhat comical, and something Cheyenne hadn't ever expected to experience in relation to herself. *Jealousy.* That Angus was sixty-seven and very married with five grown children was something Cheyenne supposed she could have shared, but Will's obvious dismay had bemused her. And warmed her, whether she wanted to admit it or not.

What they'd done in the shadowed forest of Devil's Tower continued to haunt her. Even with all that had happened since, the memory clung. The deep rasp of Will's voice, the roughness of his hands, the pleasure of his mouth... The stolen moments they'd shared would tear through her at random, unexpected, *potent*, and heat would burn in her veins. Sometimes she could *feel* him, still holding her, still stroking her, still using his mouth to drive her toward orgasm.

Orgasm.

What a fine how-do-you-do that had been! No wonder people lost their marbles over sex. Such pleasure... Cheyenne had never imagined such a thing existed. Mindless and unbound by morality or self-awareness. *Free.* Utterly and completely, for the first time in her life. Without care, wholly unconscious of her fears, her anger, her scars. Pure physical being; lost in ecstasy.

She knew it would not have been that way if she didn't trust Will. If he hadn't gone out of his way to try to give her back something that had once been taken from her. And *that* realization had shaken her.

Deeply.

Because what he'd done wasn't about sex—not really. It was about giving. About trust. Maybe even love.

Love.

"You are so fucked," she whispered.

Love. Something she'd spent most of her life scoffing at.

Oh, she'd loved Hank—and Whitney, too, she supposed. And maybe even Angus. But that wasn't what she felt for Will.

Not even close. How was it possible? That in—what? Six days she could *love* someone...?

"That's just *stupid,*" she told herself.

But was it, really? Because she was pretty sure she'd fallen head over heels for Rafe—and that hadn't even taken one day. And in spite of all she didn't know about Will—his past, his dreams, hell even where he lived—she felt she *knew* him. She understood him in a way she'd never understood anyone, had never tried to understand anyone. And—terrifying though it was—he seemed to understand her.

Not that it meant anything. Will was on the hunt. He wanted justice, vengeance. *Blood.* Who knew if she'd ever see him again. And now...*Red is involved.*

Will's fox, someone he'd seemed to trust. Another betrayal, another blow. Question was—how did he know? And had he shared the location of the cache with Red *before* he'd figured it out? Was he now a target?

Fucking Afghanistan. What do you think?

Fear for him gnawed at her, but he was tough, and he knew what he was doing. Another form of trust—that he would keep himself safe. That he would accomplish his mission and get those damn bombs taken care of. That he would return.

Because there was still Malik to deal with. And Cheyenne was far beyond pissed off when it came to the Ambassador. She was ready to shoot first and ask questions later. Watching that asshole throw Rafe into his trunk had been the final straw, and the terror shadowing Rafe all day made her see red. She could almost smell his fear.

Cheyenne knew what it was to exist in that dark, horrifying place, and she would be damned before she condemned him to that. They would have to *kill* her. So tomorrow Rafe would learn how to defend himself. Ten wasn't too young to learn to shoot—not out here, where kids were bagging elk at that age—and weapons were a fact of life. She would teach him everything he needed to know and sign him up for hunter's safety classes. She would give him some form of self-assurance. Knowledge. Arm him as best she could to deal with the future.

The foggy, unknown future.

There was also the issue Will had raised: whether or not to publicly name Malik as Rafe's father. Cheyenne understood she was going to have to make that call, and while she would have been happy to let that secret lie until Rafe was older and more prepared to deal with it himself, this morning's attempted kidnapping had burned her good will to ash. If she had to go public to protect Rafe, she would. Fallout be damned.

Fuck it.

At least they would be home soon. Grand Teton Park lay to the west as they headed south down through the Jackson Hole valley. The sun was sinking slowing beyond the Teton Range, casting long fingers of light across the valley floor; flecks of gold glinted atop the surface of the Snake River, aspen trees fluttered in the breeze. The sight of those familiar peaks made Cheyenne's throat swell.

Home.

She hadn't realized what home was until she'd left it. That after all these years she did in fact have a home—and this was it. That this place soothed her soul and made her feel like she belonged. That it was far more valuable than she'd ever before understood.

She hoped Rafe would—someday—feel the same way. Because she wanted to give him a home. A life. Everything she'd never had.

"Are we almost there?" he mumbled, sitting up to rub his eyes.

"Ten minutes," she told him.

He looked out the window, and his eyes widened. "Holy shit."

Cheyenne sighed. They were going to have to talk about his language. He couldn't go around talking like a trucker—which meant she was going to have to stop talking like a trucker.

"Tomorrow," she said.

"Huh?" he asked.

"Nothing."

They traveled in silence, Rafe and Lucky staring out the window at the mountain range that speared from the valley floor like a row of jagged teeth. The lack of foothills created a stunning vista, unlike any in the world. Shimmering, blue-green lakes lapped gently at the base of the range, some sandy bottomed and shallow enough to stand in, others deep and cold and thick with trout.

"Wow," Rafe said softly. "You really live here?"

"True story," she replied.

He shook his head.

"What?" she asked.

"I never knew places like this…Yellowstone…existed."

"I didn't either, not at your age."

"How'd you end up here?"

Cheyenne considered that. Rafe would never hear the story she'd shared with Will—regardless of how old he got to be. It would only hurt him. But everything else was fair game. And she couldn't expect him to talk to her if she didn't talk to him.

"When I left Haven, I went to the bus station," she told him. "I had eighty-seven dollars and thirteen cents and no clue where I was going. And then, when I looked up at the route board, I saw Cheyenne, Wyoming as a destination—and it cost eighty-five dollars. I took it as a sign." She shrugged. "It seemed as good a place as any."

"Is Cheyenne like this?"

"No. It's pretty...but not like this."

"Then how'd you get from there to here?"

A wry smile curved her mouth. "I tried to steal a truck and got caught."

"Like...hot wire it?"

"Yeah."

"You know how to do that?"

"Yeah."

"Will you teach me?"

Cheyenne slid him a look. "We'll see."

"So what happened?"

"The guy who owned the truck was a rancher from Jackson. He told me that either I came back to his ranch and worked off the damage—I'd busted one of the windows—or he called the sheriff. So I ended up at his ranch. That ranch right there, as a matter of fact." Cheyenne pointed it out as she turned onto the gravel road that traveled along the western edge of the ranch property. "The Lone Pine. It's a cattle ranch that doubles as a dude ranch in the summer. I cleaned rooms, mucked stalls, helped in the kitchen—whatever they needed."

"And you liked it?"

She'd hated it at first. The work was hard and relentless—but it was honest, and once she'd paid her debt, it had given her the first real money she'd ever had. That Hank had never pressed her about her age or her past beyond one initial question when he'd caught her hotwiring his truck had enabled her to trust him and had allowed her a safe place to live until she'd turned eighteen. The only thing he'd insisted on was her getting her GED, which she'd done. And Mabel—

the cook—and Angus—the ranch foreman—and Hank had become her de facto family.

They'd saved her life.

"Yeah," she said softly. "He was a good man, and he taught me a lot about being a decent person. I miss him."

"Is he...dead?"

"Yes, several years ago."

"I'm sorry."

Cheyenne glanced at Rafe and smiled. Such a great little person he was. "Thank you."

"What happened to the ranch when he died?"

"His son inherited it. He runs it now."

"Do you still live there?" Rafe looked out at the large, two-story log building that sat back from the road, perched atop a small hill that overlooked the rolling pasture filled with grazing cattle.

"No. I own a small piece of property on the western edge. He sold it to me for pennies before he died."

"He was your family," Rafe said solemnly, watching her.

A thrush filled her throat. "Yes." She met that bi-colored gaze. "Like you're my family."

Rafe stared at her for a long, silent moment before nodding. "Family...it isn't really about blood, is it?"

"Some would say it is. But for those of us who don't have any blood ties, I think it's about whoever you love."

They continued on, Rafe absorbing the details of the sprawling ranch, lifting a hesitant hand to wave back at the ranch hands who waved as they rode past in the fields, rounding up strays.

Cheyenne turned into her driveway, relived to see her small, two-story cabin sitting in vivid relief against the backdrop of the mountains. By the time they pulled up in front of the garage, she could hear Dexter bleating like the crazy goat he was, and Harry was sitting on the railing of the front porch, his tail twitching as he watched them with his one pale green eye.

Lucky growled at him in the back of her throat.

"He'll kick your canine ass," Cheyenne told her.

Dexter began to bleat louder. Harry meowed. And from inside the cabin, Chuck started to bark.

"Home sweet home," Cheyenne said.

CHAPTER THIRTY-TWO

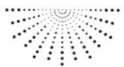

Jalalabad was, in Will's opinion, Afghanistan's most beautiful city.

Surprisingly green and lush, the capital of the Nangarhar Province sat at the junction of the Kabul and Kunar Rivers and served as both a social and financial epicenter due to its proximity to the Pakistan border. All manner of products from Pakistan were traded within the city, which also laid claim to being the capital of Afghan cricket and housed Afghanistan's second largest university.

The sun was rising over the city as Will and Brodie arrived, passengers in an aging box truck being driven by Ali Sahar, an Afghani rug dealer whose life Will had once saved. They wore traditional perahan tunbaans and turbans and were careful to keep their distinctly American features covered.

It had taken twenty-six hours to make the trip to Kabul from Denver via D.C. and Dubai. As luck would have it, Brodie had been in Estes Park visiting his sister; they'd flown out of DIA at 4:45 sharp. When they'd landed in D.C., there'd been a text from Cheyenne on Will's phone.

COME BACK ALIVE OR WE WILL KICK YOUR ASS SEVEN WAYS TO SUNDAY.

Love, C&R

P.S. Home Sweet Home!

P.S.S. Got ur message. Time to call out the hounds.

A day later—and ten hours ahead of the time zone they'd left—they arrived at the Kabul airport, where Ali had agreed to retrieve them in his rug delivery truck. Ali didn't know where they were going or what they were doing, and he hadn't asked. As far as he was concerned, he owed Will his life, and he would do whatever it took to repay that debt. A widower with three grown daughters and a fondness for American movies, Ali had been Will's friend since his first tour and was one of the few people in Afghanistan Will trusted.

It was not Will's first inclination to involve his old friend in this sordid mess, but as Brodie had been quick to point out, a native would be "damn handy" to have around. A native who understood the intricacies of Afghan society, who could come and go with little notice, who had access to a vehicle large enough to move the cache—and a wholehearted willingness to help.

But he was staying in the goddamn truck.

Brodie, on the other hand, was going to be an active participant. A friend since their mutual rodeo circuit days, Brodie was now an Army Ranger, and it was his connections at the base in Bagram to whom they would deliver the cache. Will wasn't thrilled about delivering them to anyone with bars on their chest, but he sure as hell wasn't going to sit on a semi-nuclear arsenal half of the U.S. military was actively seeking. And bars were better than bandits. He would simply have to trust—again.

But first they had to collect the weapons. Then they would deal with Red.

On the flight from D.C., Will had found himself going over every word he'd ever exchanged with Rye's brother, seeking the clues he had to have missed. Every piece of information Red had delivered, every insinuation he'd made. But there was nothing, and if it hadn't been for Red's inadvertent comment about the poppy field, Will would have called him when they'd landed in Kabul and told him where they were headed.

He hadn't made that call. Not yet. But he would.

Worry for Cheyenne and Rafe continued to gnaw at him, in spite of the text he'd received. That Malik would go after Rafe so publically did not bode well. He would do it again; Will was certain. That meant Will needed to get this shit taken care of and get back there before Malik made another move. Which also meant he had to shove the anxiety that rode him into that dark, chaotic place where all of his rage lived and concentrate on the matter at hand—or he would end up dead and of no use to Cheyenne and Rafe. No use to anyone.

The GPS coordinates that had been sewn onto Rafe's blanket led them to the industrial part of the city where large warehouses lined the narrow streets, and shipments of oranges, rice and sugarcane were in constant motion, coming and going as the market demanded. Ali parked the truck in an unobtrusive spot, and when Will told him to stay put, smiled his broad, quiet smile, his brown eyes gleaming in the bright morning sunlight as he told Will not to worry so much.

Locating the correct building was an inexact science, but none of the buildings along the street were secured with the kind of padlock the key in Will's pocket would fit except for the last one, squat and grey with a sagging metal roof and pigeons roosting along its eaves. When the key fit perfectly, the heavy beat of Will's heart echoed in his skull, and a chaotic mix of adrenaline and rage coalesced within him. For one brief moment, he couldn't breathe. But then Brodie nudged him, and the key turned, and the lock popped open, and then they were stepping into the dark, cool space where only small pockets of sunlight hinted at what lay within.

"I smell death," Brodie muttered.

Will did, too. Old death, the kind that had been overlooked. Or ignored.

They split up, each armed with an old AK-47, which Ali had managed to secure. Will went right, Brodie left, and in the dim light, they moved cautiously through the large space. The scent of death grew, and when they found the bodies—two of them, men partially decayed—neither was surprised. The men were sprawled in the rear of the building, their weapons still resting next to them, clad in black Kevlar.

Behind them sat the crates Will had watched his team die for.

"That what we're lookin' for, hoss?" Brodie asked.

But Will didn't respond. Instead, he stood there, staring at the wooden boxes while anarchy warred with cold control; the need to destroy fought with the awareness that logic and reason were the only way forward.

Gunfire and screams, and the deafening throb of the rotors; sand blasting him like crushed glass; men stalking toward him.

That fucking laugh.

Blood in his mouth, wheezing from his lips; his arm hanging at his side, damaged, useless; his hip collapsing beneath him like a broken stool. And then—

Cheyenne. Rafe.

Lucky licking him.

Will's chest tightened; blood roared in his head. Brodie reached out a hand and clasped his shoulder.

"Hoss," he murmured and squeezed.

Just breathe.

It took Will a good minute and a half to regain his precarious control. To slow his heart and make certain he wasn't having a coronary, to unlock his frozen limbs and go over to the crates and lay a hand atop the sculpted Arabic lettering that decorated the wood.

Brodie said nothing, watching as Will unstrapped the top crate and lifted it to check the contents. The bombs lay safely nestled within their bed of straw, manufactured death in neat little rows.

Relief flooded Will, so powerful his knees went weak.

"Yes?" Brodie persisted.

Will met his gaze. "Yes."

"Good. Then let's get them loaded, and get the fuck out of here."

Will nodded and replaced the lid, strapping it securely back into place. His heart beat heavily, and he wanted a fucking cigarette, but he'd left them behind somewhere and hadn't bought any more.

Brodie leaned down and picked up the weapons that lay next to the dead men. "Well, look at that: an upgrade."

He handed one to Will. Will checked the clip; almost full.

"I'll get Ali," Brodie said and disappeared.

A loading door sat along the eastern wall. As Will walked over to it, the pigeons overhead cooed and watched him with interest. Apparently living with the dead didn't bother them.

The dead.

Georgia's mercs. Will was certain. Although he had no clear memory of the men whose flesh was slowly disintegrating to the hard packed dirt floor, instinct told him they were there that night. *Something* inside him remembered them. Reviled them.

Reveled in the scent of their decay.

Had Georgia killed them? Murdered them and left them to rot with her spoils—so much easier than disposing of their bodies in a country where women were not allowed the freedom to move unaccompanied through the streets. If that were true, then no one had been here since that night. Not her. Not Red. Not anyone.

The door squealed like an angry pig when Will opened it, but no one paid any heed. Ali backed up the truck, and Brodie and Will loaded the crates silently, securing them carefully in the back of the truck with several of the rugs Ali had stored there.

Will replaced the padlock and closed the loading door. Then he and Brodie climbed into the truck.

Ali looked at him solemnly. "We go?"

"Yes."

Brodie watched the mirror. Will held his gun in his lap. Ali pulled out and turned them toward Kabul.

Rafe stared at the screen of his laptop, but the video he was watching passed through his brain, unnoticed. Pipestone, the Badlands, Yellowstone Lake...they played out before him, accompanied by brief snippets of Cheyenne and Will and Lucky chasing her tail.

But Rafe didn't see them.

He'd come out to the deck to work on his movie and to let Cheyenne talk to her friend Whitney—who kept staring at him as if she expected him to *steal* something—but there were too many distractions. Like thinking about his new room—a large, square room with a big log bed covered in a thick blue quilt and a picture window that overlooked the Tetons, a room lined with shelves of books and a built-in a desk for his computer. Then there were his new siblings: Chuck the cattle dog and Harry the Maine Coone and Dexter the goat, whose tendency to butt his head against everything—including Rafe's backside—totally freaked Rafe out.

If that wasn't enough, today Rafe had learned how to shoot. Angus—a grizzled, ornery old man who'd called him 'son' and spit tobacco to the ground every two minutes—had come up from the ranch, and he and Cheyenne had spent almost two hours teaching Rafe how to load, aim, fire and clean a .22 rifle.

Rafe had seen more than one gun in his time—in the neighborhoods he'd grown up in they were more common than cars—but he'd never held one, especially not a rifle, and he'd never fired one. The .22 had a long barrel and a pretty wooden stock and the kickback—once he'd gotten used to it—wasn't bad at all. It surprised Rafe, how good a shot he was, hitting the soda cans Angus had lined up along a downed tree two times out of three.

It made him feel good. And while he didn't relish the idea of ever having to shoot at anyone—because there'd been plenty of that in his neighborhood, too—he was glad he at least knew how. That if someone came, he could grab that gun and defend himself. Defend Cheyenne. Not that she needed it. She'd hit the cans every time.

Along with the lesson had come a lecture about guns not being toys, about always keeping the safety on, about never leaving it loaded and unattended. But Rafe didn't need the lecture. He'd seen people die from guns. He knew better.

On top of all that, Rafe was worried about Will. It had been a day and a half since Will left them in Gillette, and Cheyenne hadn't heard anything. *Nothing.* And that made Rafe anxious. Cheyenne said it would take a whole day for Will to get where he was going, so they shouldn't worry, but Rafe did anyway.

About Will. About Malik—even though no one had tried to kidnap him today—and about the future. About suddenly finding himself somewhere so foreign, he might as well be on the moon.

This place…it was crazy beautiful. Like a movie. So quiet Rafe could hear the grass whisper when the wind blew. And last night, he'd seen the Milky Way for the first time ever. The Big Dipper, the Little Dipper, Orion's Belt… He and Cheyenne had laid on the deck, ticking off the constellations, a million glittering diamonds winking down at him. And today, the scents of the ranch, the cattle, water and mud and hay; the cows mooing, the horses whinnying, the cowboys yelling "hee-ya!" as they herded the livestock from one pasture to the next. It was a whole new world, one Rafe knew nothing about. One he worried he might not fit into.

Cheyenne told him he would learn, that he was like she'd been, that it was okay. And when he looked over at the mountains that drew the border between Wyoming and Idaho, he thought maybe she was right, because they made him feel…home. They *spoke* to him. But everything else… like a fish out of water.

"Whatcha doin', Rafe?"

He looked up to see Whitney's daughter, Sasha, standing behind patio screen door that led from the living room out onto the deck, and for a moment the image of Ruby flashed through his brain, his last sight of her, and in his chest, his heart grew heavy.

"Nothing," he muttered and turned away.

He heard the door slide open and sighed. Sasha was— maybe—seven and so beautiful, just looking at her hurt his eyes. Long, curly, white-blond hair, big, bright blue eyes, cheeks rosy with color. She looked like a doll. Perfect and unreal, as far from him as the city he'd left behind.

She walked up and stood beside him, where he sat on one of the padded chairs, and looked down at his laptop with pursed lips. "What's that?"

"Nothing, I said."

He could feel those big blue eyes focus on him, but she said nothing. Just stood there, staring at him.

"What?" he asked, annoyed.

"How come you don't like me?"

The question, small and hesitant, jolted through him. Rafe turned to look at her. He didn't know what to say. He didn't *not* like her. He just didn't know her. Didn't know anyone.

"I like you fine," he mumbled.

"No, you don't. I can tell."

"How can you tell?"

"Because your face is like this." She scrunched her features into a hideous expression that almost made him laugh.

"I'm just…tired," he said.

Sasha smiled at him, so piercing and brilliant Rafe feared he might go blind. "That's okay," she told him and hurried to take the chair beside him. "You came from far away, huh?"

"Yeah."

"You're my cousin, you know."

Rafe arched a brow. "How's that?"

"You're my Aunt Cheyenne's son, so that makes you my cousin."

Rafe was pretty sure Cheyenne wasn't this girl's aunt, but then he remembered that family didn't have much to do with blood and said nothing.

"Your mom died, huh?"

She was staring at him with those beautiful eyes—as blue as the sky, flecked with odd bits of silver—her expression serious.

"Yeah," he said again.

She nodded and turned to point at the mountains. "You see that one there, like with the kinda square top? That's Mount Moran. That's where my dad died."

Rafe looked over at the mountain she pointed to—which did have a kind of square top compared to the sharp peaks of the rest of the range. "What happened?"

"He was climbing," she said solemnly. "And he fell."

"I'm sorry," Rafe told her.

She shrugged. "I was only three. I don't remember him. Do you remember your mom?"

For a long moment, Rafe didn't reply. Then, "I remember her."

Sasha watched him, her gaze alarmingly astute. "What was she like?"

He said nothing. There was nothing good he could say, and the last thing he wanted to do was to talk about his ma. Or his pop. Especially with this perfect, doll-like little girl who might as well be a Martian for all they had in common.

But Sasha laid a soft hand on his arm and leaned toward him and said. "It's okay. I don't like to talk about my dad, either. We don't have to talk about her if you don't want." She sat up and smiled at him again, pure human sunlight. "Are you going to go to Kid's Camp? Me and Kendall are gonna go. It's so cool. We go swimming and hiking and to the museum! There's games and bird watching and bike rides!"

"I don't ride bikes," Rafe replied, for lack of anything better.

She looked scandalized. "How come?"

"I don't know how."

She blinked. "You don't?"

Bikes hadn't been exactly plentiful where he'd come from, and her incredulity made him defensive. "No. So what? I don't care."

"Don't worry," she told him and patted his arm. "I can teach you."

Rafe stared at her. "Yeah?"

"Sure!" She nodded enthusiastically. "I'm good at bike riding."

"You're probably good at everything," he muttered.

"No, I'm not. I'm bad at math. And I always burn the toast."

Which made him smile, in spite of himself.

"I didn't know people could have two different colored eyes," she continued conversationally. "My grandma had a cat once, Samson. He had one green eye and one brown one. And his tail was crooked because my grandpa ran over it with the wheelbarrow." A gusty sigh. "So...do you wanna be my friend?" She tilted her head and offered him another blinding smile. "I'm very charming. Everyone says so."

That, Rafe could believe. He looked over at the mountains, aware of Sasha's small hand on his arm. He thought about the friends he'd left behind, a handful of kids just like himself—latchkey, poor, struggling for *more*—and understood that *here* could be different.

He could be different. *We decide. Not them.* And he could decide whatever he liked.

"Okay," he said.

CHAPTER THIRTY-THREE

"*D*id you just get in?"

The hair at Will's nape bristled, and he wondered how the hell it had happened, that he hadn't heard —hadn't *felt*—what was so obvious now. Had he been that fucking lost? That this asshole could play him like a fiddle from beginning to end?

Adrift in blood and sand and death.

"No," he replied, his voice even. "This morning. The Airport was on lockdown—they just opened the doors."

A partial truth, because Will was certain Red already knew which flight he and Brodie had flown in on and the exact time they'd landed. Lying about it would only tip Red off, and Will wanted him as ignorant and confident as possible. The airport *had* been on lockdown for the last five hours, because of an unknown terrorist threat, but Will and Brodie's military IDs had gotten them through security—and out of the airport—a mere fifteen minutes after landing.

The cache was now in the hands of General Roland Pierre, safe and sound at Bagram. Where it would go from there, Will didn't know. And didn't care.

Explaining why he hadn't turned them into his own Senior Chief hadn't been pleasant; connecting Ethan to Georgia Humboldt had been unavoidable, although Will had done his best to be discrete. Mostly because the whole goddamn situation sickened him.

"Where are you now?" Red wanted to know.

"On the road to Jalalabad." Which wasn't entirely true, but Will wasn't worried about Red knowing the difference; the base's techies had ensured his calls couldn't be traced.

In actuality, Will and Brodie—and the five Army Rangers the General had supplied them with—sat at various points both within and outside of the warehouse where Will and Brodie had found the cache. Ali's truck was parked outside. Ali, however, had not accompanied them, because no way in hell was Will letting him get anywhere near what was to come. He'd graciously loaned them his truck—because it drew far less attention than any military or American vehicle—and then gone to his daughter's house for dinner.

"You sure you don't need any help?" Red asked lightly, but Will could hear the fine tension that thrummed through him.

"Actually," Will told him, "I do."

A sharp breath. Then, "What can I do to help, brother?"

And Will wanted to reach through the phone and choke the shit out of him.

"The coordinates," he said, trying not to grit his teeth. "I can only get a general position with my phone. If I give them to you, can you get me an exact location?"

"Send them."

A dark, bitter smile curved Will's mouth as he emailed them to Red. *Merry Christmas, asshole.* He wondered where Red was. Jordan? Pakistan? Or closer—Kabul?

Because he would have left as soon as Will told him where the cache was. And considering Red—allegedly—ran his *Unnamed* operations out of Berlin, he was a hell of a lot closer than Will had been.

"Bih Sud Road. There's no street number." Red sounded more than a little frustrated by that. "How the fuck is anyone supposed to find anything?"

"Welcome to the third world, brother," Will drawled. "No worries. I've got it from here."

He cut the connection, slid his phone away and sat back to wait.

Cheyenne was standing in her kitchen, kneading dough when her cell phone rang. She glanced over at the screen —*Whitney*—and ignored it. She was elbow deep in flour and pie crust, and besides, ever since she'd shared what was happening with Rafe and Will and Georgia damn-her-hide Humboldt, Whitney had put her permanent freak on.

This is insane! Bombs? Bombs! I told you you would regret this. Why couldn't you just walk away? Bombs! And where's this Will guy? Why did he abandon you? What kind of person is he? I knew this was a mistake. I KNEW IT. Have you called the Sheriff? You should call the Sheriff.

And on and on it went. So Cheyenne had sent Whitney and her girls home.

"Don't come back until I tell you," Cheyenne had told her. The girls had protested—especially Sasha, who'd taken a strong liking to Rafe—but in the end Whitney had bundled them into her gleaming silver SUV and gone home.

It wasn't safe, anyway, not until Malik was dealt with.

Choo-choo! sang her cell, indicating Whitney had—of course—left a message. Thirty seconds later, her house phone began to ring.

"Go away," Cheyenne muttered and continued to knead.

Three rings and her brief, brusque message sounded. *Leave a message. Or not. Whatever.*

"Holy shit-balls, Cheyenne!" Whitney's voice burst into the quiet kitchen like the sudden, frantic yapping of a miniature poodle. "You need to see the news NOW. My phone is ringing off the frigging hook. Call me!"

Everything within Cheyenne went still. Whitney was always high strung—but that was borderline hysteria, an extreme, even for her.

Son of a nutcracker. What now?

"Hey, Rafe," she called, still kneading.

"Yeah?" he replied from somewhere in the cabin.

"Bring your laptop here, would ya?" Because Cheyenne didn't have TV—at least, not in the traditional sense. She streamed everything she watched from the internet, which meant no local or national news unless she went online.

Rafe appeared a minute later, his Mac in hand, up and running.

"Go to NewsWeb," she told him.

He set the computer down, careful to keep it out of the flour and pulled up the NewsWeb site. And there, in HD, was a frozen still photo from Georgia Humboldt's personal porno with the headline 'Busted Brass: America's Highest Officials' Orgy of Shame.'

"Hells bells," Cheyenne said and grabbed a towel to wipe her hands.

"Is that....is that *my ma?*" Rafe asked, his voice tight.

None of the participants in the video were redacted—although all of their body parts had been blurred. Georgia wore a blissful expression and a fuck you smile.

A legacy where she screwed everyone over—literally.

"Yeah, I'm afraid it is," Cheyenne replied with a sigh. "Play the video."

Rafe hesitated. "Do I want to know?"

"Probably not."

He scowled and hit play.

"The nation was rocked this morning by the contents of a package delivered to the Washington Post yesterday afternoon." The newscaster, a svelte, beautiful blond smirked. *"The package, which was addressed to the Posts' political editor, Ed McNeal, contained the following video—which we will warn you, is not appropriate for young viewers."*

Cheyenne hit the pause button and looked at Rafe. "Close your eyes."

The insult he felt was instant and apparent. "Why?"

"Because it isn't appropriate for young viewers," Cheyenne said sternly. "And you are a young viewer."

Rafe watched her with hard eyes, and Cheyenne saw the boy who'd grown up in the innermost reaches of the city. She'd wondered when they would meet.

"Why?" he asked, his voice harsh. "Because they're having sex? I know what an orgy is."

Something Cheyenne really didn't care to think about—let alone discuss. "Rafe."

He muttered and stomped his foot, but in the end he obeyed, squeezing his eyes tightly shut. Cheyenne knew he would just pull the video up when he was alone and watch it —hell, the unedited version was probably already floating around on You Tube—but that didn't mean she had to *allow* it.

She hit play again, and a clip of the video she and Will had watched in the shadow of Devil's Tower began to play. Remembering the moans and groans, Cheyenne muted the sound, watching as Georgia, Malik and Ethan Scott got down to business. The video cut off, and the blond returned. Cheyenne hit the mute button and paused it again.

"Okay," she told Rafe. "You can open them."

His beautiful, bi-colored eyes opened and shot daggers at her.

"Thank you," she told him, unwilling to bend.

Not on this.

"I'll just watch it later," he muttered.

She looked at him for a long moment. "I know you will; that's not the point. It's my job to try to protect you, Rafe. You don't need to see this—*no one* needs to see this. There's nothing of value here—just people's lives being ruined. Your mom might not have cared about whether or not you'd see this, but *I* do. Because it's nothing more than a weapon designed to destroy people."

He held her gaze. "I want to see it."

"Why? You know who she was. What she was. And watching this won't make you feel any better." Cheyenne leaned back against the kitchen counter and folded her arms beneath her breasts. "The best revenge is a good life. It took me a long, long time to understand that. Don't make the same mistake I did—don't hold on to it. Because you're the only one who cares. She never did. So fuck her, Rafe. Let it go. Be *better*."

He blinked, but said nothing. Cheyenne sighed and resumed the video.

"Participants include Andrew Malik, the American Ambassador to Afghanistan, United States Navy Senior Chief Ethan Scott, Army General Robert Forsyth, and Florida Congressman Alexander Wentworth, just to name a few. The woman is reportedly a CIA agent named Georgia Humboldt, who was killed earlier this month while on assignment. Our technical people assure us that the video has not been Photoshopped in anyway—and Washington is reeling beneath its disclosure." Another smarmy smile from the blond. *"In addition to the video, the package to Mr. McNeal also included a birth certificate for a child born to Ms. Humboldt, a boy, just ten years old. The man listed as the boy's*

father? Ambassador Andrew Malik. It should be noted that the Ambassador has been married to Elena Abadi, sister to the current Saudi Price Ahmed, for the last twelve years, and they have three children. According to our sources, the boy is currently in the custody of his legal guardian, wildlife artist, Cheyenne Elias. Stay with NewsWeb for more from this breaking story as it becomes available."

The video ended, and a commercial for internet dating began to play. Cheyenne stared at it blankly, her head buzzing.

"She was talking about me," Rafe said. "Wasn't she?"

"Yes." And they were skirting the line by talking about his age. They couldn't release his name or his date of birth—but Cheyenne was a realist. It would hit the web in a handful of hours.

If it hadn't already.

"So...what does this mean?"

Cheyenne looked over to find Rafe watching her, his gaze pensive.

"It means the world now knows who your father is," she said.

"So...does that mean I'm safe?"

"Most likely. If he moved against you now, it would be suicide—in more ways than one. I think that, right now, he's probably far more concerned with damage control."

Rafe's gaze flickered to the screen. "I bet his wife crapped a brick."

Cheyenne smiled. She couldn't help it. "Quite possibly."

But it was Malik's in-laws he was going to have the biggest trouble with. Not even the U.S. government would be able to compete with—or prevent—the punishment the Saudis would mete out. Andrew Malik would no longer be Rafe's problem.

"And his kids...my sisters. Half-sisters. They probably

hate me."

"You don't know that." Cheyenne shook her head. "And you shouldn't assume that. For right now, this is just something we're going to have to swim through. But later...you never know what life will bring, sweet pea. Trust me on that—because I never expected you. Not in a million years."

"Yeah," he said. "Sorry."

"For what?"

"All the shit I came with."

"None of which is your fault," Cheyenne pointed out. The impulse to hug him gripped her, and she gave in and wrapped her arms around him and squeezed tight. "It's going to be okay, Rafe. I promise."

"Even Will?"

Her heart lurched. "I hope so."

"You still haven't heard anything?"

"No." Which pissed her off. She'd texted Will when they'd gotten home—just like he'd asked—but she hadn't gotten jack in return. *Nothing.* So she'd texted him again. And again. And again.

Which now made her his official stalker. But he hadn't responded. No call, no text, *nada*. And that fucking terrified her. Luckily, being angry was a lot easier than being afraid.

Story of my goddamn life.

The landline rang again, but Cheyenne didn't answer it. Whitney's voice, even more agitated than it had been during the first call, sounded. "What the hell should I tell these people? Everyone wants a comment! I need a comment! Call me back, damn it!"

"What do you think we should we say?" Rafe asked. He stayed locked in her embrace, unmoving.

Cheyenne shrugged. "What do you want to say?"

"Nothing," he muttered and shuddered against her.

"Then we say nothing."

CHAPTER THIRTY-FOUR

"I've got four bodies headed toward you. Another two still in the vehicle." Brodie paused, and the radio crackled, and in the rafters above, the pigeons cooed. "Mercs, I'd guess, by the foul look of 'em. Armed for bear and wearin' armor. Be careful, boys."

Will's heart beat like a drum in the hollow of his chest, and his forearm ached like a son of a bitch. Probably because his hand was wrapped around his gun like a stripper around a pole.

"Roger," he said into his radio unit.

"Shoot to kill?" clarified Beckham.

Fuck yes. The words rose in Will's throat and locked there, almost choking him. Outside the warehouse, footsteps sounded.

"Nah, might be some valuable intel there," Brodie replied. "Best just disable."

Which was, of course, the right response—no matter how much Will wanted different. That was one of the reasons he'd chosen Brodie. Brodie had been through his own kind of hell, and he understood exactly where Will's head was at.

It spoke to the man Brodie was that he had no problem picking up Will's slack—and wouldn't hold it against him.

The warehouse door shuddered violently. Will had left the padlock in place and locked them in; clearly, no one had thought to bring a pair of channel locks along. The loading bay door only opened from the inside.

Another shudder.

Will waved Beckham and Davis forward, and they flanked the vibrating door. Somewhere behind him, Johnson and Mills hid in the shadows. Brodie and Cline were outside, Brodie on the roof of the building across the street, Cline at street level on the side that held the loading bay.

Gunfire was going to be unavoidable, but if they could take them down swiftly—and not turn the place into the fucking OK Corral—it wouldn't draw too much attention. It was only late afternoon, and there were still plenty of people working on the streets around them; a firefight with the locals was the last thing anyone wanted.

Pop pop pop; they were firing at the lock. The door rattled and burst open, and the first merc strode through, weapon drawn and aimed. Will stood in the center of the building, his own weapon steady in his hands. It was the first time he'd held an SSAR-15 since the night that had blown his life to pieces and shredded his identity, but other than the cramping in his damaged arm, his hold was rock-steady. Adrenaline speared through him, a heady slide he knew how to ride, and anticipation licked at his nerves. He was *ready*.

The chaos and lunacy he'd feared was still, as if slumbering, and he felt nothing but the sharp bite of exhilaration. The sight of the merc coming at him made his heart jerk hard and eyes sharpen; he heard the *click* of Mills' weapon, tasted the Afghan dust on his tongue.

Alive. Not dead. Damaged but not undone.

Three more mercs followed the first, weapons drawn.

Not one of them bothered to check the doorway they walked through, and Will couldn't help but wonder where Red had gotten them. Not from the same pool Georgia fished from, that was certain.

"Took you boys long enough," Will told them.

Beckham and Davis closed the door. Mills and Johnson stepped out of the shadows and flanked Will, weapons aimed and ready.

The last two mercs through the door—Three and Four— turned to face Beckham and Davis, weapons raised, but it was clear from their expressions they hadn't expected soldiers. Hell, they probably hadn't expected anyone but Will, and definitely not Army Rangers, who were some of the fiercest warriors the U.S. military trained. The men froze, their faces so full of uncertainty, Will almost smiled.

Surprise.

"Blackheart?" demanded merc One, a tall, swarthy, unshaven man of indecipherable heritage.

"I prefer Lieutenant," Will said.

"We've come for the cache. You let us take it, and you'll walk out of here upright."

Beckham laughed. "Sure he will."

"We don't want no trouble," the merc insisted, but his finger caressed the trigger of his weapon like the absent stroke of a lover.

"We like trouble," Mills replied.

The merc swept them with a glance and met the gaze of merc Two beside him. An almost imperceptible nod followed. They were clearly more experienced; neither wore the hesitation that had frozen Three and Four.

"Last chance," he told Will, his tone as grim as his features.

"You sure about that?" Will asked him.

He was ready when the merc fired; he'd known it was

coming. These weren't the kind of guys who would lay down their weapons and surrender. They were outmanned, outgunned, and out trained—the only thing that could turn the tide was an archaic hail of gunfire.

Will went left—behind a strategically placed group of empty steel barrels—and came around the other side; merc One was still firing into the empty space where Mills and Johnson had stood. Will aimed his SSR and let it rip, turning the guy's legs into pulp. Mills was beside him a moment later, firing at the merc Two, who was smarter than One: he was headed for the door. But he had no chance to escape; Mills' shots—all aimed at his posterior—put him down before he even got three feet.

"Nice," Will told him.

Mills grinned.

Beckham and Davis stood over Three and Four. Will wasn't even certain they'd fired—it looked like they'd just hit the ground and prayed. Mills and Johnson moved in, disarmed each one and cuffed them.

Ten maybe fifteen rounds fired…not too bad. Hopefully not so many that anyone came running. Except for Red.

"What's cookin', hoss?" Brodie's slow draw was tight with tension. "I need an update."

"Four down, two to go," Will replied.

"You won't have to wait long. They're headed your way now."

"Roger that."

Another shuffle of feet. Beckham moved to the door; Will stepped into place on the other side. Mills and Johnson stood next to their captives, guns pointed at their skulls in silent warning against speaking.

When the door swung open and the two men strode through, Will didn't bother to fire. He simply hit the first one with the butt of his gun, a sharp, swift blow that laid the guy out immediately. The second one had Beckham's barrel in his cheek before he could even assimilate what had occurred.

The first was clad in the same Kevlar and armed with the same semi-automatic as the others—merc Five. But the second...the second wore a shiny silver suit and bright blue tie. Pale blond hair slicked back with pomade, narrow framed, grey-tinted eyeglasses, matching diamond studs in his ears.

And no resemblance to Rye Morrow whatsoever.

Will lifted his weapon and slammed it into the guy's chest, shoving him back into the door, which Beckham had once again closed.

"Where is he?" Will grated, only minutely satisfied by the slam of the guy's skull into the door.

But the man—*boy, more like, no more than twenty-five*—only shook his head, his glasses askew, his eyes as big as saucers. Will thrust his weapon at Beckham, who took it and tsked softly at the kid.

"Where?" Will snarled and slammed his fist into that pale, narrow jaw.

Blood streamed down the young man's chin. He made no move to defend himself, staring at Will in shock. "Wh-what?"

"Red!" Will roared and hit him again. "Where the fuck is he?"

"I..."

Another hit. Blood spattered the door.

"You'd better open your mouth, boy," Beckham told him ruefully. "While you still got some teeth left."

Will raised his fist again, and the guy cried, "No, not again, please don't hit me again!"

Will crushed that fine silver suit in his fists and lifted him from the floor. *"Where?"*

"He left for the states...." Blood dribbled from the corner of the kid's mouth. His nose was busted, maybe his jaw, too.

His glasses were under Will's left foot. "Said...said he had unfinished business."

Will froze, and his blood—rushing hot and thick in his veins—instantly went cold.

"What unfinished business?" he gritted, his heart suddenly pounding with sickening force.

When the kid didn't respond, Will hit him again, a kidney punch that—had he not been holding the kid up with one arm—would have dropped him where he stood.

"I don't know, I swear I don't know!" Tears now, rolling down pale cheeks. "I was just supposed to come here with Tito and pick up the cache. He said it would be easy. He said Tito would take care of everything, take care of..."

"Me," Will rasped.

The kid's eyes widened. "Blackheart?"

"What else?" Will asked him, a hairsbreadth from snapping the idiot's neck.

"I don't know! I was just supposed to pick them up and get them to the border. I don't know. Tito had a plan." He looked over at merc number one, who was only semi-conscious, bleeding out onto the hard-packed dirt floor. "I was supposed to send a text when it was done."

Beckham reached into the interior of the kid's suit and removed a slim silver phone.

"What were you supposed to say?" he asked, his hands moving swiftly over the touchscreen.

"Package delivered." More blood, a fine mist that sprayed across Will's arms. "Blackheart dead."

Beckham scrolled through the contacts list and then showed the kid the phone. "That him?"

A weary nod.

Beckham typed. *Package delivered. Blackheart dead.*

Whoosh!

"What's up, hoss?" Brodie's voice broke the silence.

Will made himself release the kid, who fell to his knees, shaking violently, tears slipping down his cheeks. One of the Unnamed, obviously. Far more capable at hacking than war.

Red was a fucking moron.

"Just a small fish," Will replied to Brodie. "Big one's gone to finish some business in the states."

Brodie, with whom Will had shared just about everything that'd happened in the last two weeks, said, "Aw, fuck."

Will looked down at the kid. The need to get to Cheyenne and Rafe swelled within him, a massive, unstoppable tide that pressed against his skin and threatened to unleash the monster he held so carefully in check.

"Get him out of my sight before I kill him," he muttered to Beckham.

"What's the plan?" Brodie asked.

They would be okay, Will told himself. Cheyenne wasn't foolish or stupid or weak. She would hold on until he got there.

"Hoss?"

Will took his weapon back from Beckham. "I'm going after him."

"Shotgun," Brodie said.

CHAPTER THIRTY-FIVE

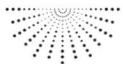

Rafe stared down at the basket he carried, which held six large mushrooms—morels, Cheyenne had called them. "They look like brains."

They'd left the cabin hours ago armed with a backpack full of sandwiches and water bottles, a can of bear spray—which Rafe thought was nuts, because what was a can full of pepper going to do against a *bear*—two fishing poles and an empty mushroom basket.

They'd been escaping. Ever since the news had gotten its hands on that video yesterday, Cheyenne's phone had been ringing off the hook. She'd finally unplugged it and turned off her cell, checking every few hours only to see if Will had finally called.

He hadn't.

They'd gone for a hike, soaked their feet in an ice-cold stream, ate their sandwiches and hunted for mushrooms. Rafe had videoed a moose they'd seen munching on willow while Lucky and Chuck followed game trails, and Cheyenne fished for trout. The sky above was bright, shimmering blue, like Sasha's eyes, dotted by huge white clouds that cast monstrous shadows down upon the land. Rafe heard his first hawk cry and had his first encounter with a raven—a giant black bird that had watched him eat his sandwich with a piercing black stare, strange sounds working in its throat. The air smelled of sunlight and sage and pine, and he thought of Will and hoped he was okay.

"Yeah—but they taste much better than they look," Cheyenne replied. "We'll dip them in beer batter and fry them up. Yum."

Rafe eyed the mushrooms doubtfully, but didn't argue. He'd come to realize in the last few days that Cheyenne could *cook*. He was going to get fat as St. Nick if he wasn't careful. And she let him eat as much as he wanted—a first in his life.

The sun was beginning to sink over the mountains as they got closer to the cabin. Far off, the sounds of the ranch echoed, and beside him, Lucky struggled to keep up, clearly exhausted from her adventure. Chuck nudged her forward again and again; Cheyenne was right: Chuck loved Lucky.

"How about fried chicken for dinner?" Cheyenne asked.

"Okay," Rafe said, his belly growling. Their sandwiches had burned off long ago, and he was hungry and tired, but happy. As happy as he could be, anyway. Worry for Will churned within him. It had been three days. *Three whole days.* And he knew Cheyenne was scared, too. Rafe could tell.

He was learning her.

"Maybe some potato salad, too. I've got—" Cheyenne halted abruptly.

Rafe froze and looked around.

"Bear?" he whispered.

"Worse." She looked behind them, at the sweeping hills that led to the narrow canyon they'd explored, but there was nothing. Chuck stopped and looked around, lifting his nose to the wind. A low growl rumbled in his chest. "Men."

Rafe frowned. "How do you know?"

She inhaled deeply. "I can smell them." Chuck's growls grew deeper. "So can he."

"What do you mean?"

"Cologne. Something strong and expensive." She shook her head and looked around, studying the stand of pines trees they stood within. The wind whistled, and the boughs rustled, but there was no crashing through underbrush, no twigs snapping underfoot. Chuck was frozen beside them; Lucky looked around, clearly confused, and whined.

"Let's go," Cheyenne said quietly. "Stay beside me. If anyone comes, you grab Lucky and haul ass to the ranch, and get Angus."

Everything in him rebelled. "I ain't leaving you," he told her.

"Yes, you will," she told him.

"No," he said. "I can help. I can—"

"Getting Angus *will* help."

Rafe said nothing else. But he wasn't going anywhere if there was trouble. Will would never forgive him if he let something happen to Cheyenne. Rafe would never forgive himself. And besides—

Chuck made a sound that lifted the hair at Rafe's nape. The fur along the dog's back rose, and his lips drew back to bare gleaming white teeth. Lucky followed his lead, growling low in her throat.

On the trail ahead of them suddenly stood a man, a big, ugly, dark skinned man with black eyes and scars on his face. He wore all black and held a huge gun, and the mirrored sunglasses he wore reflected their surprise.

"I knew I smelled asshole." Cheyenne stepped sideways, blocking Rafe from sight. Chuck quivered, snarls breaking from him. Lucky echoed him. Cheyenne held out a hand and stayed them, but they clearly sensed a threat. And wanted blood.

"Do not move again," the man replied, his voice thick with an accent Rafe didn't recognize. He moved toward them until he was only a handful of feet away.

"Seriously," Cheyenne said. "This is getting old."

The man waved his gun at them. "Up to the house. Now. Move." He motioned toward Chuck. "Control your beast, or I will end him."

Cheyenne turned slightly and looked down at Rafe. At the same time, she reached for the can of pepper spray that sat in the nylon holster attached to her belt. Her arm was turned toward Rafe, hidden from view, and she was careful not to move too quickly, slowing unsnapping the holster and sliding the slender can out.

"Angus," she said distinctly. Then she turned and and unloaded the can into the guy's face.

He dropped his gun, fell to his knees and began to scream.

"Move!" Cheyenne ordered and kicked the man over.

Rafe hopped around him and ran hell bent for leather up the trail, looking back to make sure Cheyenne was behind him. She was ushering Chuck in front of her—Chuck, who wanted a piece of the guy so badly he was frothing at the mouth—and Rafe leaned down and scooped Lucky into his arms. He lost his basket as he ran across the sage covered meadow toward the cabin. He looked back again; Cheyenne was just a few steps behind him.

Lucky barked, and Chuck streaked past him. He was almost there, so close he could almost—

A loud thud behind him. He whirled to see Cheyenne and another man suddenly on the ground, rolling away from him. They rolled to a stop, the man on top, and he backhanded her hard. Chuck snarled, a grisly, terrifying sound and tore off toward them. Rafe turned to follow, but hard, painful hands closed around his waist, yanked him from his feet and stopped him. He fought, squirming and kicking, Lucky barking hysterically in his arms.

Cheyenne reared up and head-butted the man on top of her, and his head snapped back. She followed the blow with a flat palm smashed against underside of his nose and then punched him in the nuts. Chuck was there then, his teeth sinking deep into the man's arm, dragging him sideways. Cheyenne rolled to her feet, staggered a little, and kicked him in the head. The man who held Rafe tucked him under one arm—as though his weight and his battle to be free were nothing—and pulled a gun from his coat pocket.

"No!" Rafe fought harder, slamming his head back, kicking with his heels. Lucky squirmed frantically against him, but he was afraid to drop her, afraid—

The man fired, and Chuck cried out sharply and fell. Cheyenne looked up, and the change that came over her chilled Rafe to the bone. She started toward them, her hands fisted at her sides, her pace measured and even. She walked, her face getting darker and darker until her eyes looked black, and Rafe's gaze fell to Chuck, who lay unmoving, and rage welled within him. He screamed, a loud, ear-piercing cry that hurt his throat.

"Not one more step," hissed the man who held him, and Rafe realized that the gun that had just put Chuck down was suddenly pointed at his temple, the barrel painfully hot against his skin.

Cheyenne halted, held her hands up, and stared at the man with such burning hatred, Rafe felt its sting against his skin. Behind her, the man who'd hit her was crawling to his feet, lurching toward her, murder in his eye.

"You're going to die today," Cheyenne told the man who held him, her voice cold frost.

He laughed. The man behind Cheyenne shoved her forward, and she turned on him and punched him in the throat. He went down, gasping for breath, but before she could do more, the man who held Rafe fired his gun into the air. The sound was deafening.

Cheyenne froze, and Rafe's heart beat so hard he thought it would burst.

"Inside the fucking house. *Now*," the man ordered. Cheyenne walked past them, and her gaze met Rafe's. He could see her rage.

It gave him hope. He was also aware of the Taser and the knife in his pocket, but he couldn't get to either. Not yet.

They went into the house. Rafe could hear Dexter bleating like he was dying; he hoped Angus could hear him, too. No doubt everyone at the ranch heard those shots. That gave Rafe hope, too.

They *weren't* alone. But he desperately wished Will was there.

Inside the house, the wooden blinds had been drawn, and it was dim, lit only by narrow beams of sunlight where the shades didn't conceal the windows, and two large squares of bright white light that illuminated the living room floor from the skylights overhead. Two men stood within the shadows, one tall and broad and armed with a shoulder holster like Will's and another, more narrow, clad in a black suit, a bright white shirt and shiny black shoes. He held a narrow silver phone in his hand, his fingers a blur on its touchscreen.

The man who held Rafe dropped him in the middle of the floor, and he almost landed on top of Lucky. Cheyenne moved to help Rafe up, one arm tight around his shoulders. She faced the man in the suit, and Rafe could feel her vibrating against him. Her cheeks were flushed with color, her scar paper white. Her right cheek bore an angry imprint of the hand that'd hit her.

"You've made this entire ordeal incredibly difficult," the man in the suit said conversationally. He didn't bother to look at her, his attention locked on his phone. "Who knew you would protect him so fiercely? The child of your nemesis." He looked up then, his eyes as dark as coal, and smiled at Cheyenne. "I must say I've found it quite…intriguing."

Cheyenne's hold on Rafe tightened. She said nothing. Lucky growled, and Rafe shushed her, ushering her behind him, terrified they would shoot her, too.

"Perhaps that's why his mother gave him to you. You certainly care more for him than she ever did." The smile faded. "All she cared for was herself."

"Boo-fucking-hoo," Cheyenne said.

He blinked, and a hint of the smile returned. "You're very different than she was."

They stared at one another for a long, silent moment, and Rafe shoved his hands deep into his pockets. The Taser fit perfectly in his palm; the knife was there, too, but it would take time. He had to open it. Cheyenne squeezed him, as if she knew.

"She would not have saved your child," the man said. "Why did you save hers?"

"You wouldn't understand," Cheyenne told him, so quiet the hair at Rafe's nape bristled. "You don't have it in you."

The man stilled. "No?"

"You killed your own brother. Your own *blood*."

Rafe didn't understand. Who was this guy?

"Not me. *Her*." The man's dark eyes were locked on Cheyenne. "Rye's death was never part of the plan. He was supposed to *survive*."

A harsh laugh broke from her. "You're a moron."

"Yes," he replied, and Rafe stared at him, perplexed.

There was pain there, even Rafe heard it. But he still didn't get what the hell was going on, or who this guy was, or what they were talking about—

"It's been you the whole time, hasn't it?" Cheyenne tilted

her head, her eyes hard as they raked the man. "Malik was never a worry."

"Very perceptive." The man took a step toward them. "Of course, the men I sent thought they were working for the Ambassador. How did you figure it out?"

"Will."

The man blinked. "Will?"

Cheyenne said nothing. Rafe *still* didn't understand. If this guy didn't work for his pop...who *did* he work for?

"Well." A dark smile. "I'm impressed. I didn't think he had it in him."

"That's why you're a fucking moron."

"Careful," the man warned softly.

"Why? Because discretion will save me?"

Rafe didn't like the way the man was looking at her. It was like how Will looked at her...only different. Bad different. His hackles rose, and his hand tightened around the Taser.

"What did she do to you?" the man asked.

"The same thing she did to you," Cheyenne told him.

The man said nothing for a long minute. "I shouldn't have involved her."

"Why did you?"

Another smile, but this one was sad.

"You loved her," Cheyenne said.

"Unfortunately, yes. She contacted me several years ago, looking for access to the Agency's servers. To Malik and Ethan Scott and all the men who sought to use her. She was so beautiful. So intelligent. So—"

"Insane," Cheyenne muttered.

"Yes. The realization was...devastating."

"Takes one to know one."

Rafe watched them, turning the words over in his head.

"The fox," he whispered. Cheyenne's hands tightened on him, and he knew he was right.

"Why?" Cheyenne asked.

The man didn't respond. He looked her up and down, and Rafe took a small step toward him, but she pulled him back.

"My brother was...perfect. The perfect son, the perfect soldier. While he drew accolades for fighting an illegal war and slaughtering innocents, I was berated for exposing the men who orchestrated that war. I was punished for pursuing the *true* terrorists. Rye was golden, faultless, without flaw. While I was...a criminal."

"So this was...what? Revenge?"

"Opportunity."

"To lay the loss at his feet? To wash him in blood and guilt and destroy everything he was? In addition to the valuable little nuclear arsenal you'd get to walk away with..."

The fox looked pleased. "No wonder Will guarded you so zealously."

"How did you know about the cache?" Cheyenne demanded. "Who told you?"

"Why, my brother, of course. He thought he was saving the world. Stupid fool."

"He called and told you?"

"We were speaking when they were given the go ahead. You see, our mother is dying. Stage four breast cancer. We were discussing her imminent demise when he got word... and being the heroic idiot he was, he told me."

Cheyenne stared at him for a long moment. "How did you know where he would be?"

"Baby brother was micro chipped. We both were. My father was the CEO of GenTek; he feared we would be kidnapped, and he might have to part with some of his precious pennies to retrieve us. I dug mine out years ago, of course, but Rye, being Rye, assumed the chip would make it easier for him to be found if he was ever captured. He had no idea I'd been monitoring his movements for years."

"So Ethan Scott, Malik...neither of them had anything to do with it?"

A small smile was the only answer she received.

"And the video? Were you the one who leaked it?"

"No." The smile faded. "I wouldn't have. It was too valuable a tool."

"For extortion."

"Yes. But she took that from me, too."

"You killed her," Rafe said, the knowledge instant, the words bursting from his throat. "Didn't you?"

The fox looked surprised, as if he'd forgotten Rafe stood there, listening.

"It wasn't my intention. At least, not until she'd shared the location of the cache she'd secreted away. However...I lost my temper. And then it was too late. She was the only one who knew where they were. And then...then I found you, my boy." The fox grinned at him. "And I knew she had to have left them with you. You were all she had."

Rafe wanted smash his face into bits and pieces. No matter that his ma had asked for everything she'd gotten. This man had *killed* her. Had taken her from him.

He was going to—

Cheyenne caught him when he tried to go around her.

"No," she growled at him.

His heartbeat was deafening in his head. He tried to shrug her off, to push past her, but she held tight.

"Will's going to kill you," he snarled.

But the fox only laughed, a low, deep laugh that made Cheyenne stiffen and Rafe's knees go weak.

"Will is dead," the fox said. "I received confirmation yesterday. Would you like to see?"

He looked down at his phone briefly and held it out so

the touchscreen faced them. The letters were abnormally large. Clearly the fox couldn't see worth a damn. But that thought faded when Rafe focused on the words.

Package delivered. Blackheart dead.

"You're going to die today, too," Cheyenne told him softly, and Rafe felt a violent tremor move through her. Her tone scared him.

Will is dead.

Rafe didn't want to believe it. He *couldn't* believe it. Not Will. Will was strong and brave and *good.* Will didn't deserve to die. Rage rushed up Rafe's throat, almost choking him.

His ma and Chuck and now Will...

"I would imagine he went quickly, if it's any consolation," the fox said.

Cheyenne jerked, and Rafe knew it was over. He could feel her shaking, trying to hold it together. Part of him wanted her to detonate; the other part wanted her calm. Part of him didn't give a shit anymore; the other part wanted to live. The Taser was slippery with sweat in his hand, but the man next to him wore a t-shirt, and all he had to do was make contact with skin and pull the trigger.

That's what he was going to do.

"Angus," Cheyenne said, and Rafe knew what she was telling him. He understood. But he didn't care.

"I'm sorry?" the fox asked.

"You're not," Cheyenne replied, fury vibrant in her voice. "But you will be."

And then she went straight at him.

CHAPTER THIRTY-SIX

Will had left exactly seven voicemail messages on Cheyenne's cell. He'd sent five text messages. He'd even tried Rafe's phone.

Nothing.

She'd left him five voicemails and four texts over the last three days, which made her sudden, resounding silence fucking terrifying.

He'd been forced to wait until they'd landed in Denver to contact her. Security protocol dictated that no messages were sent or received when on an official military flight, and he hadn't called her from Bagram or replied to her texts because he was afraid Red was listening. His phone might have been safe, but there was no guarantee hers was.

The last thing he wanted to do was give Red a head's up. But the price he'd paid—not being able to reach out, to connect if only briefly over a satellite connection—had left him in a place that was silent and dark and filled with quiet, suffocating fear.

Nerves massed in his throat as he and Brodie traveled the road that would lead him to Cheyenne's home. They'd caught a direct flight out of Bagram and managed to shave almost eight hours off the flight time back from Afghanistan, but he knew it wasn't enough.

Red had too much of a head start.

Stomach churning, Will flexed his hands around the steering wheel of the large black Suburban he drove. Muscle twitched and flexed along his spine; his legs were tense; his arms as taut as a bow string. In his chest, his heart beat heavily. The darkness hovered, but he refused to let it wash over him. He would be useless if he fell into that crazed, lost state. He had to hold on. Fight it. *Beat it.*

There was no other option.

"Damn, this place is gorgeous," Brodie muttered, looking over at the line of mountains that edged the valley, huge up thrusts of jagged granite that rose from the valley floor to kiss the sky. "I'm gonna have to come back here."

Will only hoped he would have the opportunity.

On the flight back, he'd learned that Georgia's porno had found its way to the *Washington Post* along with Rafe's birth certificate, and he wondered how Cheyenne was dealing, how Rafe was doing, and if Malik would finally stop chasing the boy. To go after him now would be wholly self-defeating, but considering the lack of judgment Malik had exercised regarding Georgia Humboldt, there were no guarantees that logic would hold sway.

Either Red had released the video or Georgia had—either way, the cat was out of the bag. And it would have to be dealt with.

"Jesus Christ," Brodie said.

A woman on a large bay horse suddenly leapt into the middle of the narrow gravel road they drove and cut them off, forcing Will to stop the Suburban. Dust flew, and the horse danced impatiently. A long rifle lay across the woman's lap; narrow eyes watched them from beneath the low brim of her worn straw hat.

"What the fuck?" Will snarled, but when he went to open his door he found an ancient man standing beside the Suburban, a double barrel shotgun aimed and ready in his gnarled hands.

"No trespassing," the man announced and spat a wad of chewing tobacco to the ground. "Violators will be shot. Survivors will be shot again."

Will watched him, his heart pounding with painful force.

"Can't you read?" the old man asked, his eyes two small, faded green orbs in a face wreathed in lines. "We got a sign."

It was nothing to slam the door into him, kick his legs out from beneath him and take the gun, which Will aimed back at him, hands flexing around the stock, blood rushing like a runaway freight train.

"Dad!" the woman on the horse yelled. She aimed the rifle at Will, and Brodie said, "Easy, sugar. We're the good guys."

The old man glared at Will. "Blackheart?"

Will stared at him. "Angus?"

"Christ on a cracker." Angus rolled sideways before pushing slowly to his feet. Will didn't lower the shotgun, didn't offer to help. Instead he watched the man carefully, aware of the weapon the woman had trained on him, of Brodie holding his 9 mm in his lap, of precious time bleeding away.

"Well, ain't this a shitshow," Angus said, dusting off his pants. "About damn time the Calvary arrived." He looked at his daughter and said, "Put that thing away, Prue." He turned back to Will and said, "I don't suppose those folks who got here ahead of you are part of your crew?"

Terror surged through Will. "No." He thrust the shotgun back at Angus. "They aren't."

Angus took the weapon, but as Will turned to climb back

into the Suburban, the old man stopped him with a surprisingly strong hand on his shoulder. "Now just wait a minute, son. Riding up like a herd of menopausal bison ain't going to make Cheyenne and her boy any safer. We'll go on foot. Leave your rig."

Then he turned and walked into the stand of pine trees that lined the road and disappeared.

"This just keeps getting better and better," Brodie said, climbing out of the Suburban.

The woman—Prue—rode over and dismounted, a graceful, agile movement that spoke of a lifetime of repetition. The bay horse was monstrous and eyed both Will and Brodie nervously.

"We heard shots," Prue said, tying her reins to the rail of the wooden fence that lined the road.

Will tried not to focus on those words. Panic licked at his nerves, and an ominous cloud of dread hovered at the periphery of his vision. If his heart beat any harder, it was going to explode. He turned to follow Angus and checked his .45, which he'd left in a locker in Denver; he hoped like hell Cheyenne still had his Glock. That she was using it.

"When?" Brodie asked.

"Ten—fifteen minutes ago," Prue said. "We were branding or we would've come right away. The boys are out pulling stock. There was no one we could send."

She was a pretty woman, tall and slender with hair the color of dark chocolate and her father's green eyes, but her face was strained, her mouth a tight line.

"How many of them?" Brodie asked, checking his weapons as they walked.

Prue watched him. "I don't know. I just saw the vehicle. A black Hummer with Colorado plates."

Angus was up ahead, winding his way through the trees.

Will had to force himself to walk, not run. He didn't even know where he was going; following Angus was a necessity.

Angus.

So much for the young, slick cowboy he'd pictured.

You're gonna pay for that, baby.

If she was still alive.

Angus halted at the line where the trees ended. In the small clearing in front of him sat a two-story cabin with a large deck facing the western mountains and a two car garage with one door open. A Jeep four-by-four was parked in the garage. The black Hummer Prue had referred to sat out front.

Will halted and assessed the situation. The sun was sinking, and shadows were beginning to creep across the land; the trees had stilled as the wind died at the edge of the day. Somewhere close, an animal bleat as though it were dying.

"How many?" Brodie asked Angus.

"Four of 'em, I think." He shook his head. "Can't be sure."

"We should circle around this side," Prue said. "We can—"

"You're staying here," Brodie told her.

"Bite me," she retorted, and Will thought of Cheyenne and almost smiled.

"Hell, she's probably a better shot than you," Angus added and spat tobacco.

Brodie only shook his head.

"Someone needs to call law enforcement," Will said grimly and removed his .45. "These assholes will shoot first."

If they haven't already.

A thought that pierced him as effectively as the sharpest blade.

"How you wanna do this, hoss?"

He met Brodie's gaze. "Quickly and quietly."

"Then let's go. Clock's ticking."

~

Package delivered. Blackheart dead.

That had been the point of no return.

Chuck going down had nearly cleaved Cheyenne in two; it was all she could do to leave him lying there, to focus on Rafe and the men who threatened to do much more than kill a dog. But it was hard. She clung to control with everything she had in her. Watched Rafe, told herself to *think*, imagined their pleas as she watched the men bleed out.

Getting Red to extrapolate had helped. His self-important babbling had explained more than a few things and helped to calm her to the point she could focus and think. *Plan.*

But then... *Will is dead.* And the world had gone red. The roar in her head was deafening. *Rage.* Incendiary and ferocious. She knew Rafe wouldn't listen; he wouldn't run for the ranch, he wouldn't find Angus. He was like her. He would fight.

There was nothing she could do. Pleading with a son of a bitch who'd anted up his own twin on the altar of sibling rivalry would get them nowhere. He was here to kill them. No words, no tears, no hope. Nothing would sway him.

So they would fight.

Her baton was in her pocket. She wished like hell she'd grabbed Will's Glock but it was in the drawer of her bedside table. The .22 was in the mudroom; maybe Rafe could get to it. Maybe he had his Taser. His knife.

Maybe they would survive this.

"Angus," she said to Rafe, her heart so loud she barely heard her own voice.

That dual-colored gaze met hers, his resistance clear. She wanted to shake him, to *make* him go, but there was no time for that fight.

"I'm sorry?" Red said, arching a brow. Oddly beautiful,

with long, sable brown hair and dark chocolate eyes, the fox's allure had become clear.

Georgia had always liked pretty—and if he was useful, all the better. *A game. Just a fucking game. Those men, those lives... nothing to them.* Including Will.

"You're not," she said, rage bleeding from her pores, like gravel in her throat. A red mist hovered at the edge of her vision, and her hand slid into her pocket and closed around her baton. "But you will be."

Run, she thought to Rafe. And then she went for the fox.

The first blow landed, a sharp crack against his neck. She was too angry; if she'd taken her time, it would have shattered his cervical vertebra like glass. But fury fueled her, and she was not as precise as she should have been. He went down, but not out, and as she brought the baton back for another blow, a man barreled into her from the side.

They went down, crashing against the wooden floor with brute force. Cheyenne held onto her baton for dear life and brought it down with vicious force—his head, his shoulders, his back, but he was big and heavy and still pissed off about that punch to the throat. He tore the baton away and slammed a big-boned, meaty fist into her cheek.

Intense, shearing pain and blood bursting across her tongue in a coppery wash; she reared up and head butted him—a *second* time, the dumbass—and his bruised nose cracked. He roared, but those strong, crushing hands didn't retreat. Somewhere behind her, someone was yelling and Lucky was barking, but she couldn't turn and see, couldn't—

Big hands grabbed her skull and slammed her head into the floor, hard, and stars shimmered in her brain. She bucked against the weight on top of her, grappling for her baton, which lay only a few feet away. *Too far.* The man shoved her down and climbed astride her, a bloody grin turning his mouth as he looked down at her. Cheyenne bared her teeth in response and hit him in the throat again. Then she swung her legs up and around him and slammed her booted heels into his chest. She crossed her feet and pulled him backward for all she was worth, the muscles in her thighs screaming.

He fought, twisting left then right, but she only wedged her heels beneath his chin and pulled harder, her heels slicing his throat, her elbows digging into the floor. She arched her back and leverage won; he toppled backward and slammed against the floor. She rolled over, her legs groaning as she forced him to roll with her, and as soon as they were facing the floor, she pulled her legs free and whirled to pounce on top of him, one knee landing on his spine, the other punching into his kidneys. Then she slid her arm around his throat and did her best to choke the crap out of him.

He reared against her, and she held on for dear life, squeezing his carotid artery with the forearm she'd laid against it, holding on tight when he began to flop and fight and pull at her arm where it wrapped him. Fingers tore at her hair, nails gouged her arms, his strength tested hers, and she clung blindly, her arm aching, the ride as rough as any wild mustang. Thirty seconds of brutal struggle for control later, he suddenly slumped beneath her.

Blood roared in her head; blood leaked down her chin. She pulled her cramped arm from around his neck and looked up to see Rafe standing over the man who'd brought them inside, Taser in hand, his eyes big and horrified as he watched the man writhe and scream and convulse on the floor. She stumbled off the fallen man, scooped up her baton, dragged Rafe behind her and turned once more toward the fox.

"Stop," Red said, and a faint, final golden ray of sunlight glinted off the barrel of the gun he held, a shimmering wink that made Cheyenne freeze.

His gaze was deep and turbulent, and her skin crawled when he smiled at her.

"You really are something," he whispered. "It's a shame I have to kill you."

Cheyenne stared at him, aware they were only half-way home. One more thug—half-blind, maybe, from bear spray, but he was out there—and this asshole in front of her.

Him she wanted to *kill*. Even if it took her bare hands.

Behind her, Rafe was shaking, his hands twisted in the back of her shirt, Lucky hovering around his feet. And while the guy he'd Tased wouldn't be getting up anytime soon, the one she'd knocked out would stir in just a few minutes. Then she'd have to put him down again.

"So much for saving the world," she said to Red, her voice a cold scalpel that sliced the air between them.

"I *am* saving it," he insisted. "This situation is…an anomaly."

A sharp sound tore from her. "Greed. For power, for *love*. You're no different. You're the same."

"No," he said sharply and took an abrupt step toward them, his weapon trained on her. "I'm *better*."

"Delusions of grandeur." This time she laughed. "Exactly the same."

"No!" he snarled.

Boom!

Cheyenne jerked with the sound and looked down, but there was no pain and no blood. She looked up again; crimson bloomed across Red's chest, a scarlet stain that spread across his snowy white shirt like ink bleeding through paper. A startled expression shaped his face; the corners of his mouth glistened with blood. He dropped his weapon and fell to his knees.

Behind him stood Will.

Cheyenne's heart stopped. Rafe flew around her before she could stop him.

"Will!" he cried and threw himself at Will, who caught him with one arm and lifted him against his chest.

Lucky barked, and Rafe wrapped himself around Will, his cries shearing the sudden silence, and Cheyenne could only stare stupidly at them, her hand clenched around her baton, the wild beat of her heart deafening in her head.

"Cheyenne," Will said quietly, and the sound of his voice made her bleed inside. Pale blue eyes glinted at her. "Come here, baby."

She was moving, even though she hadn't decided to do so. Even though she wanted to punch him in the face for the portentous silence he'd left her in for the past three days. Even though—when Red had declared him dead—she'd suddenly realized how much she loved him.

He reached for her with his free arm and hauled her against him, and she felt the faint, fine tremor that moved through him. His breath touched her scar, and his fingers dug into her hip, and as the scent of pine filled her lungs, tears stretched in her throat and leaked from her eyes. She dropped her baton and wrapped her arms around him and let his heat and scent and strength sink into her.

"He said you were d-dead," Rafe wept, and Cheyenne laid one trembling hand on his back.

"I'm hard to kill," Will replied, and his gaze met Cheyenne's. "I want to live."

The connection arrowed through her like live current, and she felt too much: hope, fear, need…and such incandescent joy she flinched from it. *Too much.* Rafe was shaking against her; Will was solid, unmoving, his arm like an iron band, and for a moment she wished she could weep like Rafe was, huge, shuddering sobs for all of the loss they'd endured—

"Chuck," she whispered and pushed away, horror crashing through her.

"We found him," Will said and tightened his hold. "He'll be okay. He's down at the ranch."

Cheyenne tried to speak, but tears wedged in her throat and streamed down her cheeks, and she could do nothing but battle the swell of emotion that threatened to erupt.

Bawling like a stinking baby. Buck the fuck up. But Will was *alive*. And Chuck was shot. And—

She pushed away again, but Will resisted. "There's another one. He's—"

"Dead," Will said.

Sirens sounded then, and Cheyenne's fingers curled into his shirt and clung.

"Almost done." He pressed a kiss to her hair. "Just a little longer."

But that's what she was suddenly afraid of.

CHAPTER THIRTY-SEVEN

Three hours, seven phone calls and one interrogation later, Will finally began to relax.

Red—who was still breathing—was in surgery in Salt Lake City, guarded by an entire FBI team and a dozen local cops. Will was confident the fox would make it through surgery; after all, what was a little punctured lung?

Small pleasures.

Even though Will had imagined killing the man responsible for that night of sand and blood and death a million different ways, in the end the leader of the *Unnamed* was far more valuable alive than dead. Too much lived in that brain; better exploited and explored than buried. Guantanamo, Will thought, could have him.

Not an outcome he'd envisioned. But he knew, too, that had he arrived too late, had Cheyenne and Rafe died, those fantasies of blood soaked walls—*paint the world in flesh and blood and bone*—would have materialized. If they'd fallen, he wouldn't have been able to control the darkness.

Carnage he did not want to even try to fathom.

He'd taken responsibility for the loss of his team and the

cache; Will knew that was his cross to bear. But listening to Cheyenne reiterate Red's confession had helped dilute the bitter regret that dwelled within, and he suddenly understood that—from the moment Rye had included his brother in something no one outside the team should have known—the situation had become untenable. So while he could concede that he bore blame, he was no longer willing to accept all of it. There was plenty to go around.

He would still dream of it; memory would still overlay reality in moments of stress and chaos and pain. That simply was, no use fighting it. But there was no reason—no *excuse*—to allow it to define him. To let such a thing shape the days he had left on this earth was to inexcusably shame the band of brothers he'd buried, something for which they would not thank him. Punishing himself only made their sacrifice *less.*

So he would live.

"What happens now?" Rafe stood beside him before the windows that overlooked mountains, where the moon washed the world in liquid silver. "Is it over?"

Will put his hand on Rafe's shoulder. "Yes."

The boy looked up at him, his face solemn. "You leaving now?"

"No," Will told him.

"Cheyenne know that?"

She ought to, Will thought. But she didn't trust like she should, and in the aftermath of the confrontation with Red she'd been unusually withdrawn. While she hadn't shied from him, the retreat had been palpable. There'd been nothing to do for it during the hours that followed, while he was dealing with the local Sheriff and the FBI and contacting Bagram, but the storm had finally died, and in the silence, he would act.

"I'll tell her," he said.

"She's looking for Harry. She can't find him."

"Harry?"

"The cat."

Will nodded.

"The bombs....they're safe?"

"Yes."

"Good." Rafe paused. "He killed her."

"Who?"

"The fox. He killed my ma."

Will crouched beside him. "I know. I'm sorry."

Rafe shrugged. "Least now I know what happened."

For all the good it did, Will thought, and reached for the boy. Rafe wrapped his arms around Will and clung; he smelled like sunshine and sagebrush and orange soda.

"Are you gonna keep us?" Rafe asked in a hushed voice, his small fingers digging into Will's shoulders.

"Yes," Will said. "That okay with you?"

A nod.

"You sure? I have your blessing?"

Rafe pulled back and those odd, old eyes studied Will with a seriousness that made his chest tight. If someone had told him two weeks ago that he would undertake the safety and protection of his enemy's child, he would have laughed.

If he'd known how.

But his relationship with Rafe had gone far beyond simple defense, and he wasn't sure when it happened, what it was that had grown into the space between them and connected them, but the bond was strong and real, and Will wasn't letting it go.

Even if Cheyenne sent him away.

"You don't need it," Rafe said.

"I want it," Will said seriously. "It's important to me."

"Okay," Rafe said and offered a small smile. "You got it."

"Thank you."

Rafe nodded. A moment of silence, then, "I was really scared."

"Me, too."

"I cried," Rafe whispered. "I tried not to."

"You did great," Will told him. "I'm proud of you."

"You are?"

"Hell yes." Will hugged him again, hard. "You're smarter and stronger than some of the men I've fought beside, Rafe. And you always do your best. No one can ask for more than that."

Rafe's slender arms held him tight. "I don't want to be scared anymore."

"Then don't." Will rubbed his back, throat tight. "It's over. It's time to live now."

Silky hair brushed his chin as the boy nodded again.

"I'm glad you're staying," Rafe said.

"Me, too."

They stayed like that until Brodie's voice broke the silence, where he sat in the living room watching a survival program.

"You see this, hoss? He's teachin' how to make a fire, and he's using a goddamn Bic. What a bunch of horseshit."

Will smiled and stood.

"You should tell Cheyenne you're staying," Rafe said, watching him. "I'll hang out with Brodie." He looked toward the other man. "He's pretty cool."

"He's a good friend."

Rafe shot him a sideways look. "He helped you, didn't he? With the bombs?"

"Yes."

"I thought so." Rafe turned, took two steps and then ran back to Will and hugged him around the waist, hard, before taking off again, leaping over the back of the couch to land beside Brodie, who said, "Hey, little man, you see this fool? Survivalist, my lily white ass."

Will left them discussing the lack of reality on reality TV and stepped out into the chilled night, where the only sound was the rustle of the wind and the occasional hoot of a horned owl. The moon bathed the landscape, so bright he had no trouble making his way over to the barn, where he could hear Cheyenne talking to someone.

He wondered if Angus or Prue had returned, but as he got closer, he realized it wasn't a person she was speaking to—it was an animal.

"He's down at the ranch," she was saying. "And Dex is with him. Don't worry, he's going to be okay. Before you know it, they'll both be back, annoying the crap out of you."

"Meow," came the plaintive reply.

"I know, baby. I'm sorry."

Will stepped through the doorway and pulled the door quietly shut behind him. Cheyenne stood in front of a small stack of hay bales, stroking a long-haired yellow cat with one eye. She wore faded jeans and a lime green fleece hoodie; her hair was contained in messy bun at the back of her head, and his fingers twitched with the urge to free it. A dark, angry bruise had formed on her right cheek and along her jaw, and the darkness within him stirred. In that moment, he wished he'd killed them all.

"Meow," the cat repeated and looked over at him, one large green eye staring at him.

Cheyenne followed the cat's gaze and said, "Hey."

Then she looked back at the cat and stroked him again, and Will watched her shoulders tense, her face close. His chest went tight. He strode over to them, noting the small step she took back when he halted beside her.

"You did it," she said. "Congratulations."

He didn't reply. Instead, he reached up and tugged the tie from her hair.

"Hey," she protested as her brilliant red mane cascaded down to her hips like living fire.

Will ignored her. He stepped into the space she'd put between them, thrust his hands into her hair, and put his mouth on hers.

~

It was not the kiss Cheyenne had anticipated.

After the last few hours—hell, the last week—she was wired and impatient and high on adrenaline. When Will's mouth descended toward hers, she expected the same wildness she felt, a culmination of the chaos they'd weathered, but the press of his mouth was tender, an exquisite rasp of his lips against hers.

It made her throat burn.

"Scared me," he murmured and licked delicately at her bottom lip, his mouth as light as his hands were heavy. "Thought I was too late."

His fingers clenched in her hair, and the kiss deepened before she could respond, his tongue stroking into her mouth, rubbing against hers. Her blood turned thick and hot, liquid fire in her veins. Her belly clenched, and her knees went weak, and the current between them crackled in her ears.

A low, rough sound rumbled from him; the vibration resonated through her, making her skin prickle. Her nipples budded, hard and aching, remembering his mouth, and a soft, painful sound whispered from her. Tears burned her eyes.

"I know," he muttered and rubbed his cheek against hers. "I know, baby."

Her breath hitched in her chest, but he kissed her again, slow and deep, so gentle the tears slid down her cheeks, unheeded. Her body burned beneath the languorous assault, her heartbeat heavy and erratic. She moaned into his mouth, her hands sliding up the hard plane of his chest to wrap his nape, her nails digging into his flesh.

"Missed you," he rasped. He nipped at her ear, her throat, the sensitive place where her neck and shoulder met. His hands, wrapped in her hair, tugged her head back, giving him better access, and he pressed a kiss to the frantic pulse that fluttered in the hollow of her throat. "Say you missed me, too."

She didn't want to. This man...he had the power to strip her bare. To erase every barrier and tear down every wall. With him she was terrifyingly exposed, bared of her defenses, her guard ash around her feet. He could destroy her.

"Tell me," he grated, and a tremor rippled through him, and some part of her understood she wasn't alone in the maelstrom. He was there, too.

"Pain in my ass," she said huskily. "Didn't miss you for a minute."

A smile she felt against her throat. "Liar."

"Yes," she said, her fingers digging into him.

His lips brushed her bruised cheek, so careful she shivered. "Should have killed them for this."

"Sweet nothings," she murmured. "Kiss me again."

He did, his mouth hungry, the leash slipping as he angled her head and plundered. Cheyenne slid her hands into his hair and gripped him hard, raising up onto her toes to press herself against him, and the hard plane of his body made her thighs clench, the hollow, aching pulse he always sparked growing until it was a drumbeat in every cell. Hard, callused hands traced her shape, stroking down her back to curve over her bottom. His fingers clenched into tender flesh as he lifted her against him; wicked bolts of white heat arrowed straight to her core. His cock was like granite against her, and she squirmed to get closer. She stroked his tongue with hers, swallowing the rough sound he made, hungry for every bit of him. She had thought—stupidly, foolishly—that she could somehow let him go, deny herself this wild, beautiful thing that lived between them, but she couldn't. Wouldn't. Not without at least one taste.

One memory.

Will lifted her onto the hay bale stack; Harry jumped down with an annoyed *mew*. Rough hands slid down her thighs and spread her knees, and as Will stepped between, Cheyenne clenched her fingers in his hair. She made a sharp sound of protest when he tore his mouth from hers.

"Slow down, baby," he murmured, his hands stilling her when she rose against him. "I'm not going anywhere."

Cheyenne stared at him, her breath breaking from her in unsteady surges, blood a dull roar in her ears.

"And neither," he added darkly. "Are you."

The possession in him should have made her angry, should have stiffened her spine and her resolve. Instead, it made her clench her thighs again.

"Rafe?" she asked.

"With Brodie. My man will keep him occupied."

"Then I want this," she said. "I want you. Here. Now."

His hands stroked up her thighs, and heat lashed through her veins, heady and intoxicating, as befuddling as any illicit high. "*No.*"

His blunt rejection made her jerk, and her heart fell, an endless descent that felt like death. Her hands curled into fists and slid down his chest to push against him.

"Let go," she snarled softly.

"Not in this lifetime," he replied, unmoving. "I'm keeping you."

She jerked again, and a million butterflies took flight beneath her breastbone. His eyes glinted in the dim light of the single bulb that lit the barn, pale blue topaz so beautiful it hurt. "I love you, Cheyenne."

"You don't," she denied, the words an instinctive, knee-jerk reflex. "It's just sex. Just *fucking.*"

Some part of her recognized that she sought to make him angry, to push him away, to scoff at his unbelievable declaration—because very, *very* few people had ever loved her—but she couldn't seem to reach out and stop that part of herself, too old, too ingrained to silence. But he didn't get angry. Instead, he leaned down, tucked a strand of wayward hair behind her ear and said, "Every mulish, brave, foul-mouthed hair on your head, baby."

Tears burned, and she blinked against them, words a jumbled mix in her throat. She wanted to repudiate him; loving was far easier than being loved. And when she'd thought he was dead…*such eviscerating devastation…*she wasn't sure anything was worth that. But to be the one he reached for, relied upon; to be the one at his side *always*…it was the greatest temptation she'd ever faced. Still, she wasn't certain she could be that for anyone.

What do you think you are to Rafe?

A bar she was still unsure she could meet. Not that she would stop trying…

So what's the difference?

"I can't give you babies," she whispered, the words razors in her throat. "Not ever."

"I. Don't. Care." His voice was hard, his gaze unflinching.

"You will," she whispered. "Every man wants a son."

"And I will have one."

When she realized he was talking about Rafe, a tear

escaped, and the pressure in her chest welled unbearably. "Are you sure?"

"This is the *only* thing I'm sure of." He leaned closer and rubbed his cheek against hers, his bristle rubbing her scar, making her shudder. "You and me and Rafe."

Something she had not let herself imagine. Something in the scope of her existence—her *survival*—she'd never envisioned for herself: a family of her own. Another tear escaped, and her fingers twisted into the dark gray button-down shirt he wore as though it were a lifeline.

CHAPTER THIRTY-EIGHT

"Balls," Cheyenne whispered.

For the first time in her life—she was going to lie down. She was going to *let it happen*. And to hell with the consequences.

Fuck it.

"I want my ring on your finger," Will continued roughly.

"Ring?" she repeated, and the butterflies swarmed frantically within her, a thousand wings fluttering against her heart.

"Wife," he said succinctly and nipped at her mouth. "That's what I'm going to call you."

Cheyenne could only stare up him stupidly. Ring. *Wife.*

Mrs. William Blackheart.

A wild, crazed laugh caught in her throat. "Did you get hit in the head?"

He didn't smile. "I'm fucked up and broken in a thousand different ways, but not in this."

"You've gone crazy," she said in a muted voice. "I'm not wife material. It's only been *ten days*. I don't even know where you live."

"I have a place in San Diego, just off base. And you'll make as good a wife as you are a mother." He swept another strand of hair up and tucked it behind her ear. "I told you, life happens fast, baby."

"That's why you have to hold on tight and enjoy the ride," she said, remembering.

His hand brushed her scar, his thumb tracing its shape. "Yes."

"Will you leave again? To fight?"

"No. Pierre cleared my AWOL status—hell, they'll probably give me a goddamn medal of honor for getting that cache back—but I'm done. Honorable discharge; officially retired."

"Does that make you sad?"

"No. I'm ready to move on."

Cheyenne gazed up at him, her ears buzzing. "You really want to get hitched?"

"Hitched," he repeated and smiled. Dimples slashed his cheeks. "I really do."

Cheyenne couldn't look away from the glitter in his eyes. His certainty emboldened her. And for all of the fear crowding her, the doubts, the cynicism that had scarred her effectively as the flames, she knew it was a simple thing. Just one more leap of faith. Like she had with Hank, with Rafe. With every good thing she'd ever had.

"I love you," Will said again, his smile fading, his eyes searching hers. "I just need you to give me the chance to prove it."

But he already had. With her, with Rafe…again and again. No matter how broken he thought he was. How damaged. He'd sheltered them, held them together; he'd stood in front of them, ready to take every blow aimed at them, over and over. And she knew he would do it again.

"Okay," she said.

He blinked. "Okay?"

"Yes, I mean." Color rushed into her cheeks, so hot and fierce it was a wonder she didn't pass out. "Isn't that the right—"

He swallowed her words with a hungry kiss that was certain of his welcome, and Cheyenne, lost in the dark heat of him, responded wholly, gripping his fine shirt, meeting every thrust of his tongue, demanding more.

Always more.

"Here," she gasped when he released her mouth to exploit the sensitive line of her throat. "Now."

Sharp teeth sank into her earlobe. "Patience, baby."

"No." She reached up and ripped his shirt open; buttons flew, and then the roped muscle of his chest was bare to her touch, and she ran her hands over him, tracing the slender silver bar that pierced his left nipple with her finger.

"Fuck," Will hissed, a violent tremor making the hands on her thighs clench.

"Yes," Cheyenne said. "Please."

He shuddered when she tugged gently at the bar, and her nails scored into the thick pad of muscle that covered him. Then she leaned in and put her mouth on him.

"Cheyenne, baby, *stop*," he gritted, but one of his hands lifted and wound in her hair and held her to him. The other slid up her thigh until his thumb was nestled in the tender crease where her leg and pelvis met, where he stroked her, making her breath catch sharply.

"Why?" A hushed question as she met that pale gaze, like shards of ice washed in the softest blue.

The hand in her hair tightened. "You aren't ready to do this."

"Why do you think that?"

His mouth hardened. "What happened to you will affect us, will affect *this*. You have to be sure and even then..." He shook his head. "I don't want to hurt you or scare you. I can wait."

Cheyenne tilted her head, studying him. She'd always known the rape she'd survived had the ability to reach far beyond the single night in which it occurred, that what she didn't remember about that event might suddenly emerge and shred her from the inside out...that having sex—with anyone—would test her nerve and her resolve and could, quite possibly, break her.

But this was Will...and she wanted to try.

"I trust you," she told him. "Please."

Another stroke along the seam of her thigh, barely skimming the flesh that wept for him, and a sound she couldn't halt broke from her throat. He stared at her, and she knew he was fighting himself, that he would do everything he could to cosset and protect her from the reality they faced, but Cheyenne would only accept that shield if and when she needed it.

And now was not that time.

"I want you inside me," she whispered to him.

He shuddered against her, his jaw as hard as stone. Cheyenne saw his resistance, that damned white knight streak that plagued him, and her hand lowered to the hard, blatant line of his cock, straining the zipper of his faded jeans. Deep inside, she was melting, hot and wet and throbbing for relief, and when she traced a finger down the tensile steel of his erection, her womb clenched in need.

"You're killing me here, baby," he ground out, but he pushed into her touch, and his thumb stroked her again, a slow, deliberate sweep that made her shudder in pleasure.

She rubbed him with her palm; he was thick and long and hard, and she wanted him inside her so badly she ached. His gaze held hers, an intense, erotic connection that made her breath wedge in her throat.

"Now," she said.

"Be very sure," he said, his voice rough, his eyes hooded.

In response, Cheyenne reached down and pulled off her hoodie and the thin t-shirt she wore beneath it. The dim light turned the yellow lace bra she wore into gold, and her nipples protruded through the lace, tantalizing hints of flesh peeking through the delicate nap. She was aware of her scars, the scattered pattern of smeared flesh that traced its way down her left side, but Will looked at her with such dark hunger she felt no hesitation, no fear.

"So beautiful," he whispered.

But he was equally so, the sculpted plane of his chest revealed by his open shirt, his face taut with desire. Cheyenne wanted to devour him.

His head dipped, and he pressed a soft kiss to the waxy flesh that trickled down the curve of her shoulder and pooled in the hollow of her collarbone. His tongue flickered against the sensitive skin, and Cheyenne gripped at his shirt in effort to stay upright. He followed the trail of scars down to the slope of her breast, his mouth tender in a way that made her chest tight and her throat thick. She knew it was deliberate, this gentle worship, a symbol of acceptance.

Love.

If she'd thought sex powerful, it was nothing compared to the giant swell of emotion within her, utterly inexplicable, and yet so powerful she would follow—no matter the risk. And she understood, then, why some people believed life was only about love. Everything else paled in comparison.

"Do you know what I see when I look at these?" Will murmured, tracing her scars with the lightest brush of his thumb.

Cheyenne shivered. "What?"

"Strength." Another press of his mouth, the flicker of his

tongue teasing the edge of lace that cupped her. "Perseverance. *Survival.*"

He slid her bra strap down and bared her to his gaze. The pale surface of his eyes shimmered as they traveled over her, as potent as a physical touch. Her breasts seemed to swell beneath his look, her nipples hard, aching points she wanted him to taste.

"Quit lollygagging around," she told him. "And touch me."

A low laugh rasped from him, and she felt it resonate deep inside.

"So impatient," he whispered and spread his hand between her breasts, pushing her to lay back atop the hay bales, where the rough grass poked at her. She didn't notice, not when he followed and kissed the silky plane of her belly. "So much to learn."

"Later," she said and thrust her hands into his hair. "Right now, I'm *ready.*"

His eyes lifted and met hers; hunger and amusement and something darker churned there, something she wanted to *feed.* "Are you?"

"Yes," she ground out, her thighs clenching at the glints of white heat running through her like live current.

Will turned his head and licked her nipple, a wet, teasing touch that made a low sound murmur in her throat. "I'd better check."

He popped open her jeans and pulled them from her legs in the space of a heartbeat. Her panties were gone a second later, and then he was pulling her knees open with gentle but unrelenting insistence. For a moment, Cheyenne resisted, vulnerable in a way she hadn't expected. But then his gaze met hers, and he said, "I want to see you. Show me," and she yielded, letting her thighs fall open, baring herself to his gaze. He looked his fill as she watched, fascinated by the hunger she saw; his lust, open and unadorned.

"You make my mouth water," he murmured, his hands gliding from her knees to her inner thighs, a teasing rasp of skin against skin that stole her breath. "I want to taste you again."

"Later," she gasped.

His thumb swept through the weeping, silken flesh that throbbed for him, and she arched, her entire being focused on his touch. He circled her clit, possessive and far too skilled. She was so wet, she blushed, but it felt so good, she didn't care.

"Like fucking silk," he muttered and leaned down to suck her nipple, the sharp edge of his teeth grazing her in a way that made her shiver.

Cheyenne moaned, trying to press closer. "Please."

"You deserve more than this." But his fingers joined his thumb to rub at her wetness, spreading it in a delicious slide that made everything within her clench. He nipped the side of her breast. "More for your first time."

"It's not my first time," she argued, inhaling sharply when he teased the tip of one finger into her, the intrusion thick to her untried body, the pressure exquisite. "*Oh.*"

"There it is," he said, and she could hear the satisfaction in him. "And it *is* your first time."

Her gaze met his. He was right; what she'd experienced before bore no resemblance to what she was experiencing now. But before she could tell him, he was pushing that finger deep into her body, and she was stretching and waking around him. His eyes grew dark as he watched her assimilate the sensation of him inside her.

"Do you like that?" he asked in a low, rough voice, his gaze locked with hers. Her body clenched around him.

"Yes," she whispered.

"You want more?"

The challenge in him thrilled her, and she licked her lips,

a deliberate, sensual act she would have never thought herself capable of. But his sharp, indrawn breath pleased her, and she realized she enjoyed the power she had, something she'd always shied from.

For him, she *was* someone else.

A second finger joined the first and pushed slowly into her. Her breath punched from her lungs, and Will bit her nipple again, harder this time. The whip of pleasure/pain made her groan. When he suckled her, his reward flooded his palm, and he stroked her from within; the friction of his fingers against her most tender flesh took her higher, made her body shudder around him, and her legs lifted to wrap his, her heels pressing into the backs of his thighs. Her fingers clenched in his hair, holding him close.

He was so big, he dwarfed her, but she felt no fear. If anything, his size only enflamed her further, and she wanted to climb all over him and test with her teeth the muscle that roped him. That he so carefully controlled his strength spoke to who he was—but she wanted to test that, too.

He ran his free hand down her body, over her breast, the gentle slope of her belly; his skin was darker than hers, rougher, lined with small scars and calluses. The sight of it aroused her even more, and when the fingers inside of her began a slow, wet glide in and out, she moaned softly, her legs tightening around him. Slow and steady, gentle thrusts that built an unbearable tension within her, and she couldn't get close enough, she needed *more*—and then he was plunging in and out at a pace that stole her breath, and the pleasure that tore through her was incendiary; sudden, shearing, flinging her into orgasm before she knew what was happening.

"Look at me," he demanded, stroking harder, making the orgasm deeper, longer, his pale eyes locked on hers.

Cheyenne couldn't catch her breath, her limbs shaking

with fine tremors she couldn't control. The pleasure was intense, unexpected, heightened by the hunger he wore like the finest suit. The intensity of his gaze drove her higher; such dark, uncompromising possession. Everything she once would have fought, in this moment, she reveled in.

"Now you're ready," he rasped. He leaned down and suckled her neglected breast as he pulled his fingers slowly from her, making her shudder.

Her fingers tugged at his hair. "Kiss me."

His mouth was on hers before she'd finished asking, his tongue twining with hers, one hand gliding up her body to cup her jaw. His other hand traced over her thighs, up her belly to her breast, leaving a damp trail. Her scent filled the air. She slid her hands from his hair and pushed his shirt from his shoulders, splaying her palms against the hard, supine heat of him.

He made a rough sound into her mouth as she touched him, and she plucked at the bar that pierced his nipple while stroking a hand down over the ridged muscle of his abdomen toward the hard press of his cock. He was *delicious*.

"No," he said, tearing his mouth from hers, his breath shuddering out of him.

"But I want to touch you," she protested, hunger a deep clamor within. That orgasm had been fan-freaking-tastic... but she wasn't done. She wanted to trace the tribal tattoo that decorated his arm, lick the odd, round stamp on his belly, taste him the same way he'd tasted her—

"Next time," he said and ripped open his jeans.

Cheyenne stilled and watched as he shed them, revealing strong, corded thighs and the hard, thick line of his cock, which made her pulse echo in a pounding rhythm at her core. Moisture glistened at the tip, beckoning her touch, and she couldn't help but reach out and swipe it with her thumb.

So soft.

The discovery fascinated her, such silken, delicate skin over something so hard, and she moved to sit up, intent on learning more, but he captured her hands in his and said in a tight voice, *"Later,"* and then he was kissing her again. He released her hands and slid his palms down her arms to her breasts, where he rubbed her nipples in lazy circles. She arched against the hard, heated line of him, and then those rough palms were gliding down her ribs to her hips, sliding over the globes of her bottom to pull her closer, until his cock nudged at her opening and the whole world seemed to pause.

His head lifted; his gaze met hers.

"Now?" he asked, his voice a husk of sound.

"Oh, hell, yes," she whispered.

One hand wrapped her hip; the other splayed on her inner thigh and lifted her leg, opening her further. Then he bent over her, flicked his tongue against her nipple and began to push into her.

If his fingers had been thick, his cock seemed immense. Her body struggled to yield, the pressure a mixture of pleasure and pain so intense her breath locked in her throat. Will suckled her, testing the edge of his teeth against her sensitive flesh, and moisture flooded between them, easing his way.

"All the way," he muttered against her. "Let me in."

And then he suckled her with strong, hungry pulls, and she moaned, arching beneath him, and he slid into her to the hilt, until he was so deep she could feel his pulse against her womb.

He shuddered, and the hand at her hip flexed, once, twice.

"Oh," she said, clenching around him. "That's…"

"Yes." Will was utterly still, watching her, his gaze hooded, turbulent. "More?"

Cheyenne grappled for control, her nerve endings

twitching and sizzling as though they were live wires. He was so thick, so hard, felt so damn *good...*

"Everything," she whispered.

His eyes closed, his neck corded, every muscle taut, and he was so beautiful Cheyenne knew she would paint him like this, motionless on the edge of lust and need; hers alone. And then he pulled out and thrust back into her, and the thought imploded.

"*Oh*," she said again, sharper as he began to stroke in and out in a steady, breath-stealing rhythm, and every time he plunged into her, she climbed higher, her muscles tightening more, the pleasure intensifying until she was moaning, her nails scoring the thick muscle of his back, her hips lifting to meet his.

"Look at me, Cheyenne." His words were harsh, grated between them, and she obeyed dazedly, unable to think past the pleasure that had burned away everything else. "I want you to see me."

His eyes trapped her, glinting like polished jewels, sharp enough to cut. Her arousal climbed higher as their gazes held, as he thrust harder, deeper, the connection even more intimate than the interlock of their bodies, and Cheyenne felt tears burn her throat.

"So tight," he whispered. "Hot and wet and perfect. Going to undo me."

Harder, deeper, until she was panting beneath him, her body in flames, and all the while, he held her gaze, lust vibrant on his face, his pleasure in her raw and shared. Cheyenne couldn't look away; higher and higher she climbed until she was shaking, fighting the orgasm that was trying to take her, unwilling to let the experience end.

"I love you, baby," he said, his voice low. "Come for me."

And then he pinched her clit and flung her into orgasm. Cheyenne came apart beneath him, her body rippling around his, wild cries tearing from her throat, and then he was stiffening against her, flooding her womb with his heat, a sound of such primal release snarling from him that she came a second time, her nails raking him, her body shuddering violently.

She didn't know how long she lay beneath him, his head between her breasts, his hands stroking the length of her thighs in long, soothing strokes, his body still buried within her. How long it took to stop shaking, to mute the roar of her blood, to calm the beat of her heart.

But when she could finally slide her fingers into Will's hair and tug his head back, she did. His eyes shimmered in the light, and the hands on her were possessive, petting her with a proprietary air she had no wish to fight.

"I love you, too," she told him around the sudden, wrenching lump in her throat.

His gaze narrowed. He reached up to rub his thumb along her bottom lip, spreading the wetness there. Her thighs clenched around him and, deep within, hunger stirred. That quickly, she was ready.

"Again," he said.

CHAPTER THIRTY-NINE

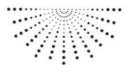

Rafe was sorry to see Brodie go.

He liked the Army Ranger. They'd hung out and watched survival shows into the wee hours of the night —even after Cheyenne and Will had come in and gone to bed —and Brodie had promised to take him out and actually— really and truly—teach him how to survive in the wilderness. How to build a fire and a shelter from scratch, how to find water, how to hunt. Rafe couldn't wait.

But Brodie had to return to his sister, who'd just had a baby, and it was a long drive down to Estes Park, so he left early, right after Cheyenne stuffed him full of bacon and eggs and banana pecan pancakes. He promised Rafe he would be back in a month, hugged Will and kissed Cheyenne and waved goodbye from the big black Suburban.

When they went back into the cabin afterward, Rafe made his announcement.

"I want to dump her," he said.

"Dump who?" Cheyenne stood in the circle of Will's arms, and she was leaning back against him, a half-smile Rafe had never seen curving her mouth. Rafe knew something had happened between them because Will was touching her *a lot*. And she wasn't arguing. They were together now. For real.

"My ma," he replied. Watching them made him happy. And hopeful.

But this needed to be done.

"What do you mean?" she asked.

"Isn't that what people do? Dump the ashes?"

"Oh," Cheyenne said, and he could tell she was trying not to smile. "Well, I think most people spread them. Not dump them."

"Whatever." Rafe shrugged. "I want to get rid of them."

"You sure?" Will asked. "Once they're gone, they're gone."

Good riddance, Rafe thought.

"This is a new start," he explained. "I want her behind me. I don't want to see her every day and think about it all."

Cheyenne folded her arms across her chest and stared at him.

"What?" he wanted to know.

"Will's right, sweet pea. You might not want them now, but someday—"

"I don't want them." He'd *decided*. He stared back at Cheyenne mutinously, having already come to the conclusion that if she didn't want to help him, he'd do it himself. He wanted the reminder of his ma *gone*. Like she was gone.

Turn the key.

"Okay," Cheyenne said. "If you're sure."

"I'm sure."

"Alrighty then. Where do you want to spread them?"

He'd thought a lot about that. At first, he'd figured they could just dump her in the driveway, but then he'd think about her every time they drove over her. So it would have to be somewhere else, further away, and maybe if he put her somewhere beautiful, it would help erase all the ugly she'd done.

Rafe always knew his ma was off, but after what she'd done to him, to Cheyenne—because he knew there was *something*—what she'd done to Will, to Will's men, after stealing the cache, after releasing the video...now he truly hated her. He couldn't forgive her—even if she *was* sick—and he didn't want to. It was over. As far as he was concerned, it was time to get rid of her.

Like she'd gotten rid of him.

The only thing that made him uneasy about his decision was Cheyenne. Without his ma, he wouldn't *have* Cheyenne. Or Will. Or Lucky and Chuck. He wouldn't have gotten out of the city, seen the Badlands, or found himself in this amazing place. He wouldn't have met Brodie or gotten to Tase someone. Not that *that* was a good memory.

But still. Some good things had come from his ma—even if she hadn't meant for them to. And Rafe was pretty sure she hadn't meant for them to. Maybe someday he would be able to sort it all out—maybe someday he would *want* to—but not today. Today, he was tired. Tired of thinking about it and tired of caring. Today it was time to move on.

"How about by that creek?" he asked. "Where the moose was?"

"Nice," Cheyenne said. "And when do you want to do this?"

"Now," he replied, eager for it to be done.

She watched him for a long, silent moment, and he thought she might make him wait, but then she turned and disappeared into the mud room. Will put his hands on Rafe's shoulders.

"You're sure about this?" he asked.

Will's eyes could cut right through a person, but Rafe nodded, certain. "Yeah."

"You're ready to turn the page?"

"Yeah," Rafe said, relieved he understood.

Will nodded. "Then we're with you." He looked over at the doorway Cheyenne had disappeared through. "Did she tell you?"

"Tell me what?"

"We're getting hitched."

Rafe's heart jerked in his chest. "Hitched?"

"Married."

Rafe launched himself at Will. That was the thing about Will: Will always caught him. And even though Rafe felt small and breakable in his arms, he knew he was safe. Like he was safe with Cheyenne. They were the only people in his life he'd ever known that about. The only ones he trusted. He thought maybe he could trust Brodie, too, but only time would tell.

"We're going to be a family," Will said, and Rafe reared back to stare at him. "That okay with you?"

"A family," Rafe repeated, dazed.

"All for one and one for all," Will replied. "Sound good?"

The sudden, painful swell in Rafe's throat crushed the words he wanted to speak. So he just nodded and hugged Will again, his arms tight around Will's neck, his belly churning. He'd fantasized about Cheyenne and Will being together, about them becoming a family, but he hadn't expected it to happen. Not really.

"What's wrong?" Cheyenne asked, standing in the doorway, her arms overflowing with coats.

Rafe shook his head, struggling to swallow past the lump in his throat, to blink away the tears that burned the backs of his eyes.

"He approves," Will said.

"Approves of what?" She dumped the coats on the couch and moved to lay a hand on Rafe's back, a frown drawing her brows into a vee. "Sweet pea?"

It was such a silly thing for her to call him, but Rafe loved her more every time she said it. And he did love her. He hadn't planned to; part of him didn't even want to. Nothing good had ever come to him from loving. The only time he'd ever told his ma he loved her, she'd laughed. Laughed and laughed, like he'd told the funniest joke she ever heard…so he never said it again. And neither did she. He really didn't want to love anyone again. But if he was going to have a family…he *had* to.

"Getting hitched," Will said. He pulled Cheyenne into their hug and kissed her, and Rafe had the feeling that was something he was going to have to get used to. But that was okay. He didn't really mind. "He's going to be my best man."

Rafe's heart leapt for a second time. "Really?"

"Best man?" Cheyenne said.

"When we get hitched."

She stared at Will, color flooding her cheeks.

"You said yes," Will reminded her, and Rafe had no doubt he was going to hold her to it. "And we're doing it right."

Her mouth opened, then closed.

"We're going to be a family," Rafe told her, the words tight in his throat.

She looked at him. "Is that okay with you?"

No one had ever cared what he thought. That Will had asked for his blessing still seemed like a dream, something he'd just imagined. But now they were both looking at him, trying to make sure he was okay with what was happening… when he'd never had any choice in anything that happened. It was so unreal, he reached down and pinched himself.

Ouch.

"Hell, yeah," he said. "I ain't never been to a wedding before."

"Me either," Cheyenne said.

Will smiled. "This is going to be fun."

"How about here?" Rafe halted next to the slender ribbon of water that split the small valley he, Cheyenne and Will stood within. Lucky sat down next to him with a big sigh, still clearly exhausted from her adventure the day before. The sun winked atop the water's surface, diamond bright. "Is this a good spot?"

Will squeezed Cheyenne's hand, where it was wrapped securely in his.

"Sure," she said softly, her gaze on the wooden urn Rafe carried.

Will knew she wasn't sure about the 'dumping' of the ashes, but she'd given Rafe the lead, accepting his decision and allowing him to make a small production of hiking out to the stream, the urn held out before him as though it contained the deadliest of viruses.

"Are you sure about this?" she asked. "Because there's no going back once they're gone."

Rafe pulled the lid from the urn and moved to dump them.

"Wait!" Cheyenne said, and he stopped.

"What?" he asked with a scowl.

"We should say something," she said.

"Like what?"

A million answers flooded Will's head, but he said nothing. He understood Rafe's need to move forward; Will was right there with him. Ready to step beyond the chaos and pain Georgia Humboldt had caused and *live*. To shed the bad and don the good. *The good*. Something, he supposed, he had Georgia to thank for.

Christ, what a crazy, fucked up thing that was.

"I don't know," Cheyenne said and sighed. "It just seems like we should say…something."

Rafe stared down at the urn, silent, and somewhere far off, a raven cackled.

Cheyenne pulled her hand from Will's, but before she could walk away, he caught her nape and pressed a hard kiss against her lips. She favored him with a small smile before turning to join Rafe at the edge of the stream.

Will watched them, content. He was still hyperaware of their surroundings, still vigilant against Malik—because that situation was fluid, nothing had been settled—and still cognizant that Cheyenne and Rafe were his to care for. He was okay with that. Even the demise of his military career seemed somehow muted, as though he'd turned off that road by choice. As though what he'd envisioned as being everything always was now just what had once been…and he didn't feel lost. He felt found. Ready for whatever may come.

Are you sure? Cheyenne had asked him in the hushed aftermath of their explosive union. To which Will had given her an unequivocal answer, one that would leave her with no doubts. He knew the word "wife" scared the hell out of her, that her world had been as upended as his. That she'd never imagined herself on this path…but they were here now. Together. And this is where they would stay.

A family.

Will's first love had always been his country; getting married, having babies, cutting a slice of that American pie… that had been for others. His only focus had been his next mission, getting his men in and out safely, accomplishing their goal. *Staying alive.* There'd been no life outside of that.

But now…it was different. *He* was different. That Cheyenne should be tied to him wasn't even a question in his mind. That he would accept Rafe as his own went without saying. That they would be a family was just…fact. One he didn't question.

He knew it wouldn't be easy. Each of them was self-sufficient. Alone. Even Rafe was used to making his own way. Bending to meet in the middle would be work for all of them. Compromise, sacrifice, communication...they would all learn. They would have to. Because after last night, there was no letting go. No walking away.

Will was all in.

"I don't know what you expect me to say," Rafe muttered.

He was still scowling, and Will knew he just wanted to dump his mother's ashes and be done. He wasn't saying 'good-bye' so much as 'get lost.' He had no desire to linger.

But Cheyenne lifted the lid on the urn, grabbed a handful of ash and said, "We commit this body to the ground, earth to earth, ashes to ashes, dust to dust." Then she opened her hand and let the ash flutter down to the water.

"Amen," Rafe added and turned the urn over, dumping the rest of the ashes into the water with a loud *plop.*

Cheyenne watched him with a frown. Will moved toward them, until he was close enough to put a hand on Rafe's shoulder and wrap an arm around Cheyenne. She looked up at him, worry dark in her gaze, but Will only shook his head faintly and kissed her.

Some things just were what they were. This was one of them.

Rafe sighed and leaned back against him, and as the wind lifted and aspen leaves fluttered overhead like gentle wings flapping, they watched Georgia Humboldt's ashes travel downstream.

Your anger issues will never go away, Cheyenne. Not until you deal with their origin. If you cannot find it within yourself to do that, you will be angry every day for the rest of your life.

Phil, that SOB, was right. Because this morning, Cheyenne had woken up...happy.

Happy.

Sore and aching, dotted by bites and love bruises and razor burn. And hungry for more. *Freaking thrilled to be alive.*

It was strange, not being angry. Not at anyone....well. Maybe not *anyone*. She'd like another shot at Red, and maybe one at Malik, although time would tell with that one... But she wasn't pissed off. Not even at Georgia. In point of fact, she was grateful. Because for all the damage Georgia had done, all she *could* have done, all she'd *tried* to do...Cheyenne had won.

She had Rafe. She had Will.

Precious, priceless gifts, ones she would not have without Georgia's machinations. It couldn't matter, what the endgame was, what Georgia had been trying to do...what mattered was the end result, one Cheyenne would not trade for any other. And one for which there was only one person to thank.

You must forgive her.

Olga's words echoed in Cheyenne's head as she stood watching Georgia's ashes slip farther downstream. Rafe rested back against Will, his small body warm next to hers, and Will's arm was tight around her waist. She felt...*home*. Like this was exactly where she was supposed to be. And while she'd rejected Olga's advice every time the words whispered through her brain, Cheyenne knew the time to listen had come.

Rafe needed to witness a little forgiveness. He needed to see her make a conscious effort to forgive his mother, so that someday he might be able to do it for himself. Cheyenne could see the hate eating away at him, as caustic as acid. His rage, as clear to her as a line of thunderheads on the horizon. His pain, which stabbed deep and made her heart hurt.

She was going to have to be the example.

"Balls," she muttered, and Will pressed another kiss to her hair, as if he knew. Since last night, he'd spent a lot of time kissing her.

Last night.

When she'd leapt, mindlessly, into the fire. When she'd decided to indulge in a little harmless physical pleasure—only to have it be her heart he touched. Her soul he'd taken. Her life he'd changed.

Getting hitched.

The man had lost his marbles. And she hoped they were never found.

"Well, hell," she said and sighed. "Georgia Humboldt, I forgive you."

Rafe's head snapped back. He stared up at her. "You do?"

"Yeah." Cheyenne nodded. "I do."

"*Why?*" Such darkness in that question. Such fury. "She don't deserve it."

"It's not for her. It's for me." Cheyenne ran her hand through his silky hair. "She ended up with nothing. I ended up with *everything*. I can afford to be generous, sweet pea, because I have a future. She doesn't."

"I don't care. What she did...." Rafe shook his head. "I'll never forgive her. *Ever.*"

"Maybe someday," Cheyenne said.

He said nothing, and Cheyenne knew he didn't believe that, but she hoped—for his sake—it was true. Will pressed a kiss to her temple, and she knew he understood, even if he wouldn't forgive, either.

Cheyenne didn't blame him.

They'd talked late into the night, until her throat was raw, and the sun was rising, and then he was inside her again, taking her with slow, relentless thoroughness, making her cry out as the birds awoke, and the first light of dawn bathed them in gold.

"I don't want to," Rafe declared, his voice harsh.

"You don't have to," Cheyenne replied calmly. "But I'm going to."

"Why?" Angry again, as if it was a betrayal.

"Because I spent the last decade hating her, and that was ten years too long. I can't forget, Rafe, but I *can* forgive. It's time."

"She don't deserve it," Rafe said again, his voice tight.

"If you spend the rest of your life hating her," Will said quietly. "She wins."

Rafe scowled, but he didn't say anything else. Cheyenne could see him turning Will's words over, considering them. Will only waited, ever patient; he was a good man, one who would love Rafe and protect him and *teach* him. Cheyenne knew she couldn't have asked for anyone better to be a part of Rafe's life. Of her life.

And she wondered how it had happened. Why. Was it just crazy coincidence? Fate? That dumbass fake rabbit's foot on her keychain? *Did it really matter?*

"Nope," she whispered, and Will squeezed her hip.

"I can't do it," Rafe said softly, his voice intense, and when he looked up at her, those dual-colored eyes were in turmoil. So much older than his decade of life that sometimes she wanted to cry. "Not now. Maybe not ever."

Cheyenne slid an arm over his shoulder. "Okay."

"Whenever you're ready," Will said.

For a long moment, none of them spoke. Rafe was tense, but the longer they stood in the shade of the pines, watching the water flow by, the more he relaxed. Finally, he sighed.

"We can't tell Sasha about this," he said. "Okay?"

"Sasha?" Will repeated.

"Why not?" Cheyenne asked.

"Whitney's kid," Rafe told Will. He looked at Cheyenne. "We can't tell her because she'll try to drag me out here. That's not happening."

Cheyenne arched a brow. "Why would she do that?"

Rafe only shook his head. "Trust me, she would. So we're not gonna tell her. Okay?"

He was serious, waiting on her promise, and Cheyenne wondered what had happened between the two kids. They'd spent a good hour together when Whitney visited, but they'd been out on the deck, and Cheyenne had no clue what passed between them.

"Okay," Cheyenne agreed. "My lips are sealed."

Rafe looked at Will, who held up his hand.

"Scout's honor," Will said.

"Good." Rafe stepped away, urn in hand and turned to look at them. "Thanks. I just…really needed to do this." And then he walked back down the trail, Lucky bouncing along behind him.

"We did that wrong," Cheyenne said, watching him.

"There's wasn't a right way." Will hugged her, his cheek rough against her scar. "We did okay. He'll work it out, eventually."

"Or not."

"Or not," Will agreed. "Either way, we'll be here if he needs us."

So pragmatic and simple. Cheyenne sighed and turned in his arms. He immediately pulled her close, breast to thigh, and she smiled as she thrust her hands into his hair.

"Such a practical man," she said softly. "How will you ever keep us grounded?"

Those pale eyes studied her, lingered on her mouth. "I'm your tether."

The truth in that statement struck deep. Her smile faded. "You are."

"And you're mine," he said. "It works both ways, baby. We hold each other to earth."

Cheyenne stared at him and felt too many things: hope, terror, giddiness, an awareness of something much larger than herself at work. But most of all, she felt love. Weird, breathtaking, wild and *powerful.* Far more potent than her rage had ever been.

Goddamn irony.

"I'm strong," she warned him. "I can stretch and bend; I won't break. You'll never be rid of me."

"Promise?"

Her heart skipped a beat at the seriousness in him. His hand cupped her jaw; his thumb brushed her scar, traced the fullness of her bottom lip. White heat simmered in her veins.

"Promise," she whispered.

Then she kissed him.

THE END....*Until next time.*

∼

Thank you for reading.

If you enjoyed *The Bequest*, please consider leaving a review. Reviews are critical to the exposure and success of independently published works. Thank you!

For a sneak peek at Sam and Lucia's story, The Getaway, keep reading...

THE GETAWAY

Lucia Sanchez has stolen two children. Two children who don't belong to her; two children she will do anything to save. Driven by a bloody past and determined to change an ignoble future, Lucia will make any sacrifice necessary to be certain history doesn't repeat itself. She has given everything she ever was, everything she would ever become, and nothing will stop her from completing her mission.

U.S. Deputy Marshal Sam Steele is tired. Tired of chasing fugitives and protecting turncoats. Tired of breathing. When he's drawn into the kidnapping plot of a woman he has no desire to help, it's just one more nail in his coffin. But duty calls, and Sam knows his duty. When the plea of a close friend makes it impossible to walk away, Sam must make a choice—to follow the rules and play it safe, or to follow his heart and risk everything.

She will give everything to win; he wants only to keep them alive. Thrust together in a deadly game of cat and mouse, Sam and Lucia must set aside the desire and distrust that flares between them and work together if they want to free two children from a sickening legacy and out-maneuver a man who will hunt them to the ends of the earth...

PROLOGUE

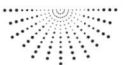

"He's going to kill you."

Lucia Sanchez said nothing.

"Did you hear me? You're *dead*."

Her gaze flickered to the rearview mirror. The boy sat in the middle of the Nova's sagging back seat, his features schooled into the remote mask she'd come to expect. Pale green eyes stabbed into hers, as hard and opaque as the jade they resembled.

"I am not afraid to die," she told him softly.

"Everyone is afraid to die."

How dismissive he sounded. How callous. It never failed to appall her.

"Even the ones who pull the trigger themselves," he added cruelly, purely for spite.

A direct, piercing hit, but Lucia didn't flinch. The boy was like a shark in bloody waters; any weakness would be devoured. No matter the chaos that churned within her, she must be unwavering. *Steadfast.* And so she only turned her gaze back to the hypnotic, dotted line of freeway. The vibration of the uneven pavement made the steering wheel shudder in her hands, an echo of her fiercely pounding, terrified and angry heart.

Thud-thud. Thud-thud. Thud-thud.

Be calm, she told herself. *Destiny is not for the weak.* But deep within, she knew better. Deep within—*ay, yai, yai, chica, what have you done? Muy estupido! You should have waited, should have planned, you will pay—they will pay—and now there is no going back*—because four hours and three hundred miles lay behind them, and the lights of the city had faded long ago. To the east, the first rays of sunlight were creeping across the desert scrub brush, and the wheels she'd set in motion were spinning far beyond her control. But the panic that sat in her chest like a lead weight was nothing compared to the fury that burned in her veins, so hot and caustic and volatile she knew she could not allow it escape. *Enough damage has already been done.* She had jumped; it was too late to worry about landing now. No matter the furious, frantic beat of her heart.

"You know he'll come," the boy continued, and his tone might have been flat with resignation, but his eyes...they glittered at her in the mirror, a bright, dizzy sheen of fear he couldn't hide.

She had pushed him with this action, right to the edge. He stood beside her now.

"*Sí,*" she acknowledged.

He growled, a low, rumbling sound few would believe him capable of. "Then why are you doing this?"

Lucia took him in: chiseled bones, hinting at the man he would become, a strong jaw and stubborn chin. Pale, jade green eyes lashed with thick ebony crescents; a tiny beauty mark kissing his right cheek. Only ten years old, but already so beautiful that sometimes just looking at him hurt. "Because someone must, *mijo.*"

"Not you," the boy said, and there was something in his

voice that made her squeeze the steering wheel until the worn plastic abraded her skin. He looked down at the small form sprawled across his lap. "You aren't...*enough.*"

An infuriating—if accurate—assessment. But it changed nothing. She would have to be enough. A grim reality, and not something she could change. She'd tried.

"You can't win," he added, as though it were fact. *What goes up must come down.*

Which only fed the fury that threatened to blind her, so toxic and unstable, something she *must not* allow to control her. But Lucia was sick to death of being told her limits, her place, of being relegated to someone else's definition of her existence. It had taken years to carve a path out of the madness of her childhood; blood, sweat and tears to travel that path. No one would tell her what she must accept, what she must *allow.* Not any longer. Because the monstrous present had raised the equally grisly past, and she would not stand idly by as it repeated itself before her.

No.

Perhaps this rash, dangerous act would change nothing; perhaps the evil men did was already written, something no one—her least of all—could change. But she refused to be complacent, to be silent. *To watch it happen again.* Others might turn away, but she would not. Because for her, evil was not merely an idea. A stranger she had never met. No, malevolence was an old enemy, one with whom she had been long acquainted. One she was introduced to in childhood, whose shape and form and scent she knew intimately.

One she recognized as if it were family. *Family.* Something she had not had in over a decade. Something that same evil had taken from her.

And now it will take even more! Your future, your dreams, your life—

But that would not stop her. She would not run and hide, not again. Not ever again.

No matter the specter of death Alexander spoke of.

"You underestimate me, *mijo*," she replied finally, darkly. "You should never underestimate anyone."

"You're nothing," the boy said, certain.

A roar filled her throat, begging for escape. She wanted to pound her fists against the ancient dash and make him understand. But that would only egg him on and—probably—crack the dash in half.

"Everyone is someone," she told him, calm, hard, equally as certain. "And anyone can change the world."

"Is that what you're doing?" he derided, his mockery honed to knifelike precision. "Changing the world?"

She met the sharp glitter of his eyes. "Your world," she said.

His gaze dropped. He looked out the window, to where the sun was steadily rising in a fiery arc of orange and pink. Fingers of light speared across the road before them, highlighting the tar lines that held the pavement together.

Thud-thud. Thud-thud. Thud-thud.

The old Nova sliced through the cold morning air at eighty miles an hour, shuddering in effort to meet the demands of her lead foot. The car smelled of aged vinyl and cigarettes, and a long crack arced along the windshield, shearing the pane in two. Traffic was light, the road littered with garbage and the occasional animal carcass.

But no police. *No Ivan the Terrible.* Not yet.

"When he catches us…" The boy shook his head. "Do you know what he'll do?"

Lucia knew; she didn't care. Not anymore. That fear was useless, a waste of time she no longer had. "*Sí.*"

"No, you don't."

But she did. She knew exactly. And even if the knowing

woke terror in her heart—because the man who would come, he would want blood, he would *enjoy* her pain—such a thing would not stop her.

Nothing would stop her.

"Some things," she told him, "are worth the risk."

"Not this. Not to me."

Her heart fluttered painfully in her chest, like a panicked bird fighting its cage. She only ignored it and watched the boy in the mirror, her resolve like steel, no matter his doubt. Her own. "No?" Her eyes fell to the child he held. "What about to him?"

The boy wanted to hit her. She could see it flaring in his eyes, the suppressed violence that always simmered there, just below the surface. The hate and rage that lived within him like a second self.

It had taken her eight months to understand. Eight months too long.

"You can make choices for yourself," she said. "But not for him."

"I can't, but you can?"

Such fury, like a whip snapping through the air, but she said only, "*Sí*, I can, *mijo*. I *am*."

The boy looked away. The stoic line of his profile and the hard, unforgiving line of his jaw where a muscle ticked uncontrollably made Lucia want to do violence. She'd known horror and pain and devastating loss; blood so thick it would not run, the sickening stench of death. The dreams still *were*, as they had always been, and she would not have believed it would become something she would embrace.

Something she would use.

She'd been wrong.

A child should not know this pain.

But Alexander wasn't a child. He hadn't been for a long time, certainly longer than she'd known him. His decade might as well have been a century. There was nothing at all child-like about him.

That had been her first clue.

"You don't understand," he muttered, a small crack in his cold reserve.

"What don't I understand, *mijo?*" Lucia asked. "What he will do to me? Or what he will do to you?"

The weight of her question filled the car like a thick, sulfurous cloud. But she knew he wouldn't respond.

He never did.

She had only her own conviction, the proof evidenced by her own eyes. The sickening truth she could not—*would not*—deny. Not even for him. She'd been too young the first time, too weak. Too ignorant and naïve and *stupid.* Not so now. And while she understood the boy's silence, it wouldn't stop her. Nothing was going to stop her—nothing but the death of which he spoke. No matter her mistakes, her panic, the regret eating at her, berating her for allowing her fury to control her, she would stop at nothing.

She would save him. Save them both. No matter the odds against her, the men who would come, the army that would hunt them. Because the alternative was unthinkable, and not something she could live with. Not again.

Never again.

She'd abandoned all that she was, all that she could ever hope to become for this mission. The phoenix that had risen from the ashes of her childhood would die a sudden and brutal death, buried as effectively as any corpse, its grave barren and unmarked. All she'd fought for would be anted up on the alter of this sacrifice: every precious, hard-won day of survival, the life she'd built brick by painful brick, the education she'd worked nearly into the grave for, the future of which she'd dreamed. *Gone.* All gone. And part of her screamed at the injustice, mourned profoundly the loss, but what drove her was unconcerned with that loss. Life *was* loss. Sacrifice and pain were nothing new. If the tradeoff was their future, she would happily make it. Because it was not death she feared, it was failure.

"*You'll just make it worse,*" Alexander hissed, another fissure forming in his diffidence.

"No," Lucia disagreed quietly. "There is no shame in truth; there is only strength."

"Truth." The boy's mouth twisted. "Yours or his?"

"There is only one truth, *mijo.*"

He shook his head again. The muscle in his jaw quivered. He wanted so badly to deny it. Lucia could see the words trembling on his lips, the cry welling in his thin chest.

But he wouldn't. He couldn't. They both knew the truth intimately, even if they did not speak of it. She had tried, more than once, but he would not be swayed. He was too ashamed—the burden of which no victim should carry—and no matter what she said, he wouldn't accept that he wasn't responsible, that he'd never been in control. A victim, not a participant.

He couldn't seem to tell the difference, which only enraged her more.

So many casualties. She hadn't expected it to find her again. More fool her.

"What will we do?" Alexander demanded tightly. "Run forever?"

A valid question.

Lucia's gaze flickered to Benjamin, who slept fitfully in his brother's arms, his ruddy cheeks flushed. She wanted so many things for them both, so many wonderful things... things she would never be able to give them. These children, who had come so unexpectedly into her life, whom she hadn't expected to change her. *To love.* And Alexander was right: they deserved more than the nomadic existence she was damning them to, more than a life driven by uncertainty and a constant fear of discovery. A life spent running instead of living.

Because the one who would come for them—*for her*—would not stop. Not until she was dead. But the alternative was worse, and one she could not allow. No matter the price.

Destiny is not for the weak.

"He's going to find us," Alexander said coldly, his belief absolute. "And then he's going to kill you."

Lucia's hands tightened on the steering wheel until her knuckles ached. "He is going to have to."

ABOUT THE AUTHOR

Hope Anika is an indie author who lives in the Greater Yellowstone area. Her books have been finalists in the Daphne du Maurier Award for Excellence in Mystery and Suspense and The Fool for Love Contest sponsored by Virginia Romance Writers, Chapter 19 of Romance Writers of America. She can be reached via Facebook, Instagram, www.hopeanika.com or hope@hopeanika.com.

Made in the USA
San Bernardino, CA
19 May 2019